POISONED ARROW

IRIS VAN OOYEN

EASTWOOD
PRESS

POISONED ARROW

Copyright © 2018 by Iris van Ooyen
The moral right of the author has been asserted.

All rights reserved. This book or any portion thereof may not be reproduced or used in any manner whatsoever without the express written permission of the publisher except for the use of brief quotations in a book review.

This is a work of fiction. Names, characters, places, and events are the product of the author's imagination or are used fictitiously. Any resemblance to actual persons, living or dead, events or locales are entirely coincidental.

First Edition. Published by Eastwood Press
www.poisonedarrow.nl

Paperback ISBN: 978-90-828220-0-7
Hardcover ISBN: 978-90-828220-1-4

Edited by Allison K Williams
Cover and interior design by Domini Dragoone
Cover art uses images by: David Methven Schrader, Li Jiuming, Burmakin Andrey, and Evgeniya Porechen Skayer. All 123rf.com.

For Oma Mer and Oma Saar

*Thank you for passing your love for flowers and plants on
to me. I could not have wished for better grandmothers!*

CHAPTER ONE

Kaale Mountains

Auran Stronghold ducked his head to avoid a jagged stalactite. Every time he returned, it took a while to adapt to the stale air and to having a mountain of rock above his head. He longed for his beloved forest and the chatter of birds.

His trip had taken longer than expected—he dreaded having to tell Iris the news.

Auran crossed the common room with long strides, not giving anyone a chance to start a conversation. Almost every area of the cave was put to use. He spotted wood shavings in a corner. *Someone worked on arrow shafts last night.* He nodded at an off-duty guard about to eat his breakfast of grains.

He met a few more guards coming off the night shift and they hurriedly saluted. Their forest-green uniforms were impeccable, unlike his own. He brushed some sand off his sturdy trousers.

Auran's feet took him toward the tower, the highest position they dared occupy in this gorge. It was a mockery to call the two-floor station a watchtower, but compared to the rest of the cave it was elevated.

It's too quiet. The absence of guards chatting made his heart beat faster.

He paused to reinforce his shield and check his dagger—around the bends in the walkways, his favorite bow was useless. Relying on his instincts had saved his life many times. He turned the corner—the tower entrance was empty.

Gods.

He alerted Merlow and Iris. They responded immediately, their presences filling his mind. Strengthened, he carefully approached the watchtower.

As he came closer, he saw black leather boots pointed toward him. *By Seth, that's Basil!* Someone had gotten inside. *Did Apex find us?*

Auran used his mindlink to show Iris and Merlow the scene: Basil lying face forward on the rock floor. *Can you locate Jacob?*

Seconds later the alarm bell went off—he heard people running to their stations and felt Iris link up with Jacob in the watchtower. Images streamed through her: Jacob had heard Basil cry out and was hurrying to check on him.

Auran knelt down. Basil had a weak pulse and his breathing was shallow. Jacob and a second guard met Auran at the base of the tower.

"What happened?" Auran demanded.

"We rounded the tower twice but saw no signs of breach or intruders. I don't know how anyone could've gotten in and out so quickly and unnoticed," the second guard said, scanning the granite walls as if he expected strangers to drop from the ceiling.

Auran cursed. "How could the nightwatch leave without their relief there?"

The guard gaped at him. "Basil released them—he said he'd finish the shift—"

Auran cut the man off with a gesture and stretched his senses to locate the source of the danger he still felt nearby.

At a sudden movement behind him, he reared back, ready to strike. He almost hit one of his own men. Choking the instinct to shout, he hissed "Don't sneak up on me. I could've killed you!"

The guard cringed.

Auran twirled his index finger, signaling his men to stay on high alert. "Keep searching the cave. Go through all the chambers and put extra guards at the outside entrance."

He knelt down again and carefully turned Basil on his back. As soon as Auran saw it, he froze.

An orange arrow.

A poisoned arrow sent across time and space. Time-traveling arrows were more dart-like than traditional arrows—though no less dangerous.

"Jacob!"

Jacob came closer and paled visibly, cursing under his breath.

"I know. Either we're out of luck or worse—someone knows we're here," Auran said. "These arrows have a way of showing up in batches. Tell the guards to steer clear from this entrance."

Jacob nodded, and crouched at Basil's side. "Get a couple of men," he told the guard. "We need to carry him to the infirmary."

Auran sent a quick prayer to the God of War. *Please, Seth, let this be a coincidence.* A deliberate arrow meant a trained magician had located them. It called for an intricate collaboration between a seer and a magically trained warrior to shoot an arrow so precisely it could take down a guard. *Damn.*

Merlow and Iris were still listening through the mindlink. The hum of magic around him intensified. *They must be strengthening the shield around the cave.* Now not even their own people could get in. Sparking on Apex's readings was less important—survival came first.

Auran wished he could return to Arbres and choke the bastard in his own plush chair.

He still sensed the presence of danger and went up to inspect the armory—the rows of glinting swords and full quivers filled him with pride. He even peeked at the leatherbound duty logs, then hurried back down.

Iris was coming down the corridor. Her blue eyes blazed with power and focus, determination in each footstep.

He wanted to yell at her to keep away, but she was their strongest magician by far. Not that she couldn't fend for herself, but old habits died hard. He was too used to keeping her hidden.

She flicked her blonde braid over her shoulder and grounded in a strong stance as she prepared to trace the arrow's flight in her mind. Merlow would monitor the energy in the cave from his chamber. Auran continued searching for physical signs of a breach, letting Iris work her magic.

••••••••••●••••••••••

Iris Springtide studied the slab of rock the arrow had emerged from at a thirty-two-degree angle, focusing on the remnant of the magical trail. She gathered more magic as the path stretched farther back.

What? She steeled herself and opened a tiny window—twenty years in the past.

Twelve warriors were gathered in a lush meadow, congratulating a bearded archer. Although the red-haired bowman couldn't know who he'd shot—the time lapse was too great—he knew he'd hit a mark. It was rare for warriors in training to hit a live target since they usually aimed at remote locations. *Which is what this mountain was before we took shelter here.*

Iris pulled her mind back. "Auran!"

While she waited for Auran to finish his own inspection, she used a powerful spell to install a magical barrier on the grey rock the arrow had shot through. The magic wouldn't block the arrows entirely but would steer their course to a hollow in the granite, making a safe corner.

As she opened her eyes, Auran came to stand before her, his aqua-blue eyes wide.

"It's a training arrow, and there are twelve marksmen." She shook her head. "We'll see more arrows soon, but I've changed their path. Keep your men away from this corner."

Auran relaxed his shoulders a little as Jacob joined them. Behind him, four guards gently lifted Basil to carry him out.

Iris held up a hand. "I need to adjust the shield first." She lowered the protective shield around the mountain, hoping it hadn't yet shown up on Apex's readings. It was still early—few readers were skilled enough to read across long distances, and they needed sleep, too. More so than usual, thanks to the constant scanning.

Jacob and Auran looked at her expectantly.

She answered their unspoken question. "We'll know in twenty-four hours if they've noticed the energy spike. I'll brief Sourni at the palace so she can alert us in case of heightened activity."

They both nodded.

Iris eyed Basil. "His aura is already paler than when I got here. Take him to the infirmary right away. We need to make sure he's only sedated. Merlow might need his potions to create an antidote."

"I'll see to it," Jacob said, following his guards and the unwieldy burden of their unconscious combat instructor.

Auran scratched his head, upending his blond hair. "Thanks to the pickets we'll likely have at least a six-hour warning."

"True."

They had five guards in outposts, monitoring the barren perimeter around their cave in the Kaale Mountains, but if they were under fire, every minute counted.

Auran called after Jacob. "Instruct the guards to wear their armor and see if they need anything else."

"Will do." Jacob strode off.

Iris trusted the preparations to Auran and Jacob and headed for her room.

"Wait!" Auran called out. "How do we know when the last arrow of this batch has arrived?"

Iris turned on her heel. "Twelve archers. Assuming this was the first arrow, we can expect at least eleven more. You could've figured that out on your own."

Auran flinched. When things got tight, they both got edgy.

"I'm sorry," she said. "Neither of us got enough sleep."

"No, it's fine. You go contact Sourni. The sooner we know the impact, the better we can prepare." Auran sounded mollified.

Iris nodded and suppressed the urge to stroke the stubble of his day-old beard and be reminded of the scent of home. She shook herself and headed for her chamber. Guards passed, scurrying to their various destinations. Iris automatically ignored their thoughts, an ever-present buzz in the background. Some she recognized from Yarden, the village she'd grown up in, others had been recruited by Auran over the past two years. Jacob had brought in a few from his travels.

Several young guards had anxious faces, so Iris smiled reassuringly. The more seasoned guards appeared smug and excited they'd finally seen some real action.

They wouldn't be so arrogant if they were the next person hit.

B asil's black hair fanned out over his pale face—a sharp contrast to the tanned young man who'd escorted her to these mountains. Most of the color was bleached from his normally olive-green aura, too. At least she had Merlow—the Master Magician of his generation—to help.

But her teacher stood at the foot of the bed—unhinged—his mouth slightly open. "Iris, you have to do this. I…I am not feeling well." He walked out of the room.

What? His aura was a strong yellow. *What's wrong with him?*

Iris grabbed Basil's wrist. His pulse was irregular. They couldn't afford to lose anyone, let alone their sole hand-to-hand combat instructor. Many of the guards were still in training and Basil worked wonders with the young men. They all adored him. Iris herself had been busy enough shielding the entire operation, she'd barely learned any of their names.

One of the newer recruits stuck his head in the infirmary. "How's Basil?"

"Unstable. Can you fetch Auran or Jacob please?" Iris groaned. She hadn't had breakfast yet, and with Merlow refusing to help— why?—she'd have to dive deep into her power and use healing magic without toppling over. But Basil wouldn't last another half-hour…

There was no time to eat.

She grounded herself and cleared her energy field. Carefully she sent her awareness into Basil. From his aura she'd already deduced the poison had spread from the wound, up to his shoulders and down to his knees—endangering all his vitals. *Whoever crafted this arrow certainly took pride in their work.* Perhaps the poison had matured over the years, becoming more potent.

Iris placed her left hand on Basil's hip and her right on his massive pectoral muscle—creating a healing space between her hands. The makeshift wooden bed creaked under his weight. She flung her magic into Basil, pouring from her chest. Since she had no idea of the poison's composition—and no time to find out—Iris swamped his body with her power. The energy encouraged his cells to expel the poison and stop the venom from spreading further.

Slowly she was able to force the poison from his upper legs, and the top boundary retreated to the middle of his torso. Leaving most of his organs exposed. *Damn. I should've focused on his heart and lungs first. Unbelievably bad timing for Merlow to bail on us.* Iris drew on more power and concentrated on Basil's heart. *Dear Layla, please guide my hands.* She was used to Merlow doing the more extensive healing. Sweat dripped down her forehead—she was handling too much power without any food in her stomach.

"Iris?" Auran asked.

She nodded, then cursed herself when a sharp pain shot through her head.

Auran stood next to her. "I heard Merlow is sick. Are you okay?"

Closing her eyes, she focused all her attention on Basil, willing his heart to continue beating.

"Gods, you haven't eaten, have you?"

Iris didn't dare open her eyes, and swayed.

Auran cursed and grabbed her shoulders to keep her upright. "You're drenched."

She noticed the perspiration, a rivulet down her back. Auran clutched her left armpit with one hand and used the other to extract a bottle of lemon oil from his pocket. Iris giggled.

"You're delirious. Jacob!" Auran hollered. "Somebody get Jacob here." He bit the cap and unscrewed the bottle one-handed, then spit the cap on the floor. He held the lemon essence under her nose. "Breathe in."

Iris inhaled the citrus scent. Invigorated, she fed more power into Basil's insatiable body.

Jacob's running feet skidded to a halt. "What's wrong?"

"Get Merlow here. Carry him if you have to. He has to take over. And bring some food," Auran directed.

Iris pursed her mouth. "Merlow says he's sick..."

"And you are so well?"

Without energy left to argue, Iris dragged her left hand to Basil's liver, boosting the organ so it could expel the toxins floating in his bloodstream.

"Iris, enough is enough. You can barely stand."

She heard people enter.

"Merlow, you have to finish healing Basil. Iris needs..." Auran strained to hold Iris up. Jacob sprang forward to support him as Iris slumped.

Auran cursed. "Stubborn girl. Help me carry her to that bed. I can't believe she didn't stop in time."

CHAPTER THREE

Yarden

Secure in the backyard of the mansion outside Yarden, Iris watched her little brother Thom waggle toward her, his blond curls bouncing. The translucent soap-like bubble surrounding his body shone with excitement. He tripped over his own feet, trying to catch one of the yellow butterflies. She smiled at him and opened her arms wide.

He got up and toddled as fast as he could, throwing himself into her arms. Iris let herself fall back and tickled him until he squealed.

Thom rolled off her and they both lay on their backs, staring at the white clouds.

"How old are you?" Iris asked.

Thom held up his hand.

"No, you're not five." Iris helped him lower his thumb and index finger. Thom needed his other hand to keep the fingers down.

"Good. And how old am I?"

"Seffen." Elation shone in his baby-blue eyes.

Iris laughed. "Yes."

Thom sat up and pointed at a dandelion. "Da-lios!" he beamed.

Indulging him, Iris went over, picked two of the delicate white seed clusters, and held one for him to blow on. He almost took a bite of the flower on his first try. The second time was only slightly better.

Iris giggled and held out her own dandelion. "Look, make your lips go like this," she pouted, "and then blow like so."

Thom clapped his hands in delight and breathed on his own flower. Laughing, Iris poked him in the ribs.

CHAPTER FOUR

Yarden

"Iris, are you paying attention?" her mother asked. Saturday mornings were reserved for Fleurisian history.

"Hmm?"

"You need to focus on the people in front of you. How often have I told you that it is important to be able to concentrate on what is happening right here? Do not let the colors distract you."

"Sorry, Mama. What's a perfectionist?"

"Where did you hear that word?"

"From Cook. He says you're a perfectionist. I don't think he likes you very much," Iris added.

"Did he really—? Iris Springtide, did you read his mind?"

"I just heard him think it."

"Iris, you simply cannot listen to other people's thoughts. It is not polite. I have told you before!"

"I wasn't *trying*. I walked past the kitchen and he thinks very loudly…"

Her mother shook her head. "Well, you should be not-trying harder. And in Seth's name—never share what you overhear." She settled herself back in her chair. "Let us talk about the Cataclysm. It is time you learned more about how this world came into being. In the old days, before the world changed forever, people studied food and its effect on the human body. Different ingredients had different effects, and they found out which vitamins and minerals you need."

Iris could tell her mother liked their history lessons, from the pink glow radiating while she spoke.

"Information was spread easily with other countries and over long distances, and they used electricity to do that."

"What's electricity?"

"It is like the wood for a fire to heat the stove, but invisible. They used this electricity to create a very powerful weapon, but when they lost control, it destroyed anything that used electricity. All dossiers have been destroyed. Since the Cataclysm, electricity has been forbidden.

"There were wildfires and earthquakes—the world fell into chaos. The disaster struck hardest in the cities, where there was more technology and machinery. The newer the city, the bigger the damage.

"The only people to survive the Cataclysm lived in small towns and remote areas, mostly local doctors and school teachers, biologists and historians on field trips, farmers, and of course housewives and children. Very few military or technologically-savvy people survived.

"Many of the survivors moved further south, because the weather had changed and their crops would not grow. That is why there live people with so many different heritages in Fleuris. It is how our language became a melting pot.

"Without electricity, people reverted to the old ways. The historians remembered much about how people lived before electricity was invented. The farmers planted new crops and over the years they all found a new rhythm and way of life. The life we now know.

"But the eruption of electricity changed the vibration of the planet. Here, place your hand on the table. Can you feel a tremor?"

Iris flattened her hand on the smooth oak tabletop, and concentrated. She shook her head.

"Try sitting on the floor."

Iris sat cross-legged and pressed both palms to the cool tiles. *There!* She smiled. "It tingles!"

"Good girl. Most sensitive people are now able to feel the earth vibrate. And some people discovered a well of magic inside themselves that had been dormant."

"Really? Those people had magic? Wow."

Her mother bit her lip. "Yes, they did, and some still do."

"What happened to the other people? Where was their magic?"

"Well, I think they were sad because so many people had died."

Iris nodded. Even though she had no experience with people dying, a glimpse of pain shimmered through her mother's words and her bubble wavered. "How come you know all this?"

"Most people were busy getting everything together, so they did not have a lot of time to write about their experiences. Fortunately, a lot of information was retained through prophe…" Mama cleared her throat. "The Wise Ones."

Iris perked up. "The Wise Ones? I like that name."

Iris, Auran and Jacob sat cross-legged on the long grass. Iris smiled, thinking of the morning lesson with her mother. When she focused back on the conversation, Jacob was drawing something in the grass. "We'll need rope to secure the branches. Also a hammer and nails for the floor. I'll ask my father."

"What are we building?" Iris asked.

"A treehouse!" Auran said. "We can use the big oak tree in the woods and have our own secret base." Both boys grinned.

A secret place to hide. "I'll ask my mom for a tablecloth, so we can have a picnic."

The boys exchanged a glance. "Sure," Auran said. "But we have to put the treehouse up first." He looked at the drawing of the house. "I thought Basil would come, too?"

"No, he had to help his dad cut wood," Jacob said.

For several weeks, Auran and Jacob scavenged the forest for suitable branches for the walls and floor. Iris insisted on a window, and the compromise was a branch that narrowed in the middle so they could peek out.

"We need to name it," Iris said.

"Why?" Jacob asked. "It's a treehouse."

"Yes, but it's our secret place. It needs a secret name."

"All right," Auran said nudging Jacob with his elbow. "What did you have in mind?"

Iris narrowed her eyes, thinking of a good name. "The Wise Men's Cabin." When the boys didn't respond she hastened to clarify. "It's like the Wise Ones who survived the Cataclysm, and we'll be up in the air like they are."

Auran and Jacob stared at her.

"My Mama told me," Iris said proudly.

"Who are they?" Auran asked.

Iris put on her reciting voice and repeated her mother word for word, "The Wise Ones were survivors of the Cataclysm who emerged as leaders and possessed particularly valuable knowledge. They were allowed to live as crossed-over souls, dwelling in their own realm but able to communicate with the living. Anyone who died before or during the Cataclysm is not found in the afterlife of this realm. No one knows where they went." Iris looked around to see if they were properly impressed.

"So, Wise Men's Cabin," Auran pondered.

Iris nodded eagerly.

"But you're a girl," Jacob said.

"So? I can still be a Wise One!" She turned to Auran for backup. "Right?"

"Sure."

"Besides, it's my backyard," Iris added. "And you already decided on the design." She glared at the would-be window.

"Okay, fine," Jacob said. "Now, look what I made." He hauled a rectangular chest from behind an elderberry bush and stroked the polished wood. The sun glinted on the red cedarwood lid.

Iris peered into the chest. "Wow. When did you make this?" It was big enough to hold four buckets.

"At night, my dad helped me. We can use it for our secret stash of food."

"Yeah," Auran said. "We can collect nuts and other stuff that'll hold."

"Yes, for our picnic," Iris said with satisfaction.

"Mama, can I borrow a tablecloth?"

"Why, sweetie?"

"For a picnic in our"—she noticed Thom—"place."

"Pinnik!" Thom exclaimed, jumping up and down.

Iris glanced at her mother for support.

"Iris, you and Thom can picnic here in the garden," her mother said. "I will ask Trevor to serve lunch outside today."

Thom hugged Iris's legs with glee, and she bent down to pick him up and twirl him around, squeezing him tight. His white shirt and navy-blue shorts were snug around his protruding belly.

After lunch, she sneaked out with an old linen tablecloth under her arm. At the edge of the woods she heard Thom call, "Ihus!" She quickly hid the tablecloth under her shirt and turned to see her little brother barreling toward her.

She took his hand and walked him back to the house, handing him over to Theresa, her mother's servant. Thom stuck his arms up in the air, and Iris sank to her knees to hold him close.

AFTER DINNER HER mother called Iris over to the sandstone mantel, handing her the traditional cream-white candle that always stood atop like a guardian. "I want you to light the candle in the fire. Before you do, we will invoke Ayna's presence."

Iris's eyes lit up. She was thrilled to be invited to this sacred ceremony of the Goddess of Love, her mother's favorite goddess.

Her mother closed her eyes and folded her hands in prayer. Iris followed suit, her hands clamped around the unlit candle.

"Dear Ayna, we ask you to watch over our loved ones. Give them strength and fill their hearts with love. Let my husband feel my presence. Let my mother—Iris's Oma—feel our gratitude. We pray you keep them safe, in this life and the afterlife. And so it is."

"And so it is," Iris echoed.

"Now hold the candle close to the fire and repeat after me while you ignite the wick: With this light, we light our love."

Iris carefully held the pillar candle to the fire and waited for the wick to catch. As soon as the candle flame flickered, she declared, "With this light, we light our love." The blue of the flame complemented her own bubble.

Her mother smiled. "Now imagine the circle of light around the candle traveling all the way to your father on his journeys, and all the way to the afterlife to Oma."

Iris scrunched her brow in concentration, envisioning the light rippling out from her hands.

CHAPTER SIX

Yarden

Phillip Springtide returned home with a heavy heart, but waited to tell his wife the tidings they'd feared for so long. He'd seen Iris squinting at him—despite his efforts to remain cheerful, she'd probably read his mood in his energy field. When the children were in bed, he glanced at Merle and shook his head.

"What's wrong?" Merle asked.

"I have news."

••••••●••••••

Apex went over the ledgers in his study. The numbers of priests had been dwindling in the past few years. But he took pride in having turned the tide by establishing the Order of the X. He touched the X on his chest and took in the lavish décor. The majestic mahogany desk was his favorite—his private world of scheming neatly tucked in four drawers.

At a cautious knock, he looked up. "Come in."

His curate slunk around the ornately carved door. "There's been an incident." The man crossed himself.

"The grand family—the fish—dead."

Apex rose. "Speak plainly, man."

"I, the…the fish from the Dead Seas. The cook says the fish must have been poisoned."

"Poisoned?"

"Or spoiled or something! Because the guests ate the same meal except for the fish, and they are all fine."

Apex nodded. Fish from the Dead Seas was a delicacy reserved for the ruling family. Even esteemed guests weren't included in that privilege. "They *all* died?!"

"His and Her Eminence collapsed at the table. Both princesses were carried to their rooms. The youngest is still breathing. The grand physician is examining her."

Apex sat down trembling. The grand family had been in his care for four years now. He was proud of his position and had developed a fondness of the girls especially. "Can I see her?"

His curate shook his head. "The grand physician asked us to pray for her."

"May the Gods guide his hands, and heal the…Her Eminence."

CHAPTER SEVEN

Yarden

"Thom, you can't come," Iris said, prying his sticky hands from her legs.

"But I want to," he whined.

She had promised her father they wouldn't show Thom their treehouse—it was too high up for him. "You can help us find acorns, like these." She showed him one. "For our secret stash," she whispered.

At this he perked up. "Shhh," he said loudly.

Iris stroked his ash-blond hair. "Yes, shhh." She kissed his chubby cheek and hurried to see Auran and Jacob in their treehouse. After a few paces she looked back and noticed Thom had followed. "You have to go back, Thom. You can't come this far." She turned him around and waited for him to take a few steps before she ran off again.

She deftly climbed the big oak and emptied her pockets in the wooden chest almost filled to the brim with acorns. Last week Jacob had sanded the rough wooden floor—after she'd gotten a splinter wedged in her thumb. She brushed leftover wood dust through the cracks.

"Thom!" Iris called. *Where did he go?* "Thom!" Her mother had sent her out to find him. They hadn't seen him since breakfast. *Perhaps he went to look for more acorns.* The day before he had been so proud, beaming while he gave her a handful. Auran and Jacob had patted him on the back.

Iris scanned the forest, searching for his pastel-colored bubble between the trees. Nothing stood out. He usually didn't go this far. Suddenly alarmed, she thought of the treehouse and set off running.

Iris looked up and saw the broken tree branch. She couldn't believe he had climbed that high. He must've followed Auran and Jacob…

WHEN THOM DIED, a grey mist appeared in the house, the world not wanting to be as bright and shiny as it had been before. Even if Mama's red-rimmed eyes hadn't given her away, Iris could feel her mother crying through the walls.

Iris didn't sleep much that night or the next. She kept finding Thom on the forest floor—a relentless nightmare turned real—her heart clenched again and again. Time slowed down, and every leaf in his blond curls stood out, forever etched into her memory. She called his name, but the response was an unbearable silence. Then she rushed home for her father but found their servant Trevor instead.

The second morning Iris woke shivering with cold sweat. The tension built underneath her skin like a string pulled tight. She stayed in her room until Theresa came to take her into the dining room. Her tall father stood hunched in front of the black wooden stove, warming his hands, his usually vibrant indigo bubble very much subdued. Iris moved to stand next to him. He tousled her hair and said, "I've asked Trevor to kindle the stove this morning. We could all use a little heat, and…"

Iris knew they would need the fire later that day—for Thom. She swallowed.

Her mother made her eat a few bites of honey-sweetened oatmeal before giving up. "All right, go help Trevor and your father outside."

Iris ran to the garden, eager to burn off some of the excess energy that kept building inside her. It was traditional for the family and anyone closely related to the deceased to build a funeral pyre. Auran and his father came and helped haul logs from the forest. The rough wood seemed out of place among the bright daisies and fresh green grass.

At noon the pyre was to be lit by her parents—those who gave life to Thom—to return him to the Gods. Iris saw the flame reflected in her mother's face, her tears illuminated like precious gems, as her parents joined hands and ignited the fire as one.

Iris stared at the flames licking the stack of wood, keeping her eyes on the bottom of the pile to avoid looking at the swathed bundle at the top. The pressure inside her increased, and the smell of burning pine crept up her nose. She dutifully joined the others in turning her palms upward and praying, "May Ayna take him in." Her mother burst into sobs. All Iris could do was stare at the flames, not noticing the heat until Trevor gently pulled her away.

CHAPTER EIGHT

Yarden

T he day after Thom's cremation, Iris fled outside. The suffocating grey blanket around the house permeated her soul, dragging her down. She wandered to the back of the garden and halted at the edge of the forest, refusing to go to the treehouse.

Not sure where to go, she turned and faced the wooden shed. A sunbeam pierced the clouds and highlighted a yellow butterfly. Iris's heart stopped. She ran toward the butterfly and chased it away, yelling, "Where did he go? Why didn't you protect him?"

Iris fell face down on the dewy grass and started sobbing. Guilt flooded her. The burning pain deep inside her touched something slumbering. A powerful energy clawed its way up her spine, and she let it. Struggling, she drew a ragged breath and the heat intensified—burning from the inside. She screamed in pain and bewilderment while the pain took on a life of its own.

From far away she heard her mother call, "Iris!"

Cool hands stroked her cheeks. "Calm down, Iris. It is all right."

She was pulled into a sitting position by two big strong hands under her armpits. Trevor—she recognized his cypress scent, but it was mixed with something smoldering.

"Do you remember seeing the clouds, Iris? Imagine it is starting to rain. Can you feel the drizzle on your face?" her mother asked urgently.

Iris was dizzy. The energy swirled all around her. It was almost impossible to focus on her mother's voice.

"Look at the clouds, Iris. Feel the coolness of the wind and breathe it in. We will do it together. Breathe in. Feel the cold air enter your lungs. Now breathe out the warmth—pfffff."

Iris gasped for breath.

"Good girl. Keep breathing in the fresh air, feel it spread through your body—nice and cold."

Slowly, achingly, the heat dissipated. After a few more minutes of breathing deeply, the phantom hand let go its tight grip, releasing her spine. She went limp when the energy left her.

"There you are. Well done." Her mother's soft hands stroked her face, wiping away the sweat. "Thank you, Trevor." Her mother pulled her into an embrace, and Iris felt the big hands let go of her.

"You are welcome, ma'am. Is there anything else you need?"

"Some water please, for my girl here."

"Certainly."

THE NEXT MORNING Iris and her mother sat in the living room when her mother put her precious embroidery away in the antique pouch table and asked, "Do you recall what I told you about the Cataclysm, and how some people had magic and some did not?"

"Yes."

"Well, there is something important I need to tell you." Her mother looked straight at her and Iris felt a jolt from her mother's bright blue eyes. "You see, you have magic too."

Iris stared at her mother. "Is that what I'm feeling?" Tears welled in her eyes. A knot she hadn't been aware of loosened in her stomach.

Her mother stroked her hair. "Yes, darling. It is why you can hear people's thoughts and see their bubbles. Yesterday your power was triggered by your grief. I will have to teach you how to control and suppress your magic when you get emotional."

"Yes, please, Mama. Yesterday—I don't want that to happen ag—again."

"I know it was frightening, but you did well. Just remember you can always find your way back to balance as long as you focus. Let us practice right now."

Iris followed her mother into the garden, and they sat cross-legged. Iris cast a glance at the scorched grass and cringed.

"Do you remember when we used to play the game where you doused the flames?" her mother asked.

Iris nodded. It was one of her favorite games.

"Imagine you feel the fire burning inside, like yesterday, and in your mind's eye spray water over the flames. Keep adding water until the fire is extinguished."

Iris hesitated. She wasn't keen on feeling the flames again, the memory still too vivid. Touching her stomach, she glanced at her mother for support.

"I am right here, you can do it." Her mother inclined her head encouragingly, the sun glinting on her golden blonde hair.

"Okay." Iris took a deep breath and closed her eyes. She focused on the hint of pain still present from yesterday. Then she let the pain grow bigger until the energy stirred slightly. Thinking back on the water dousing, she sprinkled water on the imaginary flames.

Nothing happened.

She tried again but to no avail. "It doesn't work," Iris grunted.

"Try adding more water. You will need something stronger now your magic is activated."

Iris envisioned a big bucket full of water and dumped it unceremoniously on the pain. *Was it just my imagination or did the flames sizzle out?*

"Did it work?"

"Yes," Iris breathed in relief, then caught a glimpse of pain on her mother's face as she clutched her side.

"Mama, what's wrong?"

"I am fine. I might take a nap."

Iris squinted her eyes at her mother's aura. The rose-blush hue was less bright than usual.

During dinner her father's indigo eyes trailed her. "I heard your magic woke up."

Iris swallowed. "Yes."

"Don't worry, your mother will help you."

That was the last time her power was discussed openly.

Tomorrow would've been Thom's birthday. It had been almost a year since he'd passed. Iris was glad Auran had come over after school—grateful for the distraction.

Running around outside with Auran had made her thirsty, so Iris came in for some water. From the hall, she heard Trevor say, "Before you can be accepted into this household you need to swear a blood oath."

Iris paused outside the dark-green kitchen door, not wanting to intrude.

"A blood oath? I thought only the royal family took them and that was years ago," an unfamiliar male voice answered.

That must be the new cook.

"It is not up for discussion. Either you are willing to take the oath, or we will let you go on your way." Trevor sounded very stern.

It was silent for a moment.

Trevor added, "I believe not many people are hiring chefs these days."

Iris heard a deep sigh. "I don't want to be involved in anything illegal."

"I can assure you the oath has nothing to do with illegitimate actions. It is solely to protect this family."

"All right then."

Iris heard the zing of a knife pulled out of the block, and she cringed when Trevor said, "Give me your right hand."

"Ouch," came from the kitchen, followed by language Iris didn't recognize.

"Wonderful," Trevor said.

"Now, which secrets am I to protect, pray tell?"

"Do not be surprised when you run into the little girl. Best to avoid looking into her eyes."

Iris backed away, returning unseen to the garden.

"Hey, why didn't you bring me any water?" Auran asked.

Iris kept walking and motioned him to follow. There was no fence or hedge to mark their border—the forest a natural extension of the grounds.

"What? Did something happen? You're as white as a sheet. Are you in pain?"

Iris shook her head.

"Then what?" Auran urged.

As soon as Iris reached the relative safety of the area behind the shed, hidden from view from the house, she told Auran what she had overheard. "I don't understand! What's wrong with my eyes?"

Auran looked at her like she was his baby sister. "Iris, you do know your eyes are unusual, right?"

"No. Why?"

"Well, they're really bright. Most of the time it's impossible to look into your eyes."

Iris glared at him.

"When you're upset or really happy, it hurts."

"My eyes hurt you?" Iris asked, sagging onto the grass.

"I know you don't mean to, but yes, it often does."

"Is that why people avoid me on the street?"

Auran dodged her gaze.

"You're my friend, you have to tell me."

Auran's head jerked up, and after a moment he scooted over and patted her back. "Yes, most people are afraid of you, of what it means."

Biting her lip, Iris focused hard on not crying.

"I always figured there was something wrong with me," she muttered. "The way people kept avoiding me—yet I never knew why. I assumed they just didn't like me much."

"You know, it *does* get easier. For me it did." Auran bobbed his head encouragingly.

"What do you mean?" Iris sniffed.

"Well, it doesn't hurt as much as it did before."

Oh.

THAT NIGHT IN bed Iris remembered the last time she'd been allowed to walk in the village. She'd been skipping happily alongside her mother on their way to bring homemade tomato soup to a sick friend.

A dark-haired woman and her son turned the corner. Iris smiled and waved in greeting. The broad woman held back for a moment, averting her eyes, and pulled her son to the other side of the street. "Don't look at her," the woman hissed.

Iris's mother pulled her in close, shielding her from view. "Do not worry. We are almost there." But, before they arrived at her mother's friend's house, three more people crossed the street, all pretending she and her mother were invisible.

••••••••●•••••••••

Phillip Springtide scrutinized his wife's face. "What's wrong?"

"It is not a blessing—it is a curse!" Merle said. "You know what happened to Jonathan."

"Your brother's got nothing to do with this."

"Jonathan's fate shows what happens to people who practice magic."

"One magician going astray doesn't mean they all will. You can't decide this for her."

"And her eyes," Merle continued—ignoring him. "People stare at her all the time. Today we could not even walk across the street without people scurrying away."

"She can be pretty intense."

"We cannot let her...we need to protect her."

"You're shaking." Phillip sighed. "All right, she stays in the house and gardens." He guessed this was not the time to mention Apex had annihilated an entire village.

CHAPTER TEN

Yarden

Every day after lunch Iris practiced dousing the flames under her mother's supervision, and every time it was a little easier to imagine the water and put out the flames.

Iris now felt the presence of her magic at all times as banked embers, ready to spark.

She was worried. In the past two years, her mother's bubble had gradually turned from bright rose-blush to a very shallow pastel pink. One day her mother didn't get up at all. She stayed in bed the entire week. "What's wrong with Mama?" Iris asked her father.

"She's…not feeling well."

Iris tilted her head. "I know."

Her father ruffled her hair. "That's right." He sighed. "I've requested a healer. She should've been here yesterday. I've sent Trevor to search for her."

Trevor walked in. His normally viridian bubble flared brighter green with distress. "Sir."

"Did you find her?" her father asked.

Trevor shook his head, glancing from Iris to her father and back—water dripped down his ebony hair and dark coat, forming a puddle on the floor.

"Go on," her father urged.

"The healer has been apprehended. Someone recognized her and alerted Apex's priests. They took her to the Citadel."

Her father cursed.

Iris's eyes bulged. She'd never heard her father swear before.

At last Iris was allowed upstairs. She knocked on the hardwood door to her parents' room, and her father opened it. His sable hair lay flat against his forehead.

"Come in, sweetie. Your mother just woke up."

"Hi Mama," Iris whispered. She stifled a gasp. Downstairs she'd sensed her mother's pain and distress, but nothing had prepared her for this sight. Her mother's light went out in the space between heartbeats.

"Iris," her mother breathed.

"Go on, you can sit on the bed," her father encouraged. "I will leave you in charge while I get some hot tea," he said while stroking Iris's hair.

Iris climbed on the four-poster bed and stared at her mother—hollow-cheeked, unwashed hair hanging in strands. She grabbed her mother's hand and willed her strength into her mother.

A tear escaped her mother's eye. "Thank you, sweetie," she croaked. "But it will not work." A coughing fit interrupted her. "You need to be strong. Promise you will practice dousing your flames," her mother wheezed.

"Yes, Mama." A now familiar dread filled Iris's body. She prayed fervently to both Layla and Ayna. *Please help my mother get well, please!* Crying, she said, "Mama, you can't go, please don't leave." She hugged her mother tight. "I...I...love you."

"I love you too, sweetie. I wish I did not have to go."

Iris sobbed, soaking her mother's flannel nightgown.

After a while she asked, "Will you be with Thom?"

"Yes, and Oma."

Iris cried even harder. "I want to come, too. Don't leave me here."

Her mother hugged her, and they cried together. Iris wasn't sure who held up who.

Her mother kissed her hair and whispered in her ear, "The Gods have other plans for you. I know you will make me proud."

CHAPTER ELEVEN

Yarden

I ris couldn't bring herself to go outside and help the men, their steady progress creating a heaping pile of wood from the stray logs. With each chunk added to the pyre, she felt more energy slip away.

Auran came to get her. "You must, Iris. At least one twig."

The day blurred.

Stretching her right arm to take her father's, Iris lit the fire in her mother's place. The flames ate the timber as if rushing to transport her mother to the afterlife. Theresa's face streamed with tears when she turned her palms upward. Iris could barely push the words past her throat "May Ayna take her in."

Pride had shown in her mother's eyes when she completed her first Ayna ritual, lighting the family candle.

Through the ceremony and prayers, Iris felt the suffocating heat. In the house again, Iris stripped as fast as she could and threw her clothes out her bedroom window. Thom. Mama. She never wanted to remember the burnt smell of grief again.

CHAPTER TWELVE

Yarden

I ris didn't see much of her father after the funeral. He was often away on one of his trips, which left Theresa and Trevor in charge. Since her mother died, it was now Theresa who brushed and braided her blonde hair in the morning with calm, cool hands, taking her time as though there were nothing more important in the world. Theresa skipped the caress on Iris's cheek, though, and Iris was glad she did.

She'd known her Mama was sick and getting frailer every day, but she'd never expected her to…leave. Iris hadn't practiced dousing the flames since her Mama died.

The house sounded so quiet, even the stones were mourning. The closed windows muffled the sounds from the forest. Sadness was all around her, emanating from everyone, even the cook who never liked her mother very much because she was so picky about his food. Iris saw the grief hanging around people, a grey mist that dragged them down. She had to get out of the house, feeling suffocated by the lack of air and energy.

Iris pushed the back door open and stepped onto the flattened grass, scowling at the crushed daisies. No one else bothered to side-step the flowers. She looked up at the house. The teal curtains in Thom's room were drawn. Her Mama had opened them from time to time, when she was feeling sad. Iris's gaze trailed to her parents' bedroom—the window open only a crack.

Inhaling deeply, she soaked up the oxygen, lightheaded. She'd gone outside to play in the garden, having already read all the books her mother used for her schooling.

Perhaps the Faeries will be there today. Iris didn't want to get her hopes up. They were rarely there, and never when it rained. The Faeries preferred the sun. So did she. People were happier when the sun shone.

She walked to the back of the garden, where their shed almost touched the line of trees. Behind the shed, concealed from the house, a small patch of sunlight shone through the pine trees. That's where she usually found them. The Faeries never ventured too far from the forest.

Iris peeked around the corner and tried to swallow her disappointment.

Empty.

Not wanting to go back inside, she lowered herself on the warm grass. She made a crown of daisies for something to do, and placed it on the tree stump next to her. "This is for the Faeries," Iris murmured, pleased with her creation. The Faeries were never afraid of her, unlike the people in the village. It was nice to have someone to play with, even if it was just every once in a while.

THE NEXT DAY the daisy crown was gone, so Iris looked around eagerly to see if she could find the Faeries. Giggling trickled from the forest and she skipped toward the trees. Her two favorite Faeries, Wendolyn and Maesie beamed at her.

Iris, mesmerized by their iridescent dresses, noticed how the Faeries' energy synced with their outfits.

"Why is everyone so dreary?" Wendolyn asked.

"Huh?"

"At your house. No one is happy."

"My Mama d…died." Iris wiped away a tear.

"Well, then you should dance!" Maesie declared.

They grabbed her hands and the three of them danced in a

circle—Iris making sounds as close to the ancient Faerie verses as she could. She felt so much lighter than she had in days, and some of the grey mist lifted. Once their heads were spinning, they fell on the soft moss, breathless and giggly.

Both Wendolyn and Maesie attended Faerie Garden, a fascinating concept to Iris. She'd never frequented a regular school. Her mother had always taught her at home. "Which stories have you learned?" Iris asked leaning forward.

"I want to tell her!" Maesie said bouncing, her blonde ringlets swinging. Last week they had learned one of the ancient tales each Faerie has to memorize. "This legend is called 'The Universal Words.'"

Maesie paused to make sure both girls were paying attention.

Satisfied, she continued in a grave voice, imitating her teacher. "The Universal Words date back from long before the Cataclysm. They were created in a time when humans and Faeries lived alongside one another and were granted access unto the other's domain, provided they abide by local laws. After a few confrontations during which both humans and Faeries betrayed each other, the Faerie Queen and your King decided to protect their inhabitants." Maesie clapped her hands. She particularly liked the protective part. "These wise rulers invoked a powerful incantation—forged by both Faerie and human magic—to ensure truth was spoken. Whenever a magical human or Faerie spoke these words with pure intent, it forced their adversary to speak nothing but the truth."

Maesie had done her best to learn the words by heart and glanced at Wendolyn for confirmation.

Wendolyn nodded and smiled, revealing her dimples.

Maesie stood up, wiped the wrinkles out of her dress, and removed a few strands of moss. She placed her left hand over her heart and facing Iris said, "I demand access to your wisdom and the truth of the Universe, may the Gods oversee your answers and punish your disobedience or untruthfulness." She looked at Iris with gleaming eyes. "Now we all have to speak the truth to each other, for as long as we shall live!"

·········•●•········

Iris was fascinated by the ritual. When Maesie stood, the lilac color around her started swirling, turning into a rainbow while Maesie spoke the magical words. Iris beamed at the Faeries. "We'll be friends forever!"

CHAPTER THIRTEEN

Yarden

Today was the three-year anniversary of her mother's passing. The weather remembered, too.

The rain drummed a steady heartbeat on the windows of the mansion. Iris yearned to enjoy the rain tickling her face, to escape the stale air and blistering warmth of the woodstove. When she walked toward the garden door her father called, "You know you can't go outside, Iris."

"Why not? I'll stay in the garden."

He sighed. His indigo bubble was still paler than it used to be—Iris often felt him cry at night.

Mama. Her throat constricted.

"You know we can't risk it. It's not safe," her father said.

She'd never been allowed to go into the village on her own. Her gift made her too much of a target, but her parents had usually allowed her to play in the backyard.

Her father strode over and pushed her back from the dark-green door.

So unfair! Her frail control crumbled as power thrummed inside. The energy fought its way up slamming past her barriers until her throat burned. Raw power flowed from her unchecked, her blue eyes unbearably bright. In response, the flames in the woodstove leapt up and licked the wall, creeping toward the periwinkle curtains.

Her father screamed.

Iris struggled for control, focusing her attention inward to where it burned the hottest. *It looks like a ball of fire...*

It reminded her of the flame dousing game she used to play with her mother. She tried to envision bursts of water.

Focus. Through her anger she could barely see the water and the energy in her bubble flared up.

Breathe.

She kept inhaling the stale air, nauseated by its smell.

"Take your time, sweetie," her father encouraged, rubbing his wrist.

Putting a hand on her mouth, she stumbled to the door.

Her father fumbled with the lock and swung the door wide. He stuck his arm out and let the rain fall on his seared skin.

Iris gulped in the cool air, shaking. Her mind vaguely registered a sizzling sound.

CHAPTER FOURTEEN

Yarden

"Iris!"

She stuck her head out of her bedroom door. "Yes, Father?"

"Come downstairs. I found someone who can help you."

"All right. I'll be right down." *Huh?* She was rarely introduced to strangers. Iris picked up her comb to divide her hair into three strands, then dropped her hand. It wasn't right, not without Mama. Fleurisian mourning tradition prescribed she couldn't cut her hair for four years after the loss of a sibling or parent. Hers had grown quite long.

She quickly brushed her hair and padded quietly downstairs.

Iris paused outside the dining room, surprised her father had invited strangers into their private quarters. Visitors usually stayed in his study. Their energy felt restrained somehow. She took a deep breath and walked into the room, her shoulders slumped and eyes downcast.

"There you are," her father said. "Iris, meet Head Priest Rex and his curate."

Rex's gleaming scalp was ringed by a curtain of grey hair. *That must be a tonsure.* The curate was half-hidden by Rex's belly.

Iris remembered overhearing her parents. "The priests have become increasingly violent since Apex became acting regent for Her Eminence," her father had said. "The elders have less say in what goes on in their villages and towns. I fear their interference will only increase.”

Seeing the bubbles of the priests, a menacing scarlet, that made more sense now. Iris stepped forward and politely shook their hands, instinctively avoiding eye contact. “Pleased to meet you, sir.”

She knew Apex’s name illustrated his ambition, the X a reference to the cross of his God. His most devoted followers changed their names to include an X to honor their leader.

“Your father said you have trouble focusing?” Rex said, patting the embroidered X on his chest.

Iris swiveled her head and stared at her father. *Did he tell them about my magic?*

“He said there was an incident where you almost got hurt by your carelessness.”

What?

Her father smiled encouragingly. “I thought these priests could help you focus and train your mind, so you’ll be less easily distracted.”

“Thank you, Father.”

“I’ll leave you to it,” her father said while closing the door behind him.

“Come over here girl. We will get started before dinner is served,” Rex commanded.

They’re staying for dinner?

Iris obliged and followed the head priest to the front of the room. Rex sat in her mother’s blue-striped chair. Iris flinched.

“Kneel down.”

She knelt in front of the armchair.

“Most people have no control over their body. They let hunger and sleep dictate their life, and they are weaker for it,” Rex droned.

From the corner of her eye, Iris noticed his curate light a stick of incense using Ayna’s candle on the mantel. He waved the stick up and down while he circled through the living room.

“You need to resist the urges of your body. You are its master. Assume control at all times,” Rex continued his litany.

The stench of cheap incense crept up her sensitive nose, and Iris pretended to cough to mask her cringe.

"You *cannot* let yourself be influenced by what happens around you. Your focus determines what your eyes see and what your ears hear. You need to shut out everything else."

As Rex spoke his bubble turned wine-red, and his repressed anger rippled out in waves of threatening black streaks.

It took all her self-control to stay motionless.

Rex folded his hands on his round belly and sat back in the chair. "Focus on your breathing. It will help calm your mind."

Iris tried to follow his instructions as she had once listened to her mother. But his ominous energy confused and distracted her. She closed her eyes to shut out his energy, but instead saw images of people being flayed. She winced.

"Stay still!"

Opening her eyes, she concentrated on the tile in front of her, blocking out his voice, imagining drizzling water to calm herself. She pretended to be out in the forest, feeling the cool breeze.

Slowly the familiar calm returned, and she became more aware of her surroundings. The cold of the granite floor seeped through her thin linen skirt, and Iris shuffled involuntarily.

"You moved. You will have to start again. Stay here for another hour," Rex barked. He snapped his fingers at his curate. "Get my silver cup from my saddle bag. I am ready for dinner."

His assistant bowed. "Sir."

Rex got up and seated himself at the head of the table.

Father's spot.

Trevor walked in and finished setting the table. Lighting the three-branched candelabra bathed her mother's favorite tablecloth in a golden glow.

"We will not need four plate settings. The girl will not join us," Rex said.

"Certainly, sir. I will set a plate for her in the kitchen," Trevor answered.

"She will not need food tonight. She will fast for three days in penance."

"Sir?"

"She can have two glasses of water per day while she trains her mind."

Iris's body swayed.

Iris hadn't eaten in two days. Her head hurt. Even the third glass of water Theresa had brought her last night couldn't keep away the increased pounding. That morning she'd told Auran to go home. She had no energy to even talk to him.

That priest Rex had told her to calm her mind. She understood the need for focus but concentrating became harder instead of easier. She was relieved the local friary was hosting a dinner in honor of Apex's birthday. Iris had seen the relief in her father's bubble too, when he told Cook. Her stomach rumbled. *Don't think of food.*

She knelt on the granite tiles next to her mother's armchair, pressing her palms to the cool floor to take her mind off the hunger. Today people's feelings weighed heavier on her. She hadn't been able to deflect Auran's thoughts like she usually did. The tension built from her core. She pushed her hands against her stomach—hoping to contain the power. Her body started rocking back and forth. "Gods no..." she mumbled, in an effort to keep the servants away.

No air, there was no air.

The burning started deep inside her, flames licking their way from her soul into her physical body. The agony clawing a path out, craving release. She knew it was a matter of seconds until she was fully immersed in the power and consumed by its desire to unleash.

The living room door opened. Theresa entered to light the candles.

No!

CHAPTER FIFTEEN

Yarden

When Iris came to, she was in her bed, her father seated beside her. Worry lined his face. "How are you feeling?"

"Empty, and sore," Iris said, then coughed harshly.

Her father silently handed her the glass of water from her bedside table, his face solemn.

She barely had the strength to sit up, and her hands shook—spilling water on her already drenched sheets. The liquid was smooth and cool in her parched throat.

"Theresa?" she whispered, dreading the answer.

He shook his head and swallowed. "Her funeral was yesterday."

Iris started sobbing and her chest heaved, sloshing more water. "I don't—I didn't…"

Her father took the glass from her and looked at her with red-rimmed eyes. "I know."

She opened her arms, yearning for a comforting hug, but he grabbed her hands and leaned back. "Better not set you off again…"

It felt like a punch to her stomach. Iris hugged herself in an attempt to hold everything together. When her sobs slowed, she wiped the salt from her face with the sleeve of her white cotton nightgown.

Yesterday? "How long have I slept?"

"Almost two days. When Trevor found you two, you were unconscious, so we carried you upstairs. You haven't stirred since. We weren't sure you would wake up."

Iris shut her eyes, tears still spilling down her face.

"What, how, who?" She was afraid to voice her questions.

"Mercifully the priests remained at the friary for Apex's celebration. I've told them you were incapacitated from lack of food and forced to rest in bed. That we didn't need their services any longer." Her father cleared his throat. "We kept the cremation ceremony small—just us."

Iris heard what he said but had difficulty processing the meaning. Her eyes glazed over thinking back of what'd happened downstairs. She winced. *Theresa.*

Her father got up. "I'll let Trevor know you're awake. I think you need to eat something before you get out of bed."

Iris nodded, understanding she was confined to her room for now. *Good.*

Trevor arrived shortly after, carrying a tray with a warm bouillon. "Here you go, miss. The cook thought this would be safest on your empty stomach." He placed the rectangular tray on her lap and handed her a napkin.

"Thank you, Trevor." She didn't dare look him in the eye, afraid to see his judgment.

"Miss."

Steeling herself, she looked up. "Yes?"

"We, I, we were worried for you."

Iris noticed his eyes were red too. He looked exhausted—his ebony hair lifeless. He must've kept vigil with her father. She nodded. "Thank you."

He inclined his head but didn't leave.

The savory smell of the bouillon made her mouth water, and Iris devoured it. She hadn't eaten in days.

Trevor hovered until she finished her last mouthful. He took the plate from her, then moved his other hand gently toward her face. He ended up patting her on the shoulder. "You take care, miss. We will have to wait for about an hour before you try to eat more. Is there anything else you need?"

She started to shake her head, but then said, "What will happen now?"

Trevor avoided looking at her. "I am not sure, miss. I will take this downstairs now." He picked up the tray and turned on his heels.

Iris tightened her lips. She knew the village elders were informed of each passing in the village. Killing a fellow citizen was punishable by death. She wasn't sure the same rules applied to children. She'd felt Trevor's worry and sensed more despair from downstairs.

First light was always magical, his favorite time of day—the golden light a promise of wonders ahead. But today was bleak and no miracles were forthcoming. Trevor observed his master pacing the room like a caged animal. Outside, the contours of the roses in the front yard were now visible. The light chased away the darkness outside. He wished the rays could obliterate the shadows inside him, too.

Trevor wrung his hands, fear blossoming in his chest. "I promise to take care of Iris, sir. You have my word."

His master dragged his gaze up, too tired to register his vow before shuddering. "Thank you, Trevor. My family owes you. Your loyalty..." He shook his head.

Trevor placed a hand on his heart. "As if she were my own, sir."

Iris's father inclined his head, eyes half-closed while tears dripped down his face.

Trevor walked over and brushed some imaginary dust off his master's shoulder. "Should I wake her, sir?"

"No, she can't know..."

CHAPTER SIXTEEN

Yarden

I ris woke after the heavy front door clicked shut. She sat up and scanned the energy around her. The house felt empty.

Worry snaked up her heart, and she flung her blankets aside, stepping hastily into her slippers. She walked downstairs in her clammy nightgown, holding on to the wooden railing after her steps faltered. She sensed Trevor in her father's study and navigated her way there. "Where's my father?"

Trevor slowly looked up to her—his dark brown eyes vacant.

"Where did he go?" She was distressed by the weakness of his sickly-pale viridian bubble. Dread filled her and drove out the oxygen.

"Sit down, miss." Trevor patted the weathered armchair and waited for her to get settled.

She plopped down on the cool leather and pulled her legs under her—tugging her nightgown over her knees.

"The council took him into custody this morning."

"They'll kill him!" Iris cried. "He should've waited for me. I would've explained." She ran to the front door and turned the knob, but it didn't budge.

"Miss," Trevor tried.

She pushed past him making for the back door, twisting the handle again and again. "No!"

Her energy burned inside, and the monster reared its ugly head, clawing for a way out.

Trevor pulled her back from the door and visibly forced himself to maintain eye contact. "Please, remember the water dousing."

Iris made herself take big breaths. She turned her focus inward and flinched at the sight of the flames. With sheer willpower—imagining buckets of water—she managed to bring her power down to a simmer. She slumped down to the floor and leaned against her mother's striped armchair.

Trevor bent down and placed both hands on her shoulders. "Do not squander this gift your father gave you."

"But I don't want it!" Iris wailed. "I don't want it. I don't want it!"

A knock on the front door made Trevor jump. He hastened to open the door a tiny crack and was relieved to find Auran standing there. He opened the door enough to let the boy through. "Please come in."

Auran came into the living room and stared at Iris, clenching the armrests as if her life depended on it. "Iris."

Trevor stepped back but stayed in the room, mindful of the promise he had made.

Auran walked to the chair and clumsily patted Iris on her shoulder.

To Trevor's surprise she let him, and he turned away to stare out the window.

"My Dad told me," Auran said. "I came as soon as I heard."

The rest of the day passed in a haze.

If not for Auran, Trevor was not sure they would have managed. The boy had a way of calming her down.

CHAPTER SEVENTEEN

Yarden

For the third night, Iris had been the only person sleeping upstairs. The servants were all housed in the hall down the kitchen. She hadn't drawn the curtains fully—allowing the moon to shine in.

Her father's execution was scheduled for noon. The entire village was required to attend.

Iris wiped her damp hands on her navy-blue skirt, and tucked in her blouse. She knew she would need all her willpower not to erupt at the scene, nor to confess at the sight of her father. Trevor had explained in detail that her confession wouldn't set her father free. He would still be killed for perjury.

Auran and his dad came to lead the macabre procession from her house to the town square. They both looked like they had a wakeful night, too—their crumpled faces did not match their formal attire. It was the first time Iris had seen Auran in dress trousers, his white longsleeved shirt matching the color of her blouse. The servants filed in after them.

Auran squeezed her arm and she peered at him. His eyes asked whether she was still in control. Iris nodded. She knew it was vital her magic remained hidden—especially today.

They walked in silence, villagers joining their sad parade as they came closer to town. When they walked past the bakery, the baker's wife stepped outside, still wearing her apron. She nodded at Iris, heartening her. Everyone had closed shop to witness the event.

They halted as one at the heart of the village where a rickety wooden platform graced the center. A few stray nails loitered around the hastily erected structure and the smell of wood shavings hung in the air.

The sun had almost reached its zenith. On cue, the dark wooden doors of the municipal building swung open and the village elders filed out—her father up front, hands bound. Rex and his curate brought up the rear.

They lined up around the dais, and the principal elder raised his hand imploring silence. "We are gathered here today to witness the execution of a member of our community. Phillip Springtide has confessed to killing one of his servants."

Iris swallowed her bile.

"He claims her death was an unfortunate accident and the deceased was cremated in private before the authorities were informed. His testimony was confirmed by…"

Iris zoned out, unable to listen. She willed her hearing to go numb—relieved when silence replaced the elder's voice. She focused on her father's face, feeling the goodbye in his stare. His bubble was bright indigo, brighter than it had ever been. He was using up the remainder of his energy in his last few minutes, staring at her even as he was led up the two steps on the platform and tied to the pole.

Auran grabbed her sweaty hand, and his father put a protective arm on her shoulder with a surprisingly firm grip.

Iris kept blinking away her tears, wanting to maintain eye contact until the last second. When a hush fell over the crowd she knew the moment was near, and forced herself to smile—pouring all her love in that gesture.

Her father smiled back, as if simply wishing her goodnight.

At the release of the arrow she closed her eyes, engraving his smile into her memory.

She fought against the ripple of pain and fear mingling with the emotions of the crowd, some leaning forward eagerly, but most shuffling their feet.

Iris focused on her own breathing. It took all her strength to sweep the hostile energies away from her physical body. The crowd's emotions weighed her down, clinging like an oily smudge.

It felt like eternity until Auran pulled on her hand, edging her away from the platform. Concentrating solely on her feet, she let him guide her. People stepped aside, but their anxiety pressed upon her like a physical weight, each wave of worry and despair squeezing more oxygen out of her lungs.

Each footstep pushed on her frazzled edges. She kept blocking their conversations and forced herself to keep moving. She noticed the dirt on her sandals, the grey and brown coating on her feet, the pebbles in the sand, the rougher, darker soil outside the village, Auran's callused hand a beacon to safety.

At last Iris smelled the roses at the front door. Going inside would be too suffocating. She veered around the house, Auran trailing behind her, and sank to the ground behind the shed. Kneeling in the shaded grass, she focused on the green blanket beneath her, its coolness below her palms, inhaling its crispness with each breath, willing herself to calm.

The more she tried to squelch her energy, the harder it fought back, unwilling to cave. She panicked, and her hearing returned like she flipped a switch.

"Iris?" she heard Auran ask, his worry evident.

Suddenly all the sounds she thought she'd blocked out flooded in, her subconscious dutifully replaying everything.

She heard the release of the arrow, and her father's gasp when the broadhead hit his throat. Time slowed down, the tear of the arrow point piercing his flesh playing again and again. She clamped her hands on her ears, shaking her head to lose the echo of his rasping breath.

Iris sensed Auran's hand on her shoulder before he touched her, and her head shot up.

Auran pulled his hand away as if bitten by a snake. His forehead wrinkled, and he opened his mouth to speak.

"Don't, not safe," she choked out.

His eyes bore into her, not moving an inch.

The energy pushed harder on her insides. "Leave!" she bellowed.

She could no longer focus. The pressure inside erupted and she tried to aim away—praying the Gods to spare Auran.

Auran turned to sprint for the shed. He felt the blast behind him and the pressure of the wave carried him away from her. He stumbled the last few paces and grabbed the corner of the wooden building to haul himself around its edge, ignoring the splinters in his hand. He pushed his body against the hard wood, breathing heavily, praying the structure would remain standing.

Sweat dripped down his back from the heat. *Please keep us safe.* He leaned his head against the wall, unwilling to consider the alternative.

After the pressure subsided, he peeked around the corner. His heart hammering in his chest, he watched Iris. He gasped and clutched the wall for support. She was lying on her back, her left arm covering her face, the smoldering and blackened grass surrounded her like an inkblot pointed at the forest. Several bushes caught fire—the flames greedily licked the resin-rich pine trees.

Auran jumped forward, grabbed her by the shoulders and brusquely dragged the dead weight of her motionless body behind the shed. He prayed to Layla to keep her safe and ran to the house for backup. He knew the land was dry.

CHAPTER EIGHTEEN

Yarden

The next morning most of the staff were gone. Though sworn to silence, they couldn't be forced to stay. Iris didn't blame them. Frankly she was glad they'd left. Fewer people to hurt.

Trevor placed a steaming bowl of oatmeal in front of her. "I hope you like it, miss. It has been a while since I prepared a meal."

She wafted the vapor toward her and inhaled its scent. "It smells different."

Trevor smiled tentatively. "It is what I grew up with."

Iris nodded and sliced into the bright yellow farm butter. She watched the golden puddle melt and glaze her porridge before she stirred and took her first bite. It was rich and refreshing. After eating another spoonful she sensed Trevor's stare and looked up, questioning.

"I am pleased you are eating, miss. You need your strength."

Iris grimaced. Given the result of her fasting, she wouldn't ever try *that* again.

CHAPTER NINETEEN

Yarden

The black-roofed house stood outside the village, nearly hidden by trees. The front garden had once been well kept, but weeds now grew across the path and no one had bothered to trim the wilted yellow roses or boxwood hedges. The white-brick manor had about twelve rooms, judging from the number of windows.

Merlow used the brass knocker on the dark-green front door, but no one answered. He turned the knob and to his surprise the door swung open. Merlow stepped inside, right into a cobweb.

Muttering, he removed the sticky strands from his face and beard, wiping his hand on his grey cloak. The house was cold and damp—the woodstove not burning despite the autumn chill. He walked through the long hallway past several rooms and into the kitchen. Each space had the same deserted feel—the kitchen counters empty. He strolled into what must be the living room and noticed a large black stain on the floor—the granite tiles damaged. Iris was nowhere to be found.

Merlow realized the house was completely devoid of furniture—not even a curtain on the wall. All he noticed was a stale loaf of bread on the windowsill. *She must be living somewhere else.*

He went outside toward the back of the yard, checking for clues to her whereabouts. He approached a rough wooden shed when the energy flared, and his senses went to high alert. A pulse like a lighthouse sent out bursts of light, the energy so bright it was almost

~ 54 ~

visible. *That must be Iris.* He recognized the energy signature, but something felt off.

Her energy was fighting its way out and she kept clamping it down. Like a volcano trying to spew fire, then being corked and bursting through the stopper again. Merlow knew in his bones that at any point the power could erupt, and he pulled up a strong shield. He turned the corner and saw Iris jumping up and down, a blond boy her age behind her.

"Maybe if you get tired the energy will get used up." Merlow heard the boy say.

Iris grumbled something, sounding out of breath. She must have been jumping for a while. The boy spotted Merlow, and Iris stopped jumping long enough to pivot and freeze in place. She turned on her heels and stomped off into the woods.

The boy approached him warily. "Who are you?"

"I am Merlow, and I came to aid your friend." Merlow extended his hand, but the lad did not shake it.

"How do you know she's my friend?" the boy asked him with surprising authority. "And how do you know who she is? Who sent you?" the boy said, blocking Merlow's path to the trees, taking a defensive stance.

Merlow folded his hands in front of him. "Her grandmother Oma has sent me, and I have sensed Iris's energies from far away. I am a magician, and I am here to help Iris control her magic."

The blond boy narrowed his eyes. "Why?"

"Because I want to assist, and because it is dangerous for her to remain out of control. I assume you were trying to support her just now?"

The lad didn't respond, leveling a stare at him, jaw set, as he took him in. He seemed to conclude Merlow spoke the truth for he said, "Wait here, I'll go talk to her."

Merlow nodded his consent.

The boy disappeared into the woods with an ease and lightness in his tread suggesting he had been hunting from a very young age.

A few minutes later Iris and the boy emerged from the pine

trees, the young man a few steps in front of her. She looked at Merlow and the brightness of her blue eyes hit him like lightning. They were unbelievably bright with an intensity that was palpable.

Her stare went right through him, the energy shredding his shield as easily as tearing through paper. Merlow felt naked, even with his traveling cloak tight around him, as she sensed everything about who he was. He was shocked by the ease with which she broke through his protection. Merlow sensed it was crucial to maintain eye contact, although he was not even sure he could break her stare if he wanted to. She squinted to take a last deep look, and released him.

Merlow exhaled with relief. He had passed the test.

Iris said, "Auran told me Oma sent you."

"Yes, she did."

He still remembered the moment vividly. It was a moonless night and he had been waiting to fall asleep when he sensed someone's energy—strong and vibrant. It did not feel like a physical person approached, but it reminded him of the connection with his now deceased mentor—a crossed-over soul. However, this energy was feminine.

He lay still, waiting for her to speak. She had evidently been a powerful woman when she had been alive. She still was. Crossed-over souls were able to assist those whom they bonded with during life, and they often took their gifts with them to the afterlife. He had never met her, but she seemed to know him.

The woman spoke, *"I have been keeping an eye on you for a while. I came to request your assistance in training my granddaughter, Iris. She needs to master her magic and you are the only one strong enough who can teach her. The only one strong enough whom we trust."*

Merlow knew she had been referring to Thorn, a vile but powerful sorcerer. At no time would Merlow cease regretting the day his former friend started dabbling with sorcery, crossing the line to dark magic. He shivered to think what havoc Thorn could wreck with a young, unsuspecting girl. A girl with formidable powers no doubt.

Several nights ago, when Merlow had scanned his surroundings for breaches or weaknesses in his security spells, he had noticed a flare in the energy—an uncontrolled outburst quite a distance away. From the raw way the magic was shaped he knew the magic user had been a greenhorn. It must have been Iris, and the eruption must be why her grandmother now summoned him. He might have refused had he not been so intrigued by the girl's powers and what she might become. Apart from Thorn—and Merlow's former mentor—he had never come across anyone who came close to his own power. Yes, he was curious.

The thought of officially wielding his powers again appealed greatly—he still had a score to settle. Besides, he was tired of lying low.

"I accept."

"Splendid. The Earth Faerie has helped her ground, an emergency intervention, but we both know my granddaughter is in need of solid magical education. We thank you. Tell her Oma sent you." Her voice sounded tender.

Merlow refocused his attention on his surroundings and on Iris and the boy in front of him.

He smiled at Iris. "Your grandmother looks out for you."

Iris merely nodded. "Where will you stay?"

The boy shuffled his feet.

"Do you have guest quarters I can use?" Merlow asked her.

The boy's head shot up and he stared at Merlow.

"This is Auran," Iris said.

As if this gave him permission to speak, Auran said, "You can't stay in the house," and glared at Iris. They stared each other down until Auran gave in. "Fine," he said louder than needed, and turned around. "See you at dinner," he called over his shoulder, kicking the grass with each step.

Iris watched Auran until he disappeared behind the house and then angled her head to observe Merlow. He experienced the intensity of her gaze again. Without speaking she turned and walked toward the mansion.

Merlow followed her into the house as she strolled through the long hallway to the back.

"This is your room," she said, pointing at another empty room. "I sleep in the living room. It's closest to the garden," she added.

Merlow pressed his lips together, not sure what that explained but sensing this was not the time to demand answers. He stepped into the light, spacious room and dropped his travel bag and cloak on the stone floor.

She lingered at the doorstep. "Thank you, for answering Oma's call."

Merlow inclined his head.

"If you need anything, there are things in the shed." She swallowed.

"Thank you," Merlow said. "I have all I need right here," he padded his jute bag.

CHAPTER TWENTY

Yarden

The next morning Iris woke up in the living room of the mansion and for an instant wondered what was different. She sensed Merlow's energy in the back of the house—a bubble of warm yellow light bobbing about—and she recalled what had happened yesterday.

Knowing Oma was watching over her warmed Iris's heart and made her feel a little less alone. After she'd sent Trevor away two months earlier—terrified she might hurt him, too—she fully understood no one dared take her in. Auran did his best and his mother often invited her over for dinner—even tried to look into her eyes. But others in the village muttered and averted their paths when they noticed her on her way to the Stronghold's.

Iris sighed. She shook off the remnants of the nightmare that kept plaguing her—the horrible smell of seared flesh still in her nostrils—and got up. She found Merlow in the kitchen putting some grains into a pot he must've brought with him. He wore a distinct cobalt-blue robe, unlike anything she'd ever seen a man wear.

"Good morning. Are you admiring my tabard?"

"I like blue."

The corner of his lip curled upward. "Would you care for some oatmeal?" he asked.

"Sure." She curiously observed how he held his hands above the copper pan, as if he warmed them. After a few seconds the grains started boiling. Iris took a step back, a precaution for when the porridge would spill over, but to her surprise it kept simmering slow and steady.

He made using magic look effortless, and it didn't seem like he was in pain nor did it smell like fire. It felt like…breathing.

It was a stark contrast with how wielding magic felt to her: massive, painful, overwhelming and dangerous. *Perhaps, perhaps he can truly help me.*

Merlow added a few herbs and a pinch of salt.

"What did you put in there?" she asked him, not recognizing the smell.

"Sage," he said. "It bolsters your focus. Sage is a powerful herb and one of my favorites."

Iris eagerly leaned forward to get a closer look.

"We shall start with some basic exercises today, laying the foundation for your magical education. Food is equally important as spells. Most people do not realize the power inherent in nutrition and how it can either aid or hamper you."

Iris hadn't known. The servants had never allowed her into the kitchen.

They went outside and sat on the grass to eat the porridge. It tasted good and Iris devoured another mouthful. It felt as if a hole was being patched up deep inside. A hole she hadn't noticed until now.

When she swallowed her last bite, she focused on Merlow, on the lack of thoughts buzzing. She squinted and prodded his bubble.

"Are you trying to read my mind, young lady?" Merlow asked.

Iris's cheeks flushed. "Why can't I hear your thoughts?"

"Because my mind is none of your concern. Do not ever try that again."

Iris thought back to her mother's scolding. "Okay," she muttered.

"Not only is it rude, but you cannot ever unlearn what you overhear. People need their privacy—especially people you spend a lot of time with. For us to get along we must respect each other's space. Having special powers is no excuse for abusing them. Use it as a last resolve, and only when you are in peril," Merlow lectured.

"How do you know what people are plotting when you can't hear what they think? I mean, we've just met."

Merlow raised his brow. "You shall have to be content with the old-fashioned way. Pay attention and you will know. If you do not have faith in me, at least trust your grandmother."

"I didn't mean…yes. I have to brush my teeth."

Iris stomped up the stairs to the bathroom. It was the only room she dared used upstairs. She'd tried sticking to the kitchen sink for a few days, but she craved a regular bath too much. Focusing on the wooden floor she walked past the door to Thom's room, ignoring her parent's room at the far end. Light streamed in through the bathroom window, illuminating the sea-green tiles. She picked up her bamboo toothbrush and squirted some of the salty white paste on the hairs. *Stupid to try to read his mind.* Iris vigorously brushed her teeth—rinsing and spitting hard to get rid of her embarrassment.

After she had brushed her teeth, Merlow took her to the back of the yard. "Your tunic complements your eyes."

Huh? Iris glanced at her dark blue shirt. "Thank you."

"Show me the grounding exercise the Earth Faerie taught you," he said.

Iris stood straight, feet firmly planted on the ground a hand-breadth apart. She closed her eyes and turned her focus inward. Placing her right hand on her lower belly, she focused on her breathing. With each breath she slowly sent her energy downward. With each exhale, her feet felt heavier, anchoring into the earth. She kept breathing at her own pace until her lower legs were like lead. She stopped and opened her eyes.

Merlow watched her intently, a hand supporting his chin—half-buried in his white beard. "Well done. Now can you feel there is room to ground even further?"

Iris explored her body, and feeling the lack of weight in her upper legs, she knew she could go deeper. She nodded.

"Close your eyes again and focus on your feet," he said. "If you look through your mind's eye, can you see into the earth, beyond the grass? Search for the roots and go past those. See if you can stretch your anchoring even deeper."

Iris extended her senses beyond her feet, putting feelers out. A huge stretch beckoned. She let it lead her downward.

Hidden from view was a whole new world, where the insects and creatures beneath the surface had their kingdom. She sensed how her anchoring cord wove its way through the grassroots and into the earth, without disturbing the balance there. The soil opened a pathway for her to use. It was a peculiar sensation—the earth seemed to not only grant her permission to pass, but throbbed with jubilance as she merged her energies, gaining courage and stability.

She opened her eyes again and stared straight into Merlow's twinkling deep blue eyes.

"Yes!" he said. "That is it! Astonishing how quickly you were able to go deeper." He beamed at her and the weight on Iris's shoulders decreased. She smiled a small smile.

"Grounding is the first rule of safety in magic. Anchoring yourself to the earth helps you to stay balanced and focused. It is like a big oak tree. It starts as a small sapling. When the roots grow wider and deeper, the tree receives more nourishment and gets stronger and bigger. The network of roots below the ground will be just as big as the span of the tree branches. It is like a mirror image. The same goes for wielding magic. Your ability to ground needs to be equal to the strength of your power so you can maintain your equilibrium. Otherwise you risk collapsing, handing over control and the magic can consume you," Merlow said.

Chills ran down her spine. Images of flames flashed in her mind and the pressure built in her chest.

"Once you enter into this downward spiral it becomes nearly impossible to break out of that bind. That is why anchoring yourself is crucial. Now let us take the next step. I want you to focus on staying grounded and connected with the earth below while you start walking around. See whether you can keep that connection," Merlow gestured at her.

"Should I keep my eyes closed?" she asked him.

"Yes, it is easier to focus when you are not distracted by what you see."

Iris shut her eyes and reconnected with the earth beneath her, searching for the cord that had almost slipped from her consciousness. She quickly grabbed it and tied the thread around her waist. Picturing the garden, she rooted her feet firmly in the fresh grass.

Putting her arms in front of her she started moving, inching her feet forward as if she were bumbling through clouds. Somehow the energy around her was even more tangible than usual. She often noted colors around people and saw these colors shift with their moods, like the grey mist after the funerals. Now she honestly *felt* the energy like a soft cloud embracing her, brushing off her as she went by. The sensation distracted her, her focus slipped from the cord and she stumbled forward. Iris opened her eyes in time to avoid a broken tree branch ripping her eye out, and fell face down on the damp grass. She looked behind her—Merlow was only a few feet away—and glared at him.

"Go on, try again," he encouraged. His deep blue eyes calm as if nothing had happened.

Iris got up, her bright eyes shooting daggers, and straightened her shoulders. Pulling a hair tie from her pocket she fashioned her loose locks into a ponytail. She closed her eyes and tried to turn her focus inward. This time it was harder to concentrate—her emotions got in the way. She pushed her annoyance down but it kept coming back up. Frustrated she shoved her irritation down with force, putting a lid on top to close it off.

"Hold on," Merlow said. "Come over here for a moment."

Iris walked back over to him, trying not to be angry.

"What you just did, strong-arming your frustration and closing yourself off, do you do that often?"

She cocked her head, ready to defend herself. Her power started to build again.

Ignoring her questioning expression, Merlow said, "I want you to sit down cross-legged. You have taught yourself to shut down your emotions because they trigger your magic, am I right?"

Tears welled in her eyes. She wasn't sure how to respond. It was like he'd pushed a button. Years of feeling inadequate rose to the surface like a tidal wave of emotions.

"Do not over think it. We will talk more later. For now I want you to direct your emotions downward, but not into yourself, let them seep into the earth. Feel how they leak into the grass from the bottom of your spine. See them dripping down. Focus on that alone."

Tears ran down her face, warm and then cold on her cheek. It took all her willpower not to be embarrassed, to concentrate on her spine, to see the emotions slide into the earth.

At first, she sensed some resistance, a barrier, but she remembered the way it had felt when she weaved her anchoring cord. Using the same piercing focus while asking the earth to open, she was able to shed the pressure into the ground beneath her like the tears rolling down her face. But the space soon filled, and the emotion backed up, tensing her physical body. Panicking, she opened her eyes and glanced at Merlow.

He smiled. "You are making great strides. Do not worry. I will not let you explode."

Iris wasn't convinced. She didn't believe he could genuinely prevent that from happening. The sheer force which overtook her on such occasions was beyond control.

"Get out of your head and into your body!" Merlow told her firmly.

Iris snapped her head up. People rarely commanded her anymore.

"Note my energy," he said. "Sense it and see how I steer it down. It is not about forcing the energy into the earth but collaborating with it. Your energy is your friend—not your enemy—embrace it like you would someone you love. Be gentle yet strong, and tell it where to go. Your emotions are merely a vivid form of energy. There is no need to be afraid of them."

Iris glared at him unbelievingly. *He has no idea.*

She was about to tell him when Auran approached. He was still on the other side of the house, but she recognized his calm, rock-solid energy. Today there was a spike to it somehow—he was annoyed about something. Iris could've read his thoughts to know what bugged him. She had a pretty good idea, but she'd taught herself to skip around what he was thinking—a courtesy to her friend and to protect herself.

With most people, she sensed the energy of their mind but chose to ignore their thoughts. It usually worked, unless they were emotional. Then, they broadcast their feelings and there was no missing their state of mind.

"Look at me!" Merlow barked at her. "Your energy is boiling and about to spill over, yet you do nothing to prevent it from happening!"

Iris instinctively took a step back, surprised by the force of his tone.

"Don't you speak to her like that!" Auran yelled. "You're upsetting her, can't you see?" He marched over to Iris and scanned her—making sure she was all right—then positioned himself in front of her.

As Auran blocked her view of Merlow, she felt the energy from both men tearing at her. She cringed at the physical pain of her body trying to do two things simultaneously. Iris struggled to command her power—afraid to hurt Auran—and tried to follow Merlow's instructions to root herself. With her last shred of control, she managed to lock her power back inside.

Iris covered her ears with her hands and screamed "Leave me alone!" Dodging trees left and right, she ran deep into her beloved forest, making a beeline for the clearing in the center. Having expended some of her energy into running, she sat on the damp moss and ran her hand over a tree stump—tracing the brown growth rings with her fingers. Her heart hammered in her throat. It had been close, too close.

She lay down and let the soft moss caress her cheek. It was good to feel the solid earth beneath her. She inhaled. *Pine.* Somehow this place always helped her calm down, perhaps because of the happy memories of playing with the Faeries. This had been one of their favorite spots. A few twigs poked at her face and she let them.

Iris missed her Mama. Well, she missed them all, but she'd expected her Mama to teach her how to handle her...power. She'd turned fourteen on the autumn equinox a few weeks ago, but her parents hadn't been around to give her the traditional coming of age ring…

She sensed Auran's energy coming closer.

"You okay?" he asked

Concern rang in his voice and she made herself sit up. "Yes." She sighed from the bottom of her lungs.

"If he bothers you, I'll tell him to go," Auran said vehemently. "You don't need to listen to him."

Iris bit back a smile. "I know." She stroked the moss, drawing circles around a few leaves. "I think he's trying to help."

Auran sat down beside her. "You truly believe he can?"

She stared him in the eyes, and Auran flinched but held her gaze. She nodded. "When we began, the exercise worked. It's a practical way of being more centered, but then I messed up and lost it. And—" she shook her head, not knowing how to voice the feeling of how Merlow went straight for her weak spot, her loathing of her own inadequacy.

Auran's shoulders slumped. He stared at the earth and picked up a twig of his own, stabbing the moss like he was trying to puncture someone's flesh. The twig broke and he grabbed a more solid branch, testing its balance. He set to spearing a few leaves.

Iris detected his inner turmoil—it radiated off him like heat waves.

He met her eyes with a pained look and threw the twig at the nearest pine tree. "I don't know. You're sure this is the right thing?" he spit out.

Iris looked sideways at him.

He ignored her stare and got to his feet. "I don't like him making you mad," he muttered.

Focusing on her hands, she braced herself for another argument. This morning's exercises had been exhausting and she was too weary to fight. She stifled a yawn.

Auran studied her. He ruffled his sun-bleached hair and said, "If you want to try this then at least let me help, too. There must be something I can do."

She knew he wanted to keep her safe. At times it was suffocating, but he'd been there when she most needed support, so she nodded.

Some of the tension ebbed from his stance, and he attempted to cheer her, saying, "It was only your first try, you'll figure it out. I know you will." He looked down at her, his eyes so full of faith it tugged at her heart.

To hide her feelings, she stood up abruptly. "Let's go back to the house."

When they broke through the trees there was no sign of Merlow. Iris sensed his energy in the mansion. They found Merlow in the kitchen examining some sachets. "What are you doing?" she asked.

"I am preparing tea for you, with herbs to help restore the minerals you burned off this morning," he answered. "Would you like some too Auran?"

Auran craned his neck to get a closer look at the brew, wrinkling his nose. "I'll pass."

"I will make you a different one," Merlow said. "This is especially for Iris." He handed her the light blue cup, steam wafting off of it.

Iris inhaled the smell of the tea and smiled. "I like it!"

"Okay, I'll try it," Auran said.

Merlow perused his bundles of herbs and picked two.

"What are you putting in his?" Iris asked, moving closer.

Merlow held out the two sachets. "Cedar and pine, they will support his strength."

At this Auran stood up a little straighter.

"What did you use for mine?" she asked.

Merlow showed her the herbs. "Smell for yourself and see what you recognize," he encouraged.

Iris took one of the bags, opened it and stuck her nose in. She inhaled deeply and ended up coughing. She rubbed her nose, not fazed by the interruption. "I think it's rose hip!"

Auran gaped at her.

"Mama used to make this for me," she explained.

"Well, that makes sense," Merlow said. "Rose hip is one of the best dried sources of vitamin C. Before the Cataclysm, people called scientists discovered vitamin C and rose hip is full of it. The magnesium replenishes what you use when wielding your power. What else do you recognize?"

Iris scrunched her brow in concentration, peering into the next bag. "Cinnamon!" she said and smiled.

"Very good," Merlow said. "Do you know the properties of cinnamon?"

"No. But I like the warm smell." It reminded her of Auran.

"Take a sip of your mélange and try to feel what it does for your body," Merlow instructed.

Iris sipped from the brew and closed her eyes, focusing on the warmth sliding down her throat. She took another sip and paid attention. Her body let go of some of the tension. "Is it to relax?" she asked Merlow eagerly.

"Yes, cinnamon helps you to unwind. Now can you determine the next ingredient?"

Iris took a few more sips but the rest of what she tasted was unfamiliar. She was also unable to sense other effects on her physical body, except the warmth from within. "I don't know."

"The third ingredient is angel's trumpet. This root is also a poison—"

Auran inhaled sharply.

"—but used sparingly and in the right combination, it can be a powerful tonic. It stimulates digestion and aids the release of toxins."

Iris was intrigued. Herb lore was fascinating.

Merlow finished stirring Auran's herbs into his mug and handed it to him.

Auran accepted the brown mug cautiously and took a whiff of his drink. "It doesn't smell bad."

Merlow smiled. "Usually our body likes what is good for us. I believe the body recognizes what it needs."

Auran took a sip. "It's spicy. Different from yours!" He bent over to smell Iris's brew again and pulled back instantly. "Yours is hideous."

"Speak for yourself," Iris said. "At least I'm not drinking trees." Auran ignored her comment and swallowed a mouthful. She was fascinated by the effect the herbs had on them both. *I want to learn more.*

CHAPTER TWENTY-ONE

Yarden

Merlow woke up with a jolt. A high-pitched scream pierced the night—Iris. He immediately scanned the house for intruders, checking the wards he had installed around the perimeter once he had set foot on the property. His wards showed no sign of breach, but powerful magic swirled through the house.

Another scream—muffled this time.

Merlow got to his feet, summoning his power as fast as he could while running down the hallway, and reinforcing his personal shields. He pushed the living room door open while a third cry chilled him to the bone. It sounded like death.

Dawn streamed in through the curtain-free windows, and he saw Iris on the floor thrashing and turning, fighting off an invisible force. Merlow examined the room for danger, noting the magic was contained to this part of the house, then quickly scanned her body for injuries. He stopped abruptly when he smelled scorched fabric.

The cuff of her floral nightgown smoldered and was about to singe her wrist. Merlow pulled up a spell to douse the fire and kept the cloth away from her skin with another spell. The smoldering flames went out with a sizzle, and Iris woke, first terrified, then shocked and confused.

Merlow held up his hands. "I heard you scream and came running to see whether you were hurt. It was only a nightmare. There is no one here."

Iris desperately clenched her fists, pale as a sheet and drenched with sweat. "She's dead," Iris choked, and stared horrified at the corner.

Merlow pivoted, half expecting to see a corpse, and was relieved to find the room empty, save for the woodstove.

Iris broke into sobs.

Merlow assumed she meant her mother. Relieved there was no real threat, he slowly dispersed his magic, using it to reinforce the shield around the house. No sense wasting the power, even if it wasn't needed now. At a loss for words he mumbled, "I will make you a cup of chamomile tea." He hastily retreated, utterly unprepared to deal with crying girls.

Merlow found solace in the rhythm of preparing the brew. He added a touch of lavender, to help her fall asleep again. He resolved to talk to her in the morning. His intuition told him this nightmare was a regular visitor, and he needed her well rested. He put the sachets back into one of the linden-green cupboards and looked around the kitchen, wondering again why there was no furniture in the house. He stirred the tea and walked back into the living room.

Iris sat hunched, a blank look in her eyes, miles away.

He offered her the drink. "Here you go."

She looked up at him with such desperation it hurt him physically. The strength of her emotion broke through his barrier. That was twice now that she tore through his defenses, and he was pretty sure she was not even trying. *Goodness.* She accepted the cup with a feeble thank you.

Merlow wondered whether he had made the right decision to accept this charge. She seemed so frail at night, a harsh contrast to the girl who had ordered Auran off with such sternness. He pondered whether the exhaustion from today's exercises might have triggered the nightmare.

He glanced at Iris. She was warming her hands on the cup, blowing on the tea. A paternal instinct kicked in, and he asked, "Do you want me to stay in here tonight?"

She shook her head and smiled a small smile. "It's okay, thank you for the tea." She sniffed. "It smells lovely."

•••••••••●•••••••••

The next morning Iris woke with a headache, although the hammering was not as severe as usual, perhaps thanks to the herbs. She frowned at her singed sleeve. Merlow was already awake, judging by the sounds coming from the kitchen.

She got up and observed him from the doorway. He looked focused, softly humming to himself.

"Morning," she said.

"Good morning to you," he answered. "How are you feeling?"

Iris shrugged. "I'm fine."

"Are you?"

She gave him a pointed look.

Merlow added, "I need you to be honest about how you feel while we are training. The slightest imbalance may have a big effect. I am usually good at reading other people's energies, but you cannot rely on me alone. What if I am distracted or not present? You must be aware of your own well-being and be able to assess what you need quickly. Your life may depend on it."

"What do you mean?" Iris asked.

"Do you remember the first rule of safety in magic?"

"Being able to ground is equal to your power and to stay balanced."

Merlow nodded. "There are two more. Proper nourishment is crucial, and we will look at what that means later. Rule three is about getting enough deep sleep."

Oh.

He regarded her knowingly. "How often do you endure nightmares?"

Iris's heart sank. "Almost every night," she whispered.

"Do you know what causes them?"

"Memories…" her words barely a breath.

"Let us first try different potions to see if they might help you sleep through the night. It is also a great opportunity to teach you more about different herbs and their purpose."

Iris looked up. The idea of taking back control over her sleep was appealing, and it would be lovely to learn herb lore. The herbs and spices spoke to her on a deep level—she knew what the plants told her. "I would like that."

"Excellent." He handed her a breakfast bowl.

Iris followed him outside, glad he hadn't asked more about the nightmare. She inhaled the porridge steam. "It smells different than yesterday."

Merlow smiled at her. "Yes, indeed. Can you determine what I added this morning?"

Iris stuck her nose in the milky-white china bowl, eager to discover more about this intriguing scent. It smelled vaguely familiar. She knew she'd gotten a whiff of this aroma somewhere. She shook her head. "I can't remember where I smelled it."

"Make sure you mark this scent in your mind. Next time you come across this smell let me know, all right?"

Like a game. Iris nodded eagerly.

After breakfast they got back to grounding. Iris stood with her spine straight and searched for the anchoring cord. It took a few moments to sense it. Once she did, she grabbed the thread and tucked it right into the earth.

"Excellent," Merlow said. "Now try walking around while staying rooted."

This was where she'd messed up yesterday. Iris positioned herself away from the trees, closed her eyes and made sure she was balanced. Slowly she put a foot forward, taking the cord with her and took another step. After a few paces she noticed the anchor dragging, and backed up.

"Well done." She heard Merlow say. "Can you feel why the cord lagged?"

Iris turned her focus inward and realized she had seen the cord as a piece of rope—unliving, unaware. "I guess I didn't see it as something alive…maybe if I envision it like a living bond breathing my energy it'll move with me."

"Exactly!" Merlow beamed at her. "Go ahead, give it a try."

Iris imagined pulling the cord from her energetic bubble. She cast the flame-blue rope down into the earth and sensed even more of the liveliness there. Now when she put a step forward, the cord danced along, a long tail trailing behind her. She picked up her pace and walked normally. The connection held. Iris opened her eyes, happy with her achievement, and stumbled.

Merlow chuckled. "You need to walk before you can run. Do not rush. Magic requires steady steps and full control. I want you to practice this for at least an hour every day, until you can stay firmly grounded with your eyes open."

It took Iris several days until she was able to walk around with her eyes open while staying firmly rooted.

"Excellent," Merlow said. "You are ready for the next phase."

CHAPTER TWENTY-TWO

Arbres

Apex stared out the window, watching Her Eminence stroll through the palace grounds supported by Esmeralda. It was the first time he noticed Her outside since he'd moved the household to Arbres. *I hope She enjoys the rose garden.* He'd had his priests emulate the prize garden with fragrant wine-red roses from Her family's estate at the Dead Seas.

Apex's assistant unrolled a parchment with care. "I located the official Bright Eyes Prophecy in the palace library. Recorded four years after the Cataclysm—the first time the Oracle of Phortàk prophesized."

Apex waved a hand, his ring flashing bright green. "Read it to me."

His curate cleared his throat. "You will rebuild from the rubble and find new ways to live. For several generations you will experience peace. Until crepuscular forces gather and the imbalance occurs again. When times become dire, a female with bright eyes and immense power will emerge. She will drive out the dark with her light and sacrifice her life for the greater good. Balance will be restored."

Apex took the fragile scroll. "I expected more details."

"The children's songs are quite accurate, sir."

"Keep looking." Apex rubbed his ring—emerald stimulated clairvoyance and purposefulness. He knew his God had spared Her for a reason. He would make sure he did all within his might to prepare for the moment that bright-eyed girl would come calling.

CHAPTER TWENTY-THREE

Yarden

Iris yawned, not yet fully awake despite the brisk morning air.

"Always remember the first rule of magic," Merlow said. "It is where you should start until it is as automatic as breathing. Make sure you are grounded before trying to wield magic of any kind. Are you ready?" Merlow asked her.

She verified her grounding cord was in place. "Yes."

"We will start with something simple: heating water for tea. Find a clay mug in the kitchen and fill it with water," he instructed.

She came back with her favorite light blue cup, filled to the brim.

"I want you to sit down and place the mug before you on the grass. Hold your hands close like you are warming them, but do not touch the mug."

Iris glanced around and asked, "Can I sit with my back against the tree?"

Merlow looked up with surprise. "Why would you want to do that?"

She shrugged. "It feels more solid."

He pursed his lips, then gestured at the tree. "By all means, if you think it will aid you."

Iris positioned herself with her back against her favorite chestnut tree, the trunk lending her support. Leaning sideways, she grabbed a few chestnuts from under herself and put them aside. *That's better.*

"When you heat water or apply your magic for healing," Merlow explained, "it needs your constant focus and attention because you direct the energy and what it does in that moment. When you stop the flow, the alteration stops."

"Okay."

"Now focus on where you feel your power inside you and direct the energy through your hands toward the cup, with the intention of slowly heating the water." Merlow held his palm above the mug. "Like this."

Iris sensed the magic around his hands and how the power connected with the water. He stopped before it started boiling. "Now you attempt it."

She focused on the power inside her and tried to imagine the energy coming out of her hands.

Nothing happened.

She peeked up at Merlow. "I feel my power but I can't get it to move."

"See if you can sense the way my power advances," he said.

She studied him with intense concentration. As soon as his power stirred, she noticed a tiny yellow thread traveling from his abdomen, through his arms and out of his hands. The yellow thread circled the mug. More magic arrived, turning into a cloud surrounding the water. The yellow cloud dipped into the water, mixing with it, but not quite. The water slowly started to boil.

"What did you notice?" he asked her.

"It was like you pulled a thread of energy out of your magic reservoir, like pulling a thread out of a carpet, and then encircled the mug with it, stirring it into the water."

"That is an interesting way to describe it," Merlow said. "Did you *see* the energy?"

"I always do."

"That might prove useful. Now try again. Tap into your reservoir and direct the magic toward your hands."

Iris focused, willing the power to go to her hands, and failed. The energy kept getting stuck in her upper body. "I don't know how to get the power from my chest into my arms, it won't move farther," she grunted. "It keeps swirling around my heart chakra. It's like your magic supply is in your lower belly and mine is in my chest. My magic wants to come out there."

···········●···········

Merlow was not able to see the colors she described, although he sensed the presence of her magic, lots of it. "I have never heard such a thing." Something was different about her power, not necessarily wrong but off somehow.

If she was not able to get the magic into her hands, he was not sure how he could teach her to focus and steer it. That is where mastering magic began.

Perhaps... "If you will permit me, we can connect mind-to-mind so I can sense your magic supply and where it gets stranded. I can help you get the energy in motion so you can replicate the process," Merlow offered.

Iris wrinkled her forehead. "What does it mean when we connect mind-to-mind? Can you see all my thoughts?"

"I will only be able to sense what you are thinking in that instant. I cannot wander off and look at your memories at will," Merlow said. "However, you should only do this with someone you trust," he added. "Later I shall teach you how to connect with people telepathically over a distance. We call that a mindlink. This is slightly different for it will allow me to feel what you feel, so I can sense your magic and where it is located."

"Is it dangerous?" Iris asked.

Merlow was glad she did not accept his offer lightly. It was crucial she was able to discern people and their intentions and ensure they were honorable. "It could be, if neither of us knew what we were doing. Or if one of us had bad intentions. You see, you need to open up to my mind as much as I need to open up to yours. We take a similar risk here. However, if you do not feel comfortable we shall devise another way."

Iris was silent for a moment. "How do I stop if I don't want to continue?" she asked.

"We will grab hold of each other's hands to allow for this kind of connection. When you release my hands, I will no longer be able to sense what you feel. To also stop me from seeing your thoughts, you can shove me out of your mind by you imagining to sweep my presence out of your conscious."

He saw she was weighing his words. "Okay, I'll try it," she said.

Merlow stood in front of her and extended his hands, inviting her to stand. She gently placed her hands in his. Her fingers were long and elegant—great for playing the piano.

"First confirm you are still grounded," he said, giving her a chance to do so.

Iris nodded.

"Now see if you can sense my presence tapping your mind, and imagine opening a small door to let me in."

"It tickles!" she said with surprise.

Merlow laughed. "Yes, it tends to do that. Now slowly create a small opening so our energies can connect."

"It's like our colors mix—your yellow and my blue—it's turning green!"

Merlow was astounded. He had never heard anyone describe magic this vividly. "Is it entirely green or do the individual colors remain?"

Iris took a moment to respond. "It's green in the middle but the yellow and blue surround it like a ribbon."

He picked up the wonder in her assessment and smiled to himself. "Now bring your focus toward your magical supply. Slowly lead me there." He felt her tug on his energy, moving toward her chest and soon arrived at a cave overflowing with magic. The power thrummed through his veins.

Merlow endured the pressure in his eardrums. Her magic had one narrow exit, pointed toward her heart chakra. There were no other openings. Magicians directed their energy through both arms and hands, like a conductor leading an orchestra. He did not sense any of the delicate, sophisticated magic here. It was raw power.

"Can you gently guide some of your power out through your chest?" he asked Iris.

The energy moved right away. Many things happened simultaneously. Connected to her senses, Merlow heard his own voice reverberate within her—echoing in her mind—he sensed how she perceived his energy, how she noticed Auran approaching the house, the mood Auran was in, his sapphire energy bubble—and how Iris set her overwhelming power in motion. It fought its way out of her chest—a tidal wave crushing everything in its path. It knocked him out cold.

CHAPTER TWENTY-FOUR

Yarden

Merlow's presence left Iris's mind and she blinked at the abruptness. She opened her eyes and watched her teacher fall. Time slowed, and she observed everything with heightened clarity.

Merlow dropped like the stones Auran used to shoot across the pond, his billowing tabard the only thing moving.

He hit the ground with a thud. The impact resounded in the earth beneath her. Her knees buckled. Time ran normally again.

Merlow still didn't move.

His face was as white as his beard, his frozen expression a look of surprise. He lay stock-still.

Not again. Not another one. Just as she'd started to get used to him, to like him even.

"Auran!" she yelled. "Auran!"

Merlow's face blurred with Thom's, his blond curls ruffled, leaves in his hair and green-brown bark on his face, hands, smudged all over his clothes. She shook him. "Wake up, wake up!"

Auran came running—bow at the ready—scanning for danger. "What?"

"I killed him. I killed him Auran!" Iris fell to her knees, sobbing violently. The force of her despair crushed her, a gaping abyss. Terrified to look down, utterly convinced she could never return once the darkness claimed her, she gasped for breath.

Auran dropped to his knees and checked Merlow's pulse, then

leaned closer and put his right ear on the magician's chest, blond hair hanging over his eyes. "Shhh," he said to Iris. "Be quiet."

Iris bit back her tears and waited.

"I can hear his heart beating faintly," Auran said. "Help me get him inside."

Auran hauled her to her feet, and together they dragged Merlow inside. The magician was more substantial than he looked. They lowered him onto the brown woolen blanket where Iris slept.

She fidgeted.

Auran stared at her. "Can't you use your magic?" he asked her. "Scan him to see what's wrong, heal him, whatever it is you do?"

"We never got that far!" Iris exclaimed.

Auran placed his hands on her shoulders, the weight a calming presence. "Why don't you start by grounding," he suggested.

Iris was ashamed it hadn't even occurred to her in her panic. She focused her attention inward and tried to ignore her fear as best she could—gently pushing the worried clouds aside—concentrating on her feet and her connection to the earth.

Within seconds her training kicked in and she sensed the anchoring cord. With relief she tied it around her waist, feeling instantly calmer. Iris surveyed Merlow and scanned his body in what she hoped was an effective way to discern his health. Hardly any color surrounded him—it was mostly transparent—and she sensed he was low in energy. She grabbed his hand and willed her energy into his body, going on instinct alone.

After a few minutes Merlow stirred, and the color surrounding him revived. A pale blue emanated from him. Iris kept holding his hand, sending more energy to Merlow until he opened his eyes.

"Hey," she said. "How do you feel?"

Merlow blinked a few times. "Like I was run over by a herd of bison," he croaked.

"Shall I make you some tea?" she offered.

"Sage," he whispered. "And mace. Not tea."

"Okay." She knew he meant she should let it simmer longer, making a stronger concoction for healing rather than herbal tea.

"Auran, can you light the stove?" She wasn't going to experiment with magically heating the brew now.

"Sure," Auran said, walking over to grab some kindling.

Iris retreated to the kitchen, shaking. *What's the point of having magic when it only hurts people?* She browsed through the different spices to find sage and mace, pausing when her eye caught *Lavendula angustifolia*. Merlow hadn't mentioned lavender, but she sensed it would round off the potion nicely: calming, relaxing, mildly sedative and a stimulant to the immune system. Yes, it would do.

She poured water into a pan and added the herbs one by one. With each herb she said a prayer for Merlow's full recovery, a silent request to Layla, Goddess of Hope.

Back in the room, Auran had the stove going, and she placed the copper pan on top. She let the brew simmer for a few minutes, and poured a little bit in a cup, placing the pan back on the stove so the rest of the concoction could continue to steep. After it cooled enough to drink, she took the brew over to Merlow. "Can you sit up?"

Merlow made a feeble attempt to get up, but Auran grabbed his shoulders and supported him into a sitting position. Iris held the cup in front of Merlow, and an approving look flashed across his face when he smelled the mélange. He took a few sips and leaned back, Auran slowly lowering him to lie down again.

After they repeated this procedure three more times, Merlow was finally able to sit up by himself. The color slowly returned to his cheeks.

Merlow gazed at them. "Adding lavender was a nice touch," he said to Iris. "It is good to know you have a feel for herbs."

Iris smiled at the compliment.

"What happened?" Auran asked.

"I am not quite sure," Merlow pondered. "If you do not mind I think I will take a nap."

Iris and Auran both got up and went into the garden. They silently walked back behind the shed, where Auran eyed her questioningly.

Iris sat on the grass and held her head in both hands. "I—I think he was repelled by what he saw," she said.

"What do you mean? What did he see?"

"I had trouble directing magic the way he showed me, so he wanted to look in my mind," Iris explained. It took all her strength to keep from crying. "It was fine at the beginning. I sensed his energy in my head, but when I showed him my magic, it nearly killed him. I *hate* my magic! I don't want it."

She could no longer hold back the tears, and glared at Auran, daring him to say something.

He stared right back. "It doesn't sound right. Why would looking at your magic hurt him? You didn't use it on him, did you?" he asked.

"No!"

"Okay, I'm sorry. I know you wouldn't do that—not on purpose."

She shot him another dirty look. *Grounding, I need to ground, to control my anger.* She got to her feet and walked into the woods, needing the calm presence of the pine trees, she inhaled their fresh, resinous scent. Auran's energy trailed behind her.

When she arrived at the clearing, she sat on a soft patch of fresh green moss. As Auran entered her line of sight she held up a hand. "Don't."

He nodded, respecting her need for silence, and sat at the other end, facing her.

She ignored him and thought about what had happened. She had honestly believed she had killed Merlow. She couldn't stand the idea of losing another person. She flexed her shoulders to release the burden and sighed.

As soon as Merlow recovered she should ask him to start with healing lessons. She wondered what was wrong with her, why her power worked differently. For a moment she'd felt genuine surprise in Merlow's thoughts as he took in her magic supply, followed instantly by worry and concern. She snorted. *Of course something's off with my magic. The events in the past have shown that clearly enough.*

She met Auran's gaze and smiled, grateful he'd been near when Merlow dropped like the dead. Her cheeks flushed when she thought of her panic—another thing she needed to master.

~ 85 ~

Yarden

Merlow took two days to restore his strength. After Iris prepared breakfast, experimenting playfully with different spices—he grimaced at the memory of her dill and cinnamon combination—he decided to start with herb lore.

After searching the bare house—the work of a moment—he found a beautifully worked linen tablecloth in the shed. Merlow made a note to ask Iris why all her belongings were stacked there, then spread the embroidered cloth on the grass and laid out his sachets—all ecru, the color showing them safe for ingesting.

Iris gaped at the white cloth.

"Did your mother embroider this?" he asked gently.

Iris lovingly stroked a pink flower. "Yes, she often did needlework and she loved flowers."

"Well, perhaps her spirit can support you in memorizing suitable combinations for seasoning." He tried to mask his chuckle.

Iris grinned. "You didn't like my breakfast, did you?"

Merlow laughed. "Not my favorite, no. As a rule of thumb, you can select the spices you want to combine, hold them together and take a whiff. See whether the blend smells balanced. When in doubt, experiment with other sachets."

Iris nodded enthusiastically.

"We shall focus on herbs for sleeping first. You get to make an herbal concoction for yourself for tonight. A well-balanced potion holds at least three elements. The first herb acts as a base, like the fabric you use for a dress. The second is to enhance a specific effect, as the design emphasizes the waistline or whether it will be work clothes or a fancy dress. The third holds the brew together and integrates the three elements, similar to the stitches that hold the dress together. Does that make sense?"

"I've never had a fancy dress."

"Well, yes." He guessed there was no point for fancy dresses, not when you didn't have anywhere to go.

Merlow grabbed a few sachets and held them up. "Later on you can use multiple herbs for each of the three elements and make a more advanced potion. Each herb influences the other, and they can fortify or diminish each other's qualities, hence the importance of balance."

"You mean like making a dress with different fabrics and colors, and making sure they match?"

"Yes, something like that indeed." *Thank you Layla, for steering us back to herb lore.*

"Is that why dill and cinnamon didn't work together, because their colors clashed?" Iris asked.

"Yes," Merlow hummed, distracted because of a thought that she sparked. "Do you see colors around herbs, too?"

Iris stared at the different ecru cloth pouches and picked up dill and cinnamon. "I do." She studied the two herbs. "Dill looks purple and cinnamon is orange." She wrinkled her nose. "It's like they repel each other." She held the sachets together and bumped them against each other—like bouncing magnets.

Merlow was intrigued. This was a whole new way of looking at plants. Perhaps he could use a more intuitive way of teaching instead of making her memorize lists of herbs and their properties. He remembered how tedious that was. Besides, he did not possess the lists…

"All right," he said. "Using the colors, which herbs would you pick for your deep sleep mélange?"

She perused the sachets, laying aside lavender, chamomile, neroli and rose. After a moment, she added sandalwood.

He was impressed she was able to select the appropriate herbs. It had taken him months to progress beyond a three-herb potion. For her to select neroli and sandalwood—both exclusive and highly expensive—she could not have come across those aromatic plants in this neck of the woods. "How did you do that?"

"I thought about relaxation and how I feel when I'm calm, and the color that's around me then. I tried to create the same color with the herbs. When I squeeze my eyes and peek through my lashes, I can see the herbs connected to that color."

"What do you mean?"

"It's like each herb has different colors which make up the final color. Like lavender. The overall color is blue but when I look deeper, I see the blue is made up of sky-blue and white with a hint of cherry."

Merlow saw the picture she painted in his mind's eye, a flower with three petals, each of a different color. *Fascinating.*

"Perhaps each has a different vibration, that's why some don't go well together!" Iris exclaimed. She started sorting all the bags, creating different piles. Just when it looked like she was done she started moving more bags around.

Merlow was confused. "What are you attempting now?"

"It keeps changing!" Iris grumbled. "Once I shift focus, all the colors change."

The colors change? "You lost me."

"Well, I sorted the herbs for relaxation, and then I looked for which ones to use for more energy and other colors came forward. It was like they changed clothes."

"It sounds as if you are able to tap into the different characteristics of the herbs, and they show you what you are looking for." Merlow could hardly believe it. "Let us not try to do everything at once. We shall go back to the sachets you selected for today's mélange."

They went over the five herbs one by one. Lavender served as the foundation, chamomile enhanced the relaxing properties, and rose rounded the blend off. A concentrated dash of neroli, or orange blossom, was a quick note for going mentally deep and known to aid with depression, fear, sleeplessness, and calmed the nervous system. Sandalwood tied everything together as a festive ribbon.

Iris held the five herbs together and sniffed. "I love the way it smells."

"Excellent. After dinner we shall boil these herbs for twenty minutes and let the blend steep for one hour before you sift the brew," Merlow instructed. "I want you to take notes on how you feel before and after you drink it, and as soon as you wake up in the morning. Write down anything that stands out so you can document the effects. It will be the first entry in your botany journal." He handed her a tan leather diary.

"A gift?" Iris's eyes opened wide.

"Yes, for you. All magicians have a journal to monitor progress, or develop spells or potions."

"Thank you," she whispered, her eyes now lit with gratitude.

Iris untied the leather strap and opened the notebook, leaning forward while carefully turning the pages—already enticed by her future writing.

"Make sure you keep track of everything. You never know when you might have a need for it."

Iris nodded eagerly. "I will." She sat up clutching the journal to her chest. "Auran is coming." She got up and ran off, calling, "Auran, look what I got!"

Auran studied the leather cover and traced his fingers over the spine. He picked at the top. "Cool."

"Don't break it!" Iris tried to grab the journal back.

Auran lifted the diary out of her reach "I'm not! Look. The spine is hollow."

Iris stood on her toes. "Let me see." Auran tilted the book for her to examine the opening.

Her eyes lit up. "Oh, I bet I can fit some acorns in there."

Merlow smiled at her excitement. He was glad she had a knack for potions. Herb lore was often one of the least popular parts of magic. Most magicians never found herbalism appealing, but Merlow knew concoctions would prove crucial, especially in this country so devoid of nutrients. Thorn had certainly thought medicinal herbs beneath his standing.

CHAPTER TWENTY-SIX

Arbres

Apex leaned back in his armchair—stretching his legs in front of the fire.

Thorn's raven-black hair dripped water on the carmine rug. Outside the arched window, it was still pouring with rain.

"Why have you summoned me?" Thorn demanded.

"I need an update. Have you found the bright-eyed girl yet?"

"Trust me, if I had found her you wouldn't be asking me that."

"Watch your tone," Apex said, angling his head.

Thorn leaned against the mahogany desk, water drops trickling on the waxed wood. Apex squinted but decided to let it go.

"Someone must be shielding her. I've traveled half the country— trying to locate her."

"So travel the other half," Apex instructed.

"I was, until I was summoned to Arbres…"

"Join me for dinner. I found some scrolls I want to discuss." Apex pulled the cord.

Servants entered and placed silver platters piled with food on the mahogany table—even the dinner chairs matched the reddish-brown desk.

"This is intriguing," Thorn said, putting the scroll aside long enough to stuff his mouth with pheasant. "If I can train some of your priests to scan for energies from a distance, we could monitor from here."

"That's what I thought." Apex swirled the wine and drained his glass. The butler refilled the crystal goblet from the decanter. "Take this week to select my most apt novices, and they're yours to drill."

"Excellent." A dark smile spread over Thorn's face.

CHAPTER TWENTY-SEVEN

Yarden

A whole new world beckoned in Iris's herbal lessons. And somehow Oma felt closer when she was around plants—both of her grandmothers did.

She couldn't wait to write the first entry in her journal. She pulled it from underneath her pillow, sat on her blanket, and chewed her pencil. *Where to start?*

Iris wrote *Healing properties of lavender*, and narrowed her eyes. *Yes, that sounds like a serious entry.*

Dutifully she recorded what she'd learned until her hand started cramping, her muscles no longer used to writing so much. Shaking her hand, she reread her notes, giving the book a satisfied nod. After closing the notebook, she retied the strap before tucking her treasure back under her pillow.

When they had finished a simple lunch of rice and carrots, Merlow suggested Auran stay to watch her next magic lesson. "So you can learn to distinguish between stable magic and when it becomes unbalanced," Merlow said.

"What should I do when the magic is unstable?" Auran asked.

"In general? Get away as soon as you can."

At this Auran took a half-step back.

"No need for concern. We shall experiment with small amounts of magic first," Merlow reassured.

Auran gave him a pointed look. Iris knew he was thinking of the accident a few days ago. "Why did you pass out?" Auran asked.

Merlow's cheeks colored. "Your friend is stronger than most. We shall work on channeling the energy first." He turned to face Iris. "Your magic flows from your heart chakra, so we will focus on dispersing the energy through your chest."

Iris was relieved she didn't have to force her power into her arms again. *I hope I can get my magic to flow out of me safely.*

"Do you remember the first steps?" Merlow asked.

She nodded and searched for her anchoring cord while she leaned against the chestnut tree. She closed her eyes and focused on the energy in her upper body, seeing it swirl calmly. As she reached out in her mind, with the intention of opening up her chest, her energy woke up. The swirling increased its pace and the power built. She imagined a door in her chest, similar to the door in her mind through which Merlow had entered, and a surge of energy burst out.

Merlow swore, "In the name of Seth and Layla!"

Iris opened her eyes as he deflected her power and directed the blue haze upward, defusing the magic as if dispersing mist.

Once the magic was disarmed, Merlow stood and shook his head. "You cannot do anything slowly, can you?"

Auran chuckled.

She glared at them both. "I got it to move, didn't I?"

"You sure did. Let us mark this as full power—"

"This was *not* full power!" Iris exclaimed.

"—and start the flow at a soft ripple," Merlow concluded.

She scowled.

"Are you done?" Merlow asked sternly.

Iris shot Auran one more look for good measure and relaxed her shoulders. "Yes."

Merlow noticed Iris shoot a dirty look at her friend before she was able to release some of the tension.

"Iris, you need to pay more attention to your mood…" Merlow swallowed the rest when he noticed her glare.

"Don't! Don't preach to me about mood swings. All I do is worry about my power erupting. I'm afraid to do anything!"

"I told you not to upset her!" Auran added, walking over to her.

"Iris, I did not mean to unnerve you, nor do I want to hurt you. Nevertheless, I *am* your teacher and thus responsible for your well-being," Merlow said. "You have not gone up in flames because you taught yourself not to feel, but you *are* overburdened, and your senses are continuously overwhelmed. Grounding and the potions will take the edge off, but only practice—lots of practice—will get you to mastery."

Iris watched him intently, blue eyes blazing.

Merlow took this as acquiescence. "Take a short break and make a relaxing herbal tea for all of us."

Iris turned on her heel and stalked toward the kitchen, muttering something under her breath.

Auran stared at him and followed Iris into the house.

Merlow released a breath he had not realized he had been holding. *What a pair.*

He was glad he had answered Oma's call. After laying low for so long he truly enjoyed teaching and using his Gods-given talent. Part of him still chafed at the loss of his best friend. Merlow rubbed his chest—the ache might never fully cease.

But if he was right about Iris—and Merlow was convinced he was—he had another, more important, reason to aid her in mastering her power. Being installed as the Master Magician was one of the proudest moments of his life. Merlow had not forgotten his vow, pairing his magic to the future of Fleuris.

He sat down to await the arrival of the tea. When it came to directing magic, he was relieved she had been able to release the energy through her chest, but he had no clue how to teach her the different levels. Typically he would instruct a student to release magic through one finger, then two and so on, slowly building intensity. Merlow was stumped for a solution, with her way of steering magic. He prayed her instincts would guide her.

They drank the chamomile tea in silence. Merlow said, "All right, try again. This time move the magic as slowly as you can. Let it trickle out."

To his amusement Merlow noticed Auran inching behind a pine tree after her second attempt.

It took several hours. Each time Merlow had to neutralize her magic before Iris was able to get a grip on her energy. Merlow sensed her agitation and decided to end the afternoon on a playful note. "Well done. Remember the second rule of magic—proper nourishment? Using magic depletes your body. It uses certain trace minerals and nutrients. You will need to replenish those."

Iris nodded. Auran moved closer, letting go of his tree.

"Can you scan your body and see which herbs it craves?" Merlow asked Iris.

Iris looked dubious. "Can I go over to the kitchen and choose the sachets?"

"No, I want you to tune into your body first."

Iris frowned, then sighed, closing her eyes. After a few heartbeats she said, "Iron, magnesium, chromium."

Did she just deduct the depletion of her body on a nutrient level? "How did you work that out?" Merlow choked out.

She shrugged. "It came to me when I focused on my body."

"Can you...can you see which herbs it relates to?"

"No, but I would like some hot chocolate."

Merlow started laughing, a deep rumble from his chest, and he let himself fall backward into the grass.

"What? What did I say?" Iris huffed.

Merlow allowed himself to enjoy the mirth. It had been a while since he had laughed out loud. "There is an ample supply of all those nutrients in raw cacao," he kept laughing. "I have some in my travel bag. I guess you deserve some." He waved her off.

"Did my body use minerals too, being around magic?" Auran asked.

A bright young man. "Excellent question," Merlow said. The possibility had never even occurred to him. "Did this afternoon cost you energy?"

"Well, I was worried"—Auran glanced after Iris, who had disappeared into the house—"and I feel like I stood too close to the fireplace." He rubbed his skin and yawned.

Merlow wondered whether Iris and the boy were so connected Auran sensed when Iris worked magic, or whether he was merely more sensitive than most people and his body responded to the flow of power. "I am not sure. I can examine your nutrient level in a healing session, but it will only show big fluctuations. Perhaps Iris detects a difference in your aura? We should ask her."

"I don't want her to worry about me."

"As you wish. Perhaps we should brew you some herbal tea too. Or in this case, chocolate for everyone."

••••••••••●••••••••••

When Iris got back to the house Merlow was chopping up roots in the kitchen. "What are those?"

"This is fresh ginger. I am adding it to the sauce for dinner."

Iris picked up a piece and held it to her nose. "It smells peppery and refreshing."

"What else can you tell me?"

Iris studied the tan root with its yellow interior. "Something with heat, and it makes me think of my stomach."

"Both pepper and ginger are warming from within. What do you think the ramifications are for your stomach?"

Iris sniffed the chopped pieces. "Flow, it's got to do with flow."

"Indeed. It aids digestion and helps reduce nausea. Always good to remember."

"It that why we're eating it?"

"Well, I have missed its lovely flavor, and it supports our immune system, too, which is most welcome in the fall. I will teach you to dry the rest tomorrow. We shall have to start growing our own herbs and spices."

"Why?"

Merlow sighed. "Apex is monopolizing the herb market, claiming spices for his priests and followers."

Oh.

"We will need to be more careful of how and when we use our store."

CHAPTER TWENTY-EIGHT

Arbres

Apex stared at his ring, urging the emerald to spill another vision. "Why don't you let me try it?" Thorn suggested.

There was not a hair on Apex's head that considered lending his father's ring to the sorcerer. He cocked his head.

"Suit yourself," Thorn said. "Have you tried recreating the circumstances of that first vision?"

Apex huffed. *What didn't I try?* After that first lucid dream he hadn't taken the ring off even for bathing. He'd been completely taken by surprise when shown a cave. Upon waking he knew the location would at some time shelter the girl from the prophesies. He'd instructed Thorn to coax Lord Ashen to have his Gemini Squad shoot at different caves. Who knew what a lucky shot might do?

It was unfortunate that, given the time lapse, Lord Ashen's magician hadn't been able to deduce which caves they'd targeted. Apex hadn't dared travel the mountain range since.

The heavy oak door of his study flung open, and his curate rushed in. "Monsignor."

Apex frowned at the lack of decorum.

"Her Eminence, the fish," the young man panted, leaning on his knees.

Apex's eyes bulged. *Not again.* "Is She well?"

"No monsignor. The grand physician requests permission to solicit aid from the sorcerer."

"Granted."

Apex was stupefied She'd been able to get the kitchen staff to prepare Her fish from the Dead Seas again. Some of the staff were loyal to a fault…

Ever since the ecological disaster, fish from that former sea were virulent to anyone except Her. The grand physician had surmised the small doses She had ingested as a child had made Her resistant—though not immune.

CHAPTER TWENTY-NINE

Yarden

Iris knew how to block out the colors around people. She did it when she was worn out. She'd stumbled upon the ability when she'd been sick as a child, perhaps five years old. When her body needed to preserve its energy for healing, the bubbles vanished. She recalled the moment clearly, the world becoming flatter, less vivid— none of the remaining colors of clothes and furniture as vibrant as the living colors emanating from people. Now, when she needed to, she could turn the colors off by shifting focus in her mind.

The grayish landscape had lasted two days until her father came home with a secret stash of acorns. When her health returned, so did the colors. It happened when she woke from a slumber. Theresa walked in with a cup of broth, surrounded by her usual vibrant violet bubble. That very instant something shifted inside Iris, an extra room opened in her head, allowing her to see with her eyes *and* her mind.

Those two days were still one of the bleakest times of her life, feeling cut off from her life force, but not as dark as… She cringed from the memory, willing herself to look for something, anything, to shift her mood. She got up and went looking for Auran.

CHAPTER THIRTY

Yarden

"I love your mother's bread," Iris sighed happily.

Auran tore off another piece. He mumbled around a mouthful.

She held the crust against her nose and breathed in. *Mmm.* She always saved the crispy delight for last.

After lunch Merlow announced, "Iris, you are ready to learn more about healing."

Yes. After a year of practicing the basics she was going to learn something useful.

"Now it is best to practice on a real injury." Merlow spotted Auran.

Auran scampered to his feet and held his hands up, "I'm fine."

Iris giggled.

Auran glared at her and quickly added, "I saw a squirrel this morning, I think his leg was hurt. Should I go find it?"

Merlow stroked his beard, hiding a smile. "That is a lovely idea." He turned to Iris. "You know how to prepare yourself."

Iris nodded and got to her feet.

"I found it!" Auran hollered.

She smiled. Auran was great at tracking animals. She opened her eyes and saw him walk out of the forest, clutching the red-brown squirrel against his navy-blue shirt.

Merlow beckoned him closer and pointed at the big chestnut. "Can you seat yourself against the trunk and hold the squirrel in your lap?"

"Sure." Auran sat down, gently cradling the animal.

"Iris, place yourself in front of him and see if you can figure out what is wrong with the creature. Do not disclose the problem, Auran."

Auran shook his head "I won't."

Iris sat cross-legged in front of Auran and focused on the animal. Its bubble was pale—the same as when someone was sick—and she noticed the energy was almost translucent on his left hind leg. She pointed at it. "This one."

"Yes," Auran and Merlow said in unison.

"Can you get a feel for what is wrong with it?" Merlow asked.

Iris held her hands over the squirrel, but Auran pulled the animal away.

What? She felt the betrayal in her stomach.

"I'm sorry, I acted on impulse. I know you won't hurt it on purpose," Auran said, looking contrite. He continued clutching the squirrel, and asked Merlow, "Are you sure it's safe?"

"I would not let her practice on live animals if I thought she was not ready," Merlow answered.

Auran held the squirrel as if making an offering.

Iris released a breath, then reached out to stroke the soft pelt. She bent over and whispered, "I'll do my best to heal you, okay? I'll go slow."

She met Auran's eyes.

"I'm sorry, Iris, I truly am," he said.

His pain emanated from him, mingling with hers. She swallowed. "I know."

"All right," Merlow said. "Make sure you clear your energy, check your cord and scan his energy to determine the problem."

Iris nodded and closed her eyes. Her emotions swirled, and she noticed Auran's energy too. She took a few calming breaths and with each exhale she released some of her own hurt until her energy calmed down. Her stomach settled.

Keeping her eyes closed she reached forward and searched for the squirrel's faint energy, moving her hands to where it was weakest. Exploring with her mind's eye, she saw where the energy flow was interrupted, an entangled mass of muscles and tendons. "I think he broke his leg." As she said that an image flashed by—a chase, a tree branch snapping—she zeroed in on the leaf-covered forest floor and a flash of pain. She flinched.

"Excellent," Merlow said. "Tell me how you propose to heal him."

Iris retraced the energy, thinking of how to restore it. "I'll redirect the flow of energy and knit the bone together, take away some of his pain, but not all. We don't want him to use his leg yet, and I think we should splint his leg and feed him some herbs," she concluded.

Merlow nodded. "Well done. I am glad you remembered that though magic can fuse bones the body needs time to strengthen the connection before a person, or squirrel, can put their full weight on the bone. Which herbs would you recommend?"

"Well, assuming he, no wait, let's check his energy," she murmured. "He would need something to prevent inflammation like ginger or coriander and calcium to mend his leg."

Merlow smiled. "If he were human, we would certainly make such a concoction for him. Since these spices are becoming scarce, what else can you give him? Something from the forest maybe?"

She considered the alternatives, scanning through the forest. "Tree bark!" Iris exclaimed. "For the inflammation. He could chew on it. From the, the Copaiba tree!" She beamed at Auran. "My Mama told me."

"I know where to find one," Auran said.

Iris clapped her hands. "We'll fix him!"

"Very well," Merlow said. "Yet the patient is still waiting. What will you do first?"

Iris narrowed her eyes. "Prepare," she said determinedly. "Find a splint and something to tie it to his leg." She studied the squirrel. "You think he won't try to take it off? Chew on the strings?"

"We will have to see. Auran cannot hold him forever."

Iris got up. "Perhaps I will keep him in the house, to make sure he eats his bark." She walked to the house and came back with a teaspoon and a ball of brown yarn. Showing it to the men, she asked, "You think this will work?"

"That spoon is way too big." Auran laughed.

Iris put her hands on her hips. "I know that," she said indignantly. "I thought if his brace is heavy and unwieldy he won't try to run around with it."

Auran peered at the scrawny thing in his lap. "It could work."

"All right," Merlow said. "Let us keep an eye on the time, the patient is in pain and he could be in peril."

"Sorry." Iris sat down. "Auran, you have to hold him still," she instructed.

He nodded.

Iris held both hands above the broken leg, focusing on redirecting the energy flow. It was mostly blocked where the muscles were torn, and she gently drew on her magic. She watched the shards of bone blend back together and the bone restore to its original position. The instant it snapped back in place, some of the tension left the animal, and she looked at Merlow for confirmation.

"Well done," he nodded. "Now you can splint his leg."

She took the silver teaspoon and cautiously aligned it with his leg. "Merlow, can you bind the string around it?"

Merlow tied a complicated knot. "It is time to get your patient inside."

Iris carefully took the squirrel from Auran and together they walked inside. "I'll find him some of that bark," Auran said.

"Okay," Iris said. She gingerly placed the animal on her blanket. "You have to stay still, okay?" She wagged her index finger at the critter. "Or you'll hurt yourself."

She thought of her mother and the healer that had been apprehended. If only she'd known what to do then…

Iris perched on the other end of the blanket to keep watch, and pulled her notebook from underneath her pillow. She leafed to a fresh page. *Healing. First patient: red-brown squirrel.*

CHAPTER THIRTY-ONE

Yarden

I ris squatted on the grass to catch dew drops with her fingertips. The nights were getting colder again. So much had changed. After she'd gotten used to Auran's deeper voice, she now had to suppress giggles when he stroked the fuzzy blond hairs on his upper lip.

"You are ready to start learning spells," Merlow announced, stepping out the back door.

Iris sat up eagerly. *Finally.*

"The difference," Merlow continued, "between using magic for healing or heating and spells is the continuity of your focus. Through the use of spells you project your energy outside of yourself—giving the magic a life of its own. The spell is able to exist apart from you, without your constant attention."

Wow.

"Now you remember the three rules of magic, right?" Merlow asked.

Iris nodded.

"There is a fourth rule. Never use magic when you are sick. You can heat water, unless you have a fever, but not much more than that. When you are ill, using magic strains your body, not only delaying your healing but actually endangering your health. Plus, when you are unwell your magic becomes unstable..."

She shuddered and pushed aside the smell of scorched flesh.

"We shall start with protective spells. A shield is a spell you cast to safeguard yourself. A ward is a spell to ensure the safety of the perimeter, building or room. We will commence with shielding. Are you ready?"

Grounding, calm. "Yes."

"Imagine you pull a hood of magic over your head, then make the hood so big you fit entirely inside it. Pull the magic all the way around you."

"Like a tent?"

"Yes, something like that. Can you feel it?"

Iris shook her head. "It gets stuck at my face."

Merlow squinted. "Release the magic and try again. Use your hands to steer the magic."

Iris focused on the magic swirling in her chest and forced it to come out slowly. She grabbed the magic with her hands and pulled it over her head and behind her back and her legs—all the way to her feet.

"Very well, now make sure you place it under your feet as well. The ground is not a barrier for magic, so you need to protect your underside too."

Iris tried to push the magic into the earth, but it kept bouncing back. "It doesn't want to go through the grass."

"Remember how you weaved your cord into the earth? Have your magic merge with the ground. Do not try to force it in."

She imagined the soil opening beneath her feet to allow her magic in, then pulled the energy from her heels to her toes—it tickled the soles of her feet—and up again. Keeping her eyes closed she managed to draw her magic up all the way to her chest. The beginning and end of her shield hovered over one another.

"Excellent. Now merge the two ends so your shield is seamless. Try it," Merlow encouraged.

Iris tried to persuade the upper end to come down, but it pushed the lower part away. She thought of sewing and roughly stitched it shut. The edges were now connected, but it felt frail.

Merlow observed her curiously. "What did you do?"

"I sewed it together."

Merlow smiled. "That is very creative. Does it feel solid?"

"No," she said, annoyed.

"Try to fuse it as you did with the earth. See the colors blend."

Iris searched for the magic. She noticed the blue pulse of her power and joined the two ends, realizing they were one and the same. As soon as she did, the magic flowed all around her like a living breathing cocoon. She opened her eyes in surprise.

Merlow pressed his palms together in excitement. "Wonderful! From now on add a shield each day after you ground."

"Okay. Will my shield be active all day?"

"In the beginning a spell usually holds for several minutes or hours—depending on the complexity of the spell. As you get more experienced, spells should hold for one or two days."

"Are protective spells the ones that last a day?"

"Not necessarily. The stronger the magician, the longer a spell will last. Simpler spells hold longer than layered ones."

"Layered ones?"

"Yes, we will get to that later. Once you are fully trained I expect most of your spells to last two days at least."

Oh.

WHEN IRIS WOKE the next morning she was disappointed her protective shield was gone. The spell had still been active when she went to bed, and she hadn't sensed the magic dissipate. She went to find Merlow in the kitchen. His yellow bubble a sunny touch in front of the linden-green cabinets. "What does it feel like when your protective shield ends?"

He continued stirring their oatmeal. "It depends."

"On what?"

"If the spell is coming to its natural end, it peters out. If it is an important or complex spell you will want to feed your magic into the spell before that point though, to prolong it. Maintaining the spell is usually faster than casting it anew—especially with layered spells."

Iris was intrigued. Layered spells sounded exciting.

"However, if another magician or sorcerer disrupts your spell, the feeling is more abrupt. Like someone took your coat off, in the case of a shield. If the spell is farther from you, it is…as if an energetic bell sounds. You are tied to your spells, you will notice."

"How can someone break my spells?"

Merlow laughed. "Shall we eat first?"

Iris nodded and followed Merlow outside, rubbing her arms. It was a bit cold to sit on the grass. She glanced up surprised when she sensed a warm breeze. Merlow's eyes twinkled.

"Is that a spell?"

He nodded. "Technically we would call it an enchantment, referring to a more complex or multi-layered spell. Warming air is considered a luxury though. It takes a lot of magic to keep warming the air around you, so only use it when in peril."

Iris stretched her right hand out to feel the flow of air, searching for magic. She didn't feel anything, so she studied Merlow's hands and followed the butter-yellow magic flowing out of his fingers. She narrowed her eyes. His magic turned into a cream-colored cloud—a warming mist. Then it floated away. "It's gone!"

"A warm breeze takes up quite some magic, and you should always keep power in reserve. You never know when you might need it. It is good custom to only use magic when required."

"Okay." Iris dug into her hot porridge. Today it was flavored with cinnamon, sweet and warming. She chewed slowly. Auran teased her about how she took forever to eat. She'd never been able to explain why she preferred to savor her food.

After breakfast she took the bowls to the kitchen and rinsed everything in the white porcelain sink, keen to learn more about spell casting. While she put the bowls and pan away, she felt Auran approach, and ran outside. "Auran!"

He walked around the corner. "Hi!"

"I made a shield yesterday. I made a shield!"

"Nice! Where is it?"

"Huh?"

"Your shield."

"You can't *see* it."

"Why not? Show me."

"No, it's a spell—a protective shield."

"Really? You can make magic shields? Wow." Auran's eyes were alight. "Can you make one for me?"

"I don't know. Merlow!" She looked around, then used her senses to locate the magician. "He's behind the shed. Come on."

They ran to the edge of the forest. "Merlow, can we make a shield for Auran?"

"Good morning Auran. What do you need a shield for?"

"Well, I don't need one now, but it could be useful. I don't always carry my alderwood shield."

"A powerful magician can cast shields outside himself, but the person needs to stay in range of the magician or the protection will not hold long. Unless…" Merlow studied Auran, circling him.

"What? What do you see?" Iris probed.

Merlow rubbed his chin. "Do not get your hopes up, but if I am not mistaken, you have the potential for basic magic, Auran."

Auran took a step back. "What?"

"Really?!" Iris exclaimed, jumping up and down. "You have magic Auran. You have magic too!" she clapped her hands.

Auran was white as a sheet. "What do you mean, I have magic? What if I don't want it?"

Merlow held both hands up. "I said you have the *potential* for basic magic. We shall know for sure as you age. Common magic settles around the age of eighteen. I could give you herbs to support that process, to nudge it, so to speak."

Auran sat down, staring bewildered at the grass.

Iris squatted beside him. "Are you alright?" His sapphire bubble was fainter than usual.

"Iris," Merlow said. "Perhaps you can make him some tea."

"You want tea?" she asked Auran.

"Sure." He sounded unenthusiastic.

Iris looked at Merlow. "Maybe Auran needs hot chocolate, too?"

"All right, but only for him. Let the herbs steep twice as long while you keep an eye on it, and add only one teaspoon of cane sugar to the cacao."

Iris got up and ran toward the house, yelling "Okay!" over her shoulder.

"Auran," Merlow urged.

Auran looked up at him. Devastation lined the boy's face. "I don't want magic. I don't want it."

"There may come a time when it is important you can protect yourself with more than arrows or swords."

Auran's eyes widened.

"I think you know Iris has a purpose. There is a reason for her power. She is not ready yet, but she will be. At that point anyone close to her shall need extra protection, too."

Auran swallowed. "My father wants me to train in the Amazon."

"I think your father senses that someone must balance the power in this country, and that person must be an extremely powerful magician."

"Aren't you powerful?"

Merlow shook his head. "Not enough. Thorn and I are almost equal in strength, and with the majority of magicians killed or usurped by Apex, Iris and I do not stand a chance. Not yet." Merlow thought about the handful of friends that Apex—well, Thorn—had subverted. He pushed the sense of betrayal aside.

"Will they kill her?"

"Once they know who she is they shall certainly try. That is why her parents moved here—to live secluded. It is our job to ensure she is prepared."

"Does she know?"

"No, and she cannot know. Not until she is in control of her magic. We do not want her to erupt again. You *must* keep it a secret."

Auran nodded. "I promise."

"Do not worry about your power. You shall never have to be

afraid of losing control. If you preserve your magic, assuming we can indeed awaken it, you will have only enough for shielding. You can never use it for anything else. I want you to think about it. Consider why it may be useful for you to uphold your own protective shield."

Auran took a big breath. "Okay."

"And be mindful of your thoughts around her..."

CHAPTER THIRTY-TWO

Kaale Mountains

Iris walked back to her chamber in the Kaale Mountains—leaning sideways to let one of the guards pass, hauling armor. She automatically deflected his thoughts, though there was no missing his anxiety.

That's it! She's seen the archers in the meadow but hadn't picked up the buzz of their mingled thinking. *Someone was shielding their thoughts.* Shooting time-traveling arrows required a skillful magician, but she'd never heard about one capable of hiding the minds of others. *Well, Merlow knows how to conceal his own thoughts.*

After the—intense—healing on Basil she'd been knocked out for a day. Iris still felt the toll it had taken, slowly recovering and refilling her magic reservoir.

Until now it had never been fully depleted. Though Merlow said, she hadn't reached the bottom of her power but the limit of her physical ability to sustain while handling magic. *Something I need to work on.*

Iris entered her chamber and sat down. If Apex was behind the attack Sourni might've heard something. Slowing her breathing she reached out to Sourni.

Crickets.

Apex must be around.

Iris knew Auran would come find her as soon as he'd finished his rounds. She bit back a sigh of relief every time he returned safely from his trips to solicit more supporters. He wouldn't want her to worry, and she'd seen him fire a bow often enough to know his skill, but worry she did.

She smiled when he walked in. "How's Basil?"

"Merlow is stuffing him with potions—"

"Yes, he does that."

"—He said we'll know more by the end of the day."

"Good. It helps that Basil is in good shape." She eyed Auran. *He's in good shape, too.*

"Have you been ogling his muscles?" Auran teased.

Iris laughed. "His biceps are hard to miss."

The son of a woodsman, Basil had learned to swing his axe at a young age. Auran always marveled that a man with his bulk had a knack for stealth.

She handed him a bowl, her thumb brushing his hand. "Here's breakfast."

"Thanks." Auran dug in.

She'd abstained from adding cinnamon, her favorite spice for porridge. The warm scent reminded her of Auran, so she saved it for when he was gone.

"Nice to eat something warm," Auran said.

"You must be getting tired of deer jerky."

"Ahuh."

She smiled and watched him eat, pretending she was a house-wife sharing dinner with her husband. *I would be bored out of my mind in a week.* Though being allowed to hug him on a daily basis...

Auran spooned down the last bite. "I needed that."

Iris leaned over, extending her hand to his face, then pulled back. "You have porridge left on your lip." She cursed herself. *What made me do that?*

He wiped the smudge away and tilted his head. "What's wrong?"

Her hand tingled. The sensation traveled up her arm. Power stirred within her chest.

No. Iris pushed her feelings down into the bottomless pit where she kept them. "Nothing." She sat on her hands to make sure she wouldn't do anything stupid. The length of Auran's last trip must've shattered some of her iron control.

He leveled a look at her. "I missed you, too." He winked.

Iris grimaced. *Ayna might've dealt us different cards.*

"Do I smell that bad?" Auran asked. "I'm going to take a quick bath."

Iris nodded.

Auran's trips back to Arbres were getting too dangerous. It was only a five-day hike back from the coast, but he couldn't enter the gorge after first light. One overly attentive priest or early riser could prove fatal.

Her eyes lit up when Auran returned. When he was around it was impossible not to turn them on. It was automatic. *By Seth.* Soon she'd have to tell Auran to keep his distance. *Good luck with that.* Though better to risk his anger by setting out on her own than jeopardize this entire enterprise.

Too many people had already died. They'd come so far, so close. Just a few more weeks according to the stars that whispered to her in her dreams, and sometimes when she was awake. She felt their soothing presence even here in the cave. Everything was speeding up. A time would come when she would have to cut everyone loose and complete her mission. But not yet.

Auran hung the cotton cloth that served as his towel on a piece of rock jutting from the granite wall.

"What took you so long?"

Auran raised his eyebrows. "My bath?"

Iris rolled her eyes. "Your trip."

"The road was crawling with spies. Taking the back roads and traveling after sundown increased the length considerably."

Iris clenched her hands. "Are people still going missing?"

"Yes, and not just for hoarding acorns or apples. The arrests are increasingly random." Auran swore. "They're cutting down extra trees to install more gallows. The woodsmen and carpenters are working overtime. The gravediggers, too. The last safehouse I stayed at, they'd just buried their newborn niece and sister-in-law."

He shook his head. "The baby was so malnourished it didn't last a day, and the mother was sorely in need of a healer…"

Iris nodded. Several years ago, Apex had decreed acorns and apples holy property and, therefore, strictly reserved for priests. The powers in the food were considerable and they helped most people replenish much-needed vitamins and minerals. Without these nutrients women were unable to give birth to children with magical abilities—the main reason behind this ruling. That it lessened the strength and vitality of the population was a bonus.

The snap of a twig brought her back to the present. Auran was breaking wood for the fire. Silly man—he knew they could never light it. The smell of wood brought back memories of home. Playing in the forest, when her gift still seemed bearable, blissfully ignorant of the lonely path she'd have to travel.

Iris moved closer to Auran and the branches, breathing in his freshly washed scent, with a tinge of sweat. *He must've run back.* She would give anything to lean in and hug him. Have him tell her everything was nothing but a nightmare. That there was no need to keep a tight leash on everything.

She was tired of tiptoeing around her emotions, and living more in other people's feelings than her own. She sighed deeply.

Auran looked up. "Having a hard time?" he asked gently.

Iris shrugged her shoulders. "Just fatigued."

He closed the gap between them and looked into her eyes. "I do worry. You should rest more. I know the strain you are under, and one of these days it'll be too much."

She nearly blushed. Good thing *she* was the mind reader.

Iris forced the corners of her mouth up. That was the least he deserved after his perilous journey. She didn't want to ruin what might be their last days together.

She got up to pour them filtered water, and fetched three acorns for Auran—the sign of resistance. Nowadays even thinking about them could cost your head. A small reward for all he'd given up in his efforts to protect her. Her and the cause. This wasn't the life he'd have picked, but he never complained. Ever since it became clear Apex wouldn't stop until all strong magicians were eliminated or joined his ranks, Auran had encouraged her to take a stand and use her power.

He threw her an acorn.

He really should eat all three. He needs his strength.

Auran nodded at the acorn in her hand. "You need one, too."

One acorn gave the strength to go for hours and replenished vital minerals—a true power food. That's why they were strictly reserved for warriors.

She smiled. "Thanks." It would help keep her dreams away.

CHAPTER THIRTY-THREE

Bois des Sangliers

"Auran is coming." Iris looked up from the herb sachets Merlow had her studying.

"We shall take a break," her teacher said. "You have come a long way in a year—despite our long concealment in these woods making a less-than-ideal classroom."

Iris rose and walked softly along the path, pulling up short when she caught sight of Auran standing tensely beneath a tree. *Why isn't he hurrying closer? I haven't seen him in months…*

She startled when he spun sharply and kicked the trunk—orange and gold leaves raining down on his frustration. Iris swept her eyes through the thicket, praying no one had heard, and quickly pulled up a muffling spell. They'd been hiding for over a year—it would be a shame to get caught now.

"What's wrong?" she implored.

Auran pulled a crumpled sheet of paper from his pocket and held it up. "This is what's wrong!"

She grasped the pamphlet, but he yanked it right back.

"Don't read it," Auran urged.

"What, what does it say?"

Auran shook his head. "It's a warrant—for you and Merlow."

"A warrant? What on earth did we do? Merlow!"

Merlow took the bulletin from Auran and scanned the content.

"Iris…" He paused, combing his beard with his fingers. "You may want to sit down."

"What? No! What's wrong? You're scaring me!"

Auran put a hand on her shoulder. "Do you know the Bright Eyes song that children sing?"

Huh? "No."

He looked at Merlow for support.

Merlow held up his hands. "I cannot carry a tune."

"Okay." Auran took a deep breath and sang with a warm voice:

"From the ruins you will build,
A new life shall find its way.
No more blood is to be spilled,
'til there comes a darkened day.

When famine sweeps across the land,
A girl with eyes both bright and blue,
Will drive the dark out with her light,
Balance will be brought anew."

Auran paused, not sure how to continue.

Iris shook her head—bewildered. "You think that's me?"

"We know it is you," Merlow stated. "So did your parents. That is why they kept you sheltered. It seems now Apex knows too."

Energy started swirling inside her—bitterness coated her tongue. "Why has no one told me before?" she yelled. "What does it even mean?" All she wanted to do was run away. Sadly, she knew Auran was faster, and Merlow might tackle her with a spell. *Damn.*

"Your parents did not want to burden you too soon. And I decided we should wait until you were more in control of your powers. We could not risk another eruption."

Iris kicked at a leaf, not ready to give in.

"There is a third verse to the song," Merlow confided.

Auran jerked his head up. "No! This is enough."

"She should know." Merlow's voice was firm.

"What?" Iris demanded. Both Auran's and Merlow's auras flared with distress.

The magician cleared his throat. "Rather than try to sing, I shall tell you the last part of the Bright Eyes Prophecy."

Iris looked between the two men. "There is a prophecy?"

Merlow nodded. "She will drive out the dark with her light and sacrifice her life for the greater good. Balance will be restored."

The silence hung heavy between them. Numb, Iris didn't utter a word.

She was too restless to sleep that night, though she pretended to be asleep when Auran tried to talk to her, unready to forgive him.

"I DON'T UNDERSTAND. You can't stay in hiding forever. What good does it do you, or anyone?" Auran called out.

"You know I don't want to put anyone else's life in danger. It's bad enough Merlow has been dragged into this." She was tired of their old argument.

"You don't understand." he yelled. "We're all a part of this already. None of us has access to the food we truly need if we want to stay healthy. You can't even keep a fire going during the night because the concealing spell can't be used that long. We're like lambs for the slaughter, waiting for Apex's whim to take us out. Who knows what regulations he'll come up with next? You're our only chance to change this. You're the only one who can take him on," Auran said. "You tell her, Merlow," he gestured at the older man.

"Auran is right," Merlow said,

Huh? He never takes sides.

"I believe you have to honor your gift and use it for the greater good. You were not born to spend your life sleeping on barn floors or in the forest. It is not much of a life anyhow. You are trained now. You are ready."

He made it sound like this was something he'd seen coming for ages—perhaps he had. Iris had never allowed herself to look beyond her current situation, needing all her focus and attention to learn to control her powers and survive.

She put her hand up to indicate she needed time to think. She hadn't seen the sun in ages, only able to go outside at night for a while unless they were deep in the forest. Sometimes they stayed in a place where she could catch a glimpse of the stars at night, which was soothing. Most days dragged by slowly. She put all her energy into mastering her skills, honing her talent. Her throat tightened. "All right, I'll consider it. I'll think about actively using my powers."

IRIS CAREFULLY PLACED her feet, sidestepping twigs and dry leaves. The unnatural silence of the forest screamed a warning. The hair on her arms stood on end. Iris glanced at her companions to see if they felt it, too.

Merlow looked intently at the lanky trees. Auran reached into his quiver and notched an arrow. The soft green moss masked their presence.

Merlow held up his hand, motioning them to halt. Iris moved next to him, Auran flanking her.

Abandoned cabins stood in a semicircle, weeds growing in the window openings. Iris inhaled sharply. "What happened here?"

"Use your senses," Merlow answered.

She slowed her breathing, centered herself and opened to her surroundings. The energy radiated such chaos she had to brace herself.

Iris let her instincts guide her to where the energy intensified and paused. She took a deep breath and let the magic lead her back in time. From where she stood, her awareness opened a window in her mind's eye, into a sleeping village just after dawn.

A tall raven-haired man entered the semicircle of small timber houses. He must be a potent sorcerer— power radiated off of him. Men carrying swords and bows accompanied him. Without warning the sorcerer blasted away the wooden doors, "Get outside— now!" he bellowed.

The armed men spread out, each taking up a stance by one of the rough wooden cabins.

Slowly the dazed villagers filed out of their homes in their nightclothes, carrying children, some wrapped in blankets.

"Stand over there." The sorcerer pointed to the middle of the clearing.

A woman carrying a baby pulled a half-asleep toddler along. One of the soldiers pushed her and she fell into the brown dirt, landing on her elbows to shield her infant.

The soldier hauled her up by her hair. "Move!"

The children started crying, the young boy calling "Mommy!" The mother staggered forward, clutching the baby, and urged her little boy along into the clearing.

All the villagers were herded together, away from the small homes.

The sorcerer motioned to one of his men.

The soldier stepped forward, unrolling a piece of paper. "This village has violated regulation number thirteen: Each oak tree and every acorn shall be immediately reported and handed over to the closest Order of the X. Failure to do so constitutes an act of treason."

The sorcerer spoke. "Not only have you failed to report this oak to the priests so the tree could be added to Apex's sacred groves, but some of you dared to eat the acorns. These sacrilegious actions resulted in the birth of a magically able boy, which you conveniently failed to report as well. Since none of you complied with his ruling, you are all guilty of treason and shall be punished accordingly."

Iris swallowed, smelling a tinge of the villagers' fear.

The sorcerer pointed at the mother, her light blue nightgown streaked with mud, and said, "Get him."

The closest soldier moved to take the baby, but the mother hunched, hiding her newborn in her arms. The sight tore at Iris's heart. She stepped forward to help and lost the connection. Iris backed up, scrambling to tap back in, and heard the mother begging "Please spare him—raise him to be a sorcerer!"

The soldier yanked the boy from her arms.

"No, no," she cried, clinging to the baby's feet. The other child cried even louder.

Tears started rolling down Iris's cheeks.

A second soldier slapped the mother across the face until she let go, wailing.

The soldier handed the baby boy to the sorcerer.

The sorcerer dangled the baby by his swaddling cloth. "This is what happens when you disobey. This is Apex's punishment for those who believe they can oppose the law!" He smashed the baby to the ground—its crying stopped.

Iris yelled, "No!" She felt Auran move closer and vaguely heard Merlow say, "Do not touch her."

A shock went through the crowd and the mother sank to her knees, staring at the heap of a boy in the mud, arms stretched forward. Several villagers turned and made for the cover of the trees behind Iris, hauling their children with them, but only took a few steps before they all fell, as if struck by lightning.

The sorcerer barked a vicious laugh. "There is nowhere to run." The armed men stepped forward. In minutes, the soil was soaked red. The atmosphere vibrated with violence, weakening Iris's connection with the past. She struggled to keep the window open.

"One of the huntsmen left for an early trek. Wait here and take care of him, too," the sorcerer instructed.

Tears streamed down Iris's face. She opened her eyes and looked at both Auran and Merlow. "I had no idea." Then she lurched sideways, throwing up, pouring all the cruelty out.

I was meant to see this. Someone had to stand up and fight back.

THE NIGHT AFTER stumbling upon the abandoned village, Iris relived it again and again, crying out in the dream but unable to rouse herself. She woke up sore, her muscles aching from the strain and her throat raw from stifled screams.

Something must change. She knew deep down that even though she trained daily she could do more. Until now, she'd focused on gaining control of her curse, and she had. *Well, most of the time.*

But if she were to take down Apex, she needed more than control. She would have to exploit every inch of her abilities and actively use her power.

"Acceptance."

Iris looked around. *Who said that?*

"Close your eyes."

She checked her surroundings once more—scanning the trees for signs of movement—and strengthened her shield before shutting her eyes.

An image of an ebony-haired man hovered before her. *Father!*

"Hello, darling. I'm glad you can see me."

"Father!" Iris reached to touch him, but her hand was unable to grasp hold. The familiar shape of his physical body lacked an aura and was no longer tangible.

"I'm here honey, I wish I could hold you, too."

Iris blinked away a tear. "I've missed you."

"I know. I've watched you training. I noticed you sensed my presence from time to time."

Oh.

"I'm so sorry, Father! I didn't mean to kill her!"

"I know."

Iris wiped furiously at her tears.

"Remember your mother told you the rules for assisting from the afterlife?"

She nodded.

"So you know I'm allowed to help you. I'm here to tell you to stop resisting."

Ouch. Her mouth suddenly dry, Iris fumbled for her canteen of water.

"I'm very proud of you. You've learned to control your gift."

"How can you call what I have—what I did—a gift?"

"There's a reason for your power. You'll never fully control your magic until you embrace it."

Cold fear gripped her stomach.

"I know you're scared. But I trust you."

His image started to fade. Iris stretched her arm. "Don't go!"

"I love you darling."

Iris sat back, the sound of her father's voice still ringing in her mind. She opened her eyes and stared into the distance. Day was breaking, but this sunrise failed to lift her spirits.

Auran woke, and came immediately to her side when he noticed her tear-stricken face. "What happened?"

She shook her head. "Later."

AFTER BREAKFAST SHE told Auran and Merlow what had happened.

"How will you accept your magic?" Auran asked.

Iris looked at him sideways—*was he growing a beard?*—and shrugged.

"One step at a time," Merlow said.

"What's the first step?" Auran asked.

Merlow faced her. "You decide. You consciously choose to embrace your gift, and then follow the signs."

"The signs?" Iris asked.

"You shall know. You will feel a nudge or a clarity. Sometimes it is about refraining from action."

It sounded a bit hazy.

Auran leaned forward eagerly. "What's the first sign?"

She rolled her eyes.

"Your father's visit from the afterlife is a clear indication. Embracing your gift requires you to come to terms with who you are, and what you have done. In the interim, devote yourself to controlling your gift further and more deeply."

"Okay."

IRIS PLACED HER feet a handbreadth apart on the forest floor, ready to ground. To her surprise she felt a new sense of determination. She purposefully fastened her cord. "I'm ready."

"I have wanted to teach you this new spell. Do you believe your-self ready?" Merlow asked.

Iris stared into his deep blue eyes. His aura showed it was something big. "I want to do this."

"It might hurt," Merlow warned.

"That's okay."

"Auran, you may want to step aside," Merlow said.

Auran hastily retreated. "I'll go hunting."

"I shall teach you how to stop time," Merlow declared.

Iris's eyes bulged. "Stop time?"

"Well, pause it—to be precise."

Wow. "Okay."

"Place your hand on your heart, feel it beating."

Iris complied.

"The spell appears to be one layer, but it is a stacking of incan-tations."

"Then why isn't it layered?" she asked.

"You will notice," said Merlow. "This spell is more a continuous stream than separate layers."

"Okay."

"I shall demonstrate. Pay close attention to what you sense and stay attuned to the beating of your heart."

Iris focused on Merlow's magic—his yellow reservoir stirring as he tapped in. He pulled his power up his chest and through his arms and hands. The hum of magic increased as he cast the spell.

Suddenly the droning in her ear stopped. She glanced around the forest—everything was suspended midair. *My heart.* She focused on her heart and noticed its steady drum. *Huh.*

After a moment the buzzing in her ear returned.

"What did you discern?" Merlow asked.

"The forest went quiet, and everything was frozen still. My heart kept beating and my mind still worked."

"Indeed. Pausing time does not affect magicians in the same way, or any humans within their aura. Now it is your turn," Merlow said.

Her heart beat faster.

"I will show you the spell via mindlink first, and then I shall prompt you."

Iris paid close attention to the yellow threads of magic spun by Merlow. *This is seriously complex.*

"As you can see it is a multifaceted spell. I know you can cast it," Merlow encouraged. "Now with your hand resting on your heart, draw on your power."

Iris gathered magic. *Here we go.* She imitated what Merlow showed her. Her muscles stirred.

Halfway through the enchantment, her tendons hurt.

She stretched her right calf, hoping to preempt a full cramp.

"Keep going at a steady pace," Merlow warned.

Iris wiped her sweaty hands on her shirt. The pressure on her ears increased—the sign of a powerful spell. She plowed through. The pain spread from her muscles to her abdomen. A spasm took her by surprise.

"Focus!" Merlow barked.

Iris held on to the spell as if it were her lifeline, scrambling to keep all the pieces together. If she hadn't been firmly rooted she would've tipped over. She forced the last bit out, like pushing a boulder uphill. The enchantment fell into place and she experienced the same sense of weightlessness. *I stopped time!*

Merlow started time back up.

Thank the Gods. Iris fell to her knees. In the corner of her eye she noticed Auran's return. He held some animal. *Dinner.*

"You can come closer," Merlow said to him, beaming.

Iris swayed. She couldn't decide what hurt most.

Auran ran up to her, placing two rabbits at her feet. "You okay? Maybe you should lie down."

With Auran's support, she limped to her sheepskin blanket.

Merlow handed her a concoction. "Drink this."

Iris sniffed.

"Just drink it."

She had no energy left to roll her eyes. *Maybe it'll ease the pain.* She downed the green brew. "This is gross."

"What is good for you is not always tasty." He winked.

Iris scowled, though the potion gave her a bit of a lift. She said to Auran, "He's trying to kill me."

"Shhh," Auran said.

"Let me take your pulse," Merlow said, ignoring her comment. "A little high. Now look at me." He monitored her pupils. "Follow my finger."

If Merlow hadn't taught her the importance of checking a magician's vitals after casting intense spells she would've refused.

"Hmmm. You should rest."

Oh, really?

Auran passed her his flask and Iris drank thirstily, eager to rinse the bitter taste out of her mouth. She narrowly stopped herself from spitting out the first gulp—water was scarce. "Thanks."

"What did I miss?" Auran asked.

"Torture, complete torture."

Auran shook his head.

"A new spell." Her eyes widened. "Auran! I stopped time!"

"Really? Isn't that dangerous?"

"That I don't know. But it sure is painful."

Auran leaned against the granite wall and swallowed the last bite of acorn, its power already nourishing his physical body. "I sometimes dream about it, you know."

"About what?" Iris asked.

"All the things we can do when we're done fighting."

"Ha, I'm not even sure what Fleuris would look like."

Auran took a sip of water. "Of course you do. No more people dying for lack of healers or nutrition. No more fear for having magic, and no more people getting arrested for no good reason."

"It sounds like a mirage." Iris undid her braid. "What would you do?"

He took a few more sips. "Marry. Start a family."—

Oh.

—"Not right away. First I would travel, for fun. Explore places and meet new people without having to worry where their alliance lies… And you?"

Iris turned and grabbed her brush from her satchel. "I don't know." She brushed her hair intently.

"Everything is in place at the Citadel. Try to get some sleep. I'll keep watch," he reassured.

He was good at keeping away the Lonely Ones. The crossed-over souls of those with no one in the afterlife never meant her any harm, but it was exhausting to keep fighting them off, to deny them the warmth and energy they sought.

Iris could never see past the battle, and feared it meant she wouldn't be there to see it. Not that she'd ever tell him.

There was so much more to say. But her rest had to be a priority—otherwise, she was an open flame near dry wood. Not that there was much to set on fire with all these rocks, or that some warmth wouldn't be welcome. Iris huffed. This gorge hid her well, but the numbing cold was ever present. *I might get lucky tonight and dream of sunshine.*

Once Jacob discovered this place, he'd created an ingenious system of pipes leading warm water from the wells to keep the chambers from freezing. His days apprenticing in his father's building workshop had paid off. Staying here kept their secret supply of acorns hidden—and Apex's people couldn't read these mountains. Three hundred meters below ground they were safe. Anywhere else her power radiated too strongly. She dreaded having to tell Auran they were leaving in the next few days.

Iris curled up next to the would-be fire and inhaled the smell of wood. Just a few branches to remind her of home. Auran put his traveling cloak around her. The idiot would be freezing in an hour. She paced her breathing to a meditative state, feeling the protection of the shield Auran held firmly in place.

Auran watched her do her breathing. She soon drifted away in what he hoped would be a dreamless sleep. *Stubborn woman.* Even though it cost her a lot of energy, she never let her exhaustion show, but he'd learned to recognize the signs—the way she moved, and when she used more herbs in her meals.

A faint light hovered at the edges of the grey granite. The floor was empty save for two sheepskins serving as sleeping mats and their would-be fire. Iris's leather satchel was tucked in a corner—her precious herbs safely stashed inside. Not many people would call this place cozy, but she never complained. Perhaps in shielding other people's emotions, she cut off her own ability to feel discomfort.

She looks younger when she's relaxed. The hard part was watching the nightmares crawl over her face, knowing what she relived. He'd learned the hard way not to wake her up. It had backfired—literally. He was grateful she still allowed him close. There would come a time when he would have to fight for the privilege, and it was approaching fast. *I know her too well.*

They had to be ready before then. Auran counted on Sourni to buy them time—to not be caught off guard.

After her shift, Sourni walked home via the village. She patted the apple in her pocket. Though the red star-apple hadn't fully ripened, she'd eagerly collected part of her monthly bonus. Her mother desperately needed the vitamins.

Boots scraped against the uneven stones. *Sentries.*

Sourni froze, heart pounding in her chest. Across the street, two sentries dragged her mother along, her bare feet bouncing off the dusty cobblestones. Sourni made to follow them, but someone grabbed her arm. She jerked her head up and stared into the face of a blond stranger.

He shook his head.

"That's my mother!" Sourni hissed while trying to break free from his hold.

Another man, dark-haired, stepped up. "You'll only cause more trouble for her."

She glared at him and pulled again but the first man had her in an iron grip. He stared her down, determined, but not unkind.

Sourni knew he was right, but she couldn't let her mother be taken away like cattle up for slaughter. She dropped down, trying to take him by surprise, but he simply yanked her back, and the other man moved in to block her view.

"Listen," the first man said. "We have friends here. We can ask around to hear what's going on with your mother. Once you know the details, you can decide what to do."

She shot him a withering look.

He stepped back and let her go. "All right, do as you please."

Without his restraint she felt her energy drain. The adrenaline no longer held her up. She slouched. There was no point in following those sentries. They would only take it out on her mother, perhaps even take her into custody too. "I'm an overseer here," Sourni said defiantly. "I can find out myself."

He gave her a pointed look.

"Thank you for your offer. And your help," she added reluctantly.

"Look," he said. "I understand your hesitancy. I'm Auran, and this is my friend Jacob. Is there somewhere we can talk in private?"

Sourni considered. There was nothing to do for the next hour while her mother was no doubt taken to the local dungeon. She might as well hear them out. "Follow me." She pointed to an alley, intending to take them to her favorite alehouse.

"We prefer something in the open," the man who called himself Auran said. "How about a little hike?"

She cocked her head. Surely they didn't think she was that stupid.

His friend looked around nervously—did he not agree? But Auran scanned her up and down, not like a man appraising a woman, but like a fighter assessing a potential threat. He held up his hands. "We mean no harm. We don't want to draw unneeded attention. Besides, you look like you can hold your own."

"All right," Sourni acquiesced. "There's a clearing right outside the village, past the river."

Auran stepped aside. "You lead."

She set a brisk pace and they silently fell into step behind her, far enough away it didn't appear they were together. *Smart move.* Sourni resisted glancing over her shoulder. She barely heard them walk. *They must be hunters.*

They walked past the church, the bells chiming for the eventide mass. She usually avoided the open dirt area they called "the square" to avoid being accosted by the priests, though they seemed less inclined to convert those already in Apex's employ.

Sourni crossed the wooden bridge over the stream that led past the orchard—providing ample water for the trees.

Once they got to the clearing she turned and faced them. "No one can eavesdrop now. Let's hear it."

The men exchanged glances and Auran spoke. "When I restrained you, I acted on instinct. I didn't want anyone else to fall into Apex's hands. His sentries do enough damage already."

She knitted her eyebrows. That hardly sounded like a reasonable explanation.

"People I care for have been taken. I know what Apex can do." Auran looked hurt.

Sourni relaxed her stance slightly. "Okay, now what?"

"Now we figure out what happened." Auran gave Jacob a nod.

"We have a friend, someone who can ask around to find out what occurred to your mother without raising suspicion," Jacob said reluctantly.

Who are these men? They were more muscled and well-spoken than average hunters.

"For safety reasons we can't say who our friend is, as I'm sure you understand," Auran continued. "It will help if we know a bit more about your mother and what might've caused her arrest."

"My mother works in the apple orchard, picking apples. She has for years. The last few weeks she wasn't feeling well, a lingering cold." Sourni remembered her mother coughing up green slime. "I don't know what happened, she's never gotten into troub—ble..."

"What do you do?" Auran asked.

It couldn't hurt to tell him. "I'm an overseer in the same apple orchard, different shift."

"Anything else we need to know?"

She shook her head.

"Let's meet back here tomorrow, at noon?" He peeked at Jacob, who nodded.

"I can slip out on my lunch break and pretend to go for a walk, something I already do occasionally," she said.

"If I may, I recommend you feign nothing happened to your mother. Try and stay neutral if you can," Jacob said. Auran shot him an approving look.

Sourni knew he was right—ignoring her mother's arrest was the only way to stay out of trouble—it was so counterintuitive. She resisted the urge to salute them. "Thank you. I appreciate your effort, although I still don't understand why you bother."

Auran inclined his head with a smile. "Take care."

THE NEXT DAY they met at noon. Both men wore grave expressions. "We have news about your mother," Jacob said. Apparently he was the one with the connection. "Allegedly she ate a half-rotten apple she picked up from the grass."

No! Sourni felt as if someone had punched her repeatedly. Her knees buckled.

Jacob's look was compassionate.

"And?" she heard herself ask.

"They punished her severely. She's still alive though."

"How bad is it?"

Jacob paused before responding. "Are you sure you want to know?"

Sourni nodded.

"They broke her collarbone and nose, snapped her left arm in a few places, probably broke her ribs. They stayed away from her legs, so she can still walk."

Sourni felt numb, her head processing the information, but she didn't allow herself to feel it. *His friend was well-informed. Her legs... that means...*

"She'll be hanged, come Friday noon."

Taking any food without permission was punishable by death. Even if it was rotten. Apex didn't take half measures. The three-day delay was to inform the neighboring villages—they would be forced to watch. It served as a reminder, as if anyone could forget.

Shortage of food was the leading cause of illness—the Fleurisian people didn't receive proper nutrition, with Apex and his men hoarding the good food. As an overseer, Sourni was entitled to two apples a month, an extremely valuable perk, and she always shared those with her mother. Though her mother worked in the orchard daily, she'd never had access to apples herself. *She must've been desperate, to eat a spoiled one and think to get away with it. Three more days...*

Of course her mother was relatively lucky. Death by the gallows was fairly humane, if done properly. Noblemen got shot in the throat with an arrow, to choke on their own blood, to set an example. It was even worse when they had betrayed the country they were supposed to honor.

Sourni shook herself. Both men were watching her, one pair of light blue eyes and one hazel, both concerned and kind.

"Is there anything we can do for you?" Auran asked.

"Can you...can you get a message to her?"

The men exchanged a glance. "We probably can," Auran answered. "But you may want to consider the consequences."

Sourni looked into the woods, as if the answer were written on a tall pine. They had a point. Trying to contact a prisoner was a serious offense. Dangerous for both the messenger and herself. *Is it worth it?*

She walked around the clearing, turning the question over in her mind. Sourni didn't want her mother to think her daughter had abandoned her. She was hurt enough. Perhaps it was possible to inform her mother without a verbal message. If someone added a pebble to her food, assuming the guards allowed her the watery soup they served, her mother would know. She always teased Sourni about her fondness for stones.

Sourni searched the area for a suitable pebble and found a small grey one—perfectly oval. She went over to Jacob and handed him the rock. "Can you see to it she gets this, please?"

"I will," he said, securing the stone in his pocket.

His confidence in getting the token to her mother, and get back out unscathed, took her off guard. She turned to hide tears fighting their way out. After a few calming breaths, she faced them and said, "If there is anything I can do in return, please let me know. I owe you both."

To equal out her debt to them required a favor in return—one equally valuable and potentially dangerous as what they had done for her.

Auran inclined his head.

He must be the leader.

"We'll pass by Verger again in fourteen days. Perhaps we can meet again?"

"Okay."

Auran squeezed her hand. "Be safe."

CHAPTER THIRTY-SIX

Verger

Two weeks later Auran watched Sourni approach, the dark circles under her eyes accentuating her haggard face, her russet hair unkempt.

Jacob flanked him after having rounded the clearing. "Are you sure about this?"

"She's got no one left to protect, and she'll be motivated," Auran whispered back.

Sourni joined the two men, and for a few heartbeats their small circle stood silent, until Auran said, "May Ayna take her in."

Sourni extended her hands, palms upward, in ritual acceptance of the comfort he offered. "May Ayna take her in."

She stared at her hands as if they didn't belong to her. "At least she didn't die at the gallows, in front of everyone. She would've hated for me to see her die."

Auran gently cupped her hands. "Strange times that we must take a beating as a blessing."

Sourni nodded, too worn out to talk. But even if she was hurt and in mourning, these men were still taking a huge risk, especially since she was an overseer—she worked for the government, and by extension, Apex. Only something life-or-death would cause them to seek her out.

Auran released her hands. "How are you holding up?"

Sourni shrugged. "I'm coping."

"We have a proposal for you," Auran said. While he spoke, Jacob, his bow and quiver strapped on his back, moved to scan the perimeter again. Auran knew he could fire a shot within a heartbeat.

Auran noticed Sourni trailing Jacob's movements with her eyes. *Perfect, she's still alert.* "A proposal regarding the offer you made."

He liked how she stared him straight in the eye.

"I'm listening," she said.

"We're with an organization that wants to do things—differently. We feel there's room for improvement." That was the understatement of the century, but he had to feel her out first. "How do you feel about this idea?" Even the question was dangerous. If he worked for Apex, he could have her hanged for agreeing. If she worked for Apex, she could have him hanged for asking.

She studied him, then looked back at Jacob. "I guess some things might be done otherwise."

Auran suppressed a sigh of relief. "Are you interested in doing things in another way yourself?"

She spoke bluntly. "I won't betray you. I owe you for what you've done for my mother, for keeping me out of harm's way. I appreciate what you've done for two strangers, with risk to yourself. I swear on Seth I will guard your secrets with my life." She held up her index finger and middle finger in a V and spit through it.

Auran inhaled sharply—her pledging an oath was unexpected. He signaled Jacob.

Jacob reached into his quiver and smoothly notched an arrow, scanning the trees.

Auran took a deep breath. "We believe things should be done differently. We believe magic should not be restricted to Apex's people and all food should be available to everyone. We believe the people deserve neither suffering nor sickness. We believe we can stop him and make Fleuris a better place for us and our children."

Sourni's amber eyes widened.

Auran waited for her to respond.

"I...I didn't expect this." She looked baffled.

He gave her some time to process.

"What do you need me for?" she said.

"If you want to contribute, we'll discuss several options and make sure it aligns with your skills."

•••••••••••••••••••

"All right, what do you have in mind?" Sourni said.

A hawk's cry pierced the sky. Auran followed the bird's flight before training his eyes on her. "Are you attached to this village?"

Sourni gazed at the trees as if she could peer through and see their cabin. Well, her cabin now. Verger was home. Though when she thought of her long days in the orchard, and her increasing aversion to…She closed her eyes…

Their borough's chief overseer had sat in her orchard office, in her chair, the golden X gleaming on his chest.

"Well, well," he drawled, leafing through their employee roll. "I see this Angelica person is missing."

"She called in sick—she's got the flu," Sourni answered. She realized her tone was overconfident and ducked her head.

"Did she now."

"Yes, sir."

"Your logbook says she called in sick yesterday, too. Going soft on them?"

"No, sir." Sourni swallowed.

"Go get her."

"Sir?"

"Lost your hearing? I said fetch her!"

"Yes, sir. I'll be right back." Sourni motioned her second to offer him a drink, and sprinted for the village. She couldn't believe he called Angelica in to work. Last night her fever still hadn't broken. Sourni had gone by on her way home. She raced on, avoiding the bogs in the forest, and entered the village. The place was deserted save for some infants and those too old to work, who watched the children.

She knocked firmly on the wooden door. "Angelica!"

"Yes," a feeble voice answered.

Sourni opened the rickety door and went inside the stuffy cabin. The one-room hut was scarcely furnished. Angelica sprawled across the narrow bed—fever burning her cheeks. "I'm so sorry, but you'll have to come with me. The chief is here, and he insists you come to work."

Angelica opened her watery eyes. "What?"

Sourni hauled her up. "We need to be quick. Where are your shoes?"

Angelica pointed, and Sourni grabbed the worn shoes from under the only chair and started to squeeze Angelica's feet in. "Do you have something to drink or eat? You'll need your strength."

"There is some oatmeal left over from yesterday."

"You'll have to eat it cold on the way up." Sourni helped her stand up and grasped the wooden bowl with her other hand. Angelica's heat burned through her rough cotton tunic. *I can't believe he's making me do this.*

As they set foot in the forest, Angelica stumbled on the first tree branch. Sourni fought to keep her up. If Angelica had weighed more, she would've hit the dirt.

"Eat a few more bites," Sourni encouraged.

Angelica had difficulty swallowing due to her swollen throat, but somehow she managed to empty half the bowl. Sourni chucked the bowl to the side. She'd pick it up on the way back. *The chief best not see the attempt to eat.*

At last they arrived at the apple orchard, and Sourni released Angelica's bony shoulder before they came into view, sending a silent prayer to Layla for support. Angelica stumbled the first few steps, then somehow managed to keep herself upright.

The chief stood in the dirt-ridden square outside Sourni's office. He leveled a stare at them. "Well, well, at last they have arrived."

Sourni turned to Angelica. "Go right to your station."

The chief blocked Angelica with his arm. "Not so fast."

Sourni frowned.

"First she pays for her disobedience."

"Sir?"

"Have you not read the rule book, woman?" the chief spat out. "Fifteen lashes for unauthorized absence. If she can walk, she can work."

Angelica swayed and Sourni resisted the urge to support her.

"Gather your workers. We'll install some discipline here."

Without breaking his stare, Sourni motioned her second to approach. "Sound the bell and lead everyone to the square."

Her second nodded and sped off. Sourni heard the bell ring thrice—the signal for urgency.

The orchard workers filed into the center and formed a semicircle around the post across from Sourni's office. A strangled cry broke their silence—Rolf. Sourni knew he had an eye for Angelica, often lingering after his shift to walk home with her.

Someone grabbed Rolf's sleeve, and Rolf turned with a snarl, ready to strike. Rolf pulled back when he noticed the skinny boy— barely fourteen—wide-eyed, with a white-knuckled grip on his sleeve. Rolf relaxed.

Sourni went into her office to fetch the whip and pressed her hands on either side of the polished copper hook, resting her brow on the leather. *Dear Seth, please give me strength.*

When she came back, the chief finished tying Angelica to the post, giving a last hard yank on the sisal rope. Sourni felt Rolf bristle. Angelica leaned her forehead on the splintery wooden beam, shivering with fever.

Sourni drove her nails into her palms. If she objected, the chief would only take out his anger on Angelica, maybe strike Sourni herself in the process. Her predecessor...his defiance hadn't helped him or the worker he'd refused to whip on two consecutive days. The chief had selected Sourni, hoping a woman would prove more malleable.

She willed strength into her voice. "Angelica Bowsman, your penalty is fifteen lashes for unauthorized absence."

A few feet shuffled while the last apple buckets were set down. A raven crowed nearby.

Sourni flung the whip forward. "One." She knew the chief was watching her.

Sourni gritted her teeth and struck again. "Two."

Angelica hissed.

"Three."

Her beige tunic ripped apart and her skin burst open.

"Four."

Sourni tried to aim the lashes so the wounds wouldn't get too deep.

"Five."

Blood soaked Angelica's shirt and dripped down her bare legs.

"Six."

Angelica's high-pitched scream pierced Sourni like a shard of glass.

"Seven."

A shudder went through the crowd.

"Eight."

Angelica threw up. Oatmeal now coated the pole.

Sourni swallowed her bile.

"Nine."

Angelica sagged against the slimy pole.

Rolf roared. Sourni shook her head at him. *He cares more for her than I thought.*

He stiffened when a skinny arm snaked across his chest. Rolf whipped his head around. The kid behind him was red with the effort of holding Rolf back.

"Silence!" Sourni barked, schooling her face as much as she could.

"Ten."

From the corner of her eye, Sourni saw Angelica's sister faint into her neighbor's arms. *Gods above.* She forced herself to close off everything but Angelica's back, aiming for the last few patches of unbroken skin.

"Eleven."

Sourni's hand was slippery, but she dared not wipe the sweat on her clothes.

"Twelve."

The skinny boy buried his face in Rolf's sleeve. The movement caught Sourni's attention and she struggled to maintain her focus, wishing she could avert her eyes, too.

"Thirteen."

Angelica hung from the ropes—unconscious. Sourni darted a glance at the chief.

He smiled.

Sourni swallowed. "Fourteen."

She eased her grip on the leather—just one more shallow hit. "Fifteen."

The crowd let out a collective sigh. Rolf rushed forward to untie Angelica and her second came to his aid, sidestepping the puddle of blood. Rolf and her second carried her to Sourni's office without so much as a glance at the overseer.

"Back to work," Sourni said to the rest.

Coiling the bloody whip, she briskly walked toward her office, ducking behind the cabin, where she retched and hurled until there was nothing but dry heaves. She didn't know how she could ever face Angelica again.

The chief had waited for her next to the pole, arms crossed. "I trust next time I won't need to remind you?"

"No, sir. Will that be all?"

"Make sure you reach your quota. Last week you barely made it."

Sourni had jutted her chin and stared at him. That was not true. Last week they even had extra. *Did he take the surplus?*

"I'll make sure we deliver our portion, sir."

"Great. Until next month."

Sourni opened her eyes, pine needles stinging her palms and knees. Her heart hammered in her throat—sore and dry. She scanned the dirt in front of her, nauseous from reliving the lashing. *Thank Gods I didn't throw up here, too.*

Auran squatted before her "Are you alright?"

She leaned back on her heels. "I'm sorry, I..." She shook her head and dusted the needles and sand off her hands.

Would I mind leaving all this behind? Her sense of relief stood out. "I…I could move." As soon as she said the words she got goosebumps. She took those chills as confirmation and immediately felt a sense of calm.

Auran studied her face. She wondered if he'd noticed the response of her body with his steady aqua-blue eyes that missed little. He gave Jacob another signal—a twirl with his right index finger—and Jacob nodded.

How Jacob was able to focus both on the tree line and the signs Auran gave him was beyond her. There was an ease between them. She instinctively knew they would be able to teach her many things, and she looked forward to doing something besides keeping her head down.

Part of her wondered how she could so easily engage with them and trust them with so much, but her soul recognized them. They felt familiar, and their rapport showed so much of their faith in each other.

Their idea to do things differently was crazy and unfathomably big. There was no doubt they meant serious business. Through her fog of sadness, Sourni sensed a glimmer of excitement, a future. She thanked Layla, Goddess of Hope, for answering her prayers.

As all this went through her mind, Auran seemed to reach a conclusion. He sat and patted the coarse sand beside him. "We might as well take a load off. Jacob will see to it we won't be disturbed."

Sourni sat down across from him.

"What do you know about the situation in the Citadel?" he asked her.

She considered her answer carefully. "I know Her Eminence is too fragile to rule, and she left the country in Apex's hands." She stopped herself. "Why do you trust me? I work for Apex!"

Auran merely smiled. "I think you work as an overseer because it was convenient, and because the supply of apples supported you and your mother. If I'm informed correctly, your father died from a case of pneumonia that shouldn't have been lethal—you enlisted shortly after."

He was well-informed indeed. She'd been devastated by her father's sudden death and vowed to do what was needed to support her mother. The benefit of having two fresh apples a month—of being able to take in those vitamins—had swayed her. Her heart had never been in it and she hated flogging the slow workers, though she did it only hard enough to leave a red mark without breaking their skin. She'd endured it for her mother.

All right. "I know Apex outlawed magic for anyone outside the Order of the X, and he controls all the food—hogging all valuable provisions such as apples and acorns. Without these nutrients, it's said to be impossible for children with magical abilities to be born alive."

"We need an informant around Her Eminence. The timing is perfect because there is an opening for someone to oversee Her household. As an overseer you have the necessary experience with logistics and working with people, and the benefit of being on the payroll already. The work is not difficult although the hours may be odd—you'll need to fulfill Her Eminence's whims."

"What do you need from me?" Sourni asked. "How dangerous is it?"

"We'll need intelligence about Her whereabouts, when She meets with Apex. Even though he hides a lot from Her, he still needs Her seal of approval for some things, and we want their numbers. Ideally we would place someone with Apex himself, but no one gets in there from the outside, so we'll start with Her Eminence. If you accept we'll teach you to communicate via mindlink. Most Fleurisians possess just enough magic to establish a mindlink. We can't risk letters which are easily intercepted, and we'll keep in-person meetings to a minimum."

"Can I sleep on it?"

Auran nodded. "Just know we're keeping an eye on you. We won't risk this information getting out."

CHAPTER THIRTY-SEVEN

The Road to Arbres

I t took Sourni six weeks to apply for the job and get ready to leave her village.

Jacob was waiting for her in the clearing, a full quiver on his back. "Is that all you're bringing?"

Sourni glanced at her jute knapsack. She'd brought a canteen of water and her set of spare clothes. The few bits of furniture she'd given to Angelica. There was nothing else to bring but memories. "Yes."

"Are you all set?" he asked.

Sourni nodded. It was strange to leave the home she'd lived in for so long, but part of her was excited, too. She'd never been to Arbres and longed to see the ocean. "Is Auran not coming?"

Jacob shook his head. "He's in high demand," he said with a warm smile.

Sourni understood they didn't trust her with all their secrets yet. She had no idea how many people were involved or where their headquarters were. *Our headquarters*, she corrected herself.

Ever since she'd said yes to Auran, she'd felt elated. The ecstatic feeling had overpowered the sadness and fear—and she'd consciously let it.

They walked most of the way in a comfortable silence. She noticed Jacob was on alert—his hand never far from his quiver, and they mainly used back roads. After three days even the dirt roads got busier. She thought back to what Jacob had told her the night before.

"Once we get closer to Arbres, you'll see more people around. Tomorrow we'll travel apart because we don't want people to place us together. I'll lead the way into the city and visit a tavern owned by one of our people." He studied her intently.

Sourni opened her pack. "All right."

"You'll follow me in there and order an ale at the bar. When you order, leave three guilders on the bar with your left hand. I'll come stand at your right and do the same. That's the signal for our local contact. He'll be your emergency backup. When all else fails, when mindlinks don't work, you'll report there."

"Very well. What's his name?" Sourni asked.

"No names. Don't worry, you'll recognize him."

"You told me your names…"

"Yes, but you don't know our location," Jacob answered.

That night, he taught her how to mindlink. "I wish one of the others were here to instruct you. I still have trouble initiating a mindlink myself. But receiving is much easier. Give me a moment. I promised to let them know once you were ready for practice."

Them? Them who? She took a sip of water from her canteen.

Jacob closed his eyes and she studied his face. As his features relaxed she realized he was handsome with his dark brown hair and strong jaw. A flash of concentration flickered over his face, and he opened his hazel eyes.

"All right, are you ready?" he asked her. "Just relax and open your mind like I told you to when you feel a nudge."

Sourni closed her eyes, not sure what to expect, and took a few deep breaths. On her third exhale, she sensed a slight pressure on her forehead. *That must be the nudge Jacob spoke of.* She tried to open an invisible door, but it was like her hand slid off a slick surface. *Perhaps I need a handle.* In her mind's eye she pictured a door with a solid handle and grabbed it. She pushed the handle down and to her relief the door opened.

Powerful energy entered her mind, and she leaned backward instinctively. Jacob steadied her with his long arm. She straightened, and heard a voice in her head as if someone spoke to her directly.

"Sourni, I'm so pleased to meet you," the voice said. "I'm Iris."

Iris? The Iris? Sourni's eyes flew open and she lost the connection. "Iris?" she whispered.

Jacob grinned at her.

"You could've told me!" she yelled.

"What? And ruin the surprise?"

Sourni glared at him. "Now what? Some first impression I made."

"Don't worry. She's nice."

That's a strange description of one of the most sought-after magicians of Fleuris.

"Go on, try again. She won't hold it against you," Jacob urged.

Sourni shot him a look and forced herself to calm down. She placed a hand on her stomach to draw her inhale down into her belly. After a few deep breaths, she felt confident enough to open her mental door again. This time the energy waited right outside the threshold and Sourni leaned forward into the energy. She sensed a welcoming smile—the energy was less overwhelming.

"I'm sorry if I took you by surprise," Iris said kindly. "Mindlinks take some getting used to. I want to thank you for your contribution and your willingness to put yourself at risk. I appreciate all you do, leaving your home and supporting our cause."

Hearing this gave Sourni chills.

"You can talk back by thinking of what you want to say," Iris said. "It's a matter of pausing regularly so we can hear each other."

"I…" Sourni stuttered. "Thank you for your trust. I'm honored."

"The honor is mine. Auran told me you're smart and fierce and that's perfect for what you're about to do. Just a few practical tips. I wish I could provide you with a magical shield, but unfortunately a shield will tip Apex off. None of the palace staff are supposed to have any magical abilities or associations. Being yourself will be your most important tool. Respond as you normally would, or it will be very hard to keep up appearances. Make sure you only engage in mindlinks when Apex is not around. If you ignore me, I'll know it's not an appropriate time and will try again later. Do not take any risks with answering mindlinks. It's about the only thing which can truly give you away. Do you have any questions?"

"Is there anything I should watch for in particular?"

"Jacob will brief you on specifics. He'll also provide you with a local emergency contact. I have to go now. We'll speak soon. May Ayna watch over you."

The connection had ended, and Sourni's mental door closed on its own. She'd spent the rest of the night turning the conversation over in her mind.

Sourni tripped over a rock and was suddenly back from last night. She blinked against the glare of the sun.

Jacob's head whipped around, and he eyed her up and down.

She smiled at him to indicate all was well. He gave her one last look and turned back. Straining her eyes, she made out the silhouette of what must be Arbres. The capital was bigger than anything she'd ever seen, but she'd never traveled beyond her own borough.

As they got closer she noted more details. The city was shaped as an arrow pointing toward the sea. The green tip ended in a fortress on top of the cliff. *That must be the palace.* Narrow streets lined with yellow stone houses meandered up the tongue of land.

A wall surrounded the city with sentries stationed at the gates. Sourni reached in her pocket to touch her letter of appointment. She reminded herself she was here on official business.

No reason to get nervous.

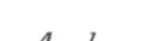

CHAPTER THIRTY-EIGHT

Arbres

Sourni took confidence from Jacob's passing through the city gates without drawing attention. She walked up to the armored sentry and presented her papers.

He ruffled through them. "Have you been here before?"

Sourni kept her voice firm and quiet. "No, I haven't."

He pointed to the middle street. "Follow the main avenue until the fountain square, then keep right until you see the palace gates."

Apparently she still looked nervous, for he added, "You can't miss it."

She was glad Jacob had taken the middle street as well. Sourni kept one eye on him. Her sandals slapped against the cobblestones. She couldn't wait to examine the shops in more detail soon. She glimpsed colorful rugs, carpenters modeling chairs and even a bakery—the smell of fresh bread taunted her.

Right before the fountain square Jacob took a left into an alley.

As Sourni turned the corner she saw him duck his head to enter a doorway. A weathered sign showed this was the Blue Lantern.

Sourni stepped inside and squinted at the dimly lit space. A red-haired man stood behind the wooden bar, wiping the surface with a rag. She swallowed and walked up to the bar, ignoring Jacob, and placed three guilders on the scratched wood with her left hand. "Can I have an ale, please?"

"You're no city folk," the bartender said, revealing several missing teeth.

Sourni peered around perplexed, not sure what she'd done wrong.

Jacob stood next to her. "Ale!" he said and slammed his coins on the counter.

Aha.

"Aye," the bartender said and drew up two ales.

Sourni tentatively took a sip from her beer, darker than the one served in her local pub, and fought to control her features. The brew was bitter as dandelion greens.

Jacob had instructed her to drink her ale without lingering and report straight to the palace. She didn't want to insult the barman— her emergency contact—but wasn't sure she could finish her beer without gagging.

The red-haired bartender eyed her, noticing her discomfort. "Not used to dark ale, eh?"

"No, not yet."

The barman howled and used the smelly rag to wipe away tears of laughter. "Next time you best order a malt."

Jacob smiled, drinking from his mug.

After a few more sips, Sourni decided to leave the rest and grabbed her knapsack. She nodded at the barman. "Thank you." The words were meant for Jacob.

The barman held up a hand. "You take care now."

Jacob gave her a polite nod.

She strode out the door and walked past the fountain to the palace gates. There were three sentries at the gate while several others patrolled a high fence overgrown with ivy. It was better-manned than the city walls.

The sentry checked his list and made a note, then took the papers into the watchhouse while his colleague kept his eyes on her. Sourni heard a bell ring in the distance.

The first sentry came back. "Wait here. The administrator will come fetch you."

The palace was immense, dating back to before the Cataclysm. It was sturdily built with large yellow stones, like the rest of the city. An arcade lined with pillars faced the lush gardens and gate.

Towers crowned three corners. The closest tower was directly ahead and lower than the rest of the building.

A man came out of that corner and walked down to the gate—his mousy hair blending with his blue-gray uniform. He stopped right in front of her. "You must be Sourni. Follow me."

Sourni wasn't sure what she'd expected, but this felt a bit cold. She heard one of the sentries whisper, "I bet she won't last a week." The others snickered.

We'll see about that…

She followed the administrator past the gardens into the palace and up the stairs, almost bumping into him when he stopped abruptly in front of two large oak doors guarded by two sentinels.

He nodded at one of them and the sentinels uncrossed their halberds and shouted, "Sir Robbert to see Her Grace," in unison.

A latch unfastened with a click, and the doors swung open. The administrator strode in as proud as a peacock. The receiving chamber, with a polished marble floor, was grander than any room Sourni had been in—more spacious than the clearing in the forest even. She glimpsed a stretch of blue behind a set of double glass doors leading to a balcony.

A dark-haired woman lounged on an elegant sofa bed in front of the open doors. She wore a heavily embroidered robe of coral lined with ochre.

Sir Robbert bowed. "Your Grace, I present you your new head keeper."

Sourni hastened to bow too.

Her Eminence scrutinized her. "Get her properly outfitted."

The administrator practically dragged Sourni out of the room and downstairs to an office, handing her off to a striking woman who stood up from behind a table covered with fabric. "See to it she gets clothes." He slammed the door behind him.

Sourni was determined not to let his foul disposition get to her, and she smiled at the woman. "It's a pleasure to meet you. I'm Sourni."

The woman returned her smile. "If you can still smile after grumpy Robbert has seen to you, you will do fine here."

Sourni felt her own smile extend to her eyes.

"Did he really force you to meet Her in your traveling clothes?"

Sourni looked at her plain flax trousers and shirt, wrinkled from sleeping outside, and brushed off some dirt from the road. She nodded. "I didn't know where we were going."

The woman shook her head and extended a hand. "I am Marie, the head seamstress. As you can see all head servants wear maroon. The color will suit your complexion." She tucked a loose strand of auburn hair behind her earlobe, the skylight illuminating garnet strands.

Sourni wasn't really concerned about her own appearance but said, "Thank you. That'll be lovely."

Marie clucked and made Sourni turn around. "My, my, you do not have much to spare, do you?"

"Excuse me?"

"I shall allow for some extra room," Marie said while making some notes.

"Extra room?"

"Yes, you will need it once Anne gets her hands on you."

Sourni took a step back.

"The food. You are skinnier than a stray cat." She shook her head.

The woman was kind enough, so Sourni held her tongue.

"Your clothes should be ready by tomorrow afternoon. I will also get you some slippers." She eyed Sourni's well-worn leather sandals. "Has anyone shown you your room yet?"

"No, I've just arrived."

Marie tutted. "Since the last head keeper—left—Robbert has been in charge of new personnel, and he is not fond of extra work. You will be staying in the former head keeper's room. You best lay low. Her Eminence finds proper garments and etiquette extremely important."

Holy Pears. "Thank you so much. When's dinner served?"

"I will have one of the maids bring you food. Best stay in your room until you get your uniform."

SOURNI WAS SURPRISED at the size of her new room. It was bigger than the two-room cabin she'd grown up in. Her chamber was situated in the left wing of the palace and even had two windows. She noticed the rectangular dining room table with six chairs, next to the fireplace. *This space will double as my office, just like Marie's.*

Sourni walked toward a decorated folding screen in the back, which matched the midnight blue velvet curtains. She peeked behind the screen and discovered her bed. It was big enough to sleep two. Smiling, she walked over to the windows.

She stuck her head out and craned her neck, enjoying the feel of the breeze on her skin and the smell of salt in the air. *That must be the sea.* Her heart skipped a beat. As a child she'd loved her father's stories about travelers and their voyages. Now she was having her own adventure. She turned around, thinking. *Mother will love—* Sourni's enthusiasm evaporated, and she swallowed the lump in her throat.

Leaning back against the windowsill, she looked over her room. The furniture was nice quality, but it wasn't very cozy. The big, dark, wooden dining set made her feel more alone. After a few minutes she shook herself and started to unpack her few belongings—placing one of her favorite pebbles on the mantelpiece. *There.* Something to remind her of home.

A knock startled her, and Sourni reminded herself there was nothing to be afraid of. She opened the door to a maid holding a tray with a plate, cutlery and steaming bowl.

"Your dinner, ma'am."

She beckoned the maid in and pointed to the table. To Sourni's horror the maid curtsied. *What?*

"Apologies from the kitchen, there was no time for dessert today. They're busy with the luncheon." The girl looked like she expected a lashing.

"That's fine. Thank you for bringing this over."

The girl's eyes widened and she backed out of the room, scampering away before Sourni had a chance to say anything else.

Sourni closed the door behind her and stared at the steaming bowl of food. It was enough to last her a full day. She sat facing the windows and ate in silence. The stew was nicely spiced and rich—she couldn't even finish it. She ended up jabbing vegetables out of the tomato-red sauce.

After dinner she looked out the windows and noticed the sky had turned pink. She walked over to get a better look and was reminded of the day her mother had died. She'd been walking back from the orchard after her shift—worried about tomorrow's hanging—when the sunset turned the sky blood-red. In hindsight she was convinced the world had told her about her mother's passing and was mourning with her.

This night's sky was lighter, more forgiving. Sourni yawned. *Time to turn in.* When she lay in bed she stroked the cream-white cotton sheets and marveled at their softness—a world apart from the rough sheets at home, which felt like sandpaper. Soon she was lulled to sleep by the sounds of the ocean.

CHAPTER THIRTY-NINE

Arbres

Sourni jolted upright—her heart hammering in her throat until she remembered. *I'm at the palace.*

She lay back down, exhaling deeply. Whether it was the sea air or exhaustion from her trip, somehow she'd slept through the entire night for the first time since her mother had died. Sourni took it as a good sign. Layla must approve of her mission.

Breakfast was delivered by the same timid maid. Afterward, Marie brought Sourni's uniform and matching silk slippers—Her Eminence preferred soft sounds. "Report to Robbert at noon. His office is down the hall, second corridor to the left and two doors down." Marie paused. "Her crystal heirloom needs to be dusted every day—the maids do not dare touch it. The vase belonged to Her great-grandmother. Do not bring up roses. Or ask about Her family's estate. It is best not to address Her unless absolutely necessary."

Sourni tilted her head waiting for more. Marie kept plucking her maroon skirt. "Her Eminence needs the—the reassurance of routine."

"All right. Thank you for your advice," Sourni said earnestly. "Is there anything else I need to know?"

Marie's verdigris eyes darted around the room, which struck Sourni as odd since they were in her private chamber with the door closed. "Hierarchy, structure and etiquette. Those are the main rules to go by. There is no room for standing out unless it is in punctuality. The administrator and the captain of the guard are in charge of the palace. Officially you are next." Her voice barely a whisper. "You seem like a nice girl. I hope you do well. Your predecessors were not malleable enough." Marie hastened out of the room, softly closing the door.

Chills ran up and down Sourni's spine. *Third in rank? What have Auran and Jacob been thinking? How in Seth's name did I get this position?*

She sat on one of the hardwood chairs, needing support. This might be harder than she'd imagined. *Concentrate.*

She took a deep breath forcing the air in and out of her lungs, looking for an upside.

Marie. She thanked Layla for sending her this angel.

Sourni's eyes strayed to her uniform. She fingered the material. The robe was sturdy but pliable. She changed into the maroon attire and looked in the mirror. *Marie was right.* The warm color did suit her russet hair and amber eyes. In the orchard, Sourni had always worn trousers, as she often lent a hand. Besides, the overseer's apparel had clearly been designed for men. Hers had never fit well—too tight on the chest. This was tailor-made. Marie was truly a master. Sourni stroked the fabric across her thighs. *Much softer than my flax trousers.*

Sourni rose and reported to Robbert's office right on time. Mustering her courage, she knocked and heard, "Come in."

She opened the door and stepped inside.

"Shut the door behind you."

Grumpy Robbert indeed. Sourni closed the door and waited for him to finish writing.

After signing three more letters, Robbert put his fountain pen down and looked up, glanced at her maroon robe and back to her clean, scrubbed face. He held up a sheet of paper as if it were a piece of dirty laundry. "This is a list of your duties. See that it gets done. There's a luncheon tomorrow, check with the kitchen. A list of guests is included. Any questions?"

"What are my hours?"

He stared at her icily, and the temperature dropped in the room. *Wrong question.*

"Your hours are whatever it takes. Make sure you do your best or I'll ship you back to the hole you call home."

"Yes, sir. Thank you."

He flicked a hand. "Go make yourself useful."

She quickly left the room and closed the door softly behind her. Studying the list, Sourni realized she had no idea how to find the palace kitchens, or who any of the people were that she was supposed to command.

When she got to Marie's room, she found her talking to a stout woman with bobbed blonde hair and flushed round cheeks.

"Sourni, meet Anne, our head cook. You want to keep her as a friend, in case you miss dinner." Marie winked.

"I'm pleased to meet you, Anne," Sourni said. "You're just the person I needed."

"The luncheon, eh?" Anne sounded exactly like the bartender.

"Yes," Sourni said. "I was hoping to find the palace kitchens."

"I's on my way there, walk with me," Anne said, waving to Marie. They hurried through a sunlit corridor, the floors paved with smooth ivory marble with starkly contrasting cardinal veins. Anne pointed straight ahead. "Ye can find the kitchens all the way in the back. This hallway is mostly head servants. There's the office of the captain of the guard." She indicated a deep turquoise door. "Them sentries stay in the barracks outside. The rest of the servants share rooms in the back or the attic. But ye isn't supposed to go up there. Ye is the head keeper, ye see?"

There was no lack of windows or blooming flowers and Sourni had never seen such exuberant gardens. At home the only thing blooming were the orchards in spring or the occasional wildflower. No one had time to care for flowers, even if they had access to the invaluable seeds.

Sourni smelled the kitchens when they got closer. She sniffed, trying to decipher the lovely aroma.

Anne's eyes twinkled. "Cardamom and cinnamon, I's boiling down the sauce for tomorrow. Come, I'll show ye."

Sourni stepped into a cacophony of clattering pots and pans, the warmth of the ovens and an abundance of smells. She noticed about twenty people dressed in impeccable white trousers, short-sleeved shirts and matching chef's hats stirring pans, kneading dough, cutting vegetables...*Cutting vegetables?* Sourni saw more vitamins on display than she'd ever seen, not counting the orchard.

Anne pointed out the room next to the kitchen where the palace staff ate their meals and introduced Sourni to the head butler, who would oversee the table setting.

Then Anne pulled her into a quiet corner next to a large burlap sack of potatoes, strapped on a white apron and rolled up her sleeves. "Let's go over the list, eh?"

Her attention on a pile of carrots, Sourni handed her the papers.

Anne caught her stare and patted a chair. "Come." She regarded Sourni knowingly.

Sourni swallowed and sat down.

Anne gestured and a young man walked up with two bowls. "Thanks." She took a whiff, then stirred one bowl. "Add more salt and a tinge of pepper. The pink one from the top shelf, eh." The young man nodded and took the bowl.

Anne presented the remaining bowl to Sourni. "The head keeper needs to approve the menu." She winked. "Go ahead, eh."

Sourni eyed the wine-red creation dubiously, took a bite and her eyes widened in surprise at the explosion of flavors in her mouth.

"Gieser Wildeman pears," Anne said. "Her Eminence's favorite and a must on every menu. Robbert imports them from the north, for as long as the borders are open."

They went over the guest list while sampling several dishes. Sourni was thoroughly impressed. Anne knew each guest's favorite foods and dietary restrictions. "Ferdinand has a weak stomach, so not too much wine for him, eh. Esmeralda is a—a friend of Her Eminence. She gets served after Her Eminence and Apex, and she likes her dessert. Apex—" Anne glanced around and lowered her voice, "he's allergic to the cinnamon in the pears so I makes him a special bowl, eh."

Sourni wondered about her own role, but Anne didn't seem to need any support. "Is there anything you need me for?" she asked.

"Aye, ye needs to keep Robbert happy, so he doesn't come snooping in my kitchens. Ye has the overview, makes sure everything matches, right?"

Like a buffer. Not unlike her previous job then.

"And ye needs to balance the budget." Anne grinned.

Sourni didn't think Robbert would be lenient when it came to overspending. "All right, when can we go over your kitchen budget?"

"Aye, the day after tomorrow's luncheon."

The more people Sourni met, the more her task weighed on her.

Anne gently pushed her out of the kitchen. "We continues preparing. I's a bit busy. The luncheon is tomorrow, eh."

CHAPTER FORTY

Arbres

Sourni was nervous about the luncheon. It was only her second day at the palace, and she'd seen Apex's name on the guest list.

The instant he walked into the room, she instinctively knew it was him. He wore a black soutane with a small golden X embroidered right above his heart and a larger X on his back.

Sourni wondered whether a dresser had helped him fasten the row of tiny buttons stretching from top to bottom on his soutane. The black silk robe showed his every curve, and the clerical collar hugged his double chin. Apex was the first overweight person Sourni had ever laid eyes on. She forced herself to look at something else and choked down her fury.

His light green eyes—cold and calculating—scanned the room. His hands were heavy with golden rings inlaid with stones reflecting his eyes. The emerald ring throbbed.

Sourni blinked. She focused her attention on the table, memorizing the right order of the forks and their size. She'd been surprised at the amount of cutlery and chinaware for a lunch. The butlers had set the table and ensured every piece was in place, while the head butler had explained the procedure.

Her Eminence was to sit at the head of the table facing the ocean, Esmeralda beside Her, with whoever else was in favor. Apex sat at the foot, flanked by high priests. The flowers were to match Her Eminence's dress, and the arrangements, placed in front of

Her like a colorful wall, were large enough to provide privacy. The flowers—only showing Her from the neck up—didn't obscure Her ocean view.

The head butler had warned her the timing of the meal depended on Her Eminence's appetite, which changed per Her mood. Sourni had to pace the courses from her observations, pulling a cord to signal the kitchen to send up the next item.

During the luncheon, Sourni stood near the glass doors. She was paying close attention to Her Eminence when she felt the tap. She froze. What unbelievably unfortunate timing to receive a call for a mindlink. For a moment she was unsure. Then she glanced at Apex and caught him staring at her. *Holy Pears.* He must feel the energy. *Ignore, ignore!*

She didn't know how to end the call instantly—she'd answer the mindlink briefly, to let Iris know she was unavailable and stop the flow of magic. Sourni looked at her shoes and tried to calm her breathing. She pictured a door in her mind's eye and added a handle. As she was about to grab the handle, she remembered what Iris had said: "*Do not take any risk with answering mindlinks. It's about the only thing which can truly give you away.*"

Sourni opened her eyes abruptly, focused back on her shoes and exhaled. She scanned the room, pretending to take in what was happening. She carefully monitored one of the servants, as if checking up on him, and ignored Apex, whose stare she still felt. As soon as possible, she excused herself and slipped out of the room as the last servant left, softly closing the door behind her with trembling fingers.

CHAPTER FORTY-ONE

Arbres

On her third morning Sourni swung her feet out of bed and found her silk slippers. *Everything is so soft and smooth here.*

She had a meeting scheduled with Marie and then Anne about their budgets, and prayed their finances would add up. After breakfast, which she ate next to the kitchen with the rest of the staff, she walked with Marie back to Marie's office. Her Eminence wouldn't wake for a few hours, so there was time. "All right, how are you doing with your budget?" Sourni asked.

Marie opened the books and they went over the bills. Sourni flipped through the pages adding up the numbers in her mind. "But...this exceeds your budget!"

Marie looked contrite. "I am always overspending."

Sourni gasped. "Why?"

"Honestly?" Marie cocked her head.

"Of course, I'll be held accountable, so yes, why?" A knot built in Sourni's stomach.

"Her Eminence, it is always Her Eminence. We cannot complain or even refuse. Apex makes us keep a budget, but no one restrains Her. There is no end to Her expenses. Anne will tell you too," Marie answered heatedly.

"What did you spend it on?" Sourni asked.

"I spent at least double, all on dresses. The embroidery She requires takes forever. Also, the price of fabric...silk is scarce, and

She will not wear anything else. Half the time we cannot even find what She desires." Marie was building up steam now. "She is terrified people will notice Her wearing the same dress twice."

"What happens to the ones She no longer uses?"

"I think Her chambermaid throws them out after a while."

Sourni chewed on her lip. "Can't you reuse them?"

Marie opened her eyes and mouth wide. "Goodness no! She would never allow it!"

"What if you use the fabric creatively in a way She won't recognize it's the same dress? My mother used to cut up her old clothes to make me something new."

"I...I guess. I like the idea..." She grabbed her notebook and started scribbling. Sourni peered over her shoulder while Marie added a sketch. "Look! We can reuse the underskirts. We can always reuse them. I cannot believe I have never thought of that. Plus the sleeves. You are brilliant." Marie got up and hugged Sourni in her enthusiasm.

Sourni wasn't used to hugging—especially at work—and she returned the hug clumsily. But Marie didn't notice. She was already summoning her assistant, her eyes bright. "I will rework the budget. Perhaps we can salvage it after all."

Sourni nodded. "All right. Perhaps it's best to keep it a secret. I'm not sure She will appreciate recycled clothes—even when they're Her own."

"I will swear my seamstresses to secrecy, no need to worry," Marie said gravely.

"Wonderful."

Sourni walked to the kitchens. Robbert must know Her Eminence was the main reason for the budget deficit. *Why would he punish his head keepers for overspending?* She sensed there was more to it. He didn't come across as the type to obediently comply with his superiors, not without personal gain.

Anne beamed at her and patted a kitchen chair with flour-coated hands. "I's almost ready. Taste this for tomorrow's dinner, eh."

Sourni accepted a slice of dark brown bread and bit off a piece. The crust was hard, crisp and—she took another bite—salty?

Anne smiled broadly. "I's trying to make it taste like the sea. She likes the sea. Look." Anne pointed out flakes of salt on the crust.

Sourni smelled the bread. "It's unusual, but I like it. She'll have something to show off. Perhaps you can do a whole range of sea-food—a special ocean dinner—with seaweed or whatnot. When's Her birthday?"

Anne paled like she'd seen a ghost. "No, not Her birthday," she whispered. "Ye can never mention Her age!"

"All right." Sourni ate the last bit of bread to hide her confusion. "Are you ready to go over your budget?"

"I's almost done. Try this," Anne handed her a bowl of broth.

Never mind two apples a month—sampling the dishes alone provided Sourni with more nourishment in just these few days than she would normally get in a month. It was a lovely bouillon. Everything Anne prepared had a special touch.

Anne dried her hands on a blue-and-white checked towel. "I's ready."

They went to the room where the palace staff ate their meals. Anne carried her notebooks with her.

"How's your budget?" Sourni asked.

Anne glanced around to make sure no one overheard them. "Well, I's always a bit tight. Them suppliers in town sell on a current account and them often send too much."

"Don't you send it back then?"

Now Anne looked as contrite as Marie had done. "Aye, sometimes." She folded her hands in her skirt and met Sourni's gaze. "They's my friends, I…they suffer, eh," her voice barely audible.

Sourni swallowed. As an overseer, she'd often been confronted with friends and neighbors who crossed the line—not even intentionally. There were so many rules and new ones shot up like mushrooms. Her heart ached. She knew she walked a fine line, and to cover someone else's omissions on top of that… She sighed. There was no need to decide right now. "All right, what else?"

Anne plucked her apron. "Mostly it's the Gieser Wildeman pears and the fish from the Dead Seas."

Sourni jerked her head up. "What do you mean fish from the Dead Seas? Eating those will kill Her!"

"Nah, She'll just get sick—throw up for hours. She won't even be able to hold on to water." Anne lowered her voice. "For some reason, She's resistant. A real pity Her parents and sister was not so lucky, eh."

Sourni's heart contracted. *Mother.* "What's the purpose then?"

"Reminiscence makes Her do it."

"Huh?"

"You see, eating the fish was a family tradition. Nobody noticed the fishes was sick—salt in the water, eh."

That must be the ecological disaster father spoke about…

"…and Apex helps Her now."

What did I miss?

Sourni shook her head unable to grasp the ways of the palace. "All right, the pears. Do we need them for every meal?"

"Just for lunch and dinner."

"Do we need them for everyone? Can't we limit the pears to—I don't know—certain people, like a favor or an honor?"

Anne sucked her chapped bottom lip while she considered this. "Aye, perhaps that could work. But Robbert needs to approve it and convince Her. He ain't gonna like it, eh."

Sourni thought he wouldn't like the budget shortage either.

CHAPTER FORTY-TWO

Kaale Mountains

Auran studied the lichen on the roof. The lime-green moss had grown. Last he'd heard, no ships got through the blockade. But the Morgenstar was swift and almost invisible in the hands of the capable captain. Much depended on the weather—highly unstable in this season. A good, timely fog might help them though…

Iris stirred and Auran realized he'd dropped the shield while thinking about the ship. He quickly reinforced his shield and saw her relax again.

Remembering she was never fully safe put things in perspective whenever something went wrong in his own travels. The closest she came to safety was in moments like this, asleep at his feet. *So much weight carried on those fragile shoulders.* It was a shame her mother had died before teaching Iris to use her gift. Auran fought to suppress the anger he felt against the Gods for the cards dealt to his friend. *And Theresa.*

Though Iris's mother's eyes were undoubtedly bright, they had never impacted him as Iris's did. Their gift got stronger with each generation. As if nature knew their power was most needed now.

Iris inspired hope in so many, whether she was aware of it or not, whether people knew it was her or not. Ever since that abandoned village, he'd traveled the country as often as possible, discreetly spreading word that the girl from the prophecy was alive and fighting back—recruiting supporters. The most powerful magician in the country was on their side.

Iris stirred and opened her eyes. His thoughts must have woken her. Auran shrugged apologetically. To his surprise she took his hand and drew him down beside her. It was good to feel some of each other's warmth—his bones ached from the cold.

He squeezed her hand. "Let's have it."

She sighed. "Let's scoot over."

They leaned against the rough wall, tucking one of the sheepskins behind their backs. He felt pressure on his eardrums as she soundproofed the room.

"Sourni has been at the palace for almost two weeks. We need to make sure you can connect to her. A messenger may take too long," Iris said.

"But..."

She held up her hand. "I may not always be around, and you have trouble initiating a mindlink with anyone else. I'll create a magical connection between you."

He narrowed his eyes. "What do you mean?"

"A direct pathway, so you can easily initiate a mindlink."

What is she planning for? "All right."

"Sit very still. Your energy must be neutral, not imbued with my connection to you. That'll only cloud the energy."

Auran sat stock-still and felt the cool touch of her hands on his temples. The energy shifted, like someone painted his picture in one stroke—for a blink he saw an image of himself in his mind's eye. The energy was palpable and familiar. He snorted. *Of course it is.*

She gave him a pointed look—the advantage of a mindreader. Although she rarely let it show. He remembered her complaining when her mother scolded her for reading the cook's thoughts. She'd gotten smarter about not sharing what she picked up, and he knew she'd finally taught herself the habit of not invading people's privacy.

Iris shifted and the air shimmered. A familiar presence filled his consciousness—Sourni. He felt the instant a connection was made, as if a tiny flag was planted in Sourni's mind, a beacon to pinpoint each other. A few breaths later the transfer was complete.

He opened his eyes, staring, and gratefully accepted the cup Iris held out for him. "Thanks."

"To ease your nausea."

Auran peered into the clear, bitter-smelling concoction.

"The queasiness lessens with practice," Iris assured him.

Perfect, especially when I have to use mindlinks while on the road. Auran remembered the bottle in his pocket. "I need a refill of lemon oil before I leave."

The essential oil had kept him going plenty of times—a welcome surge of energy and focus when he needed it most. He suddenly realized it was still the middle of the night. "Was Sourni awake?"

"No. When you're asleep the thinking mind won't interfere and push us out. People have to learn to lower their mental fences to allow someone else's energy in their system."

Auran was glad he didn't have to use mindlinks often. He could think of more fun ways to use that same energy. Not that he had time for any of that now. He would be relieved when this fight was over. *Assuming we are still alive.*

Iris leaned back against the wall. "Now you can mindlink with Sourni at any time. She's walking a fine line and may need more protection."

"I've asked our contact in Arbres to keep an eye on her. Can you link mentally with him as well?"

"No, I don't want to risk spreading myself too thin. And if they arrest someone with that kind of access to me it'll cost a lot of energy to fight off their attacks. So don't put yourself in unnecessary danger with the kind of detailed information you have..." Iris swallowed.

"Don't worry, I have no intention of getting captured. Plus I always have a vial of devil's tail with me. I won't be caught alive."

"Make sure you contact me before you use it. I can scan their minds to see if you need to take it." Iris jabbed his chest with her index finger. "Promise to use it as a last resort only, Auran. Don't play the hero."

CHAPTER FORTY-THREE

Kaale Mountains

When Auran left to check on the guards, Iris propped herself against the cave wall, adjusting the sheepskin. *I care for him too much.* If she were to lead this uprising successfully, she couldn't stay upset about individual suffering. But Iris still heard Theresa scream in her nightmares. She never slept deeply, never knew if some of their own people might turn against her—bribed by Apex or Thorn—or an active priest might stumble upon her presence. Someone mentally skilled enough could evade her guards or pretend to be an ally. They simply didn't have enough magically able individuals.

The bloodlines of magicians were weakening, thanks to the priests' forbidding intermingling between the magically able. This slowed the exchange of knowledge and diminished the chances of two magicians producing offspring. The handful who did emerge were hogged by Apex for his order. *Appeasing his God.*

The few times magicians were born, look what their magical abilities brought them. Bile rose up as the image of the baby in the dirt flashed through her mind. Even though her father had few magical capabilities and never learned to use his power, Iris was convinced the combination of his kernel of ability with her mother's lineage had resulted in her own extraordinary gift. Or curse.

I need more sleep. Perhaps she could let Auran stay one more day so they could both rest. Iris gathered a few herbs and prepared breakfast, holding out her hands to heat the porridge with magic.

Auran stepped in, annoyed. "They were only passing travelers, but those moron guards wanted to step down last night's high alert. They acted disappointed, like they hoped to catch some action." Despite his words, Auran looked like he wouldn't mind some excitement, either.

Iris threw him a pitying look, not dignifying his comment with an answer. "Breakfast is ready."

"I always like the way you prepare it—makes me think of home. Must be the herbs."

"I brought them with me but I'm almost out. Breakfast is about to get boring too."

They ate in companionable silence, both lost in thought. A sudden noise made them look up. Auran narrowed his eyes, listening.

Iris got up. "Another rock must've fallen. Heating the rocks through the pipes was bound to have an effect." She stretched her senses upward. "I'm afraid we'll have to leave in a few days."

Auran looked up like a deer caught in a flash of magic. "You know they have readers scanning for flares of your power. It'll be suicide to step outside this cave and the wards." He stood and paced the room.

"I know it's a risk, but one we must take," Iris answered without blinking. "If this gorge collapses it not only gives away exactly where we are, it'll ruin this location for future use. People in the villages are already suspicious. All we need is one overactive priest and we'll have the Strong Ones come down on us." She thought of the battalions trained for years, molded from humans with latent magic. "No matter how well Basil trains our men, a Strong One is worth at least two normal soldiers."

Auran gestured wildly at the walls. "Can't you strengthen the roof with magic and cool the rocks down? Shield the place?"

"Not without raising the vibration of this gorge. Their readers are scanning for anomalies. And it still wouldn't help with what the villagers notice. I need to pick Merlow's brain. You figure out a way to satisfy the locals."

"I'll get Merlow. Will you inform Sourni?"

Iris resisted laughing out loud at Auran's dislike of mental communication. "You could use the practice. What if I hadn't been here yesterday when Basil got shot? Would you've been able to connect with Merlow?"

His shoulders drooped. "You're right. It wears me out."

"I know. If you'd let me, I could teach you how to be less affected by mindlinking."

He sighed. "All right. I'll be right back."

⋯⋯⋯⋯⋯●⋯⋯⋯⋯

Auran rushed out. The risk of bringing her out of the safety of the Kaale Mountains made him shiver. Any encounter with a passerby could be fatal. One look at her bright eyes would tip them off and ruin everything.

Where was Merlow when you needed him? He certainly hovered enough the rest of the time.

He found Merlow sitting next to his own would-be fire in a meditative trance. *Why is it that the sight of wood prepped for fire makes us feel more comfortable and at home?*

Even though Auran hadn't made a sound, Merlow opened his eyes. "Good morning, Auran. Did you sleep well?"

"Iris needs you."

"You two are off to an early start."

Auran snorted. For him it was merely another day without any sleep. Good thing he'd had two acorns for dinner last night. They would keep him alert until lunch.

Merlow pushed himself off the floor. "Given your air of urgency, I will probably need all my senses today."

Auran checked his energy and increased his shield. No need to get anyone worried. The guards were already paying close attention to his every move. He didn't blame them. It was boring down here. *Not counting the constant threat to their existence.*

CHAPTER FORTY-FOUR

Yarden

I ris woke up sore. *Gah, I feel like I am sixty rather than sixteen.* Thanks to the deep sleep potion, she'd slept through her aches, but they returned full force. Yesterday's training session on the grass behind the mansion still resonated throughout her entire body. She groaned and pushed herself up, glaring at the light streaming in through the curtain-free windows.

Merlow had already gone to the regional market, his yellow bubble absent.

In the kitchen she reheated the porridge Merlow had left for her. The oatmeal bubbled and a hint of cinnamon wafted up. *Nice.* She smiled, proud of her control.

Iris ate inside, not yet ready to brace the chilly fall air. After her last bite she took stock of her body, rotating her shoulders. *Not too bad.*

Perhaps I can practice that new spell. Iris walked into the patch of sunlight behind the shed, grateful for its warmth. She turned her face to the sun and forced her mind to go blank, removing any emotion. It took longer than usual to calm herself down—so long, she was unable to attain the perfect level of serenity. Pushing past her exhaustion, she played with Merlow's 'power gauge.'

Diving deep into her well, she changed the dosage of magic from low to medium. *Ouch.* Pain coursed through her stomach. She pressed a hand against her abdomen, losing her grip on the gauge entirely. Magic rushed up and out of her. *By Seth.*

Iris toppled on the grass, fighting to stay conscious. *The shed!* Flames crept through the dry grass toward the wooden shack. *No!* She crawled forward, determined to stop the fire, digging her nails in the yellow grass. *Please Gods, not our belongings.* She'd put all valuables in the shed for safekeeping.

An orange flame licked the wood and climbed hungrily upwards. Iris collapsed—her body unable to carry her further.

Closing her eyes to shut out the blaze she turned to the darkness. She had no tears left.

A SHIELD CLICKED in place around her and the crackling of flames abated.

"Grab her feet Auran," Merlow instructed.

They hauled her back to the house.

"You okay?" Auran urged.

Iris nodded and started coughing.

Auran clutched her arm to help her sit up.

The pressure on her ears increased, and—silence.

Auran glanced at the blackened shed. "Perhaps we can salvage some stuff."

Merlow shook his head. "What have I told you about rule number four?"

"I'm not sick!" Iris objected.

Auran cleared his throat.

Merlow towered over her. "You were in no condition to access big magic. You were supposed to take the day off. Why do you think I let you sleep in?"

Oh.

IRIS WAS CRADLING a cup of herbal tea designed to expel the toxins she'd inhaled, when five men rounded the corner. She squinted her eyes. They looked vaguely familiar.

Merlow inhaled sharply.

"The village elders," Auran muttered. He hadn't left her side.

"Stay here," Merlow commanded. He strode over to the men and invited them inside. They shook their head.

They were too far away to hear what was being said, but Merlow gestured wildly, clearly upset.

After she'd drank her cup he came walking back, shoulders slumped. *He looks older.*

Merlow sat next to her so she didn't have to crane her neck and sighed. "You have been evicted from the village. The elders feel it is their duty to protect the rest of the villagers. You are not to return here."

Auran shot to his feet, reaching back for a quiver that wasn't there. "Damn!" He stomped his feet.

Iris stared at Merlow. *What?* The fire had worn her out and she couldn't fully process what she'd heard. Everything was numb.

There was not much left to bring. All their heirlooms had been stashed in the shed. She grabbed her father's leather satchel and pulled her notebook from underneath her pillow. *What else?* She glanced at the mantel. *Ayna's candle.* She wrapped the family candle in a shirt and clutched the satchel to her chest as she took in the room—unable to grasp the goodbye.

In the end she added two sets of clothes, the only ones that fit, and her comb and blanket.

The elders had ordered her to leave at first light but Merlow didn't want to wait. Given their need for secrecy, they would only travel at night. She wasn't sure where he'd take her, but right now she couldn't care less—as long as Auran caught up with them at some point.

·········•·········

The story reached Arbres within days. The news about a girl incinerating her own shed showed up in Apex's daily report.

Apex smashed his crystal wineglass against the gorgeous needlepoint tapestry, red liquid staining the apple orchard in bloom.

"Why have I not been told about her before?" He crumpled the report and chucked it in the bin.

"My sincere apologies, monsignor. Her family kept her existence a secret. The servants never spoke of her. It is only because the elders have evicted her that the story traveled beyond Yarden."

"Find this girl and destroy her. Kill her on sight. We can't have rogue magicians on the loose." Apex was fuming now. "Make sure you take a few strong sorcerers with you. Consult Thorn—he took care of that disobedient village nicely. He knows Merlow inside out. Put Merlow on the list of conspirators, too." He paced up and down the room. "Dispatch bulletins to every village and town. Failure to report sight of any of the convicts will result in death by the gallows."

CHAPTER FORTY-FIVE

Kaale Mountains

As soon as Iris heard a thud, she knew another arrow had struck. She stretched out her senses to see if anyone was hurt. She felt Jacob nearby and viewed through his eyes—he graciously allowed the mindlink. The second arrow had missed the guard on duty by only a handbreadth. *Thank the Gods they're wearing armor!* The anxiety of the nearby guards increased. This arrow had come from a different angle. *I need to bend that path, too.*

As Iris was about to get up, she sensed another arrow. Jacob acknowledged her nudge as it emerged from the rock like a knife through butter. Before Jacob could shout a warning, the arrow grazed the armor of a guard coming around the corner before striking into the rock wall. Jacob checked the man over and sent him, pale and shaken, to the armory to change out his breastplate, as Iris cautiously examined the third arrow.

The same thirty-two-degree angle as the one that hit Basil. Would the fourth arrow repeat the sequence?

Few warriors were skilled and strong enough to control time-traveling poisonous arrows. They were the Robin Hoods and Wilhelm Tells of their squad, snipers who could kill over distance and time. It was unusual to shoot alternately—especially in training. Normally an archer released several arrows in a row without waiting for his comrade. *Perhaps Merlow remembers.*

Iris felt him enter the room as if he'd materialized from her thoughts. She broke the mindlink with Jacob and saw Merlow had sensed the arrows, too.

"Was anyone injured?" Merlow asked, bending down stiffly.

"Just a scratch on the armor."

"Thank you Seth and Layla."

As he spoke Iris felt the thud of number four. It was uncommon for time-traveling arrows to arrive so close together, as each slowed while piercing the veil of time. The delay increased when more arrows used the same track. *Maybe that's why they're using different angles.*

Iris spoke to Merlow. "I need to bend the curve on the second batch of arrows. Do you know if we can lower the vibration of the cave when we use magic to fortify the rocks? Balance it out somehow? Auran got me thinking..." She left him to muse on the concept.

As Iris wound her way through the cave, she passed several people who all avoided looking at her. She knew why they did it, but it still hurt. She sighed.

Few were able to look straight into her eyes and even then not for long. She could force someone to hold her gaze, but she reserved that for her enemies.

Iris turned the corner and observed the watchtower. *Where did everyone go?*

Jacob stuck his head out of the entrance. "We're inside—no point being shot like sitting ducks." He rapped on the watchtower wall. "The arrows have no power left to penetrate more rock, especially since this one is strengthened by magic."

Great idea. "We can reinforce your armor with magic, too." Iris proclaimed. The downside was the spell had to be maintained. If the owner didn't possess enough magic to uphold the spell, it would lose power in a day or two. Still, that left two days of increased safety.

Jacob nodded enthusiastically.

Iris walked into the tower. "I thought to bend the curve on that second batch, or do you prefer to keep it as is?" she asked Jacob.

"I wish you could teach me," he said. "Bending arrows would be very handy in battle."

She smiled. "Yes, except it asks so much of your concentration. While you are avoiding the arrow, someone might stab you in the back."

"You know I won't let anyone come so close," Jacob joked. "But alas."

"How about bending that batch?"

"Yes, please. Can you direct the arrows to the same hollow so they're easier to avoid?"

"Sure thing." Iris approached the rock and felt another arrow coming. "Stay back." She gathered magic and focused her energy on the projectile.

An orange flash emerged from yet another angle but clattered to the ground when it met her shield. Iris grasped the fresh trail and let her mind travel back. She braced herself when she saw the warriors in the meadow. Three archers held up their bows shaking their fists while the others cheered, like an initiation rite. *Perhaps that explains the difference in angles, so it's easier to determine who shot which arrow.*

Iris let her mind stretch further into the meadow. Power radiated on her left. *A magician.*

She instinctively blocked herself from view and peered through a tiny hole. She gasped.

On the side of the field stood a skilled magician with twinkling deep blue eyes and a short beard. She sensed his shielding spell and felt him gathering more power to prepare for an attack. *What?* Reluctantly she drew back her mind. *Could it really be?* She firmly closed the connection to the past and snapped her eyes open. That energy signature was less polished than she was used to, but...*by the Gods...*

Oh, she would've loved to take a closer look. It seemed these warriors were receiving special training. She prayed the archers remained in the meadow, although most likely their magician would move them now he knew they'd been spotted. *Did he realize I was seeing him from the future?*

Not likely. Few magicians were able to stretch this far. She hadn't known it was possible until she stumbled upon it. But if she figured it out, others might as well…

As her awareness returned to the cave, she wondered how much to share with Jacob. It would be interesting to see whether the arrows kept coming. *I won't mention the magician just yet.*

"It looks like they're shooting their arrows in pairs, like a special ritual. Have you heard of something like that?" she asked Jacob.

He frowned. "When Auran and I trained with his father, he did mention a highly skilled group, famous for twin arrows. They called themselves the Gemini Squad, and they backed every arrow up with a second one whether in training or battle. It became their signature. Their precision is legend."

"Please keep this between us, will you? Be prepared for arrows from all angles. Best to stay in the watchtower with your armor on."

"Will do." Jacob was clearly eager to get back upstairs.

She smiled to herself and drew on her magic to pull up the spell. "Make sure the guards steer clear from this corner," she told Jacob.

Iris ambled toward her rooms. *What's the point of being able to read people's thoughts if I fail when it counts?*

CHAPTER FORTY-SIX

Kaale Mountains

I ris was still pondering what she'd seen and what it meant for them and their plans, when she almost bumped into Auran. He smiled at catching her off guard, then frowned at her vulnerability. Before he could scold, she tugged at his muscled arm and drew him into a chamber. She quickly explained what she'd seen in the meadow.

Auran swore.

"What do you make of a younger Merlow with the archers?" Iris pressed.

"I don't know. It's so unlike him." Auran scratched his head. "Have you told him?"

"Not yet. He'll expect me to figure it out at some point. Merlow knows my skills at looking across distances. We can read his response when we ask him," Iris pondered.

"All right," Auran steered her out of the chamber and toward her room.

As they walked in, Merlow looked up expectantly. "What news do you have?"

Iris sat down. "Trevor, could you make us some tea, please?" she called out. Like most servants he possessed enough magical abilities for simple domestic tasks like boiling water for tea.

Trevor stepped into the room—his dark brown eyes supportive. "Certainly, miss."

She nodded gratefully at Trevor and faced Merlow. "Have you been involved in training warriors?"

He sighed. "I wondered when you would figure it out. When you left to bend the second batch, my mind went back to that meadow twenty-two years ago, and how frightened I was when I realized I had been spotted. I remember shielding myself. I could not see you, so until now I had no idea who had been watching me or why. All I knew was it had to be an exceptionally powerful wizard. I suggested we move to another location but my warlord insisted we stay and complete our training. His marksmen were quite famous, you know. It is a part of my life I am not proud of."

Iris listened in silence, goosebumps on her arms. She intuited some significance to the story, but couldn't pin it down. "Why have you hidden this part of your past? It's nothing to be ashamed of—is it?"

"I did not tell you because I hoped we were in a different cave—we shot at several remote locations. And, I am embarrassed by some of my actions. It was easier to pretend it never happened..."

The silence stretched.

When it was clear Merlow wouldn't elaborate, Iris said, "I'm disappointed you let me figure it out on my own. Why didn't you tell us as soon as the first arrows arrived?"

"I guess I hoped you might not notice?" Merlow tried.

Auran glared at Merlow. "This is unacceptable."

"I—yes. You are right." Merlow's shoulders slumped.

Iris sensed his despair and increased her shield, not wanting to be burdened by his emotions.

Auran glanced at her. "All right. Tell us more about the archers and their ceremony. Why the separate batches? We need all your insights."

"Our employer—Lord Ashen—thrived on competition, therefore, he came up with the idea of separating the batches, so each shot could be attributed to its owner. To be allowed into the elite membership of his Gemini Squad, an archer had to undertake several tests, one of which was successfully shooting a poisonous arrow through time."

At this Auran perked up.

"Lord Ashen was fierce when it came to outshining his neighbors. He made me erect a shield around the meadow so his competitors could not glean any information. In addition, he encouraged his archers to shoot the arrows farther in both distance and time. That is where my abilities came in. I have never encountered another group skilled enough to shoot time-traveling arrows across such a distance. They reached up to 200 kilometers and over twenty years."

Iris saw the eagerness in Auran's sharp eyes. She knew he was itching to have Merlow work with his bowmen to improve their skills. Before he could start an in-depth conversation about marksmanship, she asked Merlow "Why this place? Why shoot the arrows here in this gorge?"

Trevor walked in with their tea and flinched at the mention of arrows.

Merlow continued as if he hadn't noticed Trevor's reaction. "Lord Ashen suggested these mountains. We were aiming for an empty place. It strikes one as being fated though."

"How so?" Iris asked.

"As though we were meant to discover the arrows now and discuss the time-travel element for future actions. The Gods have a wry sense of humor," he murmured.

Iris noticed the sadness in his eyes. There was more to the story. She considered it—sipping her tea. Trevor had prepared her favorite—rose hip tea. It always strengthened her from the inside out. Probably thanks to the high amount of iron, as if she needed to arm herself and build her strength from within.

She bolted upright, suddenly remembering where she'd heard the name Ashen before. She saw her younger self at the dining room table. Her mother was sick in bed and her father spoke to Auran's father while seated in the big chairs at the front of the room. They seemed to have forgotten about her.

"Stronghold, what do you know about Lord Ashen?" her father asked.

"I know he's trouble," Auran's father responded.

"You can say that. Lord Ashen is determined to be the first to break new ground. His magician is extremely talented, and he's created a spell to send substances along with the arrows. The warriors are going through a steep learning curve and many animals have been slaughtered in their early attempts. My wife is from that area—we've heard Ashen's magician is starting to regret his post."

"Can't blame him. This is disturbing."

Iris remembered wondering how, if the spell killed the animals, it could have worked on people. The very thought chilled her to the bone. It was murder to use that spell on humans. She met Merlow's eyes.

Merlow spoke gravely. "Now you know."

Auran looked baffled, not clear at all who knew what and why.

"I'll explain later," Iris told him. She got up and sat next to Merlow, his anxiety rolling off him in waves, his aura flickering. "Yes, now I know," she swallowed. "I'm not judging you. I know what it's like to hurt people with your power."

"For you it was an accident. I was fully trained, fully aware of possible implications," Merlow choked out.

The pain was evident on his face, in his aura. She caught images of burning skin and cringed.

"What's wrong?" Auran asked.

Iris shook her head. "I understand the burden you carry," she told Merlow. "It's similar to my own." Force or accident—she wasn't sure which was worse. She stood up and hugged Merlow, hoping her touch might help him relax.

Auran looked increasingly bewildered.

Impulsively she hugged him too, more for her comfort than his.

As she rarely touched him, her hug only added fuel to his confusion, and he started to look really worried. "What?"

She smiled a sad smile and glanced at Merlow.

He nodded. "You can tell him." Merlow got up. "I shall check on Basil. I have no desire to hear the story again. Those events haunt me enough."

As soon as Merlow had left, Iris told Auran what she'd remembered.

His face was grave when she finished. "That explains why the Gemini Squad isn't still revered. I wouldn't be too keen to be known as a member once this got out. I've always thought it odd how quickly their reputation died. We must ask Merlow whether any of the bowmen are still alive."

"Yes, but first let him catch his breath. This is painful for him."

Auran gave her a look, illustrating why he was the commanding officer. She knew she had to toughen up, but when it came to others, she often found it difficult to hold them to the same rigid standards she held herself to.

Trevor reentered, and Iris realized he'd been lingering. "If I may disturb, miss, I could not help but overhear. Your father instructed me to tell you something once you remembered this story."

Iris jerked her head up.

"You may not know this, but once your parents got married, your father took your mother away from where she had grown up. Her brother Jonathan had been used for the same experiment you spoke about. He was in the wrong place at the wrong time and no one realized who he really was. He had a gift—like you and your mother—but it had made him turn inward and become unworldly. Jonathan was never really aware of his surroundings, which is probably why they used him for the experiment. Losing her brother in such a brutal way scarred your mother. They buried an empty coffin. Only parts of his body were recovered—weeks after the funeral."

She saw a tear glistening in the corner of his eye. *So much violence.* Iris had always thought her mother's mood swings odd. She'd holed up in her embroidery. The colored threads growing into pink and purple flowers—each blossom strengthening her thin hold on life.

Merlow came back in. He must've known what Trevor would tell them. He sat back down. "Trevor, please have a seat." He stroked his beard.

"It is time for a thorough and honest self-evaluation," Merlow said. "I need to speak openly about things that have been hidden for so long. I am embarrassed, as well as relieved, that you now know this part of my past. And I am eager to apply the knowledge I have accumulated at such cost, for the uprising."

Iris's hands tingled. Things were coming together at a deeper level than ever before. She'd seen that people were placed so timely in positions that it felt like magic. Having this information about the archers fall in their lap now was exceptional.

Auran cleared his throat and they all looked at him. "Let's be clear. I need to inform Jacob. I think Iris and Merlow need to explore how we can use this knowledge to our benefit. Last but not least I want Merlow to work with Jacob and myself on these time-traveling arrows."

As he said the last bit, Iris noticed his enthusiasm. *Boys and their arrows.* Auran had always been a crack shot with Jacob a close second.

"There are a few basic rules for tying the time-shift to objects," Merlow said. "I prefer to commence with the two of you first. I shall use a fair amount of magic to demonstrate the procedures and I am not convinced Jacob is…prepared."

Trevor nimbly unfolded his legs and got up. "I will ensure you are not disturbed."

Auran paled considerably. "We don't have to do it right away."

Iris glanced at Auran. "You'll be fine."

"Do not be concerned, Auran," Merlow assured. "It will not be more arduous than attending one of Iris's magic lessons."

Auran threw Merlow a withering look and Iris tried to hide her chuckle.

CHAPTER FORTY-SEVEN

Clairière

Auran had traveled for days to get to Clairière Forest, where Iris and Merlow had sent word they were now encamped. He hid the bundle behind the shed under a blackberry bush. The lodge was owned by sworn supporters of the uprising, but it never hurt to be cautious. Merlow would retrieve the goods the next morning. Auran picked one of the last berries and popped the reddish-black fruit in his mouth. He wrinkled his face. *Sour.* He swallowed the berry anyway not wanting to waste the nutrients. Merlow would be proud.

••••••••●••••••••

Merlow approached the lodge with caution. When they had mind-linked the previous evening, Auran had shown the location as best as he could.

Even though this was supposed to be a safe house, Merlow had not risked revealing his true identity. The charm was taxing but certainly worth the effort.

The charm showed anyone—except magicians—a twenty-year-old Merlow. A pity appearance charms did not work for Iris. *Her eyes burn through everything.* He wished the magic transformed his entire countenance, not just disguised his age, but alas.

This will have to do. He knocked on the door.

The rough wooden door opened a crack. "Yeah?"

"It is a good season for brambles," Merlow said.

"One moment." The door was pushed closed.

Merlow longed to hear what was being said inside but could not jeopardize the hold on his concealment spell. All he made out was what sounded like heavy furniture being moved around.

He tugged on his beard—feeling utterly naked knowing he could not visibly use magic without drawing attention, risking being tracked by Thorn and his cronies.

Merlow smoothed the pockets on his trousers, unused to the rough fabric. It had been a true find when Auran had brought them this extra pair of clothes.

The door opened. A broad-shouldered man squeezed himself through with a bundle under his left arm. He towered over Merlow. "Follow me."

In the dimly lit shed the man handed Merlow a jute bag. "I hope your brother gets well soon."

"My brother?" Merlow asked.

"Yeah, the lad who's fallen ill."

"Yes, of course. Thank you." Merlow cursed himself.

The man stared at him.

Merlow held up the bag. "I am sure these nutrients will make all the difference." He cringed inwardly—Auran had warned him not to speak too formally.

The owner turned around—Merlow's heart rate shot up—and placed a shirt on top of the bag. "From my wife. Used to be our son's. Boys outgrow their clothes so fast."

Merlow swallowed his breath of relief and smiled. "Thank you." His eyes watered. These people were giving away so much… "It is very much appreciated."

Back in the woods Merlow put both bags down with shaking hands, relieved Auran's deposit had still been in place.

CHAPTER FORTY-EIGHT

Kaale Mountains

Auran and Iris watched in silence as Merlow prepared for his tutorial. On the rough granite floor of Iris's chamber, he laid out a wooden stick, a russet stone and a water bowl filled to the brim.

The objects reminded Iris of his old ways. Merlow had access to ancient wisdom—things he'd learned from his own mentor, the Master Magician of his age. *A powerful ally on the other side.* One they must access when needed.

Iris returned her focus to the circle in front of her when she heard Merlow murmur a spell—the hum of the energy resonated in her bones. *He's casting a protective shield.* The enchantment kept out energies and noise.

Auran pulled up his shoulders. Iris squinted. Auran was less bothered by magic than Jacob, but he'd never gotten fully comfortable with magic this close. His sapphire aura dulled.

The three of them sat cross-legged as Merlow led the initial ceremony. "Take your time to ground and clear your mind."

Iris focused on her breathing, forcing herself to slow down and become fully present. Next to her she felt Auran's tension. She sent soothing energy his way, and slowly his breathing deepened.

As the energy pulsed around them, the flow intensified. Their energies blended—Merlow's yellow embraced her flaming blue and Auran's sapphire. Merlow no longer needed to hold back from his hidden past. Something uncurled in herself as well.

Her body followed the rhythm of Merlow's incantation, and their visions merged. With a jolt Iris realized Merlow was taking them back to the archers' meadow. *Remote viewing, in the past, together.* The magic destabilized, and she took a deep breath to curb her excitement.

Merlow reached out for her power, and she fused her magic with his—the image of the meadow floated to the middle of the circle, hovering above the objects.

Four archers lined up on the fresh green grass under a clear blue sky. Each had a full quiver strapped to his back, left forearm covered with a leather armguard—sturdier than what Auran used. What stood out was an embroidered red dot on top of the leather. The first archer nocked an arrow.

Merlow pointed at the archers visible within the circle. "Endeavor to sense the moment when the arrow is touched by magic," Merlow said.

Iris clearly saw the energy flow from the archer's belly, through his arms and into his arrow. Auran's sharp inhale told her he'd sensed the magic, too. As the arrow flew, the archer's magic trailed behind.

"As you can see they still had much to learn," Merlow said.

"That was a perfect shot!" Auran exclaimed.

"I was not appointed to teach them archery, but to merge their magic with the arrows."

The image faded and with an increase in magic in their room, the scene jumped ahead to another afternoon in the meadow—the sky now overcast, and the archers viewed from behind.

"They improved quickly," Merlow said.

They watched another archer take a shot, and magic flowed from behind him, merging with the arrow, right before he let the projectile fly.

"Was that you?" Iris asked Merlow.

"Certainly. I instructed them to anchor their magic to the arrow and not release it until they sensed my magic join theirs." Pride rang through Merlow's voice.

Iris was astounded he'd been able to teach them such intricate magic. The bowmen must all have been extremely gifted. She wished she could transport them forward in time so they had access to these warrior magicians now. She needed to ask Merlow about the end result of the horrible experiments, and whether they'd figured out a way for people to time-travel—and still be breathing.

The image petered out.

Auran beamed. "I can't believe you worked with the Gemini Squad. You need to teach us, too."

Now he's excited about magic, thanks to arrows? Iris realized Auran looked different. Not just more determined but more open, too. As if he'd allowed a part of himself to come forward that he'd been resisting.

"Okay," Auran said. "When can I start practicing these exercises?"

Merlow responded with a smile. "Iris and I can both help you get started. As things get more advanced I shall demonstrate how we did it back then."

"Yes," Iris said. "But you need to be rested before handling magic so let's wait until tomorrow morning. We have enough trouble avoiding attention without adding magical accidents to the list. Which reminds me, I have to check with Sourni."

Auran and Merlow both nodded absently. Iris shook her head and got up. "Auran, will you tell Jacob? Merlow, we still need to explore options to strengthen the cave's structure if we intend to stay longer. How about we discuss that after dinner?"

"Sure, sure," they said together.

Iris chuckled. They'd responded as if the mindlink was still present. She noticed the bowl, stick and stone and realized they hadn't been used. She was about to point that out to Merlow when she understood—they represented all the elements: wood, water, earth and the reflection of light in the bowl. The items were now charged with the energy of the visions and would be more powerful later when they practiced the exercises.

This old magic was rarely at the forefront of her mind, and she kept underestimating its power. She was glad she had Merlow to remedy that. It reminded her there must be a way to charge the stone of the mountain—this earth element they were living in.

CHAPTER FORTY-NINE

Arbres

Sourni finally knew what to do. She would go to Robbert and confront him with the budget deficit. Interviewing Marie and Anne had pinned down the reasons—Her Eminence's whims for fish from the Dead Seas, Gieser Wildeman pears, fancy dresses. All highly expensive, all underestimated. Sourni calmed her mind before leaving her room, similar to when she connected for a mind-link. She found it soothing, and it helped clear her head.

Sourni walked to the administrator's office and was told to wait on the hardwood chair in the hall. She counted tiles up to five hundred and twenty. Honestly, she'd expected him to make her wait longer.

His secretary announced, "He will see you now."

Sourni wiped her hands on her skirt and got up. Upon entering she curtsied. "Sir."

"Yes?"

"I would like to go over the budget. A few things have caught my attention."

Robbert stared at her with narrowed eyes. "Did they now."

She cleared her throat—willing herself to stay composed and focused. "Yes." She handed him the overview she'd prepared last night. "As you can see, there are a few items which cost more than budgeted."

He tossed the paper on the desk. "How will you solve this—shortage?"

Sourni quelled her fury. She couldn't believe he was pretending to be ignorant about the deficit. He approved all bills before the treasury paid them. "I spoke to the head seamstress and we're working on a way to save on fabric to bring expenses down."

He pressed his lips together.

She quickly pushed on. "As for the Gieser Wildeman pears, perhaps…perhaps we can reserve such a unique product for a handful of distinguished guests during important dinners. Receiving the pears would be an honor…"

"And who will tell Her?" he scoffed.

Sourni's heart dropped. She resisted the urge to fidget and kept her head down. "I hoped you could advise me, sir."

After a few heartbeats of silence Sourni peeked up. Robbert still stared at her, his hands folded in front of him.

"How would you decide who gets the pears? Have you thought of that? This could cause mayhem—or at least a tantrum."

Sourni barely heard the last words. "I…I'm not sure," she stammered. Marie had said malleable. Sourni didn't think she was supposed to be weak. A predator like Robbert would crush her like prey. She straightened. "I'm still learning the ways of the palace, sir. I would appreciate any suggestions you have."

"Hmm."

She had a flash of inspiration. "What if we only serve the pears for Her Eminence and Apex and whoever flanks them? Getting those seats means receiving the pears."

Robbert put his head on one side. "How much would that save?"

"For this week's luncheon we would've served six portions instead of twenty-three. Rationing it ensures enough stock to cater for Her Eminence. It seems we can expect a shortage of pears."

Regarding the fish from the Dead Seas, they both knew it was a lost cause, so neither mentioned it.

"I will consider your suggestion."

"Thank you, sir."

"Are you going to stand here all day?"

"No, sir." She bobbed her head.

As Sourni softly closed his heavy door, chills ran up and down her spine. She glanced around to see what had stirred this reaction. Nothing stood out. *How peculiar.*

She went right back to her room to catch her breath. Leaning against the windowsill, she enjoyed the salty breeze. Perhaps Her Eminence was on to something with her obsession for salt. It did have a clearing effect.

Sourni relaxed her shoulders. She was surprised Robbert had let her get away so easily. *Is he hiding something?*

Over the years she'd honed her instincts and getting chills usually served as confirmation. Somehow this time was different— resembling the time when the hair on her neck stood up.

WAS THERE NO end to how often she had to be reminded of that cursed day? Sourni had walked home with a heavy heart. She'd let Rolf off early to take Angelica home after the overseer had left. Sourni rolled her shoulders in an attempt to release the strain from the lashing, and more importantly—the images. She wasn't going to eat oatmeal any time soon. Suddenly her hair stood on end. Immediately alert, she stared straight at a grey wolf on the path.

She froze.

The wolf growled and eased a paw forward. Her heart pounded in her chest and she forced herself to stay rooted. *Can it smell my fear?* She tried to control her breathing, grasping for a relaxing image. *Clouds, fluffy white clouds.* She willed the gentle clouds into her being, praying to the Gods for a miracle. *Am I supposed to stare it down— or avoid eye contact?* She breathed out slowly. The wolf watched her awhile longer, then turned away, deeming her uninteresting.

Sourni had trudged back to the village clutching Angelica's breakfast bowl, the day forever etched into her mind.

She assumed Rolf had eventually worked up the nerve to ask Angelica for a drink in their local alehouse. *I hope they're doing well.*

SHE WONDERED WHAT Apex was doing. She hadn't seen him since the luncheon. He spent a lot of time in his hometown—or so they said. Somehow, she felt darkness when he was around, and she hadn't sensed it in the past few days. She asked herself whether he snuck out of Arbres. She also wondered when she would meet his sorcerer—Thorn. Jacob had warned her about him.

Jacob...

Holy Pears. This was not the time. And she didn't get paid for wondering. She got up and went to the kitchens to make sure Anne hadn't accepted any more excess goods.

CHAPTER FIFTY

Kaale Mountains

Iris slowly opened her eyes. *Sourni must be busy. I'll try again after dinner.* She yawned. It was going to be a long day. *Perhaps a quick nap.*

She strengthened her protective circle and lay down.

In her dreams she noticed her mother waving at her, as if apologizing for not being there more often. In the background she saw someone who could be her Uncle Jonathan—given the blue eyes— his as dreamy as Mama's were sad.

Without warning she was floating above Arbres and the Citadel. With a bird's eye view, Iris scanned the capital and its surroundings. Open fields led up to the city walls. On the right of the city a pier jutted into the ocean—several cutters lay moored.

On a training ground she recognized the Strong Ones and their number, moving as one. Thanks to their magic, they were synced like a flock of birds or a school of fish—fully aware of each fellow warriors' positions.

Sunshine drenched the orchards, hammering on the row of soldiers on the battlements. She noticed the priests and how they cowered. A large group of armed men marched out the city gates.

Her attention was drawn to the ocean. A ship became visible when the sun burned away the mist. It drifted on the waves— sails flapping.

Iris zoomed in closer and realized something was wrong.

Even though she'd never been on one, she saw none of the activity expected as on the ships mentioned in her father's stories. After she drew nearer she saw sickness had killed most of the crew. *This is the ship we've been waiting for.* Without a second thought she applied healing energy to the captain and the ship's mate—the only two men still breathing.

Iris never stopped to wonder how it was possible to do this in a dream state, as if something prevented her from thinking altogether. The curative energy flowed through her and she coaxed the captain's heart to a steadier rhythm. She prompted the mate's kidneys to expel the toxins. When she came to the end of her healing abilities she reached out to Merlow via a mindlink and had him help.

Only when both men breathed evenly did she allow herself to be pulled away. As her energy left the ship, she was drawn back into her body and woke up.

She opened her eyes and found Auran and Trevor hanging over her. Apparently she'd made some noise that alerted them. They pulled her into a sitting position.

"I'm okay. I just need to catch my breath."

Auran sat beside her and took her hand. His strength and warmth flowed into her as if she'd inhaled cinnamon oil. She relaxed, and the energy trickled back into her body and muscles. *I must be drained from what I gave the captain and his mate.*

Iris had seen the name of the ship on the bow. She let Auran support her and asked him, "What's the name of the ship we're waiting for?"

"The Morgenstar. Why?"

She told him about her experience.

"That's the ship we commissioned. Its cargo is invaluable," Auran said after she finished. "They should've arrived in Arbres weeks ago. Will they be fit enough to continue their voyage?"

"I'm not sure," Iris said. "I can try to check back in tonight."

"Have you done this before? Heal someone in a dream across such a distance?"

"No, not that I remember," Iris answered thoughtfully.

"You need something warm. There's no color left in your face."

He can be such a mother hen.

Trevor walked in the room with their supper.

They ate in silence. The stuffed pumpkin was warm and nourishing. Trevor had worked wonders with a handful of potatoes, several sticks of celery and cardamom. Iris allowed herself to enjoy being taken care of. Not having to cook dinner took away some of the pressure.

After dinner Auran gave her a pointed look. "I know you were going to talk to Merlow about strengthening the structure of the cave, but I really think you should wait until tomorrow. You're still drained, and you're explosive when you're tired."

It wasn't very often he spoke this plainly about her need to stay in control. "You're right," she said.

Auran tilted his head, surprised she gave in so easily. But she was too tired to fight him. Besides, it was true. It wasn't a risk she could take.

............●............

"All right," Auran said, not sure whether she was teasing him. "Shall I walk over to let Merlow know?"

"Relax, I'll tell him via mindlink. You're just as tired and have slept even less than I have. We need our commander fit and healthy." Iris winked.

Auran laughed. He liked it when she was playful, which was none too often. "Is there dessert for this commander? Or should I fight someone to earn that privilege?"

"I'm sure I can get Trevor to fetch you something, no need for more violence. Let us eat in peace," Iris said with an even bigger smile.

It reminded him of dessert at his place, when she often joined his family for a meal.

"Besides, there are a few acorns left. You may want those rather than dessert," she added.

"You really are spoiling me," Auran said, and meant it. Acorns were sacred. There weren't that many left and they were extremely valuable. Warriors always had some handy when sent off.

"I know," Iris answered seriously. "With what happened today and the shifts I sense in you, it's important you recharge, and this is the fastest way. Those two guards down the hall are supposed to be my last line of defense, but in truth, you are."

He couldn't take all the credit. "You're forgetting Trevor. He'll die defending you."

She blinked. "I need you now. I need your brain, your memory and your strength." After a pause she added softly, "Your friendship, too."

Auran spoke vehemently. "Iris, you know you have my complete allegiance—never doubt it. You're the reason I'm here, why we fight this war. Because of you we have a shot at making Fleuris a better place, a healthy place."

•••••••••••••••••

"I know." Tears welled up as she heard the truth in his voice. *Dammit. This is no time to cry.* She had to set an example. "I'm just tired. Can we sit by the fire?" Glancing at the empty fireplace, she realized there wasn't going to be any warmth.

Auran got up and returned with a blanket. "You're not thinking straight because you're cold from exhaustion. Do you want me to ask Merlow to brew you something?"

Iris nodded. If she was going to allow people to support her, she might as well go all the way. Besides, it would please Merlow. He liked taking care of her. "Take the acorns with you." She handed Auran two of the precious acorns from her personal supply and sat back under the blanket.

She must've dozed off, because she woke smelling chamomile and sandalwood. Auran stepped in the room with a steaming bowl. She sniffed. Her familiar deep sleep brew was packed with additional powerful herbs. *Merlow must've brewed a special concoction.*

"Merlow said you were to drink all of it. He added herbs to help you regain the strength you lost in the dream healing. He was impressed you were able to link with him in that state while staying present at the ship. He says your powers are increasing," Auran said.

"Well, I guess that's me too," she mused aloud. "It seems we've all expanded today. Must be the moon."

"All the more reason to turn in early tonight," he said. "The tower guards are bracing for another attack, but they seem to be enjoying themselves. They must have a lot of faith in your ability to bend the arrows."

"You mean they actually believe I can work magic?" She snorted. "I was getting worried they joined me for the fun of it."

"You're incorrigible." He sat down and popped the last of the acorns in his mouth, clearly savoring the earthly taste. "I can get used to this. Sure beats traveling and sitting outside in the rain."

She watched him, cradling the warm mug with both hands. This wasn't the life she'd have picked for herself either. But there was no choice other than moving forward best they could. Perhaps if everything worked out...

There were too many things she knew she could never have, not even if they won this war. But he could. That's what she wished for him. Iris lifted the mug to her forehead and felt the scalding pottery, willing the hollow feeling to disappear. *Dear Ayna, please give me strength.*

She sipped her drink and some warmth flowed back into her. She tasted old magic in Merlow's potion. One day she'd love to sit down and learn all he knew about restorative brews. Compared to his talents, her herbal skills were basic. Iris emptied her mug and put it down beside her.

Auran smiled—pleased.

"What do you need before you can sleep?" she asked.

"I'm worried about you," he said. "What you do to yourself when I'm not here. You're not invincible. I worry you'll exhaust yourself and lose control."

Does he really think I can't take care of myself? "I know what my boundaries are and what I can and cannot do," she said, trying to keep her voice level. "I wouldn't have gotten this far if I didn't. I know you mean well," her voice rose, "but you need to trust me like I trust you when you venture out and refuse to communicate for weeks. We need to believe we'll both be all right and do the best we can. I can't afford to worry about you, and you can't lose time and energy fretting about me."

He leveled a stare at her. "Let me do more. I know the intensive use of magic hurts you physically, even though you try to hide it. I can see the stiffness in your body, taking extra care sitting down."

Oh.

He knew her too well. He'd seen her grow, even from before her gift had revealed itself. She grabbed his hand and squeezed it. "Thank you. I don't know what else you can do."

"Let me be near you. I know you sleep better when I'm around. You need your strength. *We* need your strength."

Her insides churned. *This is going to get complicated.* And she needed her wits about her. "I'm tired," she said. "Can we talk about this tomorrow? When we know if we can stay here longer, it'll be easier to make plans."

"Okay. Let's sleep. It'll be another early morning. If we're not woken up by more arrows first. Layla spare us."

Iris laid her head down and inhaled the greasy smell of the sheepskin. She closed her eyes and imagined a starry night. It was one of the things she missed most—the fresh scent of the wind and the twinkling of stars. She hoped the stars didn't whisper too much tonight.

Right before she fell asleep, she remembered her promise to check on the captain. Thinking of him moved her to the ship. He lay in his bunk with more color on his face—his breathing was less labored, too. *Good.* The ship's mate looked stronger as well, though he'd lost a lot of weight, considering the fit of his clothes. The boat swung, and Iris realized they were drifting toward the rocky coastline.

She drew on more magic, hoping to heal the captain enough to navigate the ship.

Slowly the fever left his body. She used the last of her strength to pinch him awake and slipped away into a dreamless state.

The next morning she remembered two things. The stars had whispered to her but only briefly. Their message had been concise. "Open to receive." She also recalled visiting the ship's captain, making a mental note to check on him after breakfast.

She opened her eyes and looked straight into Auran's. Apparently he'd been studying her face. She scooted away but regretted it immediately. The floor was cold, and it hurt him. Disappointment flickered in his eyes. So she scooted back. "Sorry," she said. "I acted on impulse."

Iris silently cursed herself for apologizing. She needed to put distance between them and this most certainly wasn't helping. Instead, she told him about the ship and what she'd seen.

CHAPTER FIFTY-ONE

Arbres

S ourni was on her way to Her Eminence, pleased she'd learned a few shortcuts in the two weeks she'd been in the palace. As she got closer the feeling of darkness intensified. *Apex.* This time it mingled with a sharp, jagged presence. Instinctively she slowed down, thanking the Gods and Marie for her soft, silent slippers.

She halted around the corner, pretending to check the lavish arrangement of flowers on the golden pedestal, her ears pricked up. Luckily the men weren't trying to hide their conversation.

"Genius!" Apex said.

An unfamiliar voice responded, "We struck before dawn. Those peasants were still rotting in their beds. They never knew what hit them."

That must be Thorn. She focused on pulling dead petals from the flowers, catching bits of what sounded like a battle report.

She barely dared to breathe—frantically memorizing the details Thorn shared with Apex.

"How many were you able to obtain?" Apex asked.

"Sixty-three—"

Sourni stifled her gasp.

"—mostly girls and a few older...did you hear that?" Thorn demanded.

"Hmmm?" Apex asked.

Sourni scurried away, then remembered Jacob's advice and slowed to a normal pace.

Someone grabbed her arm. "Who are you?" A raven-haired man towered over her.

Sourni's heart hammered in her chest. "Sir? I'm the head keeper, on my way to Her Eminence for Her morning routine."

Piercing grey eyes took her in and a weird sensation crawled over her skin.

"Humph."

"Yes, that is indeed the new keeper," Apex added.

"I gathered that," Thorn responded. "Carry on," he motioned at Sourni.

She curtsied. "Thank you, sir.

....

Without warning, Iris felt an urgent call from Sourni. She pulled Auran in the mindlink with her. "What's happening?" Iris asked.

Sourni's distress was apparent. "There's been a raid. Apex's men went to a village on the coast and turned everything upside down. They took all girls and even some of the older women."

"How many were taken?" Auran cut in.

If Sourni was surprised he was partaking in the mindlink she didn't show it. "Sixty-three in total. They took some men too, the older ones. What will become of them?"

They could only guess but chances were they'd be taken to the mines. Why they took little girls didn't make sense though, unless they needed more workers, but that didn't add up. Children would never be up to the strenuous labor.

"What do you need?" she asked Sourni. "Is there anything we can do from here?"

"No, but I had to share. Should we warn other villages?"

"There's no need," Auran said. "News will travel fast enough and it's best not to meddle, not yet anyway. The other villages will take precautions, but they can never keep Apex's troops out if they want in." Auran voiced the thought that had crossed Iris's mind, too. "Were there any sorcerers present?"

"Thorn was there," Sourni said. "If he's tall, raven-haired, and has piercing grey eyes. Is it important to know if there were more?"

"Yes," Iris heard herself say. "Be careful. We'll try to arrange more safe houses." She sensed Auran's surprise—the mindlink revealed all. But it felt important and connected to the ship's captain and his mate. *Perhaps they'll need a place to stay.*

Auran asked a few more questions and reassured Sourni.

Iris wondered if they'd ever been intimate. *Not that it's any of my business.* Apparently Sourni was beautiful. Iris dismissed the thought and focused her attention back on the mental conversation. Iris considered updating Sourni on the time-traveling arrows but hesitated. *Best not have too much sensitive information so close to our enemies.*

"We'll reconnect tonight," Auran said. "Remember, act as if you're not worried about these raids."

Iris terminated the mindlink.

"It has begun," Auran said.

"So it seems. Did you notice anything strange about her?" she asked him. His expression made her wonder whether he'd picked up on her thoughts. It was always risky—people sensed a lot when mindlinking.

"You mean other than her worry and concern? No."

"Why did you ask about sorcerers, then?"

"It was a hunch, why?"

"Because I feel there's some connection. I need to speak to Merlow. There's a lot to discuss."

Auran leaned forward. "I'll tell him, then you can get ready for the day. I don't have a change of clothes with me anyhow."

"Perhaps you can borrow a uniform from Jacob. This one really needs replacing." Iris chuckled. Auran's forest-green uniform was covered in berry stains and mud. Parts of it were torn by bushes and rocks from the looks of it. He looked more like an errand boy than the commander. What made him stand apart was his demeanor.

That rung with authority through and through. That's probably why she'd barely noticed his clothes until now.

"Yeah, yeah. I guess you want me to shave, too," he said.

"I'll leave that up to you," she answered. "I imagine it's warmer with stubble than a clean-shaven face." She got up before he could go into it any further.

CHAPTER FIFTY-TWO

Kaale Mountains

Iris walked to the alcove they used for baths, although it was impossible to immerse herself fully. She could've warmed the water by magic, but she preferred the cold freshness.

It kept her humble.

Besides, it was how most people here cleansed themselves. She and Merlow were the only ones who possessed enough magic to warm that much water. They simply used rainwater, gathered in tanks. *A pity the water from the well is too harsh to soak in or drink.*

While sponging herself down she reflected on the day to come. She sensed it would be as full as the previous one. *I wouldn't mind a dull day for a change.*

After the refreshing bath she returned to her room and hung her flimsy towel to dry.

She was dying to get to Merlow and get a few mysteries solved. Someone was orchestrating a more complex offense than they'd anticipated.

When Iris arrived in Merlow's chamber, he was sitting cross-legged on his sleeping mat for his morning meditation. She slipped in quietly and browsed through his herbs. Back home the linen sachets would've been neatly arranged in the kitchen cabinets rather than collecting dust from an overhanging stone. Picking up the top pouch, she inhaled. *Cardamom.* She hadn't noticed it in her drink last night. *Merlow must've used it for his breakfast.* Dread loomed, thinking of the day they would run out of herbs.

Merlow exhaled deeply. "You are an early riser this morning. Auran came by too but did not have the patience to wait."

Iris nodded. "I'm afraid we have news from Arbres." She told him about the raid and the little girls. "What do you make of it?"

"Apex is getting more audacious. This is the largest number of women they have captured. They must be in need of something to risk that much." Merlow stroked his long white beard.

Iris always wondered how he was able to keep it so pristine. *He must be using a permanent spell.* "I know. Something feels odd about this attack. Why so many children? It…it made me think of a ritual. What did you use for your time-traveling experiments?"

Merlow's shoulders sagged.

"I know it's a painful memory, but we need to know," Iris said.

"I fear you are right. There is—ancient magic. And with Thorn…" He shook his head. "We can expect anything. Thorn is creative and he has power, but no scruples."

A shiver snaked down her spine.

"Ancient tales speak of the power inherent in virgins."

Iris gawked at him. *Seriously, virgins?*

"The power lies in their magical potential. If the girls have never…lain with anyone and they have magical powers, their energy is still relatively neutral. It is possible to tap their potential and transfer it to a magician. If they *have* been intimate, their sense of self is enlarged and their magical supply is imprinted with their own stamp, so to speak, rendering the power useless for someone else.

"Of course, there are other ways to imprint your energy, but the more remote and less-educated a village, the larger the chance of finding girls whose powers they can steal," Merlow said, thinking out loud. "That means Apex is ramping up an army, and a magical one at that."

It dazzled Iris. She thought she'd been ready for anything, and she knew, expected even, people would die in the process. But using humans as fuel, harvesting them like a bunch of wheat was beyond her. "What happens to these girls once their power is tapped?"

"It depends whether they want the girls alive, or sane. When someone forcibly drains a person's magic reservoir, it damages the sense of self, often to the point that the person can no longer take care of herself. Since the women are casualties of war, best to deplete their life force entirely," Merlow murmured.

Hang on. When did we go from ancient tales to casualties of war? Her insides squirmed.

She was surprised Merlow knew so much about these grossly inhumane tactics. "What do you mean? Has this happened before?" Leaning forward, she watched his aura.

"I bore witness to it once." Merlow breathed in and out deeply. "I was training the archers in magical assault and several marksmen lacked the conjuring power to complete an attack. Some were unable to loose more than one or two arrows, and our strategy involved a volley. It so happened Thorn came by." Merlow shut his eyes.

Iris held her breath. Merlow's aura intensified and his anguish washed over her like a black wave. She scrambled to throw her shield up.

"Thorn is about as tall as Auran and Jacob. It was a sunny day, but he looked immersed in shadow wherever he walked."

Merlow's magic stirred and without warning she was drawn into his memory. She recognized the meadow and immediately spotted Thorn—his eyes menacing.

"Fetch one of the farm girls. Take the blonde one we saw working in the field," he instructed his assistant.

The man rode off and returned with a frightened girl of about ten.

Thorn plucked her off the black gelding. "You get to assist us today. Aren't you lucky." He handed her to one of the archers. "Hold her."

The bowman reluctantly held the girl by her shoulders.

Iris frowned.

"Now, who wants more magic?" Thorn asked.

The archers glanced from Merlow to Thorn. Lord Ashen unbuttoned his dark green gabardine. "Great idea."

"Don't be shy," Thorn insisted. "You!" He pointed at a broad-shouldered archer. "Come here."

The man sauntered over to Thorn and hooked his thumbs behind his leather belt.

"Place your feet parallel to your hips and stay moored." Thorn placed his right hand on the archer's broad chest and rested his left hand on the girl's stomach. "Make sure you hold her still."

Thorn recited an ancient incantation.

It made Iris shiver and her stomach contracted.

The spell built to a throbbing intensity, and when Thorn's magic found its release the faint supply of magic in the girl's belly stirred. As if drawing a strand from a spider's web, the sorcerer pulled the girl's magic through her navel and into his left hand. Purple thread traveled up his arm and into his chest.

To Iris's surprise the girl's purple energy didn't mix with Thorn's brown energy—it was like oil in water. She followed the purple thread and watched it stutter in Thorn's chest. With considerable effort he pushed it on toward his right shoulder. Sweat gleamed on his upper lip, and he paused.

Thorn took a deep breath and forced the girl's magic into his right arm on an exhale. It trickled down slowly. He gritted his teeth and yanked on the purple thread.

Iris's head swiveled back to the girl—her aura extremely faint—and watched in horror as the sorcerer kept pulling on the girl's magic. *Doesn't he see she has nothing left to give?* It felt like he tried to pull her intestines out.

"What is going on? What is this girl doing here?" a woman's voice demanded.

Thorn swore profoundly. The interruption had broken his concentration and he stumbled into the broad archer as if he'd been pulling with his physical weight as well.

The girl collapsed on the grass. Iris saw the last of her purple life force leave the body.

No, Gods, no! Iris opened her eyes and retched.

Merlow stared at her. "I never imagined he would endanger the girl's life."

Iris stared back. "I…how…what…"

"I believe Thorn intended to keep her alive. The disruption by Lord Ashen's wife proved fatal."

"At what cost? Her aura was drained. She was already extremely weakened before the interruption!"

This was horrific. How were they to fight and conquer men who played by a different set of rules altogether? She had to inform Auran and Jacob immediately. They needed to strategize. Iris tried not to look judgmental as she looked back at Merlow.

"I know," Merlow said. "It is beyond anything we can comprehend. Thorn has no conscience. I am certain Apex hired him for that reason specifically. Thorn is a force to be reckoned with, but so are you."

Iris made a face.

"Do not be intimidated by him. Your powers exceed his, but you are not willing to let others suffer. He must become the recipient of your wrath. I think you would not mind hurting him, given how many he has condemned."

Merlow was right. Being afraid to hurt others got her nowhere. But willingly putting innocent people up for slaughter wasn't something she'd ever consent to.

Iris ached to train at her peak again. It was impossible to unleash the fullness of her power here, not without spiking on the readings. "All right, let's round up Auran and Jacob and find a secluded place where we can meet."

Merlow reached out for a mindlink. To Iris's surprise Auran responded quickly and they agreed to meet beyond the baths in a chamber that was easy to shield. Iris noticed Merlow gathering several herbs. *Are they for a brew or the war meeting?* She could barely bring herself to wait for him. Merlow sensed her anxiety and increased his pace.

Auran and Jacob approached from the common room, shoulder

by shoulder, almost touching the granite walls on either side. They looked like brothers. Although Auran was blond where Jacob had dark hair, they had similar stances and jawlines. Their eyes were alert and investigative.

Together they silently walked to the far-off chamber. Auran barricaded the entrance and Iris installed a muffling spell. In the corner of her eye, Merlow walked around the roughly oval room and sprinkled herbs in a circle. *Not for tea, then.* They all sat on the hard floor. *I should've brought a cushion for Merlow.* The cold ground increased his stiffness.

Iris got up, energy coursing through her veins—the foreboding of an outburst. She had to keep moving to channel her power in less devastating ways. Auran followed her with his eyes as if tracking deer. She felt Merlow's eyes, too. "I'm fine!" She glared at them. "Just give me a minute."

As Iris walked, the energy became manageable. "Merlow and I have a theory. The girls might've been abducted for their magic. Merlow has seen how Thorn extracted magic from a little girl. It was—horrific." Iris swallowed.

Jacob blinked while Auran kept his gaze steady.

Merlow added, "Lord Ashen fabricated a story on how she was trampled by cows because he could not risk telling the villagers about magic."

Auran rose. "I wish we knew more about Apex's strategy. I'm worried about the increase in Strong Ones."

"Is that possible, to speed up the process with magic?" Jacob asked.

Merlow gently tugged his beard. "It seems beyond their ability to hide so many warriors in training for ten years. Nor is it likely Thorn constituted a way to bring fully trained Strong Ones back from the future."

"Fact is they are here and ready to fight," Auran said.

"Can we take away their magic?" Jacob asked.

These seemingly naive questions made Iris remember why she liked him and why Auran had picked him as his second. "What would you do if we could?"

"Well, if the Strong Ones are molded through magic, would they be disabled without magic?"

Great question.

"We need intelligence first." Auran looked at Iris and Merlow. "Only a trained magician can access this kind of information."

"No point in remote viewing," Merlow said. "Thorn will have set up a spell to prevent that. Someone must physically infiltrate."

CHAPTER FIFTY-THREE

Kaale Mountains

"How about the Faeries?" Jacob asked.

Iris could have kissed him. Bless him, sweet, smart Jacob. The Faeries were perfectly capable of veering into enemy territory without being spotted. They usually didn't pick sides but now that little girls were involved, the chance to get their cooperation multiplied. "That's brilliant!" Iris almost yelled. "You are brilliant!"

Jacob smiled his shy smile. "Who will ask them?"

"I will," Merlow said. "I have done them a favor and they must still remunerate me."

"Great, what else?" The momentum built, and Iris returned to pacing around the room. It didn't bother the others this time. "We need to check on the ship and find a place for me to practice."

Jacob folded his arms behind his head. "What's aboard the ship?"

They looked at Auran.

"A friend. And a supply of cacao beans. I figured we might need all the help we could get," he mumbled.

Wait. It dawned on her. "Is he a good friend?"

Auran flashed a look at Merlow. "Why do you ask?"

"Your aura shows you care for him."

He scuffed his feet. "Ah, yes, we're close friends. Baruch grew up in the jungle. He can speak to plants and animals—even harness their power."

Wow.

"He's a natural wizard, although he has no power of his own. He channels the energies of nature and shapes those according to his will."

"That's an incredibly powerful gift. How come you've never spoken of him before?"

Merlow said nothing.

Good thing I visited his ship. Her attention moved to the vessel—it called her again. Automatically she slipped into a trance and sought out the frigate. She saw it blundering toward the coast.

She lent the captain some of her power—pouring it into him as if filling a container—and he glanced up in surprise. Baruch quickly applied his newfound strength, taking the helm with both hands, and steered away from the cliff. Iris fueled him with what she hoped was enough magic to sustain a safe course.

The others were silent, awaiting her return.

When she opened her eyes she registered the surprise in Jacob's face. It still startled him when her consciousness left her body and she froze in place.

"The ship was about to crash on the rocks near Arbres."

"What?" Auran gasped.

"I fed him some of my magic and he was able to steer clear." Relief flooded through Auran. *Good.* If she was giving away her energy, then best for a worthy cause. The benefit from dispersing her magic was she no longer needed to pace around the room. Her stomach rumbled.

"You need nourishment," Merlow said. "These long-distance sessions devour quite some fuel."

Suddenly they heard muted voices outside the room and when Iris focused, she felt the agitation of the guards walking around. *They must be looking for us.* She released the muffling spell.

Auran shot to his feet and removed the barrier at the entrance. "What's going on?"

"More arrows arrived!"

Iris realized that with both Auran and Jacob here, and Basil in the infirmary, they must be scrambling for someone to tell them what to do. She walked to the entrance when Merlow signaled for her to stay. "You guys go ahead. I'll be right along," she said.

She put the muffling spell back in place. Merlow looked grave. The past twenty-four hours had aged him considerably—the lines in his face were more pronounced. He pushed himself up and paced.

Iris suppressed a smile.

"Are you sure Sourni is to be trusted?" he asked.

"Why do you doubt her?"

"Neither of us has met her in person. What if she fooled Auran and Jacob? She worked for Apex before she worked for us."

"Sourni still works for Apex."

"Is that supposed to help?"

Iris realized the real problem wasn't Sourni or her allegiance. She placed a hand on Merlow's arm. "Thank you for sharing. Thank you for assisting us and this process with your past experience. It's extremely valuable and we wouldn't stand a chance without it."

She didn't say she understood how painful it must be for him. She didn't have to.

Gratitude filled his eyes, and her heart overflowed in return. *Where would I be without him?* She'd invented a few spells on her own but Merlow was indispensable—a walking library with loads of practical experience.

Auran strode back in and Iris quickly lifted the muffling spell so they could hear him.

"Merlow, we need you at the tower. One of the guards was grazed by an arrow and the impact suggests the poison is stronger. Did you change the formula back then?"

"No, I personally crafted the venom since it had to sustain both the trip and the lapse in time. There was advanced magic involved." He looked keen to investigate the product of his own making.

What were the chances he would end up at the exact site where arrows had been sent twenty years earlier? Iris understood his eagerness.

She wanted to trace the arrows once more. *Perhaps I can catch another glimpse of the archers.* Now she knew Merlow was the magician she had to shield against, she might risk staying longer. The closer they got to the watchtower, the more she sensed the distress rippling toward them in waves.

As they crossed the final corner, Auran gasped.

Jacob lay face down on the granite floor, several guards hovering around him, wringing their hands. Iris and Auran sprinted forward as one, kneeling on either side of Jacob. Auran's hand hovered above the orange shaft.

"What happened?" Auran exclaimed.

One of the guards pointed needlessly toward Jacob's unprotected back. "Another arrow arrived."

"Merlow, shield us," Iris instructed. The arrow was lodged in Jacob's lower back. She carefully placed her hand below the dart and searched for the poison with her senses. A web of venom spread from the arrowhead in all directions, damaging his cells. She closed off the vein to prevent more toxin spreading throughout his body and registered Merlow's presence opposite her. "What poison did you use?" she asked him. He showed her the plant images through a mindlink.

It annoyed her he used a situation like this for teaching, but fortunately she recognized the leaves. *Nightshade.* And a more rural herb she forgot the name of. Luckily she'd seen it often and knew the remedy.

Iris positioned her hands next to the arrow shaft and focused on the entrance. On her nod, Merlow pulled out the dart and the flesh gave way reluctantly. She used magic to steer the poison toward the opening. She had to purge Jacob's blood before she could close the wound. She encouraged his liver to sift out the remaining traces and sped up his kidneys.

Even though the entry wound was small she used a knitting spell to stitch the fissure, not wanting to risk infection. It reminded her of her first healing session. She smiled slightly at the memory of the squirrel.

Now Jacob's body had to continue the healing process. He took a deep breath and regained consciousness. Iris opened her eyes and looked into Auran's once more. She nodded, and he sighed with relief. Together they gently turned Jacob onto his back.

"Help me lift him," Auran instructed two of his guards. "On three." They jointly raised their second in command. "We'll take him to the infirmary."

Merlow's eyes were still closed and he was white as a sheet, like the arrow had sucked the life out of him, too. *Is touching your own poison dangerous?*

Merlow's eyes fluttered open. He looked exhausted.

••••••••••●•••••••••

It had felt glorious at first—supporting an elite group, revered by the entire country. Merlow had been flattered and had reveled in the envy of his peers. The archers in the Gemini Squad could hand-pick the best of the best and they did. Joining them surely meant he was in a league of his own.

By the time he realized, he was in too deep—too entangled with Lord Ashen's sordid affairs to be let go. He attempted to induce as much common sense in the archers as he could, insisting they had to be sober while shooting. Sometimes he had blamed magic for not being able to continue, but Merlow knew caution was warranted, or he would be replaced.

Lord Ashen had summoned them to the open space, the spot selected to prevent prying eyes. The archers were already gathered and lined up in a semicircle.

"Merlow, good of you to join us." Lord Ashen addressed the magician with enough disdain to clarify who was in charge.

Merlow inclined his head. "My lord."

"Given the success with the kitten yesterday, I want to proceed to the next phase."

They had been able to send the three-day-old animal five minutes into the future.

Lord Ashen motioned to one of his men. The man pushed a small girl forward previously hidden by his bulk. She was four or five years old, two straw-blonde braids rested on her shoulders.

"Where do you want her?" Lord Ashen asked.

Merlow was eager to prove his worth again. He directed the girl to the middle of the semicircle, to the exact spot the kitten had disappeared from. "Stay there."

Gathering magic, he signaled the archers to notch an arrow. He waited until he sensed the hum of their magic aligning with their arrows, and cast a magic net from the archers to the girl, and back to him. Merlow recited the time-traveling spell and released his power—the marksmen releasing their arrows with him.

A cry strangled the silence.

Merlow's eyes flew open and focused on the girl. The spell had sent parts of her into the future—leaving holes in what remained, A monster had gnawed on her body. Her intestines spilled out and her collar bone jutted out through her skin. Her left hand was missing—one braid was dripping red.

He heaved. *I am the monster.*

Apparently what worked on cats was not transferable to humans.

"What happened?" Lord Ashen demanded.

"The mass was too big…" *Dear Seth and Layla.*

"How will you remedy that?"

"Perhaps we need to try goats first," Merlow surmised.

With hindsight he should have suggested it was beyond the bounds of possibility, that human biology was too complex to allow for such transfers. Then Iris's uncle might still be alive.

Lord Ashen might have bought it, but in truth Merlow was excited to be part of the greatest discovery of his era. He envisioned going forward in time to warn people against something or procure a certain medicine or herb. Even surrounded by warriors, his first thoughts had been on survival and healing—not war and destruction.

He had been unforgivingly naive.

CHAPTER FIFTY-FOUR

Forêt de Cèdres

Auran had traveled for days to get to Merlow and Iris's current hiding place, moving in circles at times to make sure he wasn't followed. He silently moved the canopy of leaves aside, careful not to leave a trace. His hunter's eye searched for signs of humans.

Iris had told him to turn into the woods after the big maple tree. There was no path. His instincts guided him, as if he were tracking deer.

There. A broken twig.

Auran touched the shriveled auburn leaves, he imagined sensing her presence, and scanned the forest floor for more proof Iris and Merlow had passed here.

Mindlinking would be handy right about now. Iris had scoffed at his refusal to learn how to initiate mindlinks. Receiving calls went well, most of the time. He would have to give up his resistance to using magic, the tiny bit Merlow said he possessed.

For now he had to rely on his gut feeling and the instructions she'd given him.

Auran closed his eyes and focused on the sounds.

The forest was relatively quiet. The birds had stopped their chatter when he'd entered but the animals' sixth sense must've told them there was no danger. Under the birds' warble Auran discerned a sound—barely audible—that didn't belong.

Iris.

He opened his eyes and carved a path toward the source of the noise. His feet routinely found the perfect spots—leaving no evidence.

Auran went deeper into the forest still, impressed how few remnants the woods showed of their passing.

Finally he heard them.

"Focus! You are still not using the fullness of your power," Merlow reprimanded Iris. "You can trust your control and do more than shield yourself."

"But…" Iris jerked her head up. "Auran! I knew I sensed you."

"Why haven't you kept a soundproofing spell up around here?" Auran said, walking into the clearing.

"Permanent spells are child's play to trace," Merlow said. "We might as well wave a flag announcing our presence."

"Were we easy to find?" Iris asked eagerly.

"Honestly? I expected to see more footprints." Auran smiled.

Iris beamed back at him—the intensity hit him squarely in the chest. It always took time to get used to her brightness after he hadn't seen her for a while.

He had to blink as she stepped closer. "We really did our best to walk on the rocks, not the leaves. Was it good?"

"You did pretty well on the footprints. Next time be cautious of the twigs you break."

"Oh."

• • • • • • • • • • •

Iris was glad Auran had arrived. It might give her a reprieve from Merlow's incessant pushing to use more of her power. "Are we done for today?"

Merlow saw right through her. He glanced between her and Auran. "You can start making dinner. Auran looks famished."

He's always hungry.

Iris reached for Auran's backpack. "What did you bring?"

He unslung the pack and untied the top. "I have basil, my mom had some left, but none of the other herbs." Auran looked up. "Apex has seized the apple orchards, too."

"Really?" The priest's greed was boundless.

Auran handed the sachet to Merlow. "I also have dried beans and bread."

Iris grabbed the loaf of brown bread and sighed with pleasure.

"My mom knitted a scarf for you. She's afraid you'll freeze." Auran shrugged as he handed her the bundle.

The wool pricked her hands, but Iris buried her nose in the navy-blue shawl—inhaling the familiar scent of the Stronghold house, mixed with the glorious smell of bread. A pang of longing for the homey atmosphere coursed through her. She was tired of running.

"Thank you," she said. "Did your mother not need the yarn?"

Auran cocked his head. "As if you could stop her from trying to spoil you."

Iris pressed the scarf to her chest.

They ate venison that night—a rare luxury. Neither Iris nor Merlow knew how to hunt and they survived mostly on roots and beets they dug up in the forest, and occasionally from someone's vegetable patch.

In these more rural areas, people still got away with growing their own produce. *For how long?* Iris wondered.

The next morning they feasted on bread with raw honey. Merlow had stumbled upon a wild beehive a few days earlier and used magic to break off a honeycomb without getting stung.

After breakfast Iris braced herself for another intensive day.

•••••••••••••••

Merlow was pleased Auran had showed up. Iris always tried harder when the boy was present. His presence helped balance her and provided her with a much-needed sense of stability—a requisite to unleash her power safely.

Plus he could utilize her familiarity with Auran's energy. "Iris."

"Yes?"

"We shall work a new spell today. However, first we will uncover how far you can stretch using your senses."

She sighed. "Okay."

"Prepare yourself." Merlow watched her go through the preamble of grounding herself and stabilizing her energy. Auran sat at the remnants of their fire—Merlow had hidden the smoke with a temporary concealing spell last night—and whittled branches to create arrow shafts. Auran had been thrilled at finding a tall red-brown cedar on the edge of their clearing.

Iris opened her eyes. "I'm ready."

"Focus your inner mind on the trail Auran created yesterday," Merlow instructed.

"I left no marks," Auran mumbled.

Merlow smiled into his beard. "Trace his energy back from where you saw Auran emerge from the shrubs. Can you feel it?"

Iris squinted her eyes in concentration.

"Now follow Auran's energy—feign you were walking that path physically. Be mindful of what you notice."

Iris sat down.

After a while she murmured "I'm at the road."

"Wonderful," Merlow said. "Now stretch your awareness further. Which side did Auran come from?"

Merlow said a silent prayer to Seth and Layla, requesting no sorcerer would walk the road in the coming hours. Iris was not yet able to hide her energy signature. But she had to master this skill and take it even further with the spell. It was the first line of defense—scouting the area. They were as far away from any known sorcerers as they would ever be and Auran's relatively fresh trail was a great place to start.

She bit her lower lip. "Auran came from the left, so he took a right turn into the forest."

The boy in question looked up in surprise.

Merlow took that as confirmation. "Well done. What else can you sense?"

She wrinkled her nose. "Cows."

Cows?

Iris turned her head sideways as if to avoid the stench.

She can smell cows?

"I did notice cow pats," Auran offered.

Merlow was impressed—not for her ability to sense the lingering energy of a herd of cows, but the aptitude to *smell* them. "Does anything else stand out?"

Iris closed her eyes, and Merlow sensed she dove deeper into the well of her power. *Excellent.*

"Pumpkins."

What? Merlow had never heard of anyone being able to distinguish inanimate objects from such a distance. She had not even started to use the spell. "How about humans? Or did the cattle take a stroll by themselves?"

Auran chuckled.

Beads of perspiration glistened on her forehead. "There were two. An older man and…a boy." The strain showed in her voice.

Interesting. She finds it easier to detect pumpkins than humans. Merlow wondered whether it had to do with her tendency to close herself off.

"Take a deep breath," Merlow said. He watched her chest rise and her energy settle.

He mindlinked with her and showed her the spell. It allowed him to demonstrate the casting of the spell without working too much magic.

"Two layers?" Her eyes flew open.

"Yes. Stay focused."

"Wow."

"Perhaps I should move?" Auran asked.

Iris glared at him.

Merlow folded his hands.

She sighed dramatically, but obediently closed her eyes again.

"Concentrate on the rhythm of your breathing. Say the first enchantment on an exhale." The hum of magic increased. "Hold it steady." Merlow monitored the energy closely. He had a spell ready—

should he need to disperse her magic. "When you are ready commence the second layer—while keeping a firm grasp on the first."

Iris's forehead creased.

"Relax. You do not have to force the magic. Allow it to flow—you only have to direct it."

Her shoulders came down slightly.

"Easy. Merge the second layer as if you are braiding."

The intensity of magic increased further. Auran's shoulders tensed.

Merlow felt the layers fuse seamlessly. "Now let the spell guide you to the closest human."

Auran inhaled sharply—eyes wide.

"Do not worry. The spell conceals your presence." *Unless you stumble upon a sorcerer.*

Merlow settled back against a tree trunk, crossing his ankles. This could take a while. The spell would scan the surroundings for people—and pause when encountering the first person. Adding a third layer would ensure the spell hunted the second closest individual as well.

Earlier than expected, Iris said "There's a priest on the dirt road. He travels with a servant. And a horse."

"Where are they going?" Auran interjected.

Merlow frowned at the interference.

Iris kept her eyes closed. "They are moving toward us."

Dear Seth. "Very well. Now slowly bring your awareness back to our camp." Merlow prayed the priest was a non-magician. Perhaps he had taken too big a risk.

"Auran, can you find us another hiding place?"

"Sure."

They gathered their belongings while Auran wiped out traces of their presence, then led the way. "Step exactly where I do."

Merlow emulated him—carefully placing his feet. *Crack.*

Auran's head swiveled. "No, Merlow. Not approximately, step *exactly* where I go. You just snapped a twig." Auran picked up the small branch. "Look." He stuck it in his knapsack.

Merlow's cheeks colored.

"No stepping on twigs or dry leaves, and stay well away from the bushes." Auran shook his head.

"All right," Merlow acquiesced.

Iris giggled.

Auran found them a great new spot, close to streaming water.

...........•...........

Iris put the bundle with her belongings down and rubbed her shoulders. She was grateful Auran had carried their sleeping mats and the heavy copper pan.

"Tired already?" Auran teased.

She yawned. "New spells are exhausting. And I had another visit from the Lonely Ones last night."

Auran scowled. "You should keep them away—create a spell or something."

She shrugged. "I feel bad for them—they have no one to go to. They're not dangerous." She knew they were drawn to her energy especially. It somehow made them feel more alive. She just didn't have the heart to deny them every time.

CHAPTER FIFTY-FIVE

Kaale Mountains

Auran, Merlow and Iris agreed Merlow would visit the Faeries as soon as possible.

"To meet the Faeries unannounced, I must immerse myself in nature," Merlow said.

"How so?" Auran asked.

"The veil between the Faerie realm and earth is ethereal in forests or near water."

Now Iris understood why Maesie and Wendolyn always showed up in the woods behind her home.

"To request a meeting with the Faerie Queen one must arrive—unarmed—at sunrise or sundown," Merlow explained.

"How will they know you want to meet them?" Auran asked.

Merlow smiled. "Magic."

Auran arched his brows.

"There is a spell that needs to be cast at the meeting place, alerting the Faeries to your presence and intention. No human can access the Faerie realm unaccompanied."

"Not even our Merlow?" Auran winked.

"Alas."

Iris rolled her eyes. "Do you have a place in mind?"

"How about the forest we crossed right before heading into the mountains?" Auran suggested.

"I remember that place. It had a quaint feel—not many humans have been there," Iris said. "Are you sure we can get there safely?"

"*You* aren't going anywhere," Auran said sternly. "*We* can travel under cover of darkness."

Iris glowered.

"There is no need," Merlow said. "I can distance-travel to the glade if Iris monitors the connection."

Distance-travel. She kept forgetting about that. She had tried it once but gave off too much energy to use unnoticed. Most magicians didn't possess enough magic to uphold the spell, but Merlow was well-versed at transporting himself to another physical location.

"Alright. Shall we ask the guard to wake us before first light?" Iris asked.

Even though the sun and stars were invisible in the cave, most humans were able to tell time anywhere. It was like tapping in to the world's watch to get a sense of how late it was—which was accurate enough for most things.

"I'll see to it," Auran said.

"We may need an archer, too. Just in case someone tries to dash along when Merlow returns here."

Auran nodded. "Jacob will hate missing out."

"That reminds me, I want to check his vitals," Merlow said. He selected several herbs to accelerate Jacob's healing process.

The hospital room was a separate room, off the side of the common room—one of their most reclusive spots. They had not expected to use the infirmary for anything other than colds and frostbites. Now both Basil and Jacob were lying here...

Together they sauntered over to the infirmary where they found Jacob awake. "How are you feeling?" Merlow asked.

"Sore."

Merlow took his pulse. "I am relieved you regained some color. I apologize for creating the poison that took you out."

Jacob shrugged and winced. "You were doing your job. I'm glad you did your job today, too."

Iris and Auran exchanged a glance.

"You are most gracious." Merlow inclined his head.

Basil sat up in his bed, his mocha eyes a little clearer than yesterday.

WHEN THE GUARD woke her, Iris realized she'd been so engaged in her dream she hadn't even heard him come in. *Either I'm losing my touch or I'm starting to discern whether someone means harm.* The first was cause for alarm, while the second option felt soothing. *Perhaps I'll get more sleep at last.*

The guard nodded. "Auran said he would be here soon."

"Thank you."

For some reason remote viewing always made her queasy, so she skipped breakfast.

Auran and Merlow walked in. A broad-shouldered guard trailed behind them, carrying a bow and a quiver full of arrows. *So, he's the third archer.*

"Morning," she said.

The men muttered a response.

"We won't need the archer until Merlow returns," Iris said.

"How long do you reckon it'll take?" Auran asked Merlow.

"I presume one or two hours, though with the Faeries it is hard to predict," Merlow answered.

"Stay on alert at the tower," Auran instructed the archer.

Iris sat and calmed her mind. Sunrise was nearing. She tapped into her magic and drew enough power to create a connection with the glade. She remembered seeing a large oak tree and chose to open a tiny window in front of the trunk. *At least we're hidden from one angle.* The biggest risk with viewing across distances was the window allowed seeing both ways. She squinted through the oriel. The first rays of light cast a golden glow on the forest floor, illuminating burgundy and bronze leaves. Widening the opening, she stretched her senses to detect human presence. Movement flickered to her left and she froze.

A rabbit hopped into view.

She breathed a sigh of relief. "All clear," she whispered.

Merlow gathered magic and aligned with her connection to the forest. She sent more power to strengthen the link. Merlow mumbled the incantation to use her gateway.

Iris was still watching the tree line. A change in pressure indicated Merlow had left the chamber.

He materialized almost immediately in front of the oak. Merlow scanned the glade and nodded to her.

Iris closed the window but maintained the connection to ensure a quick getaway. As Merlow moved to the edge of the clearing she kept tabs on him.

After Merlow cast a vaguely familiar spell, she'd immediately expected the distinct energy of the Faeries, but it was well past sunrise before she recognized their tingling presence.

She felt two or three approach Merlow.

Iris wished she'd left the window open so she could watch and listen. *I can't risk creating an opening now and scare them off.*

Merlow's and the Faeries' auras mingled.

"Everything all right?" She heard Auran ask.

She nodded and waved him off.

When she refocused on the glade, Merlow's energy faded. *Nothing to do now but wait.* Iris pulled back most of her power, hoping to leave only faint traces of her presence.

"Iris, do you want breakfast?" Auran asked.

She ignored him, wanting to stay fully focused so she could bring Merlow back immediately in case of emergency. She wasn't afraid he would break under torture. He could take himself out, but she shivered to think what would happen if the enemy gained access to him.

Iris spent the day in half-meditation, part of her attention on her chamber, part on the glade where she still vaguely sensed Merlow's presence.

Conferring with the Faeries took longer than she expected. She stretched her limbs to keep her circulation going and leaned down to rub her calves.

Halfway through the afternoon Iris felt Merlow's lifeforce return to the clearing. She sat up straight, searching the glade for signs of Faerie energy.

"Iris?" Merlow asked via mindlink.

"I'm here."

"I am ready to return."

"Okay. Hang on."

Iris established a mindlink with Auran. "Merlow's coming back. I need you here. Bring your best archer—arrow notched."

"On my way."

Within minutes she heard Auran and his archer enter the room.

"Stand over there and shoot at anything that's not our Merlow," Auran instructed.

"Yes, sir."

She took a deep breath. "Get ready, Merlow." He couldn't access these premises unless someone opened the door from the inside. They'd installed the most powerful wards and repelling spells to keep people out. *Thank Gods the density of the granite conceals our permanent spells.*

She aligned with Merlow's energy and opened the gateway.

Within a breath he stood next to her.

Iris slowly opened her eyes and blinked against the light. She teetered and Auran caught her before she hit her head on the granite. On cue, Trevor appeared with a steaming bowl of vegetables—a rare treat. He knew she needed something light after a session like this. His timing was often perfect. *He must have more magic than I thought.*

Auran nodded to dismiss the archer. "Thank you, Evan."

"Sir."

"How did it go?" Auran asked.

"The Faeries had anticipated my arrival," Merlow said.

Iris had forgotten the Faeries were said to have premonition-like abilities.

CHAPTER FIFTY-SIX

Kaale Mountains

Merlow sat on the cold floor, pleased to be back safely, though today the cave felt more prison than refuge. He wrapped himself in his woolen traveling cloak.

He remembered the golden light at the glade, momentarily disturbed by the power of his spell to get to Faerieland. Deep breaths of invigorating morning air had filled his lungs with oxygen. *Iris would have loved this.* He knew she relished the smell of fresh air, especially in the morning. The sun rose, casting pink hues on the colorful carpet of leaves, and the nippy forest gradually grew warmer. He'd basked in the glow, remaining alert to the slightest shift in his surroundings.

He sensed the Faeries before he heard them.

"Our Queen greets you," the short Faerie curtsied, sending her ash-blonde locks swinging. She was accompanied by two younger Faeries.

Merlow inclined his head. "I salute your Queen."

"We received your calling and our Queen agreed to hear your petition."

"I am most grateful."

"We will accompany you to our meeting place. You are not allowed to use magic."

"I am aware of the regulations," Merlow said, allowing his voice to show a hint of annoyance.

The short Faerie blinked and beckoned.

Merlow reminded himself not to mistake her gentle fawn eyes for being compliant. He moved closer and braced himself for the shift. The intense pressure of moving to another dimension was highly unpleasant. He had once visited the Faeries with a mild headache and came back with a two-day migraine not even his potions could cure.

The strain increased and Merlow opened his eyes to a lush green environment several shades warmer than the forest. He took off his traveling cloak.

"This way please," the younger, copper-haired Faerie said.

Merlow followed along a narrow, winding path. The white-blooming underbrush tickled his calves and released enticing wafts of jasmine. He ended up in a clearing reminiscent of the glade he had just left. Gazing at the oak tree, he was reminded of his mentor's philosophy.

His mentor—the Master Magician of *his* time—believed the world had split up in several identical dimensions. Over time each dimension changed according to the actions and beliefs of its inhabitants. *The Faeries must be doing something right.* Their world felt so much softer and more fertile.

The Faerie Queen strode to the middle. Power radiated off of her. She was majestic in a lavender silk robe. Faeries ceased wearing iridescent dresses when they reached maturity.

Merlow inclined his head. "Your Majesty, a pleasure to meet again."

"Merlow." The Faerie Queen's nod was barely perceptible.

Protocol required him to ask after her well-being and that of her siblings. After having established indeed both the Faerie royal family and Merlow were in good health, he proceeded to the real reason of his visit.

"Our world suffers from an increasing darkness, as you are aware. Recently the darkness has spread into our hearts once more when sixty-three young girls and women were abducted. We wondered if you might be inclined to aid us in locating them." Merlow had learned to be direct and honest when it came to soliciting support from the Faerie Queen.

"What will you do once you know their location?" the Faerie Queen asked sternly.

She is not surprised. Merlow tucked this valuable information away to mull on later. "We want to determine why the girls were taken, and, if possible, rescue them."

"You know why they were taken as well as I do."

Merlow's heart sank. Blonde braids flashed by and he swallowed. He looked the Queen straight into her jade eyes. "If we are to stand a chance to reverse the evil in our world, we must find the girls and discover what their magic shall be used for. We need to prepare."

The Queen held his gaze. "Let us deliberate."

"Thank you," Merlow said.

The Queen departed with her entourage, leaving Merlow in the clearing with the same three Faeries. *My guards.*

He resisted a smile. The girls were no match for his power, but since using magic was outlawed they might well overtake him—immobilize him even—especially since nothing was as it seemed. The fragrant jasmine-like bush was deadly on consumption. Even inhaling the scent too deeply caused an epileptic episode. In Merlow's experience, all paths leading from the human world to Faerieland were adorned with alluring traps.

The Faeries took their safety serious. Only a fool would consider them cute.

He passed time by brushing up on his knowledge of Faerie plants—using his senses to estimate their properties—careful not to stray too far from the clearing's edge or touch any leaves.

"We have reached a verdict," the Faerie Queen's warm timbre spoke right behind him.

Startled, Merlow turned around. Not many people were able to approach him unawares.

He tilted his head. "I look forward to hearing your ruling."

"We will assist in locating the girls."

"Thank you," Merlow bowed in relief.

The Faerie Queen held up her bejeweled hand. "There are conditions."

Of course. "Yes?" he asked.

"We are concerned about the developments on Earth. We require your assurance the intentions of you and your companions are honorable."

"Naturally!"

"Let Me Finish," the Faerie Queen stipulated. "You will swear an eternal vow on the honest intentions and actions of you and your companions—now and in the future. *You* will be held responsible for any breach."

Merlow swallowed.

"You are aware of the retributions?" the Queen asked.

Breaking an eternal vow meant a life sentence—either by death or by enslavement to the Faeries, if that was deemed more desirable. He knew they coveted his powers. *Quid pro quo indeed.*

He nodded. "I shall take the oath."

"Hold up your right hand," The Faerie Queen instructed, while raising her own right hand as well.

When their palms faced, a current of energy ran between their hands.

"I solemnly swear to assist Merlow and his compatriots in locating the abducted girls, and aid in their liberation, if possible. In return Merlow pledges an eternal vow to the honorability of the intentions and actions of himself and his entire entourage both now and in the future," the Queen recited.

"And so it is," Merlow declared. A band of energy had snapped around his wrist, ingraining the vow into his blood.

·········•••••••·········

"You swore an eternal vow?" Iris exclaimed. "For our entire group?" She looked at Auran for support. "What in Seth's name were you thinking?"

"It is I who will face retribution," Merlow spoke softly.

"That's exactly my point. Why didn't you consult us? Didn't you have twenty-three hours to decide?"

"Why not twenty-four?" Auran inquired.

"It is tradition for the Faeries to offer humans a sacred twenty-three-hour window before having to reach a decision. Our King established that custom to protect his people from deception," Merlow lectured.

"Don't change the subject!" Iris yelled. "Why didn't you wait?"

"I chose not to waste time. We have no alternative," Merlow answered calmly.

"Who, specifically, is considered to be your entourage?" Auran asked.

"These oaths are extremely explicit. As the Faerie Queen spoke the vow I held the image of you, Iris, Jacob, Basil, and myself in my mind," Merlow explained.

"You don't know if that worked. The words overrule the energy. You taught me that yourself." Iris glared at Merlow.

"It poses a risk," Merlow agreed.

Auran swore under his breath. "Are you saying that even though you intended the vow for the five of us, the actions of one of the guards could result in your death?"

Iris started pacing up and down. "I can't believe you swore an eternal vow."

"What did you envisage me doing?" Merlow uttered.

"You said they owed you a favor!"

"You cannot expect the Queen to meddle in human affairs without some guarantee."

"A guarantee, yes. But this?"

"Okay, this isn't helping," Auran said. "It's done. Let's focus on damage control."

Iris sighed. "You said the vow is specific. Does that mean it only pertains to people involved with rescuing the girls?"

"Hang on, now we're liberating them?" Auran asked. "We can't risk blowing our cover."

"I said we need to know their whereabouts and if possible, we would rescue them too," Merlow said.

"So if we don't free them we activate the vow?" Auran asked. "And who decides what constitutes possible?"

"The energy," Iris and Merlow answered in unison.

"The *energy?*" Auran looked like pummeling Merlow.

"It is out of our hands now," Merlow said. "The energy will detect whether the vow is broken."

"I'm siding with Iris on this one," Auran said. "It's a tremendous risk."

CHAPTER FIFTY-SEVEN

Arbres

Sourni left the heavy door ajar. Thanking Marie again for her silent slippers she tiptoed to Robbert's desk. She'd seen where he kept his ledgers and inspected the drawer. *No keyhole.* Leaning forward she explored the bottom for a hidden button, anything that might spring the drawer open. *Aiee!* She yanked her hand back. *That stung!* She frowned at the welt forming on her hand.

A tap on her mind made her look up. Hesitantly she opened the connection. "Hello?"

"Hi Sourni! Is this a good time?"

Sourni glanced at the door.

"Where are you?"

"In Robbert's office." She showed Iris the wooden desk and the red mark on her hand.

"What are you doing *there*?"

"Trying to find out how many soldiers...wait." Sourni strained to hear if someone was approaching.

The door swung open and Robbert's eyes bored into hers.

Holy pears. Sourni's heart hammered in her throat, she vaguely noticed Iris's presence leave. She forced herself to smile and pulled a piece of paper from her pocket. "I have the report on the luncheon."

Robbert's eyes went to his desk, her position. He angled his head. "Don't ever go into my office unaccompanied again."

"No, sir. My apologies. I wanted to make sure you got the information as soon as possible," she stammered.

Robbert snatched the sheet from her hand. "Go."

Iris looked at Auran. "Did you tell Sourni to go snoop around?"

"No, why?"

"Because she's in the administrator's office, searching his desk."

"What? Why on earth?"

"Something about the soldiers."

"Tell her to leave!"

"Well, Robbert just came in so I ended the mindlink."

Auran swore. "She can't risk blowing her cover!"

The left corner of Iris's mouth tugged up. "You're telling me?"

He scowled. "Get her back on the mindlink."

Iris arched her brow. "I think I'll wait for her to get back to her room."

Sourni nodded at the servants she passed, forcing a friendly expression. It took all her willpower to walk at a leisurely pace. She lifted a trembling hand to wave at Marie. "I'll come right by."

Sourni closed the door behind her and leaned against it, allowing herself a deep sigh. *I shouldn't have relied on the chills.* Apparently her warning mechanism wasn't fail-safe.

She strode to the bed and sat on the soft linen, focusing her attention on Iris and what the mindlink had felt like.

"I think she's back," Iris mused.

Auran sat up straight.

"Sourni?" Iris inquired.

"Yes. I'm alright."

Iris gave Auran a thumbs up.

"What happened?"

Sourni showed her, and Iris told Auran.

"Ask her what in Seth's name she was thinking!" Auran fumed.

"Auran wants to know your rationale for going into Robbert's office."

"I was hoping to find out how many soldiers are in the army and stationed at the palace."

"Perhaps you can ask your friend Anne. Ask for how many soldiers she cooks when you go over the budget?"

Iris sensed Sourni's embarrassment through the mindlink.

"Yes, I...yes."

CHAPTER FIFTY-EIGHT

Kaale Mountains

"**I**ris!"

Iris glanced over her shoulder and realized the caller was not audible. She listened with her mind. *Dear Seth and Layla!* The ship's captain was vying for her attention. Her pulse raced in alarm.

No one should be able to trace her energy here. "How did you find me?"

"I scanned for your energy and it led me here," Baruch answered.

"Just like that?"

"Well, I had a sense for the direction of your energy and found a narrow gateway leading to you."

A gateway? "Wait." Iris scanned the edges of the chamber. *By Seth.* The connection she'd created for Merlow was not entirely closed. She sealed the energy off, erasing any remnants of the magical trail with a powerful sweeping spell. She refocused her attention on the captain. His energy was much stronger and more vibrant. *He's healing well.*

The captain and his mate had gotten to land—the ocean held no power for the captain, as he gleaned his magic from plants and animals. The bits of seaweed and a handful of seagulls hadn't been enough to sustain him in his deprived state.

"Do you know how you all got sick?" Iris asked.

"I expect our food was poisoned," the captain answered.

"I didn't sense any toxins in your system."

"I suspect they contaminated the food with Nocent—it is a ferocious virus. If that malady contaminated the food and enters the human body, it wreaks damage from within. It is nearly impossible to survive… Thank you for healing us."

"You're welcome."

"I fear it means someone discovered our destination before we departed."

Does he know about Apex?

"We're at the coast, close to Arbres. Do you reckon we should go into town?" Baruch continued.

"No." She wanted to confer with Auran first. "Find shelter and stay out of sight."

••••••••••••••••••••

Auran leaned toward Iris. "Is Baruch all right?"

Iris nodded. "They're seeking refuge and will await further instructions."

Auran's shoulders softened. *It's time to come clean.* "I have more to share."

They sat next to the would-be fire in Iris's room. Auran adjusted one of the twigs to create a better balance.

"About two years ago I traveled to the Amazon for additional schooling," he said. "My father had connections abroad and arranged for me to receive a highly secret and in-depth training— usually reserved for their own warriors."

Iris threw him a questioning look.

"You weren't yet ready to embrace—all this." Auran flicked a hand. "We thought it best not to burden you with extra pressure…"

Iris tsked.

Auran dragged his hand through his blond hair. "I…my father had met the village chief on one of his travels and they became fast friends. They agreed to accelerate the education of their sons by sharing expertise and training." Auran looked her straight in the eye. "I didn't mean to deceive you, but we saw no other way."

"I don't like the idea of you being so far away without protection," Iris answered.

"We had your best interest at heart," Merlow added. "I convinced Auran not to tell you."

"I still don't like it."

"That's why we kept it from you—you would've worried," Auran said. "I was fine."

Iris sighed. "Okay, continue."

"The morning of my journey dad pulled me aside. I still remember his exact words. 'Son, go to the Amazon but don't expect to see a copy of the world as you know it. There are things in life for which there are no explanations. Seek not to explore with your mind but with your heart. Then you will be of most service to us all.'"

Deep down he'd known his father hinted at his allegiance with Iris, and what he'd always believed would become a battle for light and love. He'd carried these words with him ever since.

"The Amazon wasn't what I expected. I mean, Fleurisians live in real houses, and these dwellings were huts made of cane, their roofs thatched with banana leaves."

Iris snorted, looking pointedly at the bare cave.

Auran had imagined the absence of material wealth meant poverty, but once inside their homes he'd been struck by the intensity of the colors, the craftsmanship of their pottery, the tribe's legends— their life was rich and full in so many ways. It mesmerized him, and it held power, as if they'd captured the essence of things.

Merlow cleared his throat, and Auran noticed the surprise on both Iris and Merlow's face. "I was looking with my heart," he said defensively.

Iris smiled.

Trudging through the mud after a tropical rain, Auran had waved at the chief.

The tribe members all spoke the common language, albeit a formal version. They were known for their ability to communicate over long distances and they held the secret to tapping into the power of the jungle—especially the chief's son. He possessed a unique ability to communicate with animals and plants and absorb their energy. The procedure didn't kill the flora and fauna. It was as if they had given him permission to siphon their energy reservoir. This boy was Baruch.

"That's how you met!" Iris said.

Auran nodded. "We received the same training and there was an instant bond between us. Soon we became inseparable on our trips into the jungle. I'd brought my bow, obviously, and tried to teach him." He laughed, remembering the lush green glade where they'd trained.

Baruch had ruined arrow after arrow. They just...shattered. Until Auran figured out Baruch was focusing so hard on the shaft, he drew the remaining life force from the wood, leaving it brittle.

In turn, Baruch tried to teach Auran how to connect to the energy of the jungle. Auran held bright green leaves and hugged enormous trees, befriended birds and gorgeous azure butterflies— the namesake of the tribe.

"I would have given precious herbs to see that!" Merlow said.

Auran shook his head. "Nothing. We had no gift for the other's talent. The funny thing was, the more we tried to teach the other, the more our own capabilities grew. That's where I learned to take down a bird in flight at twice the distance."

One day on a hike Auran had gently pulled long woody vines that hung from the treetop, moving the liana to the side. "What about here?"

Baruch peered over his shoulder. "Yes, this works."

They'd wandered off while searching for a rare plant and had ended up deep in the jungle—too far to go back and sleep in the village. So they'd cleared an area with their machete and gathered reasonably dry wood. The place was unfamiliar even to Baruch.

Auran hunted down an animal resembling a boar, and with Baruch's plant knowledge the tropical forest provided ample food. They sat by the firing roasting the animal and some yams—the flames sizzling with grease.

Kgrck. Their heads shot up. The sound of a dry twig snapping thundered in their ears, and Auran nodded at Baruch's machete—there was nothing dry about the jungle—and grabbed his bow.

From an opening in the underbrush a woman floated near. She looked heavenly—the vines shimmered through her body, fluorescing from within.

"Auran and Baruch," she spoke in a melodious voice.

Auran's heart dropped in his stomach—there was power in names. He breathed as shallowly as possible, afraid to disturb the lady.

"I am the Wise Woman of the Styres."

Baruch inhaled sharply, and Auran cast a glance at his friend.

"The Styres are an ancient people, thought to be extinct. They are known for their prophesizing abilities," Baruch whispered.

The Wise Woman addressed Auran. He felt goosebumps again.

"Iris is an old soul and her powers are greater than those of anyone alive. Her destiny is to unite the world. There are many who will rally against her. Your job is to gather allies and be her confidant. Your friend will come when he is needed most. Trust that and trust your heart."

She'd silently drifted off, dissolving in the dark—leaving both of them baffled. Auran had known the truth of her words in his bones and remembered his father's advice. He knew he had a role to play, and Baruch did as well.

They sat in silence for several minutes until Baruch said, "That is settled then." As if they'd agreed to meet for tea.

"I'm glad you're taking it this well," Auran said.

"Are you jesting? I am honored to receive guidance from one of our most sacred beings. I never imagined to see one. The Styres have been gone for over fifty years."

Auran had never told anyone about the Lady in the jungle, but since Iris and Merlow would meet Baruch soon, he wanted them to be able to place Baruch's allegiance and commitment. He shuffled his feet on the granite floor.

"Baruch and I agreed he would come to support our cause when needed. About five months ago I called for him. He arranged a ship and set off more than three months ago. What worries me is the attempt to take out the entire crew. No one should have known about him."

Iris and Merlow both squinted.

Auran took a deep breath. "Baruch can support you with his ability to tap energy. He's like a magical battery available to both of you, but especially Iris, whenever you need more power."

Auran was proud of his idea and had often found comfort in knowing he'd arranged extra power for her safety. But Merlow was shaking his head. "What?"

"Iris does not need extra power—she can barely contain what she has, and is left exhausted most of the time. Her power is growing stronger every day."

Iris arched her eyebrows at Merlow.

He returned her look, as if dismissing a disobedient student. "You know it is true." To Auran he said, "There must be another reason. I feel Baruch's arrival is an important turning point. The Gods are aligning everyone to take their starting positions. We will know more when he gets here."

Then Merlow spoke to him directly, in his mind, "*Do not be disappointed. You have done your job, as you will continue to do in protecting her. It has not gone unnoticed.*"

Auran swallowed. The Wise Woman's voice echoed in his head. "*Her fate is to lose those she loves.*" He still didn't have the heart to tell Iris.

CHAPTER FIFTY-NINE

Kaale Mountains

"Let's focus on getting Baruch here safely. The last time took you more than a week, Auran, and he's unfamiliar with the terrain," Iris urged.

"Where is he?" Auran asked.

"They're hiding outside Arbres."

"Can you distance-travel him here?" Auran asked.

"Sure," Merlow said.

Iris sat forward. "Let's do it right away. Have you recovered enough, Merlow?"

"I can manage."

"Auran can you get that archer back in here?" Iris said. "I'll contact Baruch."

Iris closed her eyes to sink into a meditative trance. *Like I do anything else these days.* She located Baruch's energy, and found the ship's mate next to him. *We forgot about the boy.* "Baruch?"

"One moment," he said.

She noticed the ship's mate's energy leave.

"I sent the boy out to gather wood," Baruch said. "He does not know about my magic."

"A wise precaution. I spoke to Auran and we want to get you here. Have you distance-traveled before?"

"No, but I am keen to try it. When?"

"Now? Can you send the boy away?" Iris asked.

"He lives in the next village and is eager to go home," Baruch replied. To keep us hidden I convinced him we could not risk spreading the disease. He has seen the damage wreaked on the ship, so he agreed not to expose his family."

Iris mused. "Can you tell him tomorrow morning you will check whether he's still contagious, and if he's clear he can go home? He could leave at first light so most people will still be asleep. Then we can transport you here before anyone comes looking."

"All right."

"Tomorrow I'll mindlink with you again and guide you through the process. Merlow will support your distance-travel with magic."

Baruch paused. "Is it safe?"

"As long as you follow the instructions and engage with Merlow's magic you should be fine. Just don't lose focus." *No need to get him worried.*

"Do I need to prepare?"

"Make sure you're grounded and calm. Perhaps hold off on breakfast."

Iris opened her eyes to Merlow and Auran looking at her expectantly. "Not now."

Auran dismissed the archer, again. "Thanks, Evan."

"Why not?" Auran asked Iris, disappointment written on his face.

"The ship's mate is still with Baruch. The boy will leave in the morning."

Auran made a face.

"When did you last see Baruch?" Iris asked.

"About a year ago."

"Really?"

"It was when we visited the tribe of Holy Men, down in the south. My father had taken me along to teach me some of his trade, convinced it would somehow rub off on me. He always thought I would benefit from negotiation skills someday. Sometimes I think my dad has some sense of premonition—he has a knack for knowing when I need to be where.

"It turned out Baruch and his dad were visiting the same tribe.

Sheer luck or serendipity—I've never known. Baruch and I clapped each other on the shoulder hard enough to spray caked mud everywhere. He pushed me back and appraised me. 'I cannot believe you have grown again.' I clasped his biceps. 'You, my friend, have been working out!' We laughed." Auran smiled at the memory. "We had so much fun. Our dads had plenty to discuss as well. I felt sorry for the tribe. We were so focused on ourselves. Until the full moon."

That night was etched indelibly in his brain.

The village chief had walked toward them—the solemnity of his features revealed in the pale moonlight.

"My ancestors invite you to our ceremony," the chief said. The symbols painted on his face were spinach-green and cherry-red. *Edible* war *paint?* "Tonight is one of our main rites, welcoming the New Year." Pounding drums from the village center emphasized his request.

Auran scrunched his brow. *New Year in summer?*

"Their year starts with the fertility cycle of the Earth on the longest day," Baruch's father explained.

The chief led the way to the circle that surrounded a blazing fire. The four of them were assigned seats facing each direction of the wind.

The chief stood next to Auran's father on the south node and stretched both hands to the starlit sky. He invoked their Gods— Auran recognized some of the words, and the tribe members started chanting. Auran listened to their songs and drums, and stared into the flames. Mesmerized.

Suddenly the bonfire came alive. It showed a female face, clearly resembling the Lady of the jungle. Auran gasped.

He gawked at Baruch, seated across from him on the east node, his eyes wide.

The Wise Woman of the Styres ignored them and sat among the flames as if enjoying the view.

The drums subsided and she spoke. "The ancient heritage has brought us here. Sons of different bloodlines have gathered to prepare for the battle to come. Daughters will birth more power into these worlds. The distance traveled is not so far as the distance yet to be journeyed. It will be hard, and many will die. These warriors will protect the world and the sacred forest. That is their duty first and foremost. They will stay here to fulfill their task."

"Two among you will travel across distances both in the mind and in the body. They will learn to abstain from food and drink for days as they go through the harsh lands. They will find friends and allies in places both familiar as well as unexpected. Some may not be of the same species. You will feel it when they are true to you."

She shifted in the embers and turned to Baruch. "You are a legitimate son of the forest. Your powers will prove crucial. You shall come when called. Until then you shall extend the reach of your powers. Travel safe and travel swift."

The flames leapt up and shrank to glowing embers, and the Lady was gone.

Auran's heart hammered in his chest. Eerie, to see her again.

A grave silence hung over the gathered.

The chief stood back up and spoke the ceremonial words. Everyone clapped in response and Auran joined.

People started to get up, the celebration complete. The chief walked over to Auran and beckoned Baruch closer. "We were graced by her Lady's presence. She has sought you out to do her bidding. You best prepare."

They were not allowed to speak to their fathers and were sent away with the medicine man. Over the next few days he taught them about sustaining on little food and water, and on making themselves scarce.

"The knowledge we acquired then has served me well, especially last week on my trip back from Arbres," Auran said. "The road was crawling with informants."

Iris looked dazzled by everything she'd heard this evening. "No wonder you're so dedicated..."

Auran felt guilty for keeping the information on their venture from her.

She looked him squarely in the eye and said, "Thank you."

He leaned back and knitted his brows. It required no thanks and her saying so made it awkward.

She took his hands.

He tried to pull away but she squeezed his hands lightly. From the corner of his eye he saw Merlow leave.

"Don't," she said to Auran. "I know what you've sacrificed to support me. I might never get another chance to express my appreciation for what you and your family have done for me. You've always been like a brother to me."

He cringed.

She continued as if she hadn't noticed. "I love you, for all you do. You are the one person who understands me. Please don't offend me by not allowing me to express my gratitude. I need you to know what that means."

He released her hands and surprised her by grabbing her shoulders and pulling her toward him. He hugged her hard. "I know the burden you carry and I want to support you. Please let me do more."

She gripped him tight. "I can't. You know I can't."

"Why?" he asked, distressed. "Why are you so stubborn? There's no need to do this on your own. Let me help."

She confused him by breaking down and sobbing. It felt as if her body had broken in two. He'd never seen anyone so devastated. Auran glanced at the entrance. *I wish I could soundproof the room.* He held her and waited for her sobbing to subside.

She leaned back hesitantly—seemingly ashamed of her outburst, drying her face with the tail of her shirt.

He was afraid to think how long she'd restrained these feelings. The Gods knew she had enough to cry for. He grabbed her face and kissed her forehead. "Thank you."

Iris grimaced. "For what, blubbering all over your shirt?"

He ignored her comment. "You'll be fine. Together we can do this," he said looking directly into her eyes.

She blinked. "I'll think about it."

He knew that was the best he would get from her for now—it

was more than he'd expected. The sound of boots on granite reverberated down the hallway. *A guard.*

Auran got up to meet him, knowing she didn't want anyone to see she'd been crying. It was a miracle she'd let *him* see, although it felt unintentional, like a ripe peach that had burst—spilling at the slightest touch.

"Another batch of arrows has arrived," the guard reported.

"Anyone hurt?" Auran asked.

The guard shook his head. "We're steering clear from the entrance."

"Perfect. If they're getting restless you can put them to work. We need more arrows."

"Yes, sir."

"Dismissed."

Auran thanked the Gods for the guard's timing. A few minutes earlier and things would've been uncomfortable.

We best get some sleep. He instructed the guards on duty not to disturb them unless there was an emergency and went back to Iris's room. She was unrolling her sleeping mat. *Perfect.*

"You don't need to stand guard," she told him. "We're both exhausted and between the two of us, we'll wake up fast enough if needed."

He was tired enough to agree. Perhaps he was getting sloppy. *Never mind, I'll figure it out tomorrow.*

CHAPTER SIXTY

Kaale Mountains

The next thing Auran noticed was Iris rolling up her sleeping mat. *Is it already morning?* He'd slept a deep, nourishing sleep. *That's been a while.* He yawned and stretched his arms upward.

"Morning, did I wake you?" Iris asked.

He rubbed his face. "It's fine." He got up and rotated his shoulders—loosening his muscles. Sleeping in the woods was less safe, but softer on his body. He snorted. *I'm getting old.*

Iris jerked her head up. "What?"

"Just stiff." Auran did a few more stretches to wake up his body.

As he tucked his shirt back in his trousers Merlow and Evan walked in.

Auran stretched his senses upward to feel the hour. "It's right after first light."

"Yes, it is time," Merlow agreed. He sat across from Iris to prepare.

· · · · · · · · ● · · · · · · · · · ·

"Are you ready?" Iris asked Merlow.

He nodded.

Iris closed her eyes too and sought out Baruch. He was already waiting for her. She checked his energy to make sure he was grounded and calm. The procedure was relatively easy, so long as

~ 255 ~

his focus was solely on her. If anything distracted him…well, she had to trust his abilities.

"Envision a cord emerging from the center of your magic to me."

He sent out a glimmer of magic, and it latched onto her energy. She secured his cord into her own anchor.

"In your mind's eye hold the cord with both hands—remember, this requires your full focus—and when you feel Merlow's pull, you continue along this line. We'll guide you right here. Is that clear?"

"Yes. I sense your energy through the cord."

"All right, get ready." She nudged Merlow with her foot.

Merlow started the summons, and the energy in the chamber became denser.

Auran tensed beside her, and she blocked him out. She supported Baruch's energy as Merlow opened the gateway.

Baruch was transported as if he weighed less than a feather carried on the wind. She felt his presence come closer and knew Auran sensed it too. She suddenly saw a rainbow-colored connection between them, unlike anything she'd ever seen—their fates somehow intertwined.

The connection wavered. *No!* Iris fed more magic into the cord willing it to stabilize. After a heartbeat the link steadied. *Thank the Gods.*

She heard Baruch touch down lightly—a clean landing for a first-timer.

Iris opened her eyes and was surprised to see his skin was much darker than she'd expected. She'd envisioned him as a typical Amazonian, but his skin was pitch black. His lineage must be different than she'd thought.

Baruch smiled and enveloped Auran in a bear hug. They fervently clapped each other on the shoulders. She caught a whiff of cacao. It was good to see Auran so lit up. It reminded her of home and when he came in full of mischief—scavenging stuff for their treehouse or cooking up plans with Jacob. Perhaps they stood a chance after all.

Baruch turned to put his satchel down before he grabbed her

hand. "This must be the famous Iris. I have never seen anyone so radiant."

Iris wasn't used to people speaking this freely about the brightness of her eyes. The guards, and before that the villagers, usually avoided the subject. All she managed was a surprised hello.

He didn't seem bothered in the least and Auran introduced him to Merlow. Within minutes they were deep in discussion about the use of magic under different circumstances and the influence of weather on spells.

She peeked at Auran and watched him and Baruch sit shoulder to shoulder, content to listen to Merlow, not needing to catch up after an absence of a year—perfectly comfortable with each other. She liked it.

Now I need food. These early morning spells stirred up her appetite. "Have you had breakfast yet, Baruch?"

"No, I was afraid to eat, not knowing if the spell would make me queasy. Especially after your warning."

"Shall I make you some porridge, too?"

"Yes, please. I have never tried it." Baruch glanced at Auran. "Do not tell me you are not hungry," he said with a naughty smile.

Auran looked like he wanted to shoot him. "Don't start. We're on rations here."

Baruch raised his thick black eyebrows. "That bad?"

Auran shook it off and pretended to ignore him.

This must be their usual banter. Auran ate a lot—if you let him. He was never fully satisfied, but he didn't show it. She eyed him.

His athletic body was leaner than usual. That last trip to Arbres had taken a toll.

Iris added some herbs she knew would soothe Baruch after his first experience with distance-travel. Baruch gladly accepted the bowl she offered him. She handed a third bowl to Auran.

"For me?"

She was usually very strict about their portions. "To celebrate the arrival of Baruch," she explained and winked at Merlow, who she knew didn't need extra food. He could probably survive on light if he wanted to.

Baruch dug in. "Mmm. Which spices did you use?"

"I added cinnamon, cardamom and ginger."

"Cinnamon bark or leaf?"

Oh, a connoisseur. "Bark, always bark." She smiled. *Baruch and Merlow will get along well.*

"I understand ginger and cardamom, but why include cinnamon?

"It strengthens connective tissue—given the pressure your body was under, and it's a powerful tonic."

Baruch looked pensive while he rubbed his close-cut onyx hair. "I like your thinking."

She inhaled deeply "I *love* the smell."

Auran turned sharply toward the entrance, cocking his head.

Iris strained to hear what had caught his attention—a clamoring down the hall. They all got up as one, Auran and Baruch synced into a defensive position.

A guard ran in. "More arrows," he said, breathing heavily. "Basil was hit again."

Merlow groaned, and she realized it must be bad.

Iris and Auran stormed out of the room, closely followed by Merlow and Baruch.

"What's Basil doing at the tower?" Iris demanded.

"He insisted on doing something useful—he's not very good at sitting still. Also he claimed he was fit enough to get back on duty."

"And you let him?"

Auran glared at her. "It's not like they're very busy. The boys need the training."

They tore around the corner.

Auran cursed colorfully. "He's not wearing his armor!"

Basil lay motionless on the floor. A few arrows still stuck in the watchtower, close to the entrance.

Perhaps he'd thought himself safe inside. Iris sank down next to Basil.

Merlow joined her moments later. "We need to keep his heart beating." Merlow breathed heavily.

He's already out of breath?

"Too close together, the poison, shot twice," Merlow wheezed.

Auran muttered "You idiot. Why didn't you ask us to fetch your armor? Stubborn fool."

"This isn't helping," Iris said.

Auran cast her a glance and motioned to Baruch. The two warriors took up a defensive stance around them. She knew she could safely focus on the healing alone. She sank into a trance and linked with Merlow. She scanned Basil's body and nearly gasped aloud when she witnessed the damage in his system. "You work on his heart," she told Merlow. He was still the superior healer.

The effect of the poison had indeed accelerated. Basil's breathing was labored and shallow, and she focused on clearing his lungs. With every breath he struggled to stay alive. *We can't lose him.*

Magic brushed against her, bathing her in it. Baruch was providing them with magic. She drew from the power around her, and discovered she was able to use it directly. Focusing on Basil was easier without having to reach within for her magic. *His combat skills might prove crucial—perhaps we'll still have them after all.*

She forced the poison out of Basil's lungs, and slowly his breathing was less ragged. Yet there was still a lot of work to do. He'd been hit by three arrows, which meant the archers shot a volley. *Merlow could've warned us about that.* She put the thought aside and focused on the liver.

Merlow was still struggling to get Basil's heart to beat properly by itself.

She thanked the Gods she and Merlow were both present to heal Basil. She would've been hard-pressed to patch him up on her own— unable to expel the poison and mend his organs simultaneously.

Iris grunted. A downside of her sensitivity was she often experienced the pain of the wounded. She sagged—her body straining under the use of magic.

A leg pressed up against her back. *Auran.* She leaned in and let him support her weight.

With her eyes closed she searched Basil's body for the next

urgent spot. The third arrow was wedged in his formidable thigh and still leaking poison. She shifted downward to get a better angle, and Auran's support moved with her.

Iris put her hands around the shaft, afraid to pull the arrow out. The dart-like head was too close to an artery. She sealed off the venom that still coated the tip to prevent it from spreading. *What else?*

His bloodstream had spread the poison throughout his entire body. She shuddered and drew on more power, guiding the venom toward the entry wound. Purple blood frothed out. She washed out as much of the nightshade as she dared. In some places—where the poison was less concentrated—the blood loss would be too much. They worked in silence and after Iris's left leg cramped she realized they must have been at it for a while.

She roused from her healing haze, a sheen of sweat on her forehead. The rest of the world came back into focus. *Please Layla, help him heal.*

Auran turned to face them. "Will he be okay?"

Iris let Merlow answer.

"It is too soon to tell," Merlow said grimly.

Auran blanched.

I ris prayed to Layla—beseeching the Goddess to cure Basil.

Auran stared at his pale-faced friend.

She was afraid to think how he might take it when his men died in battle, although she knew he wouldn't let that stop him. *I prefer a commander who cares for his people.*

"Can we move him?" Baruch asked.

"We need to remove the last arrow first," Iris said. "I need your help, Merlow."

Merlow blinked then moved down and examined the wound. "I will shield the artery," he said. "You extract the arrow with magic and send it back using the exact route it entered from."

Iris took a deep breath. More magic swirled around her. She enveloped herself in the power and slowly guided it toward the arrow shaft. Merlow extended the shield beyond the artery into Basil's soft tissue. Bit by bit she pulled the arrow in an unhurried, smooth movement, following the exact curve in reverse. Basil's flesh gave way when the tip popped out.

Iris sat back in relief.

"Now?" Auran asked.

Iris rubbed the circulation back in her numb leg. "Yes."

Auran hauled her up and out of the way. Moving as one, Baruch and Auran gently lifted the still unconscious Basil—both groaning at the weight—and carried him to the infirmary. Iris escorted them, Merlow trailed behind.

Jacob moaned as they came in. "Don't tell me I can expect a relapse, too," he said. Auran shook his head and Jacob picked up on the gravity of the situation. "What happened? I heard people shouting in the hallway."

"Basil was shot again. Three arrows," Iris said.

Jacob turned gray. "Three?" he whispered.

Iris realized it must've hurt more than she expected. When she treated Jacob she'd seen the damage to his system, but his reaction showed how much it had hurt both his pride and his body. She needed to ask Merlow whether he'd added something to the venom that intensified pain, though such cruelty seemed out of his character.

"Jacob, meet Baruch," Auran introduced them.

"It is truly a pleasure to make your acquaintance," Baruch said, grasping Jacob's hand with both of his.

"Likewise."

They sat beside Jacob's bed—Basil remained unconscious, his olive-green aura faint. "We might as well bring Jacob up to speed," Auran said.

"How many more arrows?" Iris demanded. "Can we expect more so close together?" She glared at Merlow.

He sighed. "I did not recall the archers shot a volley, or I would have mentioned it. It has been more than twenty years."

She narrowed her eyes at him.

"Both Basil and Jacob need to steer clear from the tower. The risk of being shot twice is too great."

"You should've told us earlier," Iris burst out, gesturing at a very pale Basil.

"Basil was still too weak to walk for more than a few minutes. It had not occurred to me he would get back on duty." Merlow looked sideways at Auran.

Auran threw his hands up. "I wouldn't have agreed had I been fully informed! Nor would Basil have taken the risk…you're staying here." He glowered at Jacob.

"Don't worry," Jacob murmured.

The silence stretched.

"I believe there are four batches left. They should arrive within the next day," Merlow offered. "Give or take a few hours since they have been underway for twenty-two years."

Baruch whistled.

"You need to check with the guards," Iris said to Auran. "I sense their anxiety from here."

He nodded. "I'll stay at the watchtower tonight. Baruch you stay with Merlow."

Iris frowned. She glanced at Jacob to see if he felt left out. To her relief, he looked engaged and intrigued. Auran and Baruch didn't act to exclude anyone either. They moved in unison, like the sun and moon were cooperating. *That rainbow-colored connection. I should ask Merlow what that means.*

Iris cocked her head to listen. The stars whispered to her—unusual during the daytime—they typically distracted her at night. She gave in and extended her senses. The stars showed her something resembling the bond she'd witnessed between Auran and Baruch. An orb circling around the moon, each affecting the other and very much interlaced. As if one couldn't exist without the other—two different sides of the same coin.

Fear stirred in her belly.

Does that mean one can't live without the other? Gods no.

We need extra safety measures for both. Not that Auran would like it, or he couldn't protect himself. But the idea gave her extra peace of mind when there was a chance that if Baruch got hurt, it affected Auran as well. She needed Auran to play an important role, and it was not yet time. Her attention drifted back to the room.

"Perhaps we should eat first," she heard Auran suggest.

She chuckled.

"Back to join us, are you?" Auran asked.

"Good timing, too," she said. She enjoyed their banter—a nice distraction from all the seriousness. "Merlow, why don't you work your herbal magic on lunch? Add support for Jacob and Basil?"

Merlow blinked.

He must be tired.

Merlow rose. "I shall prepare lunch."

"May I assist?" Baruch suggested. "I want to discover more about the spices you select."

"Certainly."

They walked toward Merlow's chamber, leaving Jacob, Auran and Iris with a still-lifeless Basil. Something nagged at the back of her mind, about the three of them being together. Suddenly it came to her.

IRIS HAD ENJOYED having a rare afternoon off. Merlow had gone to the market in Yarden to stock up on herbs. She lay in the grass and watched the white clouds drift by.

On the other side of the mansion, Auran's energy approached—with someone else. She sat up to focus and smiled. "Jacob!"

He walked around the corner—flanked by Auran—and pulled her to her feet.

"You're back!" She gave him a quick hug, feeling Auran's eyes on her.

"I got home yesterday."

She squinted her eyes. "You've grown."

He stood up even straighter—smiling from ear to ear—his shoulders now level with Auran's. "Well, yeah—four months."

"I'm glad you're back. We've missed you," Iris said, glancing at Auran.

Auran nodded. "Lots has happened. Let's go to our hut and catch up there."

Iris cringed.

"I'm sorry," Auran said. "You okay? I didn't realize...I thought we would be safest in the treehouse, you know, for when he comes back."

Iris sighed. "Sure, let's go."

"When who comes back?" Jacob asked.

"Well, right after you left this guy showed up—a magician, and..."

Iris trailed behind, knowing Auran would relish telling his best friend the story.

She'd avoided this part of the forest and was surprised how much everything had grown. New pine saplings had sprouted, and the blooming bushes had matured, too. Iris stood still to admire the delicate hues of lilac and soft pink in the hydrangeas. There was a joyful buoyancy to these shades and it reminded her of something, someone.

As soon as the memory struck home, it took her breath away—Thom, precious Thom, his giggling as sweet as the pastel softness of the petals.

Iris allowed herself an instant to imagine her brother's chubby arms clinging to her. She caught a whiff of his vanilla scent and quickly tucked the memory away.

IRIS RESURFACED TO Jacob and Auran watching her in silence—the bare cave a sharp contrast to the green forest. They were used to her abrupt mental absences and knew better than to interrupt. Her abstraction never needed explaining, which made her feel less abnormal. She smiled. "I was thinking about when Jacob returned home from building that spire for the monastery, and we went up to the treehouse."

They'd been so young, barely teenagers. Jacob and Auran smiled, too, and for a split second it felt like they actually were transported back in time. She saw the sunshine on their faces and basked in the warmth of the fall sun.

"That's an important part of time-travel!" Iris sat up straight.

"What is?" Jacob asked.

"Emotion!"

Both Auran and Jacob watched her like she didn't make any sense, but were too well-brought up to object.

"I need to tell Merlow. We can use emotions to our advantage." *This is important.*

Something else struck her. They'd gone *back* in time. "Did you guys feel it too? The sunshine on your face?"

Auran touched his cheek. "It does feel warmer."

"Yeah." Jacob rubbed his forearm.

Baruch came in with three bowls, Merlow close behind. "Look what we made. I love herbs."

Merlow handed Iris a dish. "Here you go."

Everyone dug in hungrily.

Strange to sit here as if they had nothing better to do than enjoy a meal together. *Nice—time-off is important.* She should insist on that more for all of them. *We can't be alert all day, every day.* The guards had official hours for being on and off duty, but the four of them—and now Baruch too—were always busy.

She tasted her lunch. "Aniseed?" she asked Merlow.

"Star anise," he said, "to help you warm from within."

She huffed. "Then I hope you put in a lot."

"It does feel chilly here," Baruch commented.

"Good luck with that," Iris said. "It doesn't get any warmer. If Jacob hadn't installed the pipes, we would be freezing."

She stared at the pipes. *This room is warmer than mine.* "Does this space have more pipes?" she asked Jacob.

"Yeah, we figured the infirmary needed more warmth."

"That's why you're in here," Auran joked.

Jacob shot him a look.

Iris tapped the spoon on her lips in concentration. "If we stabilize the structure of the cave with more magic, could we funnel the backlash into the pipes and convert the extra energy to warmth? So we don't show up to Apex's readers as an energy spike?"

Everyone looked at Merlow.

"We might. That requires a lot more pipes though."

"We have spare ones in the storage," Jacob offered.

Iris stood up. "That would heat the place up too!"

Auran suppressed a smile.

She was freezing most of the time, unless she used a lot of magic. Iris started pacing. "If that works, we can make a special room where I can work my magic, too. I need to practice with all that extra power."

"That will be one very hot room," Auran said.

"Yes!" Iris cried. "A hotroom. I like it."

It would solve so many problems if they could stay here until ready. They still needed a solution for the food. *Perhaps Merlow can distance-travel food back in with him?* "They can't read temperature, right? Just energy and magic?" she asked Merlow.

"They will register a large fluctuation in temperature but not this deep. The cave is too well concealed. If you were to throw around magic, that would certainly show up on their ratings. However, if you use a spell to immediately transform any used magic to heat, and you build it up slowly…I believe that should work," Merlow said.

"Are we in peril for the magic we used to heal Basil?" Baruch asked.

Merlow shook his head. "We stayed well below the hazardous level. The magic was intense but small scale."

"Oh, I thought you both burned through quite a bit of magic."

Auran clapped Baruch on his shoulder. "Stick around and you'll see what they mean."

CHAPTER SIXTY-TWO

Kaale Mountains

For once Iris and Auran finished spooning down lunch at the same time, placing their empty bowls on Jacob's bed simultaneously. Auran cocked a brow at Iris's haste.

"I want to get started with the hotroom," she explained. "Who can you spare to work on the pipes this afternoon?"

"I would like to assist," Baruch said. "I am not quite sure why we are building this system, but I am intrigued."

"Can I help?" Jacob asked.

Iris looked at Merlow for permission—he nodded, adding, *Do not let him exert himself* via mindlink.

"You can supervise," she told Jacob. "You're our best architect." He'd come up with the pipe system to keep them from freezing, just as he'd been in charge of building their childhood treehouse—the only times Auran let him take the lead.

"Do you need us to carry you there?" Auran offered.

Jacob batted his hand away. "I'll walk." He heaved himself out of the wooden bed he'd built himself.

Iris thrust a pillow into Baruch's hands. "Take this."

Baruch was easy to talk to, perhaps because his energy and Auran's seemed cut from the same thread of magic.

Jacob trailed behind and Iris slowed down despite her enthusiasm. Jacob had healed quickly, considering he was shot only two days ago.

When they reached the farthest room, Baruch placed Jacob's pillow in the center. "Here you go."

Jacob lowered himself, a grimace flickering on his face.

"Baruch has experience with rocks," Iris said.

"I used to play in a cave near my village. I tried extracting energy from the stones, but it was not as easy as accessing the energy reservoir of animals and plants," Baruch said.

"Because those give their consent?" Iris suggested.

"I have considered that, but rocks have an awareness as well. Or perhaps presence is a better word. It is hard to describe and barely noticeable, but I sense life force energy in there."

Iris was intrigued. "Can we work with the granite, rather than forcing our will upon it?"

Baruch put his hands on the stone wall and closed his eyes.

Jacob sketched the current pipe structure on the floor with a piece of chalk. "I've thought about where we can add more pipes in case it gets colder." He pointed at a few spots.

Baruch turned, frowning.

"What's wrong?" Iris asked.

"This stone is different from the ones I am used to in the Amazon. The density is unusual, like the granite has pores. It feels like the wall is breathing."

Jacob was used to magic—growing up around her, and no doubt hearing stories from Auran. He drew an image including both the pipes and the pores. *Good thinking.* "Baruch," Iris asked, "Can you feel where to place more pipes without weakening the structure?" She chose to ignore it most of the time, but being 300 meters below ground meant tons of weight constantly hung above their heads...

Baruch walked over to the drawing and pointed. "Will that structure hold if we drill a new channel?"

"We don't have the tools to drill through granite," Jacob said.

"Oh, I think we can bore holes with magic."

"In that case, see this natural fault? If we start here"—Jacob indicated a place on the provisional blueprint—"we won't disturb the load-bearing sections."

The two men stayed bent over Jacob's diagram. When they started on transient load calculations, Iris turned her focus inward and reached for Sourni.

"Iris?"

"Oh, that's quick!"

"Yeah, I was in my room."

This time of day? "Are you okay?" *She seems queasy.*

"Wait."

Iris drew most of her mind back when she felt Sourni vomit.

···········●···········

Sourni relished the spread for lunch in the room where the staff ate, hers to take just by stretching her arm. *Anne has outdone herself again.* Even though the head cook thought this luxury was simple fare. Sourni hadn't eaten oatmeal for weeks—not since she'd stepped into the palace. She buttered a roll. *I could live without ever eating porridge again.* She smiled and bit into the soft bread, relishing the extravagance.

"The lashing is scheduled for noon tomorrow," one of the cooks said.

Sourni froze.

"A pity I'm on the roster for lunch."

Sourni choked on the bread, the sweet dough turning sour in her mouth.

"Is ye okay?" Anne asked, hitting Sourni's back.

"I'm fine," Sourni forced herself to say. She coughed and drank a sip of water. "I... I forgot something." She got up, leaving a stunned Anne behind.

Sourni hurried through the corridors, walking as fast she could without running. She made it to her room without throwing up. *Thank Gods.* She clutched the back of a chair, startling when the mindlink tapped her consciousness.

···········●···········

"Do you know what the transgression was? Or who will get lashed?" Iris inquired.

"No, but I can ask around. I'm sure I will hear all sorts of details tomorrow…" Sourni sounded weary.

"Good. Anything else?"

"Just more gloating about the stolen girls."

"All right. Take care."

Iris's awareness returned to the hotroom. She shook off the queasiness—the frequent check-ins with Sourni must've strengthened their connection.

"Can you take Baruch to the storage room?" Jacob asked Iris.

When Jacob had discovered the gorge as a possible hideout this summer, he'd immediately seen the need for heating and envisioned a way to use pipes to circulate warm water from the well throughout the chambers. He'd instantly consigned a large batch of pipes and each of the guards had carried at least five when they'd all convened in the cave to plan the revolution, Iris finally ready for the gathered forces to join.

Surveying the stack of red-brown pipes, Iris thanked the Gods for Jacob's foresight. She mindlinked with Auran. "Can you send a few guards to the storage room to assist? There's a lot to carry."

"Getting lazy, are we?" he joked.

"If you prefer I expose myself to some poisonous arrows, I'm happy to come ask you in person," she teased back.

"No, no, I'll send them right along. Stay there," Auran insisted.

I shouldn't have. He's worried enough as it is. "They're on their way," she said to Baruch.

"I am surprised Auran heard you right away," he said.

"He's been making real progress. I've intentionally used it more often; the Gods know he needed the practice. He still doesn't like it because he has to drop everything else he's doing. I hope he'll get to the point where he can mindlink during combat."

Baruch smiled—like he knew exactly what she meant.

His energy doesn't bother me. Normally it took her days to get used to the emotions and thoughts a new person radiated.

Iris and Baruch had sorted the pipes by the time the guards arrived. "Take these to the alcove at the far end, past Merlow's chamber."

Baruch and Iris returned with a couple of guards in their wake. Iris was surprised to see Jacob up and about. He suppressed his limp, but his back seemed stiff from the havoc the poison had wreaked on his body. She didn't want to reprimand him in front of his men, so she threw him a pointed look.

Jacob stared back, knowing full well what she meant to say—almost daring her to say it.

Baruch grabbed Jacob by the elbow and steered him over to the drawing, then sat, forcing Jacob to do the same.

Iris liked the Amazonian more by the minute.

"Place those three pipes on the top of that wall, and use this coupling unit to connect them," Jacob instructed the guards. "We'll drill a hole to the main pipes later."

"How much heat will your actions generate?" he asked Iris.

She flinched. The smell of burned flesh filled her throat, and she gagged—*a puddle of candlewax in the corner…*

Jacob kindly distracted her by adding, "We can pipe the warm water to the bathing area and heat the tanks. We can have a decent bath."

She half-smiled at his suggestion—the cold water was reason enough for most men to skip washing altogether. Cleanliness was highly overrated in their opinion, and Jacob knew she had a keen sense of smell. "That's a great idea. You should've become an engineer." *Thank you Seth and Layla for placing such valuable men on my path.*

The guards placed the pipes in the designated spots and Iris fastened them with magic. It wouldn't work in the long run—when the magic wore off the pipes would clatter down—but it should stick for at least a few days. At least two more days of safety, staying here.

They worked steadily the rest of the afternoon, filling the chamber's walls methodically with pipes—working off of Jacob's makeshift chart until Iris noticed his paleness and said, "Tomorrow we'll connect these to the baths. This will do for today."

She'd have to consult with Merlow first. Iris knew the amount of heat generated would provide plenty of scalding baths, but didn't want to frighten the men with the intensity of her magic—or accidentally boil them.

They gathered for a meal in Iris's room. Jacob had refused to go back to the infirmary, where Basil was still unconscious.

"I can't stand the sight of Basil unmoving—I've not seen him sit still in his entire life," Jacob said.

Trevor had outdone himself with an enticing meal of carrots, cabbage and potatoes. He'd tried growing mushrooms in one of the unused chambers but complained it'd been too cold for them to thrive. *We can lead some heat there, too.*

Baruch and Jacob sat together against the wall, discussing pipes and baths. Auran installed himself on Iris's right side—a vacant look in his eyes.

Merlow sat on her other side, wobbling slightly, knowing she wanted to talk to him.

"I'm worried about where to direct the rest of the backlash. I think the hotroom will be able to handle a third of my power at most," she said.

Auran listened. She didn't trust the tenseness in his jaw.

"If we disconnect the pipes from the well and connect the hotroom not just to the baths but to the entire structure, then you can pour more backlash into the pipes without overheating them," Merlow suggested. "It does mean you shall have to reheat daily, but there will be no need to fret about the maximum holding capacity."

"That's perfect." She needed to keep training if she were to be of use in the upcoming battle, and the constant strain of her power nagged in the background. *I can't wait for this hotroom to be finished.*

She felt a call from Sourni and let herself slip into a meditative state, feeling her protective circle of friends around her.

"Hello?"

Iris could hardly sense Sourni's words. "Sourni, you need to send a little more energy along when you think." *Is she still off-kilter from that lashing?*

"No names!"

Huh? "What's wrong?"

"I overheard Apex's assistant—they found a way to monitor mindlinks!" Sourni stayed quiet but her agitation was clear.

"We are preventing that with the right spells and shields. We just need to be very precise."

"No, they found a way around!"

"That's highly unlikely. A trained magician can block the connection from anyone else. The only communications at risk are between non-magicians and I don't know any civilians who are capable of mindlinking at all."

"You don't understand!" Sourni's energy blasted at her.

Iris felt Auran place a hand on her lower back as she put up a shield and let the excess energy drip away slowly. *I shall never go into a mindlink unprotected again.* She regained her balance and asked, "What do you mean?"

"It's too dangerous." Sourni was adamant. "We need this info. I can't jeopardize my position here."

"All right, we'll only mindlink when absolutely necessary." Iris drew her energy back.

Both Auran and Merlow stared as she resurfaced—concern etched on their faces.

"I've never seen you react like that. What happened?" Auran demanded.

She ignored his question and asked Merlow, "Is it possible to breach the magic securing a mindlink?"

Auran inhaled sharply.

"Nothing happened, not yet," she hastened to add. "Sourni startled me. She says Thorn can monitor mental communication now."

"I do not think anyone can tamper with a mindlink," Merlow said. "Not if you or I are part of the connection. If there were a breach we would notice immediately." He looked across their hastily-made table. "Can we confirm Baruch knows how to shield a telepathic conversation?"

"I already told Sourni we would keep mindlinks to a minimum." Iris looked at Merlow. "Have you heard back from the Faeries yet?"

His face twitched. "They had no news but promised to keep me posted."

Baruch turned toward them. "I do not mean to intrude, but did you say Faeries?"

Iris felt Auran get defensive. *Huh?*

"We do not have Faeries but a species that is similar. The beings in the rain forest are related to them. Do Faeries really have wings?" Baruch asked in earnest.

Iris held up her hand to smother her laughter. "I'm sorry."

"No," Merlow answered seriously. "The Faeries are small and elflike, but they do not grow wings. They can transport themselves between worlds though, which may be as fast as flying." Merlow's eyes twinkled.

Auran relaxed.

He's acting strange today.

Auran's head twisted toward her.

Baruch and Merlow chatted about the two species—apparently the main distinction was their appearance.

Jacob snored.

Iris caught Auran's eye. They got up and hauled Jacob to his feet.

"Hey, I can walk," he mumbled.

Auran slung a muscled arm under Jacob's generous shoulders and the three of them walked to the infirmary, where Jacob hoisted himself into bed without complaining.

Iris tugged his sheet up while Auran inspected the room. *I don't think he even realizes he's constantly verifying our safety.* In the next bed, Basil stirred and opened his eyes.

"How are you feeling?" Iris asked, concerned about the paleness of his olive-green aura.

"Trampled," he rasped.

She helped him sit up and drink a brew of grapefruit and thyme. Basil had trouble swallowing and part of the potion drizzled down his chin.

"Does your mouth feel numb?" Iris asked.

He wobbled his tongue. "Feels sluggish."

"Your body is still getting rid of the poison. Let me know if it gets worse," Iris instructed. "Even if it's the middle of the night. Just tell Jacob to come get me or Merlow, okay?"

Iris glanced at Jacob. A dip of his chin confirmed he'd understood.

"Sleep is your best friend, gentlemen," she said gently. "Sweet dreams."

CHAPTER SIXTY-THREE

Kaale Mountains

Auran and Iris stepped out of the infirmary and into the hall-way. *Best do this in private.* She pulled up a soundproof barrier. "What's wrong with you? You're so jittery. I've never seen you like this. Are you worried?"

Auran grumbled.

"What?" she said. "What does that mean?"

"Nothing. I'm going to have a look at the hotroom." He stomped off.

Men. Good luck hiding in your cave. She walked back to her chamber.

Baruch and Merlow had left. *I bet Merlow is showing him more herbs.* Trevor had already cleared away the dinner bowls.

Iris sat on her sleeping mat, stretching her tender muscles. *I can't believe Baruch arrived only this morning.* It felt like he'd been here for days. There was definitely a soul connection between all of them, the way they got along effortlessly and often needed few words.

Sometimes it was whispered a group of souls was placed on Earth for a specific task. Certain people were placed together at strategic locations to accomplish something vital. Timing was crucial, as meeting the right person and recognizing his or her value was largely dependent on what had already transpired.

She'd expected Auran to be over the moon having Baruch here, not prance around like a...

Iris stilled, then initiated a mindlink. "Auran? Can you come over to my room?"

His concern seeped through the connection. "You all right?"

"I'm safe."

"Okay, I'm coming."

Auran walked in—running his hand through his blond hair. "What?"

Iris smoothed her tunic. "I've been thinking. I…please tell me what's wrong."

His cheeks colored. "I guess you're happy Baruch has joined us?"

Gods. "Why on earth would you think that?"

Auran leaned against the wall.

Her heart sank. "I have no room for romantic entanglements— even if I wished for them."

Auran had a pained look in his eyes. "You didn't show any of the reservation you normally have around new people, and you were laughing together. I've never seen you so taken by anyone."

Iris reached up to touch his face but he pulled away. "The only reason I feel so comfortable around Baruch is because he's so much like you!"

Auran stared at his feet.

"Have some faith. You know me better than that. I…" Should she say out loud what they'd avoided all these years? "I wish the world were a different place, where we had room and time for romance. But there isn't. You know I love you." There, she'd said it.

Relief flooded his features. He grabbed her tightly, almost crushing her, and buried his face in her hair.

Auran released her, cupping her chin. For a moment she feared he might kiss her, though part of her wondered what it would be like to be kissed, and her entire body went rigid at the thought.

He leaned his cheek against her forehead. "The three of us will fit in your room if you want."

Iris shook her head. "No, you know I don't sleep well with other people around me. Baruch can stay with Merlow."

They stood together for a while.

Iris sensed the emotions coursing through Auran—the initial relief replaced by sadness and pain.

Auran cleared his throat. "I'll check on the guards."

Iris nodded.

She sat back down on her mat, feeling wrung out. *Please Gods, spare us from having this happen every time a new male enlists.*

Part of her was curious who else would join them. Their numbers were growing steadily, mostly thanks to Jacob and Auran. While she mastered her powers, they'd recruited most of the guards over the years, and of course, Sourni.

Ever since seeing what Thorn and Apex had done to the abandoned village, she understood it was inevitable that she would use her gift to battle for a better world. The guards and the villagers might think she was an anomaly, and perhaps they were right. To be honest, most of the time she agreed.

Either way, she wasn't going down without a fight. Not when she was certain having Apex and his men rule meant everyone was worse off. She shivered.

A whiff of her mother startled her, and Iris sniffed and searched the chamber curiously. Her mother rarely showed up. Even now it was just her rose scent. When her Mama had told her about her magic she'd had no clue what that entailed. In her naivety she'd been only relieved to know what she'd been feeling. To be able to give it a name.

Iris wished she'd had the time to get to know her better. Her mother might've been able to teach her more about her unique abilities. It might've made things easier, make her feel less alone—knowing she wasn't the only one who scared away people by looking at them. Only Merlow and Auran didn't seem bothered by her bright eyes.

Iris thought of Auran's mom. Mrs. Stronghold always flinched when Iris first walked through the door, but she muddled through anyway, taking a deep breath and smiling into Iris's face.

She remembered seeing his mother for the first time, the day after her father had...died. Iris had convinced Trevor to leave—to stay with his own family—while she sorted herself out. She'd been terrified she'd hurt him, too. So Auran had invited her over for dinner.

Iris had stood on the threshold of the kitchen, hesitant to enter.

"Mom," Auran said. "Can Iris eat here?"

The slender woman stirring the food in the pan whirled around. "Darling!"

Auran stepped out of the way and Iris realized Auran's mother was speaking to her.

His mother clasped her shoulders and looked into her eyes. Mrs. Stronghold flinched but kept looking. "Such beautiful eyes." She enveloped Iris in a hug. "Of course you will stay for dinner." She gave Iris a last squeeze and busied herself with her pans.

Iris recognized the grief in her bubble.

"Thank you," she said.

She'd enjoyed many dinners at the Stronghold's since. *I wish I'd been allowed to go there before...* Iris was convinced Auran's mother made an effort because she knew how much it hurt when people turned away.

Iris shook her head—no time for pity parties—and checked her mental to-do list for things that needed, well, doing. *Nothing urgent.* Or so she told herself.

Time for bed. She cast a protective spell around herself, ensuring she would wake up when needed, and lay down. Right before she fell asleep, Auran entered.

"It's just me," he whispered.

She smiled. As if she hadn't immediately recognized his energy. "Night," she murmured.

CHAPTER SIXTY-FOUR

Ruisseau

I ris lit up, and watched Auran run to the barn. She'd felt his energy approach a few minutes ago and couldn't wait to see him again. Continuously moving locations was exhausting.

She and Merlow had been lucky to stumble upon a deserted shack hidden in the woods. It was great to be dry.

"What happened to not leaving a trail?" she joked.

"Jacob found a place!" Auran's eyes were alight.

Jacob and a vaguely familiar man followed at a more relaxed pace.

Merlow joined Auran and Iris at the entrance. "Welcome back, Auran."

"Come on," Auran urged Jacob and the other man.

Iris eyed Jacob—she hadn't seen him in months. "Your hair is longer!" She playfully tugged a dark brown strand.

"Hey." Jacob grinned.

"You remember Basil?" Auran said to Iris.

Iris nodded. Now she recognized the boy with mocha eyes from her hometown.

"Basil, meet Merlow." Auran said.

"Hello." Basil shook Merlow's hand.

"You found a place for all of us?" Iris beamed at Jacob.

He smiled shyly. "Yes."

"Where?"

"Perhaps they would like to come inside," Merlow suggested.

Iris glowered at Merlow and pushed the rough barn door open. It was considerably warmer inside, out of the wind.

Jacob rubbed his hands. "Nice."

Iris surveyed the shaky walls and the remnants of straw. The only luxury were their sheepskins and canteens with water. *To think we all grew up in houses.*

"I shall make some tea," Merlow offered. "Make yourselves comfortable."

The men unpacked their bedrolls and sat down.

Iris fought to curb her impatience.

"Jacob, you better tell her before she starts badgering you." Auran laughed.

The pressure changed infinitesimally. Iris extended her senses to determine the nature of Merlow's minor spell. *He soundproofed the room.*

Iris knitted her brow. "I don't sense anyone near."

"With such valuable information you should never take a chance," Merlow answered.

Okay.

"Well," Jacob started, "my last trip took longer than planned so I took a shortcut. I didn't want *him* to start worrying." He poked Auran in the chest.

"I cut through a mountain range I hadn't crossed before—the Kaale Mountains—and noticed irregularities in the rock. I explored the openings and discovered a network of tunnels. There's plenty of room for all of us and it's deep enough to hide your presence."

"Everything is ready," Auran added. "Basil will escort you to the cave."

"Why aren't you coming?" Iris asked.

"Jacob had another brilliant idea."

Iris looked at Jacob—imploring him to tell her.

Jacob cleared his throat. "I thought we could fetch our chest of acorns."

Iris's eyes brightened. The precious acorns would make a world of difference. "Yes!" She realized this meant they would go back to Yarden, and her eyes dulled. "Is it safe?"

"We were hoping Merlow could shield us," Auran said.

Iris frowned. *He's not coming either?* She looked up, feeling Merlow's stare.

"You are strong enough to protect yourself, and nobody will suspect where you are going," Merlow said.

"We'll only travel at night," Basil added.

As usual.

Auran clasped Basil's shoulder. "He's our best stealth mover and practically invisible—you're in good hands. Not to mention his combat skills."

"Just enough to take out my two older brothers," Basil said.

Iris smiled tentatively at Basil. "Okay."

THE FIVE OF them set off at first light, after Auran and Merlow had erased all signs of their presence.

In the middle of the forest Auran stopped. "We'll go left here."

Iris examined the trees to her left but couldn't distinguish a path. "All right."

Auran smiled when he caught her look. "We'll see you in our new home." He clapped Basil on his back. "Take good care of her. You know what to do."

"Yes, sir," Basil answered.

Sir? She took Auran's measure, and realized he hadn't only grown muscles but in authority, too. *Huh.*

Merlow handed her a sachet of herbs. "Ingest these every morning."

Iris secured the precious goods in her inner pocket. She looked at Auran. "I..."

He pulled her aside. "Yes?"

She fought back her tears. "Will you say goodbye to them for me?" She'd started to realize she'd never see her childhood home again, and knowing Auran would see the mansion hurt.

Auran nodded. "I'll tell your parents and Thom you're thinking of them."

"And…and Theresa."

It was believed crossed-over souls often visited the place of their death.

Auran clutched her upper arm.

She wiped a tear away with her sleeve and squared her shoulders. "Okay."

"See you in a few weeks."

BASIL PROVED A companionable travel partner. His energy was calm and steady, and his hunting skills provided ample meat. She hadn't had this much animal protein since she'd left Yarden. Even though Auran had always left them a supply, he couldn't risk killing too many animals in the same area.

Iris was looking forward to not having to move around constantly. Ever since she and Merlow had left Yarden, they'd been on the move, never staying anywhere for more than a few days. They'd dwelled in the woods mainly, not wanting to risk the openness of the mountains. This was a welcome change of scenery.

A crystal clear stream gurgled down the mountain slope—the setting sun sparkling off the water. They'd risen earlier than usual; Basil wanted to seize the opportunity to catch fish before they set off again. He waded through the stream, peering into the water. Iris was mesmerized. She'd never seen anyone catch salmon with their bare hands.

Absorbed with watching Basil she failed to notice the brown bear's approach.

Iris sniffed. *What's that wet dog smell?* She heard a puff of breath. *By Seth.* Moving slowing Iris peeked over her shoulder—stifling a shriek at the sight of the huge bear.

A shield, I should throw up a shield. Iris fumbled for her magic.

The bear raised itself on its hind legs and snuffled.

Oh Gods.

Basil sloshed through the water and pushed past her—shoving her behind his bulk. The bear cocked its ears, moving its head from side to side.

"Leave, you baboon. We're not a threat," Basil spoke in a monotone voice.

The bear pawed at the ground.

Basil threw the salmon in its face.

No!

The animal grunted and dropped on all fours.

"Shoot," Basil mumbled under his breath. He moved backward, one arm curved back around her—forcing her to retreat into the water.

The creek was ice-cold, and Iris gasped for air. Basil stopped at the water's edge and released her. "Immerse yourself fully, and stay put," he whispered.

Iris drew back slowly, sinking down until the glacial water reached her chin.

Unhurried Basil crossed the river bank to the bundle of his boots and trousers—the bear following his every move. Basil unsheathed his sword.

Iris was freezing, but she no longer felt the ache of her blisters.

He pointed his sword at the bear, curving an arc back and forth through the air. "Shoo."

Horrified Iris watched the bear charge. She pressed her lips shut, forcing herself to stay silent.

Basil parried the bear's attack, deftly ducking to avoid a claw. The animal made a deep-throated pulsing sound. Basil gripped the hilt with both hands and heaved his sword up, swinging down full force and hitting the bear on his left shoulder with the flat of the blade.

The bear bellowed in frustration and swiped at Basil.

He yanked his head back and faced the bear. They stared at each other. Basil feinted left and when the bear moved he jumped forward—clunking the pommel on the animal's nose. "I don't want to kill you, just leave already!"

The animal shook his head, wiping a paw at its bloody nose.

Iris was afraid to look.

Basil swiped at the bear's other front leg—using his considerable strength—and swept the bear off its feet.

The animal fell flat on its face. Basil approached and clomped the bear's head. "Sorry for the headache buddy." He kept an eye on the bear and pulled on his trousers, calling to Iris, "You can come out now."

THE MOON WAS half full—lighting their way. Iris followed in Basil's wake, emulating his steps as she'd done Auran's. Her feet skidded on some loose stones halfway up the slope and she lost her balance. "Aah!" Iris clamped her hand over her mouth—horrified. *I should've used a muffling spell!*

The sound echoed several times against the mountains before it died away.

Basil had swiveled at the first sign of her slipping and steadied her with a brawny arm.

Iris exhaled a shaky breath.

He squeezed her shoulder in encouragement while scanning her face.

She held her hand up.

He nodded but maintained his grip on her.

She composed her breathing and pulled up a muffling spell. *Let's see if I can keep this spell moving with us.*

The rest of the night was uneventful—*thank the Gods*—and Iris was thoroughly relieved when Basil spotted a cavern where they could hide during the day. She sat down and stretched her legs. She wasn't used to this much exercise, especially in elevated terrain. The thin air had worn her down.

Iris was grateful for the herbs Merlow had given her, the blend alleviated her muscle aches significantly. On their first day she'd offered them to Basil, too, but he'd politely declined.

She closed her eyes and scouted the vicinity. Merlow had taught her how to hide her energy signature before they left, but it paid to be cautious. *No sorcerers.* She soundproofed the grotto. "There's no one around. I'll set up a ward to alert us of any passersby."

Basil yawned. "Thanks. Why don't you get some sleep first? We should be there by tomorrow."

Good. She lay down and was asleep before she could respond. The nightmare found her in minutes.

Iris knelt on the granite tiles in the living room of the mansion, her body rocking with dry heaves from the tears she couldn't shed. The constant stream of emotions from the people around her was overwhelming. She was drenched in their thoughts as if her mind were perforated. She couldn't cope any longer.

Anger smoldered inside her—she was seconds away from losing control entirely. She had no strength left to leave the manor even though she knew people would get hurt.

Dear Seth—don't let me set the house on fire. In an attempt to warn the handful of servants to stay out of the living room and in the kitchen, she stammered something so unintelligible even she couldn't make out what she said.

The burning started deep inside her, flames licking their way from her soul into her physical body. The agony was clawing a path out, craving release. She knew it was a matter of seconds until she was fully immersed in the power and consumed by its desire to unleash.

At last she gave in—having no strength left. As soon as she surrendered, both the glory of riding the wave and the incredible pain of the power seared through her system. Her body was not made for these kinds of outbursts. It was a miracle she didn't incinerate herself.

Iris noticed the striped chair where her mother used to sit to embroider, the adjacent table now void of the kaleidoscopic silk and embroidery frame. Iris heard Theresa enter the room—it was time to light the candles—and she wanted to shout, to tell her to leave. But her voice made no sound. She was no longer in control. The energy funneled from Iris straight into Theresa, a deadly lifeline. Iris felt the impact hit the woman squarely in the chest and heard Theresa shriek as she ignited—the flames spreading from her center and consuming her, like a sun shining its rays.

Theresa screamed until both the fire and life went out of her.

Iris fell to the floor, having no strength left and avoided looking at the charred body. The stench penetrated her nose—nausea hit her with force and she retched until she blacked out.

Iris woke up with a jolt, drenched in sweat. The cold, hard ground dug in her back. *Another nightmare.* She briefly wondered how many more times she would be forced to relive that dreadful moment.

"Are you alright?" Basil asked wide-eyed and hovering above her. "I couldn't get you to wake up. Do you want to talk about it?"

"No," she croaked.

Basil handed her his water bottle. "You're safe here."

She drank thirstily, then groaned, pressing the canteen against her forehead where it cooled her feverish skin.

CHAPTER SIXTY-FIVE

Kaale Mountains

Not again! Iris moaned as her consciousness was ripped away from the comfort of her sleeping mat in her chamber. The zing of the ward zoomed by.

She flung a drop of magic down the cord to determine where her astral body was headed. The distinct energy of Faerieland glimmered at the end. *I've been summoned by the Faeries!*

The command vibrated with urgency.

When will I ever get to sleep? Iris surrendered and descended into the Faerie realm.

The density of the air around her increased. Her ears popped when she shifted from the human realm into Faerie territory. Other than her dream visit to the oak, she'd never been to Faerieland. The sky was blacker than she'd ever seen, and the stars…her hands tingled at their brightness.

Iris took big breaths, filling her lungs with oxygen-rich night air. *Jasmine.*

"Thank you for yielding to our summoning," the Faerie Queen spoke.

Iris whirled around to face the Faerie Queen behind her. "Your Highness." She inclined her head. "Your urgency was apparent." She gawked at the firmament above. "The stars are magnificent here."

"There is a breach in the magic realm."

Iris's heart lurched.

No time for chitchat, huh. "A breach? How?"

"Someone tampered with the dimensions of the different realms. Magic is leaking into the underworld. Your defenses have been infringed as well," the Queen declared.

"What?" In her mind Iris raced through the day, scanning for irregularities. Something nagged in the back of her mind.

"We need to stop the perpetrators and halt the flow of magic leaking out."

Iris studied the Queen's face, framed by vermillion locks. A hint of steel glinted in those jade eyes. Iris enforced her shield. "I assume you know who breached it?"

"Some*thing*—rather than someone—came along with Merlow yesterday."

Seemingly oblivious to Iris's inner turmoil, the Queen continued. "This creature has attached itself to Merlow—tainted him."

Iris gasped. "What…what does it do? Is he in danger?"

"We determined it is a species from the underworld. Thorn has discharged light-suckers, and is making good use of their abilities to remain unseen. Every human emits light, and magicians transmit a significant amount more. Light-suckers are drawn to their aura."

Thorn. Her magic stirred at the mention of his name alone.

"Merlow merely functions as a carrier. Today we deduced he is not aware of the creature, hence our summons. His spell work is waterproof, and the thing cannot penetrate Merlow's body or mind, although it does feed on his energy. Baruch, however, might be seized once he is asleep."

The Faeries know about Baruch? Iris almost choked.

She shuddered at the idea of having this leech control a wizard—especially one capable of drawing magic from nature. *Would Baruch be able to drain magic from people, too?*

Is that why Auran was so adamant about Baruch sleeping in Merlow's room? Auran's behavior still struck her as odd. The uncanny feeling might've aggravated his jealousy. *Oh no!* Baruch, unsuspecting, must be asleep by now.

"Yes, you are right," the Queen answered her unspoken thoughts.

Iris's eyes flared. She wished her ability to mindread extended to the Faeries. She hated being an open book, especially when flying blind—the mature Faeries didn't have an aura she could rely upon either. Once they came of age they were taught to hide their aura.

"We believe ·Auran intuitively sensed something was wrong, though he did not know the cause for his concern—his instincts are geared toward safekeeping—and Baruch is at risk."

Iris swallowed. *That's why Auran acted like a mother hen…*

"If the being controls Baruch's mind, he will be a formidable opponent."

The Queen's left eye twitched as Iris's magic crawled over her. She read no guile in the Queen's features. Iris cursed herself for having missed this creature right under her nose.

How come Merlow didn't sense this thing in his energy field?

"You have been preoccupied, and you have too much faith in Merlow's abilities," the Queen said.

Iris forced herself to keep her annoyance in check. *It's a miracle no one's ever beaten me up for reading their mind.*

Again the Queen continued, "Always verify—even with those you trust. Those who hold your complete faith are Apex's most likely targets."

Chills crawled down Iris's spine.

"Thorn knows he cannot get to you directly, so he will endeavor to place his allies among your people. Watch your back at all times, even with those you trust. They will not turn on you willingly, but they might be overtaken."

What? She shook herself. *Merlow, focus on Merlow.* "Can we remove or destroy this light-sucker?"

"You have the aptitude, and we will teach you how. It is imperative the light-sucker gets eradicated. Once loose from the underworld, it can penetrate all dimensions." The Faerie Queen adjusted her necklace. "Under normal circumstances you should be able to work the spell."

"Normal circumstances?"

"This spell is somewhat more complex than what you are used to," The Queen waved her hand. "It should be fine."

Iris frowned. Her gut told her the spell would be...tricky.

"You will need a special component to secure the spell. Auroras are harvested during the Northern Lights and their intense luminosity shocks the being apart. We will give you bountiful stock, in case more beings surface."

By Seth.

"Prepare yourself. I will unveil the spell," the Queen instructed.

Iris checked her grounding cord, fumbling for solid ground. *Will this work in my astral body?*

"Close your eyes and open your inner sight. I will take you through the motions."

Iris blew out a breath, forcing her mind to go still.

The Queen showed her each of the steps. Not much of the spell was familiar. *The Faeries must use a different sort of magic.*

"Lastly you will release the auroras. Make sure you time it precisely. If you are even marginally off, the substance will ricochet."

Iris opened her eyes. "How will I know the exact moment?"

"I just demonstrated the spell and the timing."

Not used to questions, huh—damn. "Any other signs I can look for?" she asked politely.

"The being might pause for a few instants as you invoke the second spell."

You could've mentioned that. "Thank you. That's very helpful."

Iris knew she would need Auran's support to sprinkle the luminescence in Merlow's aura. He might have to restrain Merlow, too—she sensed the creature would put up a fight.

The Faerie Queen nodded. It was uncanny how easily she read Iris's mind. "Anything else I need to be aware of?"

"I expect not. We will observe from here."

Iris had never known the Faeries were able to peek in anywhere they wanted. She forced her mind to go blank.

"We will send you back. You will find the quintessence in your pocket upon homecoming."

"Thank you for your assistance."

Iris prepared herself for the shift in dimensions, and the pressure on her eardrums indicated she'd returned to the human realm.

CHAPTER SIXTY-SIX

Kaale Mountains

I ris opened her eyes. Auran was fast asleep beside her.

I need to tell him the Faeries hear and see everything.

She put a hand on his shoulder "Auran."

He bolted upright, grabbing his dagger. "What? Where?" He scanned the room, then looked her up and down.

"There's no attack. Not yet."

"What happened?"

"The Faerie Queen summoned me," Iris said.

By the time she recounted her night, Auran had gone pale. "You want me to work magic?"

Iris shook her head. "You only need to release these auroras." She pulled a small silver-colored bag from her pocket and handed it to him.

He stared at the shimmering bag as if it were poison.

For all we know it very well might be...

"So I just chuck this out?" he said.

"I'll tell you exactly when."

She strengthened the shield around Auran and added her most powerful protection spell.

He cringed. "Not sure if I'll ever get used to that."

Iris smiled slightly. "Probably not."

She divided the space in her mind into three slots and started building the first spells. She left them unfinished—to be completed at the scene. She couldn't risk losing a single second once

~ 294 ~

they entered Merlow's room. There would be no way to warn him without alerting the light-sucker.

Iris scanned the damp hallways for the aura of guards—she didn't want anyone close.

Around the corner of Merlow's chamber they halted. Iris extracted the spell to seal Merlow's room and added the last piece— now nothing could get out. *We don't want this thing to flee and latch on to an armed guard.*

She took a deep breath and met Auran's eyes.

He jerked his chin and went in first, then hauled an asleep Merlow upright. The muscles on his arms bulged with the effort of restraining the magician. Iris released her prepared spell, disabling Baruch. She knew he'd be able to wrestle himself loose—given the time—but she prayed he knew better.

Seeing Baruch stilled, Iris froze time, sweat gleaming on her forehead. Freezing time was not done lightly, but she couldn't risk the creature escaping to another dimension.

Merlow stared at her in disbelief, his beard for once in disarray.

She had no time to explain her actions. It would take forever if the two of them started battling, and in the melee the light-sucker might attack Baruch.

Iris felt the Faerie Queen nod her consent and turned to study Merlow. *Where's this thing?* She walked around him and noticed a wrinkle in his aura, on his lower back, the rumple barely discernible.

After rolling her shoulders, she started the complex series of enchantments she'd learned, or rather, watched.

The timing had to be exact. If the light-sucker escaped and word got out they had the vanquishing spell, Thorn would immediately suspect the aid of the Faeries. Their advantage would go right out the window.

The first invocation made the being visible. *It's tiny!*

The light-sucker shimmered. *It's almost pretty.* She admired the otherworldly glow. Well, it *did* hail from the underworld.

The creature started thrashing and Iris realized she'd been distracted for a millisecond, absorbing its beauty.

Focus.

The light-sucker was powerful. Iris sensed it began to unravel the freezing spell. *By Seth!* She closed her eyes and sped through the second incantation. Her power strained as she gathered more magic. She hesitated, doubting the order of the last invocation.

Mixing up the sequence of a spell was always messy. But with one this size…

She held the spell in her mind—sending her thoughts back to the demonstration. A good thing she'd paused to check, or she would've gotten it wrong.

"Iris!" Auran urged.

She didn't dare open her eyes, needing all her attention to complete the spell. She uttered the last words and felt the being become motionless. "Now!" she yelled at Auran.

He threw the auroras at the light-sucker, and Iris started the third spell. She'd told him to spread out the release of the luminous forces in order to give her about ten seconds to complete the enchantment. She had impressed upon him how critical timing was.

Auran had trouble counting.

By Seth! I froze time!

Now they had to wing it. She cursed herself for not foreseeing this complication. She nudged Auran with her hip.

He opened his fist to discharge the last of the auroras.

A loud crack echoed through the chamber as the creature vaporized into incandescent mist.

That was close.

Iris double-checked to ensure the leech was entirely gone and discovered no remnants. She unraveled each spell carefully. Starting time first—this was one enchantment you could not mess up—then releasing Baruch from his immobility.

Auran let go of Merlow.

Merlow rubbed his shoulder. "Thank you," he said incredulously. "I should have noticed myself." He focused on stroking his beard into orderly fashion.

Iris sat down, spent.

"How did you know?" Merlow asked.

"Tomorrow. I'll tell you all tomorrow," she said. "Merlow, you might want to reinstall the sealing spell once we leave." Then her face fell. "We better pray to the Gods we didn't spike up on the readings. I used quite some power."

Baruch snorted. "You almost gave off sparks."

Auran glared at him.

Merlow said "We shall know in the morning."

CHAPTER SIXTY-SEVEN

Kaale Mountains

When Baruch woke the next morning, he was not sure where he was. He studied the rock above him, feeling the bitter cold creep up. So foreign here—worlds apart from his beloved rain forest. *I never thought I would miss that humid, warm atmosphere.* He feared he would never be warm again. *Perhaps I can sleep in that hotroom, if it is safe with all the magic humming around.*

••••••••●•••••••

Auran stared at the ceiling of Iris's room.

The battle had truly begun. Thorn had sent this underworld species into their cave—he was on to them. *How much did Thorn know?* Iris looked bruised and worn out, her breathing shallow. She was still recovering from last night's spell.

Auran savored the rare opportunity to study her face, thinking of last night's revelations. He'd been so scared of losing her. What a piece of work she was—shaped by the burden of her past and future.

Iris stirred, and he returned to surveying the grey rock above. Her joints cracked as she stretched. He saw her wince as she tried to sit up. "Painful?"

She shrugged. "It's fine. The first time you cast a spell always feels like you're using new muscles."

A new spell? No wonder she looked beaten. *Dear Gods, please send us a slow day.* They all needed one. To invade the Citadel and take out Apex, they must be fresh and rested. Lately all they did was survive from one day to the next, using up their reserves.

Iris yawned and extended her arms. "Breakfast?"

"Why don't you let Trevor fix it?"

"Isn't it Sunday?" she asked.

Auran shook his head. "You're unbelievable."

Somehow she'd gotten it into her head her servant needed one day off per week—some pre-Cataclysm tradition her mother had told her about. On Sundays she did everything herself. *Foolish, stubborn woman.*

Her magical strength was never the problem, but her body needed to recover from overuse. No point in exerting herself making meals.

"I'll do it," he offered.

She threw him a sachet of herbs. "Use a teaspoon of these. Add some to yours too, if you want."

No way he'd use any for himself. There was no telling when they could get their hands on a fresh batch. "Sure. Will you take a bath?"

"I'll wait until we get the pipes hooked up. Plus I have a feeling I'll be covered in mud soon," she added absentmindedly.

Auran's head shot up in alarm. Sometimes she had a knack for premonition. Unfortunately it wasn't something they could rely on to strategize, as it came and went as it pleased. *This sounds like trouble.*

"I'll meditate," Iris said, retreating to one of the corners.

Auran stirred the herbs into the oatmeal, making sure they blended with the grains. *Ah, I need heat.* As if by magic the bowl warmed up. He glanced over his shoulder to see Baruch enter the room.

Baruch winked at him. Neither spoke, not wanting to disturb Iris.

After a few minutes Iris exhaled.

"Let's have breakfast," Auran said. "Have you had any?" he asked Baruch.

"Yes, thank you. Merlow prepared a lovely porridge. I am keeping my eyes peeled to learn all about these herbs. Most are different from my homeland. It is really enticing."

Iris smiled and understood Baruch's eagerness.

She wasn't sure whether Merlow would ever properly finish her education. It was all war-related spells, protection and battle healing now. She would love to learn more about homely remedies. Iris saw herself in the kitchen of the mansion creating a soothing herbal tea. Her mother's matching green curtains hung on the window. A young blonde girl with aqua-blue eyes jumped up and down, sending her pigtails swinging. *By Seth.*

"How did last night's creature penetrate the cave?" Baruch asked.

Iris forced her attention back. "It's a light-sucker. Someone's been tampering with dimensions and unleashed light-suckers from the underworld. According to the Faerie Queen, Thorn sent it."

"How did it find Merlow?" Auran asked. "Does this mean Thorn now knows our location?"

"The Queen indicated the creature came along with Merlow when he… No!" She held her head in her hands.

Auran stepped over and placed a hand on her shoulder. "Are you in pain?"

She shook her head. "I'm afraid Thorn traced Merlow's energy in the clearing when he met the Faeries, and registered it again when Merlow returned from Faerieland. He must've set up a trigger."

"Is that even possible?" Baruch asked.

"Thorn is very familiar with Merlow's energy."

"How so?"

"They grew up as friends and rivals—training together. Thorn has always had a mean streak. Merlow was their mentor's favorite and Thorn became jealous." Iris swallowed. "Merlow doesn't like to talk about it, but in Fleuris one magician per generation is awarded the honorary title by the Magical Society. Thorn and Merlow were the only two contenders as they were equal in power. Thorn violated the rules, so Merlow won."

"I was not aware Fleuris has a Magical Society," Baruch said.

"Well, we *did*. Thorn left out of spite, unwilling to settle for weeds. He told Apex all about the Magical Society. Apex outlawed the organization. Many members were killed—its secret locations were destroyed. Membership is now illegal. Only Apex-approved sorcerers are allowed. The rest are hunted, and that's why most magicians have been wiped out."

"Can Thorn trace Merlow's energy back here?" Auran asked.

"The granite and the wards shield us. Except now Merlow can't step outside again—or even send his energy out."

"What if the being left a mark, so its siblings can find us more easily?" Baruch asked.

"Or take revenge?" Auran added.

"Do you think this creature will be missed?"

"I don't know, dammit!" Iris yelled.

"What if more light-suckers already penetrated the cave?" Auran asked.

She glared at them. "The Queen would've told me if there was more than one creature here."

"Are you sure?" Auran cocked his head.

Iris made a face. "Hang on." She turned inside, recalling the energy signature of the light-sucker. "The guards are not going to like this." Gathering magic, she flung a powerful wave through the gorge—searching. Her magic brushed up against Jacob. "Jacob's coming," she muttered. Her power swept through the cave, allowing her to draw an intricate map of every sentient being in the mountain. She didn't dare push past the boundaries of granite, and pulled back when she sensed their own wards.

She opened her eyes. Auran and Baruch both leaned forward to hear her verdict.

"All clear."

They relaxed.

"Perfect," Auran said.

"For now. Let's pray to the Gods this light-sucker won't be missed."

CHAPTER SIXTY-EIGHT

Arbres

Sourni had learned to read Her Eminence's moods. Apparently her predecessors had lacked those skills, so she was determined to do a better job. As routine was crucial, Sourni paid close attention to the order of things. Breakfast on the balcony always included fish—none of the Dead Sea's, of course—and was invariably preceded by a salt bath in Her steaming chambers to open Her lungs. All Her Eminence's rooms faced the ocean, the doors opened wide in every season to let in the sea breeze. Most importantly, Gieser Wildeman pears were served for both lunch and dinner.

Compared to Sourni's work in the orchard, her duties were fairly light physically. She was more worried about the political scheming. Two camps were competing with the administrator, as she understood so far—one loyal to Her Eminence and the other vying for Apex. Marie promised to be a valuable resource because as head seamstress she measured everyone in the palace. Even Apex had her make his tailor-made soutane, summoning Marie to his home, in a part of Arbres facing the mountains. Apex's house was part of the city wall and also served as his personal office.

Sourni lay in bed unable to sleep. She still wasn't used to the spacious room, the velvet curtains which kept out any sign of light, and the softness of the bed. Not that their cabin had been so bad. She'd had much more than most, but this was—different.

Her mind went back to the last time she'd seen her mother. Tears fought their way up. Memories could be poison, and hers had seeped in deep and settled way down—indestructible like weeds. She sobbed and gripped the blankets so hard it hurt.

She wanted to feel her mother's arms around her one more time, to see her smile. They'd never talked much, but she knew her mother, recognized the grief in the way her mother carried herself. This morning Sourni had noticed the same signs in the mirror— blood will tell. She wiped her tears away with both hands and blew her nose. At least crying gave her some clarity and a temporary sense of relief. A false respite, but a respite nonetheless.

CHAPTER SIXTY-NINE

Kaale Mountains

I ris turned toward the entrance. *Jacob's approaching fast.*

He barged in. "More arrows!"

Jacob shouldn't have been running in his condition.

By Seth! Auran was supposed to be at the watchtower last night—instead he'd stayed with her. Assuming Jacob slept in the infirmary alongside Basil, that had left the tower without a commander.

"Anyone hurt?" Iris asked.

Jacob put his hands on his knees, breathing heavily. "No. I told them to stay away from the entrance. This angle is different, so I figured you should take a look."

"You've been at the tower?" Auran thundered. "Are you out of your mind? Did you not look at Basil? You're not going near there again. That's an order!"

Jacob leveled a stare at Auran. "Fine."

Iris left them to it, and ran over with Baruch. He pulled up a protective shield around the both of them. She glanced at him and nodded. His spell felt foreign. Magic developed over time and each country had its specific style, sometimes using different spells to attain the same result.

They arrived at the tower. An orange arrow stuck out the granite wall across from the entrance. Something had shifted. People thought a certain spell always yielded the same result, but magic was far from an exact science. Outer conditions influenced its result, and the presence of other magic could throw things off. *Did the arrow sense my shield on the rock?*

She must have a word with Merlow about the exact magic he'd imbued those arrows with. It was more advanced than anything she'd witnessed him create.

When magic evolved, it often became unstable. The next batch might come shooting from yet another angle for all she knew.

Baruch and Iris climbed up and found the guards on duty hovering on the second floor, some sharpening their blades. "We're down to three batches," Iris said. "Keep your armor on at all times, and steer clear from the entrance. This should be over by the end of the day." She crossed her fingers.

They nodded. Some guards avoided her eyes. One day she hoped to be able to thank them properly for all they risked. Now she simply asked, "Do you need anything?"

"Will Basil be all right?" one of them asked.

By Seth, we should've told them. Our being busy is no excuse.

"His condition is still critical. Today will be important."

Iris felt the nudge from a mindlink—the Earth Faerie. *Interesting.* She gave off a vibe to let the caller know she'd be right there, and asked the watchmen, "Anything else?"

They shook their heads.

She wasn't sure whether they'd been properly introduced to Baruch. "This is Baruch, he's a wizard from the Amazon. He's here to assist us."

She sent Baruch to Merlow's chamber and came across Auran in the hallway. She put up a hand—maintaining the energy of the call so she could slip right into it. He nodded and walked past, accustomed to her inner focus.

Once inside, she sealed her room. It wasn't a standard precaution for a mindlink—not even with the Faerie realm—but it felt appropriate. Iris strengthened her own shield and cleared the room of any remaining energies. It felt important the place was spotless, energetically speaking.

Only then did she answer the call.

She heard a calm, composed voice in her head—reminding her of the stable, constant energies of the earth. There was a groundedness to the mindlink, very much like the Earth Faerie herself, or so she imagined.

The only time Iris had interacted with the Earth Faerie was in a dream. The Faeries had been worried what she—untrained, her powers unleashed and out of control—would do to the overall balance. So they sent the Earth Faerie to help her regain command over her physical body.

She'd lain in bed tossing and turning, too tired to sleep. Exhausted after erupting in the garden, after her father was... Iris cringed at the memory of the arrow's sound and turned on her side, pulling the top sheet around her shoulder for something to hold on to. She felt a few Lonely Ones approach. *Not now!* She had no strength left to keep them at bay—or let them feast on her energy. "Go, please go!" she cried. To her surprise they left.

Groaning, she lay on her back and stared into the darkness. The curtains blocked out any light, but she sensed it was past midnight. She focused on the stars and eventually their whispers lulled her asleep.

"Iris. Iris!"

She directed her attention to the sound and sensed someone on her left side. Though her eyes were closed she saw the female clearly. Gentle moss-green eyes stared back at her.

"I am pleased to meet you Iris. I am the Earth Faerie."

The Earth Faerie? From what she remembered from Wendolyn and Maesie's stories, the Earth Faerie was one of the most powerful in their realm. Iris searched for the appropriate greeting and came up short.

"You can call me Moira."

Oh.

"I am here to help. You need to learn to balance your powers, and right now the most important thing for you is to ground. I was sent here to support you with that."

"Thank you." Iris was entranced by her green eyes and could almost smell the damp moss. "What do you want me to do?"

"Fixate on my eyes and imagine you can see the moss under the trees. Feel the softness when you stroke the moss."

Iris marveled at the velvety feeling, wondering how that was possible.

"I am helping you connect to nature and my eyes are a conduit—like a bridge. As the Earth Faerie I am one with this planet and can help you extend your senses to certain healing places. Look around and find a tree you like."

Iris's attention was drawn to a large oak tree—a spongy green carpet adorned with wood violets led to its inviting trunk.

"Good. Walk over and lean your back against the tree. You can sit down if you prefer."

Iris half-floated, half-bounced to the giant oak and gingerly sat. Resting her spine against its trunk was like coming home. A weight fell off her shoulders. She sighed and tilted her head back—the rough bark a solid support.

She sensed the tree and how old it was. It radiated a sturdy intelligence, compelling her to talk to the oak—not with words, but her senses received whatever pulses the tree sent out. It soothed her, and her breathing deepened.

"There you go. Keep connecting to the oak."

With every inhale a tinge of green coated her mouth. With her heightened awareness Iris noted the earthly breath fill her lungs. The oak's essence permeated her being, radiating out from her lungs to the rest of her body, using her veins as a roadmap, a calming antidote to the burning of her power. She vaguely heard the Earth Faerie speak.

"Stay here for as long as you want. You will wake up in your own bed wholly refreshed and with full memory of this experience. Be safe."

CHAPTER SEVENTY

Kaale Mountains

I ris relived the grounding dream in a flash and was filled with warm appreciation for the Earth Faerie, who had quite possibly saved her life.

"Hello," Iris said with a smile, knowing the Faerie would feel her positive energy through the mindlink.

"Here we are again my child."

Her tone suggested Iris was in trouble, and she prepared herself for a scolding.

"That was quite a spell you used last night," Moira said.

What? It was a Faerie spell!

"It shook us all. Did you realize these are interdimensional spells? Next time you should use more precaution."

"I followed the Queen's instructions," Iris objected.

"Did you really?"

The time freeze.

"That spell shattered our wards." Moira sounded indignant.

Aiee.

"Everything is more—intense—in our world. We can correct for most of the differences, but as you know, the moon and stars affect magic as well. As I am the most familiar with your world, I am sent to assist you in reworking another spell with appropriate proportions." The Earth Faerie paused, making sure Iris understood her fully.

~ 308 ~

Then she continued. "We will show you how this gorge can be overlooked without raising suspicion."

"Won't our own wards prevent that?" Iris asked.

"We cannot risk that a beacon has been left."

Gods.

"You will require several herbs and Merlow will serve as your calling station. You cannot be interrupted by anyone during this process—especially not by mindlinks."

That must be some spell. Iris stood up. *Never a dull moment.*

She found Merlow in a gathering. "I need you."

Jacob, Auran and Baruch got up. "Let's check the connection to the baths," Jacob said. The men walked out and Iris soundproofed the room.

Merlow looked at her. "Who is it this time?"

"Moira. We need to rework the wards and take this place off the energetic grid. She'll guide me through. We need your herbs, and you'll have to stand guard to keep out any energies."

"All right," he said, not easily surprised. "Which herbs will you be needing?"

Iris sat down and connected with the Earth Faerie again, pulling Merlow in with her.

"It has been a while my dear friend," Moira said. "We have been following your expeditions. You have been quite busy."

That's a bit of an understatement. Her poor mentor barely had time to sleep. Iris wasn't sure she'd have that amount of energy at his age—although she wasn't even sure how old he was. It was hard to tell with the beard.

Iris tuned back in when she heard the tone change.

"Merlow, I need you to select the following herbs," Moira said. "Adonis, columbine, angel's trumpet, larkspur and wolfsbane."

Iris's eyes bulged. These were *very* potent poisons.

Without missing a beat, Merlow picked five midnight blue sachets from his stash.

Wow.

"Stir the herbs together while I chant," Moira instructed. "Iris, create a shield to prevent dust from entering. The concoction must be undiluted and undisturbed."

Iris pulled up a spell that made a vacuum pale in comparison. She strengthened the soundproof spell.

Merlow started blending the herbs, and in her mind, Iris heard the Earth Faerie hum a tune. It struck a chord, the notes vaguely familiar. She felt the tones seep through the connection and watched in awe as Merlow steered the energy into the bowl—now swirling with color—using the herbs.

Iris hadn't realized magicians could use interdimensional sounds to increase the vibration of a potion and how much potency that added.

Moira spoke again, "Merlow, hold the bowl with both hands."

Merlow folded his hands around the terracotta pottery with poisonous herbs as if he cradled a precious butterfly.

"Iris, you will add your magic. Simply repeat the spell I share with you—the magic must be invoked in the cave itself. This spell serves as the smokescreen and will allow us to alter the energies of this cave without being noticed."

The Earth Faerie whispered the spell into Iris's mind, shielding it from Merlow as not to influence the herbs yet.

The power of the first spell stirred within Iris as she listened. The first layer protected the magician by driving an energetic wedge between the physical energy of the caster and her surroundings.

The second layer contained the power within this chamber, and the last layer placed a protective bubble around the entire gorge. Merlow vaporized the herbs—pouring their potency into the spell right before Iris completed the third layer. The pressure in the chamber rose unpleasantly, putting a strain on Iris's diaphragm. She felt suspended in midair.

The Earth Faerie dictated the second spell. This incantation was more complex, seven layers in total—each building on the previous one. Every element had to be cast precisely, or the entire spell would be rendered unstable.

Iris fell into the rhythm of working her magic, enjoying the flow of energy called forth by her actions. She knew Merlow monitored her like a hawk. Though for all his experience he was helpless as a newborn while she cast the spell.

Once a magician started an incantation, the spell had to be executed by that same person. All someone else could do was remind a caster of the words—which Merlow didn't know. A lot of power was unleashed through this spell, but it was contained by the first one—if done correctly. If this second spell blew, however, not even the first invocation would fully curb it. At best the energies would be slowed down.

The third spell was a staggering twelve layers.

Iris swallowed.

She'd never done anything over seven. Merlow always said only cocky magicians tried eight layers or more. She glanced at Merlow. He was blissfully unaware of her instructions. She knew he would try to stop her had he known.

There was no going back now—the balance of spells was too precarious, and no time to consult him either. Iris had to blindly trust the instructions of the Earth Faerie. *Dear Seth and Layla, please guide me.*

She understood why Merlow had been instructed to soundproof the room and prevent interruptions. Any waver in her concentration and the fallout would be catastrophic. She would not only blow up the room but Merlow and herself.

Iris smoothed away her fear.

Moira started whispering again, Iris following her instructions as if in a trance. Receiving the words and relaying them to the power within her became a dance. New muscles stirred, the energy swelling inside her heart and mind.

It was a joy to see the different layers melt together and create a captivating symphony. Iris's unique energy signature helped shape the composition. It was so beautiful she forgot how lethal it was.

A dissonant note pierced her mind. *I inverted two words!* She felt Merlow willing her to regain control.

On impulse she froze time.

"Good thinking," the Earth Faerie said. "Keep it short for there is too much energy building inside you. I will aid you in erasing the last two words by going back in time."

Merlow gasped.

"As soon as you feel the energy rekindling, cast the rest of the spell without pause or delay. This will not work a second time," Moira urged.

Iris patiently waited for what felt like eternity. A weird sensation brushed against her senses. *That must be the rewind in time.* Once the feeling stopped she felt a tug forward—as if the flow had returned to standing water. She continued casting the spell.

In the corner of her eye, Merlow blinked, unsettled. She pushed his concern aside.

As the twelfth layer fell into place, the energy climaxed. Iris's ears popped painfully when the spell left her system with a bang—like being punched in the stomach with an iron glove.

Merlow caught her, and she realized she'd been unconscious for a split second.

Iris surveyed the room in the deafening silence. The energy of the chamber had been altered. The vibration of the entire cave had been shifted imperceptibly. *That's why it will be overlooked.*

If she'd known the spell was to alter the vibration of such a vast place, she'd have been daunted by the task.

But now that she'd done it…a whole new world of spells was waiting for her. Her muscles tensed at the glimmer of excitement—to warn her against casting more spells.

Merlow examined her thoroughly, as he used to do when he trained her. He checked her pulse and her pupils, making sure she was fully present in her body before he fetched one of his famous concoctions.

Iris already knew what infusion he would give her. At first she hadn't understood how the body physically burned off minerals. Later she learned it had to do with the electrolytes helping bind the energy of the spell. That's why someone who was sick should never work magic, or nothing more than basic domestic spells, because it continued to deplete the supply the body needed to heal. That's why acorns and apples were sorely missed.

Iris accepted the brew and grimaced at the bitter scent wafting up her nose.

Merlow threw her a stern look.

"I know, I'll drink it," she said. "Though I'll never get used to that taste."

She dutifully emptied the cup in as few swigs as possible—fighting down her bile.

Merlow studied her as if he hadn't seen her for years. "The student outgrows her master," he whispered.

Iris put the cup down, unsure how to respond.

"Your powers are increasing exponentially," he said gravely. "You *must* practice in that hotroom. We need you fully in control if you are to stand a chance against Thorn."

"But…"

Merlow held up his hand "I know you are doing your best, and this situation is far from ideal. Honestly I am surprised you have been able to manage these spells with so much ease. Twelve layers."

Oh, he noticed.

"Your ability to cast progressively complex spells has amplified," he said.

Iris wanted nothing more than to wake up from this nightmare and live a normal life, despite the way she'd felt when casting that vibration-shifting spell. Regardless of the difficulty, she'd enjoyed being wholeheartedly alive in every cell of her body. She'd savored the challenge of not just her capacity to stay in control, but the ability to steer that power to where she wanted it to go—it was immensely gratifying.

They both looked at the entrance—Baruch waved his arms to get their attention on the other side of the soundproofed wall.

She nodded to Merlow and he lifted the sound barrier and the blockade that had sealed off his room.

Baruch barged in. "What happened?" he asked, bewildered. "There was a huge shift. I feared the mountain would come crashing down. I could not reach you! Are you both out of harm's way?" He looked like he was about to pat them down and check for himself.

Iris hurried to say, "We're fine. We did some spell work." She couldn't help but add, "What did it feel like?"

Baruch swallowed most of his words. "Some spell work, I will say. It was like a tornado played catch with a thunderstorm. Why did you not warn me?" He looked like a boy who hadn't been invited to come and play.

He feels left out. Left out and worried.

"I'm sorry—it was all very spur of the moment." As she spoke she received a call from Sourni. Afraid the energetic shift had somehow spiked the ratings, Iris hurried to answer. As she sat she heard Auran come in. His eyes instantly trained on her. She would deal with his worry later.

"Yes, I'm here," Iris said.

"I think I discovered another of Apex's cronies. A Lord Ashen." Iris inhaled sharply.

"He came for lunch and sat next to Apex. They served him the pears, and he will stay for dinner, too."

"Thank you. See if you notice anything special about him."

Iris brought her awareness back to the room and heard Merlow say, "The second layer of the spell…"

She didn't want Merlow to relay too many details—it felt too fragile still—so she interrupted him.

Auran looked relieved to hear her voice. She believed he would've tried to hug her had they been alone. *He worries too much.*

Auran crossed his arms. "What happened?"

Iris peered around the room, shaking off the eerie feeling of the opening in their dimension that allowed others to watch. She'd better make sure to close that gap. Not even the Earth Faerie needed a twenty-four-hour window into their world. "Some precaution," she said. "Nothing to worry about."

"Nothing to worry about?" Auran bristled. "You could've warned us. People were terrified when the winds started howling through the corridors. We didn't know whether we were under attack or the walls were giving in. Even the guards were screaming, convinced the world was coming to an end. What were you thinking?"

Oops. Faerie spells had a visibly different effect in the human realm. *I need to have a word with Moira.* Iris reminded herself to request more details next time the Faeries wanted her to cast a spell. *I've been a meek follower.*

"I'm sorry. It sounds like the effects were more intense than anticipated. I thought the energy was contained to this room. You don't think I would've cast a spell without forewarning had I known its effect?" she spit.

The air went out of him. "Of course not," he said. "Though a word of warning would've been nice."

"I'll try to think of it, but you knew Merlow and I were up to something when I sent you away. Don't tell me you were completely taken by surprise—"

"I have worked spells," Baruch interrupted. "But even I was taken aback by the sheer force of this one. It was like the walls came crumbling down. My organs were squeezed to the point of rupture—I admit I was frightened. I can only begin to imagine what it must have been like for non-magicians."

The sincerity in his voice made Iris feel bad for scolding Auran. She looked at Merlow. "I knew it was a big spell, but why was it noticeable outside this room?"

"I think we both underestimated its effects. Remember, the room was protected to allow us to work undisturbed, but we were shifting the vibration of the entire gorge. It makes sense the energy impact was perceived throughout."

She nodded.

Auran and Baruch exclaimed in unison, "You changed our vibration?"

"What does that even mean?" Auran asked.

"Why?" Baruch demanded.

Iris shrugged. The intensity of the spells had taken up most of her energy, and the boost from Merlow's potion was wearing off fast. She wanted an hour of uninterrupted naptime. *That would be a first.*

She yawned. "I'm going to bed. Merlow will tell you what you need to know." Auran's look told her he knew they'd get a censored version.

"I'll walk with you," he said, grabbing her arm before she could protest. "I'll be right back, don't start without me," he added over his shoulder.

Baruch slid down the wall—too tired to stand. The spells had taken their toll on everyone. "Where is hot chocolate when you need it?"

"Indeed, you brought us precious cacao beans," Merlow said.

Baruch patted his satchel. "Now I just need equipment to prepare the heavenly beverage."

Iris halted at the doorway. "How's Basil doing?"

"He is still asleep," Baruch said. "And so very pale."

"We stationed one of the guards in the infirmary to alert us when Basil wakes or takes a turn for the worse," Auran said.

They walked to her chamber in silence. Auran steered her away from everyone who looked like they were about to ask a question. When Jacob stepped up, Auran held up his hand, "Not now."

Once they were in her room, Auran sat her down and asked, "What was that all about?"

The confusion must've shown on her face.

"You and Merlow, casting spells together, bringing the place down. We need to be low profile! What were you thinking?" Auran started pacing the room.

Iris was so tired she could barely remember what the spells had been for in the first place. "I need sleep. I can't even think straight. I'll tell you after." She lay down.

"I'll stay here," he said harshly.

"Hmmmm," she mumbled and fell right asleep.

•••••••••●•••••••••

Auran watched her breathing deepen. That she hadn't even tried to send him away told him she was beyond exhaustion.

He didn't want to admit how much the spell had shaken him.

What Baruch had described was just a portion of what he'd felt. It had gone through marrow and bone. At one point he was convinced he would split open like ripe fruit. The buzzing in his head was worrying as well, and it had only started to slowly subside a few minutes ago.

He wondered whether Iris and Merlow hadn't noticed because it was what they always experienced when casting a powerful spell. He preferred safeguarding and combat. Much more straightforward and something you could train for.

CHAPTER SEVENTY-ONE

Kaale Mountains

The next day Iris woke up with a pounding headache.

She wrinkled her nose at the moldy smell of the lichen growing ever-wider on her chamber walls. *I feel like I've been trampled by bison.* She pushed herself into a sitting position.

It came flooding back—shifting the vibration of the gorge, the intensity, the fatigue. She reached for her bound notebook, and meticulously added details about casting the twelve-layered spell.

Once Iris had captured all her insights, she put her pen down and gazed at Auran sleeping at the far end of her room. Ever since her own father had died, Auran had taken on the responsibility of looking out for her. She knew he did it out of more than his sense of duty...

She got up and stretched, hoping the circulation would lessen the aches and pains. *Perhaps I can brew something.* Although if today was anything like the past few days, she would be casting spells and needed her wits about her. *So, nothing to lessen the pain.*

Trevor stumbled in the next room and she hastened to hand him herbs for her porridge—to regain energy and strength. Most accidents with magicians happened when they'd been too tired to realize the significance of self-care.

When she got back Auran was waking up. Before he could reprimand her for last night's spell, she said, "Breakfast is nearly ready." Men and food was usually a soothing combination.

Auran relaxed visibly and she hid her smile. They ate in companionable silence. *Perhaps today we can brew healing potions to have in store.*

Jacob walked in with more color in his cheeks and radiating more of his usual energetic self. "I think Basil is getting worse. His breathing is heavier."

"Is he in pain?" Iris asked.

"I don't know. He's asleep. And there were three more arrows last night. No one was hurt but I thought there was something odd about them. I left them where they struck the rock."

"Tell me you didn't go the tower!" Auran demanded.

"I only peeked around the corner—wearing armor," Jacob said. "Someone had to be there."

Auran grumbled.

By Seth, the arrows. Iris had almost forgotten. She was eager to see what the arrow's path looked like with the shift in vibration. Also she should press Merlow for details on these arrows. "All right, let's have a look," Iris said. "I'll ask Baruch to check on Basil."

"Merlow!" Iris hollered as she walked in the hallway—not her usual style. She didn't care. She added a quick mental call to tell Merlow to meet her at the watchtower, and asked Baruch to care for Basil.

As she arrived at the tower—Auran in tow—she stopped short.

The three new arrows had been shot in an impeccable horizontal line, spaced with near-mathematical precision.

Merlow joined her and inhaled through his teeth.

Iris turned and saw the color drain from his face.

"Here or your room?" she asked.

"Let us get closer first," he said.

She realized he wanted to sample the energy around the arrows to check for lingering power. Iris and Merlow stalked up to the arrows, as if the projectiles could leap at them at any second. She wasn't sure why, but the precaution felt necessary.

In fact, she had to *force* herself to take a step closer. *By Seth!* She yanked Merlow's arm and pulled him back.

The middle arrow jumped off the wall, whizzing past where Merlow had stood a second before. The arrow turned, and Iris ducked to avoid the missile. Her heart hammered in her chest.

Right behind her Auran instinctively hurled up his alderwood shield. The arrow penetrated the wood—the shaft vibrating from impact. Auran peeked around the edge of his shield. The arrow stayed lodged.

He glanced at her and jumped into action—the commander incarnate. "Clear the tower, gather in the common room. Two guards per hallway. On the double!" Auran boomed.

Iris wondered whether the remaining two arrows would only be activated by someone with magical abilities, but she couldn't risk it. As guards rushed past them to the common room, Iris backed Merlow away and sat him down around the corner. "You need to tell me all you know about these arrows before someone gets killed. That was some scary magic."

Merlow's face tightened. "I toyed with a few ideas, some I do not even remember. The energy flowed so effortlessly at the time. Sometimes I altered spells while casting them. It was like a game twenty years into the future in some cave I had never perceived with my eyes. I never realized actual people could get hurt. It was just practice…

Like these three arrows—it seemed funny at the time. An arrow chasing after you like game of tag…"

Baruch came running. "It is Basil. He has trouble breathing."

Iris's heart plunged down her stomach.

She was torn between the arrows and Basil. Her gut told her the arrows posed the biggest threat. "We'll be right there. See if there's any remaining poison in his lungs and clear that out."

Baruch frowned.

"Not now!" she snapped.

Iris stood up and started pacing, struggling to control her magic. After a few turns she stopped in front of Merlow. "What else have you forgotten—you're not *that* old!" she spat.

He flinched.

"Will the other two arrows come chase us too?"

"They will only be activated by a magician. The arrow can solely be triggered by a powerful aura, so it is you, I and Baruch who must be careful. The guards will not get hurt."

Iris glared at him.

"Well, not by these arrows," he added. "I made sure no innocent person would set the arrows off."

"Tell me exactly how it works," Iris urged.

Merlow ruffled his white hair with both hands. "The chasing arrow is activated by the energetic field of a magician, and only when he or she is powerful enough. The other two had something extra, let me think…"

Merlow was silent for a while and Iris felt him transporting himself back in time, reliving the whole thing. That was a trick she never used—there was not much she wanted to reminisce about.

Merlow opened his eyes and the look on his face frightened her more than the arrows. *What had he devised?*

The air tremored just enough warning, and Iris slammed a shield in front of the remaining two arrows. With a loud thunk, the second arrow clattered on the floor. "I guess we're close enough to trigger them. Anything else they'll do?"

Merlow closed his eyes and uttered a spell, a strong one. He added another layer to her shield, and she realized he was fire-proofing it.

Gods no.

Flames pushed against her shield. Iris cringed at the sight of the blazing fire—her mother's chair loomed before her in an orange-red glow. The stench of scorched flesh penetrated her nose and her shield faltered.

"Focus!" Merlow barked.

No one's hurt. Not yet. She drew on her power and strengthened her shield.

She mindlinked with Auran. "Pull the guards from the hallway and barricade the rooms."

This is ridiculous. They were getting ready to fight Apex in what would be a huge battle and instead of preparing they were fending off these stupid arrows. If she hadn't known better, she would have suspected Thorn of setting up this diversion.

Iris braced herself against the wall. "Now what?"

"Let me ponder, but keep your shield firmly in place," Merlow said.

She heard a whoosh and the pressure on their combined shield increased. Iris could barely believe the enormous power had all been contained in a single arrow.

A shudder signaled the last arrow had been activated. She wasn't sure whether it was triggered by the flames, or had been set up to act last. An implosion sucked the air out of her lungs. She created a bubble around herself and searched for oxygen. The atmosphere was thick—her arms felt like they were wading through mud.

Iris stretched her awareness past the common room, the infirmary, her own room.

By Seth. The pressure on her lungs increased. She pushed farther, not allowing herself to get distracted by what this meant for Auran and the others.

Iris started to get lightheaded and fought down her panic.

Her magic stretched up to Merlow's room.

No air.

She sensed the nudge of a mindlink—Auran. *Not now!*

Her lungs burned, and Iris forced her reach to extend to the hotroom.

There! A pocket of air. Iris pulled the oxygen toward herself and filled her bubble, breathing in deeply.

She wanted to call out to Baruch to have him monitor the stability of the rocks, but with the shield, her bubble and lack of oxygen, she didn't dare add another action. *I have to trust Baruch will do what is needed.*

Iris extended her bubble to Merlow, surprised he hadn't created his own.

Merlow took a gulp of air and continued working on what must be the counter spell.

Iris shook her head. It was reckless of him to forgo oxygen, trusting his ability to complete the spell before he passed out.

Slowly the pressure lessened. Wiggling her jaw cleared her ears. She was hesitant to release the bubble. *We need to check for gases first.* Iris added an extra protective layer to withstand the weight of tumbling rocks. It would hold—for a while.

"Are the arrows done now?" she asked. "Or can we expect more surprises?"

Merlow shook his head to indicate the worst was over.

Iris pushed herself off the wall and strode to the watchtower. The flames had been largely contained by their shield. The afterburn had blackened part of the rock wall, now smeared with greasy soot.

All that was left of the arrows was ashes.

She was furious at Merlow for not telling her sooner, at herself for not seeing the urgency and forcing him to speak up. The anger boiled inside her and she knew she needed to calm down.

She set up a mindlink with Auran. "The coast is clear. Are you okay?"

"NO! Basil isn't breathing. You must come!"

What?!

Iris sprinted to the infirmary, jumping over a few passed-out guards, knowing from the strength of their auras they'd be fine in a few minutes.

Baruch stood next to Basil's bed—the strong man's aura now with barely a hint of green. Auran hovered on the opposite side.

Iris shoved Baruch aside and put her hand on Basil's chest to examine him. She searched for his life force and barely found a glimmer. "Get Merlow!"

"Fetch Merlow's herbs, Auran," Iris urged.

"Which ones?"

"Just grab all of them! And bring some lemon oil!"

Auran cursed.

She focused her attention back on Basil. "Open his mouth," she instructed Baruch.

Iris stirred the air in the room and directed it toward Basil's open mouth. She forced the breeze down his lungs, willing him to absorb the oxygen. With her hands she steadily pressed his chest—starting the resuscitation.

She kept a continuous flow of air going in and out of his lungs. Pacing it according to her own breathing, falling into a rhythm. *Dear Seth and Layla, please help.*

She sensed Merlow by her side.

He assessed her actions and placed a hand on Basil's forehead.

Auran barged in. "Here are the herbs." He threw an armful of sachets on Jacob's bed.

"Look for a purple one," Merlow instructed.

Auran handed Merlow a plum-colored bag. "I also found lemon oil," Auran said.

"Open it and hold the bottle under his nose," Iris ordered.

Auran moved to the other side of the bed and unscrewed the cap.

"Hold it sideways so you don't block his mouth."

Auran nodded.

Iris smelled the lemon. It was one of her favorite scents, but today it couldn't uplift her spirits.

"What else can we do?" she asked Merlow.

"Clear the room," Merlow said.

Iris jerked her head up.

"You should stay," Merlow clarified.

Auran and Baruch left.

She looked expectantly at Merlow.

"I shall invoke the presence of my mentor."

Crossed-over souls could only assist when it was for the greater good—never for personal gain.

It's worth a shot.

Merlow murmured an incantation.

The hair rose on the back of Iris's neck.

She sensed a presence and in the corner of her eye the air shimmered.

The former Master Magician spoke to them mind-to-mind. *You should not have called. This soul is on its way to the light. His spirit is bound to the afterlife. The life force will not return to this physical body.*

Iris's shoulders drooped.

The voice continued, *You cannot atone for your deeds by bringing him back, Merlow. You know the rules. The afterlife cannot be used for personal gain. You are to face the consequences.*

A tendril of air caressed Iris's cheek. She watched as the shimmering died away.

Merlow's shoulders shook.

Iris grabbed Basil's hand, still warm and supple. Tears streamed down her face.

She sensed the men hover around the corner and called, "Auran, Jacob!"

They shuffled in. The color of their auras told Iris they already knew.

Auran and Jacob moved to the opposite side of Basil's bed, clutching the blankets for support.

Baruch waited at the foot of the bed, at a respectful distance.

The silence stretched—heavy with despondency and disbelief.

"May Ayna take him in," Iris whispered, hands out.

The others echoed her.

CHAPTER SEVENTY-TWO

Kaale Mountains

Iris's hands dangled next to her body, useless.

Auran eyed her. "Walk with me."

"No."

He gave her a stern look, and she knew he was right. She was too explosive right now, and he had a knack for calming her down.

They marched over to the hotroom.

Iris didn't trust herself to speak calmly, so she kept quiet, not wanting to distress the rest of the guards further.

She pulled up a soundproof shield and started pacing the room. A deep pain ached inside her.

"What happened?" Auran asked.

"Merlow has been experimenting. In the past," she hastened to add. "Today we saw some of his very impressive handiwork. It's really genius, and terrifying…" She trembled, closing her eyes. "The cruelty, of burning people alive, suffocating them…I would never have thought of that. He…he must have been immensely powerful."

"We need to figure out how we can use this to our advantage," Auran said.

Iris glanced at him, not sure how to voice her feelings. The frustration, the disappointment, the sadness for lives surely lost—inevitability hung over her like a thundercloud.

She wished there was a way forward without the uprising. Knowing she didn't have a choice didn't make it easier.

Auran opened his arms and she stepped into them—relishing the comfort of his embrace. For the length of this hug she could pretend all was well. She leaned her head on his welcoming chest and took a deep breath, feeling his warmth and his sturdiness. His sandalwood and cinnamon scent always reminded her of home.

Sobs shook her. She cried for all that might've been, for afternoons in the meadow, the embrace of her parents, a life void of so much pressure, her little brother Thom.

Auran held her as if it was the most normal thing in the world. As if they stood like this every day, as if she cried in his arms often.

The tears streamed down her face and with it the anxiety, the fear, stress and frustration seeped out. After a few minutes her tears dried up and she squeezed Auran to thank him.

She felt cleansed almost. Lighter. *This is the second time I've cried in his arms.*

Iris looked up at Auran and knew he thought the same. Well, best not make this a habit. People might come to think she was weak. Not that she was afraid Auran would tell anyone—but walls had ears.

CHAPTER SEVENTY-THREE

Arbres

E ven after several weeks the scent of lavender still overpowered Sourni.

She tried breathing through her mouth only. *How is it possible to detest a fragrance so lovely?*

Silk pouches filled with the purple herb were scattered throughout Her Eminence's lavish rooms to help Her relax and calm down—in the hopes of preventing another anxiety attack.

Marie complained the palace gardens weren't producing lavender fast enough to keep up with the rate at which She ran through them. The head seamstress had nothing left to fill the monogrammed sachets with.

Sourni tiptoed past the colossal four-poster bed—royal blue silk curtains still drawn—and into the imposing bathing chamber. She was grateful for her near silent slippers on the polished marble floor. *My sandals would've made a ruckus.*

She smiled at the thought and reached for the pink salt, mined in Phortàk, and carefully measured three and a quarter cups. No one else dared draw Her Eminence a bath. The balance of salt and water had to be perfect. Enough salt for Her to feel less heavy, but not enough to float.

Sourni stirred the salt in the claw-foot tub, making sure the pink substance was distributed evenly in the tepid water. Temperature was of the utmost importance, too.

She rearranged the cosmetic jars into a straight line on the limestone sink, and replaced the creamy soft towels while the bath filled. One final check proved everything impeccable. She carefully opened the bathroom door and headed back to Her Eminence's antechamber, noticing the heap of laundry in the corner of her eye. Only two dresses were hanging in Her closet. *Holy Pears. I need to alert Marie—she needs to hurry up with that new dress.* Sourni was startled by someone's voice.

"Did You receive my flowers?"

Apex?! Here? Sourni froze, breathing as shallowly as possible.

"Yes, they were—lovely," Her Eminence answered.

"I had my men fetch them for You specially from Your family's rose garden."

Oh no.

"The estate is still protected. The gardens flourish under the capable hands of my priests. You can visit anytime," Apex continued.

No, no, no, no, no!

Sourni heard glass fall to the floor and shatter.

I hope that wasn't the crystal heirloom.

"Are You all right?"

Sourni suppressed a gasp at the tenderness in Apex's voice. For a moment she was torn between rescuing Her Eminence and avoiding detection.

Instinct won. She backtracked and fumbled for the bathroom door.

"You smell lovely," Apex crooned.

Sourni delayed her gag long enough to softly close the door behind her.

CHAPTER SEVENTY-FOUR

Kaale Mountains

I ris slept fitfully that night after Basil died. Fragments of the day tortured her awake. Auran tossed and turned as well.

Eventually she gave up—everyone's emotions were too palpable, even in her room.

Merlow's comment had stayed with her: "We need you fully in control."

Part of her was afraid to unleash her power, but another part longed for the riveting flow she'd experienced during the twelve-layered spell. Her body quivered. *To live without restraint...*

If not now, when? Iris strode to the hotroom and sealed herself inside, containing the magic within the chamber. She linked her power to the pipes, and said a prayer to Seth and Layla. *Please have the pipes absorb my magic. I'll make it quick.*

Iris took a deep breath and connected to the center of the Earth to ground herself. She let the power well up inside her—filling her chest and pouring out. She started with a simple spell, strengthening the upholding of the pipes. *Might as well be practical.*

All too soon, the new pipes were securely fastened. *This should hold for several days.* Iris observed the hotroom, searching for another spell to invoke. Her eyes found the jagged spot where she'd stared after crying in Auran's arms. *Basil.* Grief welled up inside her.

No! She panicked.

You can't be sad when you work magic! ...a blackened corpse... Focus!

Iris breathed heavily—reeling her magic back in. But she'd called forth too much of her power. It was impossible to cork now.

Think! The only incantation that came to mind was to shield. Iris threw her power into her shield—fine-tuning it to perfection. Her control returned, her breathing normalized. A raw form of magic was usually used for shielding. The protection had to hold—there was no need for prettiness.

What if I make my shield visible? Thinking of her mother, Iris let a rose-blush pink bleed into the shield—coloring it all girly. She chuckled, imagining what the men would say. *Father.* She let the color morph to indigo. Squinting through her eyelashes, she could imagine Phillip Strongtide's aura lighting up the room. She sighed.

With more use of her power she erased the color of the shield. *What else?* Iris was afraid to create a new spell, though she was tempted to try something with eight layers or more. She settled for using two back-to-back seven-layer spells, to smooth and then strengthen the granite walls. *No more stones poking in my back.*

Iris planted her feet firmly on the floor—spaced parallel to her shoulders. She started the first layer and moved effortlessly into the second. She fell into the rhythm of casting the spell and danced from the third layer into the fourth and the fifth. Smiling, she funneled more power into the spell—establishing the sixth layer. *The seventh is always tricky.* Iris paused and observed the creation in her mind's eye.

The sixth layer was asymmetrical.

Oops. So much for having too much fun. She ran through the last piece in her mind, searching for a place to restore balance. There was only one part she dared alter. Iris cast the seventh layer with full focus—her senses on high alert should the spell crumble. *Good thing I reinforced my shield.*

She watched with a hawk's eye as the last layer fell into place. The enchantment wobbled for a moment—then found its footing like a sailor shaking off his sea legs.

Yes! Iris jumped in excitement. Then automatically toned herself down.

She eyed the pipes—they absorbed the backlash well enough. The room was less chilly. *I could use this system in my chamber, too.*

Iris started on the second, more advanced, spell—fortifying the walls. She pulled up more power and set it to a constant trickle. The energy flowed out of her, changing form as it submitted to the spell. When she reached the third layer, an image of Basil hovered in front of her.

It took all her willpower to stay in control of the magic. Tears streamed down her face when she thought of Basil's timid smile. Her body shook, and she blinked away the salty substance.

She wrestled through the third layer—grateful Merlow had insisted she'd learn to cast spells while speaking the incantation only in her mind.

Iris was pulled in two, her power clawing against the wall of her grief. Releasing her magic was not an option but neither was shutting out her pain. Not anymore.

She struggled through the fourth layer on experience—and reached a dead end.

It seemed there was no other alternative than to implode. She thanked the Gods for the foresight of sealing off the room.

And surrendered.

Grief rushed forward—flooding her. *It's my fault.* If she hadn't delegated healing Basil to Baruch, or hadn't gone to check out those arrows...

Sadness overwhelmed her and touched other, deeper parts— activating a chain reaction. Thom, Mama, Theresa, Father.

The responsibility of making her life count...Iris emptied her stomach on the rough granite floor.

Magic streamed out of her unchecked, swirling through the chamber. The pressure increased, both inside her physical body and outside. The pipes groaned under the strain.

This is it.

Images of her loved ones danced in front of her—encouraging her to hold on. To try.

When is it ever enough?

Iris hauled herself up, suddenly angry. "Why?" she raged. "Why did you all leave me? It's not fair!" Her fury surged through her—battling for space with her magic. She swelled like a balloon—the strain squeezing her windpipe shut. Her hands flew to her neck, willing her throat to open.

She thought back of encouraging the breath to return to Basil's motionless body.

Magic! On the fly, Iris crafted a spell to force the pressure aside, allowing the oxygen flow to return.

She inhaled deeply and coughed. Her airways were free, but the rest of her body bloated further. The air in front of her shimmered with the rise in temperature. She was lucky there was nothing in the hotroom she could burn. *Nothing other than myself.*

I refuse to be incinerated! Iris gritted her teeth and maintained the precarious balance between emotion and magic.

I wish I could burn away the pain.

What if...?

Iris grabbed hold of her magic and seized the fire that was about to burst forth. She increased the temperature of her magic to a white-hot flame—and aimed it directly at her emotions.

Pain seared through her, ripping stored emotions from her spine, her shoulder blades, her mind, even her legs. A big chunk of repressed sorrow was scorched from her abdomen.

The flame purified her emotional body, freeing up room for her cells to resume their original duties.

Iris knelt, braced on her hands, breathing heavily from both the effort of controlling her magic and the intense ache of release. Sweat dripped down her face and her back.

Finally the flame died down, having run out of emotions to burn.

Iris sagged and rolled on her back to relish the coolness of the stone floor.

She took deep, full breaths and was amazed at the lightness of her body. A weight had literally been lifted.

IRIS WOKE UP and blinked. *Where am I?*

She glanced at the wall and noticed an intricate network of pipes. *The hotroom.*

Sitting up, she rubbed her lower back. Her body throbbed in places she didn't even know she had. *At least it's comfortably warm.*

Iris stretched her awareness. *It's just after sunrise.*

Her magic stirred as if her demonstration had been but an appetizer. However, this time it was more a beckoning than a command.

She got up and grounded herself—curious to see how her power might be different with her newfound balance. She was reminded of her father's visitation, a long time ago in the forest. *This is what he meant.* An integration of her magic. She realized she'd always seen her magic as an invader of her body.

Iris drew on her magic and it came with ease—none of the stress that usually surfaced. The backlash poured gracefully into the pipes.

Now she was wielding the magic, instead of yielding to it. She reveled in her sense of control. Marveled at the ease with which she shaped the deathly current running through her veins. Hot liquid coursed through her blood vessels—propelled forward with each pump of her heart.

A smile spread on her face. Being able to work magic while staying in touch with her emotions opened possibilities. *I can't wait to tell Auran.*

She checked the fastening of the pipes. The strain of the spells she'd used before falling asleep had loosened them from the wall in one or two places. With ease, she secured the pipes firmly.

Once they'd discovered a way to remove Thorn's impenetrable shields, she would be the one to kill Apex. Sourni had already spotted one of the high priest's weaknesses.

Iris had always avoided fully realizing what it would mean to deliberately take someone's life. *I can no longer postpone facing the inevitable.*

She blew out a breath—anticipating a destabilization of her magic. Nothing happened. *Huh.*

Thanks to Merlow's stories and what she'd seen in the abandoned village she had a clear visual of Thorn. She might have to eliminate him in order to get to Apex. Her stomach contracted.

Then she remembered all the lives ended prematurely thanks to Apex and Thorn. *Them I can kill.*

Her magic stirred. *Best practice some more.*

She looked around for inspiration. *I wish we had more light.*

Iris closed her eyes and commanded her power. She used part of the spell Merlow had used to create lighting in the cave, and tailored it to her brand of magic.

She concentrated fiercely and willed a spark of light into being.

From behind her eyelids, she noticed a minute increase in brightness. Her eyes flew open and Iris stared at the spark in her hand—enraptured.

CHAPTER SEVENTY-FIVE

Kaale Mountains

Despite the hour, Merlow was awake—the wall a crutch for his leaning body. He slowly met Iris's eyes. "I wish I could go back in time."

Iris sat on the floor and observed her teacher for a few minutes.

"What were you thinking?" she asked. "You were the only one with the counter-curse and you forgot to get oxygen first? If I hadn't been there to supply you with air, we might've all suffocated."

Merlow blanched.

"It was completely irresponsible and contradictory to everything you've ever taught me!"

"It is testimony to your magic you were able to reach beyond the borders of the spell," Merlow said quietly. "I knew I would never get to air quickly enough so I focused all my powers on the counter-curse."

Oh. She'd encountered resistance when she was searching for air, and almost panicked. But her instincts had taken over. She'd simply pulled the pocket of air toward herself. If she'd felt even a hint of the impossibility of her task... "That was one deadly spell you cast."

Merlow's aura was palest yellow. "I have done things I am not proud of. I should have been more forthcoming about the arrows— I put everyone in danger. And Basil...I shall never forgive myself." Merlow shook his head. "Auran and Jacob should hear this too."

After breakfast they convened in Merlow's room.

Merlow cleared his throat. "I owe you an explanation.."

Auran, Jacob, and Iris waited—their silence heavy.

"The atmosphere at the camp was extremely competitive. The Gemini Squad lined up day after day to hit their mark and exceed their goals. They joked about using my abilities to increase the havoc wreaked by the arrows, and I took it as a challenge to exceed their expectations…"

He sighed deeply. "One night we were waiting for confirmation the arrows had arrived—it was the second or third batch—"

THE CAPTAIN OF the Gemini Squad had poked Merlow's arm. "What if you create an arrow that births other arrows? Surprise!"

"Yeah, like a knocked-up arrow!" A redheaded archer leered, thrusting his hips suggestively.

The men howled with laughter around the fire.

"Or one that sucks away all the oxygen?" Lord Ashen suggested with a wave of his long fingers, the copper buttons on his coat glinting in the light of the fire.

"Have everyone puke their guts out!" the redhead yelled.

The captain clapped him on the shoulders. "Like you did last night?"

"Oho, he's on to you ginger!"

"Merlow, can you spread disease with an arrow?" the captain asked.

Before Merlow could respond, a tall archer said, "Yeah, strike those bastards from a distance and disrupt their entire system."

"The enemy would collapse under the constant threat—never knowing when or where they might be hit," the captain had added. "They would lose sleep, patrolling all the time, worrying about what might happen. You should look into that, Merlow."

"No," Iris said, pale as a sheet against the granite wall.

Merlow looked at her. "Most of these things were beyond the bounds of possibility. I either did not have the herbs or the time to conjure a reliable spell. But I completed two."

A twenty-two-years-younger Merlow held up two arrows in his fist. The flames of the campfire crackled, welcoming him into the circle of archers. The men clapped, cheering loudly and clinking half-empty wine bottles.

Two archers picked Merlow up, the muscles on their back rippling, and carried him on their shoulders around the fire.

"We're the deadliest squad on Earth!" someone shouted.

Merlow tipped his head back, soaking up their praise.

They set him down in front of the captain, who held out his hand for the arrows.

Merlow carefully handed him the projectiles. "Do not touch the tips."

The captain weighed the arrows in his palm. "What do these beauties do?"

Merlow beamed. "This one"—he pointed at the left arrow—"carries an extremely potent poison."

The captain handed the arrows right back.

Merlow suppressed a smile. "Oleander nectar. Once the arrow pierces flesh, the effects are immediate. The injured will start sweating, vomiting and lose consciousness, followed by respiratory paralysis and death."

The archers roared. "Take that!" the redhead hooted.

"And the second one?" the captain demanded.

Merlow eyed the arrow. "This is its malevolent brother. The venom is highly acidic and extremely painful. It will not only slow your heart—like the normal poison—but erode your skin."

"Aiee," one of the archers said.

"No amount of magic healing will reverse the process. Once the venom touches someone's body, it is already too late to salvage them."

"Let's shoot them now!" Lord Ashen said. He grabbed both arrows and walked up to the captain and the redhead—their two best marksmen. "Get your bows."

Both men lined up and nocked their arrows. Slowly they drew their bows.

Merlow felt them gather magic, and his own power stirred in response.

The two archers yelled the command and Merlow automatically began the time-traveling invocation. Once the archers released, he'd sent his magic along—assuring the arrows' safe arrival twenty years from now.

Iris gasped. "Those arrows are coming *here*?"

Auran shot to his feet, ready to fend them off right this minute.

Merlow did not dare look Iris in the eye. "I am afraid so."

"Are you absolutely sure?" Auran demanded.

"Well, the archers had been drinking. But the arrows were loosed by the best of the best. They will not be off by more than a few meters." He shook his head. "I was a fool. I did not want those arrows to be released. I only wanted to prove I could create them. I should have known they would not hesitate. It was not until the little girl died…"

Merlow glanced at Auran and Jacob—the strongest fighters of their group. He saw understanding dawn in their eyes. Iris was not so forgiving. Her bright eyes pierced right through him—seeing straight into his soul.

CHAPTER SEVENTY-SIX

Kaale Mountains

Iris was torn, impressed by Merlow's abilities to cast such sophisticated spells, and appalled he'd actually done it. Disgust won, but part of her understood his desire to test his own skills.

Auran rubbed his hands over his face. "Their talent is impressive. Attacking your enemy from a distance," he glanced at Jacob, "holds a lot of potential. But by Seth, to be on the receiving end…"

Jacob leaned back against the wall. "So many coincidences. What if the archers hadn't been drinking, or what if Merlow hadn't brought the arrows with him?" He pushed himself off the wall. "When are these arrows due to arrive?"

Merlow sighed deeply. "I cannot begin to apologize—"

Auran broke in. "What's done is done. How can we contain the damage? Can you dismantle the spell or counteract it somehow?" He leaned forward, willing Merlow to fix it.

"I am afraid not," Merlow said. "Sadly, I was thorough. If there were a way to undo it, I would have found it by now."

"Okay," Iris said. "We've got a shield to deflect the arrows, and keep everyone out of harm's way—as long as they hit the same place. If they don't…will these arrows pierce armor?"

Merlow held up his hands. "Let us not go straight to mending. First, I must know where I stand, what you think of me." He paused. "Can you still trust me?"

Auran spoke. "I couldn't wish for a wiser man to guide us through these trying times. I think you've made up for your mistakes as much as possible. Who you are will have to be enough."

"Amen to that," Jacob said.

"I can't absolve you of your deeds," Iris said. *Even though it was an accident—Theresa was still dead.* "You need to find peace with the choices you made. I'm not saying it's easy. I still have nightmares from what I've caused."

Auran flinched, but she kept speaking. "I don't judge you for something you foolishly did more than twenty years ago…. I know you've grown into a different person, perhaps even because of that experience. I know I trust you with my life."

Merlow blinked away tears. "I have feared this moment for years, having to share my deeds. Thank you, truly."

"Let's get Baruch," Auran said. "Figure out how to minimize the damage."

Jacob asked, "Do I need to be here for that?"

"Yes!" both Iris and Merlow spoke simultaneously.

"You think as a warrior and an architect," Iris added. "Let's tackle this together. It's complex enough as it is."

"I just wanted to make sure we weren't wasting time," Jacob said timidly.

Iris felt like hugging him. He really had no idea how valuable his contributions were. "There could be nothing more important," she said decisively. "I also want to ask the Earth Faerie. She has ways of understanding how this planet operates beyond what we can comprehend, and she has access to different magic."

Iris took a moment to still her thoughts before reaching out. Jacob shuffled in his spot—he was never comfortable when things got too magical.

The Earth Faerie replied quickly, like she'd been waiting. "What is the matter, child? The room you are in exudes worry, concern and regret."

The Faeries can read minds via mindlink as well?

Forcing the thought aside, Iris said, "We would like your

insight. First, do you detect any structural damage to the cave from the fire last night?"

"Your power has expanded greatly. The rush of cool oxygen against heated rock caused a hairline fissure we must observe."

Oh.

Iris explained the arrows. "Do you want to join our discussion?"

Moira responded, "I will create a portal so I may come in person. Then you will not have to translate our mental communication."

Good.

Baruch entered the room. "You sent for me?"

"Yes. We'll meet with the Earth Faerie in an hour."

His eyes gleamed. "I look forward to it."

Iris checked in with Sourni. "We'll keep it quick, but we had to know if you have news."

"Her Eminence left this morning for Phortàk," Sourni said. "She will stay at the mineral baths for Her health. She's not expected to return for a few days, but She has a habit of prolonging Her visits, as She detests traveling."

Something nagged Iris.

She took a walk around the hallways to stretch her legs, and get a feel for the atmosphere. Since they were stuck underground, she wanted to stay abreast of what people might need. When she passed the infirmary, she paid a silent tribute to Basil. *We need to figure out where to bury him.* The smoke a pyre generated would attract too much attention. She began to push the hollow feeling down, then stood still and let the emotion pass through her—enduring the bereavement.

The off-duty guards were clustered in the common room, and the active guards hovered in the tower—all avoiding the infirmary. Their tension rippled toward Iris in waves. She would ask Merlow about serving a relaxing herbal tea for those whose wished extra support to keep grounded and focused. *I would like some, too.*

Iris circled back to Merlow's room and a tingling prickled her neck. She spun around as the Earth Faerie approached. There was no mistaking her—from her chestnut hair and moss-green eyes to the raw silk robe she wore, her groundedness was tangible. Power simmered beneath her skin. This was someone to reckon with, but for her broad, warm smile.

After everyone met—Iris had particularly enjoyed the surprise on Baruch's face, towering over her, his eyes flitting to the Faerie's back—the Earth Faerie turned to Iris. "You have changed, dear one," she said with apparent satisfaction. "You have gone through yet another stage. I can feel the power building up inside—you are ready for the culmination of your priesthood."

What? Iris had no idea what the Earth Faerie was referring to, nor did she have any desire to become a priestess. Her disinterest showed on her face.

"Not your kind of priests," the Earth Faerie added with a sly smile. "We will welcome you into our order. You have a task to carry out that will cross dimensions. It was prophesied long ago. Your becoming a Faerie priestess allows for a cooperation that has not been seen in ages."

Iris knit her brows.

"There is a reason you can hold so much power, so much that things go up in flames," Moira added.

Iris paled. Auran cursed under his breath.

The Earth Faerie ignored his response. "You have been prepared, Iris. In the last few days you were tested."

Iris felt like a puppet on strings, like someone else was deciding her fate again.

"Wait a minute," Auran said. "What does Faerie priestess mean exactly? Will she owe you anything, or is she obliged to protect your realm?"

I can always count on Auran to have my back.

"It does not mean she chooses us over you humans," the Earth Faerie answered with disdain. "Yet it allows us to communicate without restraint—"

Does that mean I can finally read their minds, too?

"—and enables Iris to move freely between our dimensions while drawing power from them. That will prove crucial in the upcoming battle. She will need places to hide, and to secure each dimension before Thorn attempts to command them himself."

"What's the downside?" Iris asked.

"Once you accept, you become a priestess for life. Even after the war is over we may call upon you when we need your support." She nodded at Auran.

"And?" Iris said.

"We expect our priestesses to focus solely on their calling."

What's the catch? Iris bit her lower lip. "Seriously?"

Moira inclined her head.

Iris turned to Auran. He blanched, pursing his own lips in response. Iris's heart dropped into her stomach. *Do I even have a choice?* She'd secretly hoped she might find a way to love and conceive without passing on her curse. It was highly unlikely she'd survive the war, but this would be irreversible. The Faeries were never lenient.

"When do I have to decide?" Iris asked, dreading the answer.

"As I spoke the words, the sacred twenty-three hours started. After tomorrow, the window is closed forever—we do not offer second chances," the Earth Faerie said.

Gods forbid I'll get bored. Iris faced Auran.

His eyes conveyed he'd support her choice, but willed her to consult with him before she decided.

Iris nodded—they would talk. She wished her mindreading skills worked on the Faeries, too—something big was missing. She pushed her hair back. "Let's put this priestess thing aside for now and focus on the arrows."

"These challenges are connected," Moira added, pride ringing through her voice. "As a Faerie priestess, you would have more options with which to fight."

In the corner of her eye Iris noticed Merlow frown—he didn't want to be responsible for weighing the scales in favor of the Faeries. Well, she wasn't going to be forced into hurrying this major decision. Iris spoke, her voice laced with steel, "Since I have not yet decided, I suggest we look at 'options' that are available now."

She caught a glimpse of Auran's smile, but forced her own face deadpan when she turned to the Earth Faerie. *Two can play this game.* Appreciation flickered in Moira's eyes.

CHAPTER SEVENTY-SEVEN

Kaale Mountains

Merlow spoke. "I have pondered these arrows for years. Our only option is to seal off the watchtower. Even if the archers were less on target due to alcohol, both arrows will land in the proximity of the tower."

"Let's assume we find a way to close that area off. How do we contain the horror inside? What if some goat herder stumbles upon the arrows six months from now?" Iris asked.

After a moment, Baruch spoke tentatively. "It reminds me of an Amazonian legend—a way to strengthen everyone's immune system so the poison cannot harm them, a way to make them resistant."

"Like a vaccination?" Merlow asked?

"I do not know what a vaccination is," Baruch said.

"It is something the scientists developed before the Cataclysm," Merlow said. "No one has been able to reproduce it."

"Go on," Iris encouraged Baruch.

"As part of my training I was required to memorize the formula." Baruch grimaced. "You gather under a full moon and collect the herbs you need, as they will be most potent. You let the herbs simmer in pure water collected from a sacred stream by a virgin."

Auran cocked his head.

"The village elder will sieve the concoction and seal it in a silver bottle. The potion must ripen for three days before it can be ingested. The fire must be built with branches from an elder tree, and the five magical ingredients are stardust, laymen's kiss, coriander, holy blue and star anise."

Baruch looked up, as if he dared anyone to comment. He continued softly, "The next full moon you gather under the biggest tree in the village. You hold hands and chant as you dance a sacred dance." He gestured, indicating it was impossible to explain the intricacy of the dance moves.

"At the height of the dance, the village elder will pass around the bottle, and everyone will take a sip. You can feel the energy move through the village—protecting everyone from harm."

Iris almost felt the warmth of the fire and the intensity of the dancers. She swore she saw a glimmer of the fire reflected in Baruch's eyes.

She suppressed a shiver. Ancient legends held strong powers.

The magic broke as Baruch blinked.

Auran rolled his shoulders, as if to release the tangible energy in the room.

Merlow stroked his beard. Iris recognized it as his way to untangle formulas.

"There is often a lot of truth in stories," Merlow said. "What you call holy blue is known as forget-me-nots. Lots of power is contained in that plant. It actually does what it suggests—a friend once told me," he added absentmindedly. "Stardust is similar to ours. Laymen's kiss though, do you know what it resembles?" he asked Baruch.

Baruch blushed—you would think Merlow had asked him to strip down naked.

"Come on," Auran nudged him. "It can't be worse than the unicorns."

This made Iris sit up. *When ever had they come across unicorns?*

Baruch's orange aura flared. He closed his eyes and blurted. "A laymen's kiss is the first time a magician kisses a girl after his initiation. It is traditionally done right after the ceremony, and ideally by a girl who has never been kissed to add potency. The kiss must take place in the center of the circle, overseen by the village elder. There is no privacy." The last bit sounded like he was criticizing the process, even after all this time, and with no little frustration.

Baruch cleared his throat. "The kiss lasts thirty seconds and the village elder collects a sample of the girl's blood afterwards—rife with pheromones. That is the recipe for the laymen's kiss."

Iris understood his hesitancy to share, and also why the ingredient was pretty rare.

"What if the magician is a woman?" Merlow asked. "Is there any literature on that?"

Iris snorted. *Literature.* As if any of this were written down.

Merlow looked at her with disdain—eyebrows raised—indicating she was missing the point.

Oh Seth, this means trouble. Her blood chilled. *What is he thinking?*

The Earth Faerie giggled, and it dawned on Iris. *Gods no.*

Merlow held up his hand to silence her before she could object, and he looked pointedly at Baruch.

"I do not recollect instances where the roles were reversed—or combined, but I do not see why that could not work," Baruch mused aloud. "As long as the girl is unkissed..."

Iris took a few steps back until the rock wall embraced her.

Auran cast worried glances at her.

"The other ingredients are uncomplicated," Merlow added, ignoring her discomfort.

"Even if we could collect all the ingredients," Iris said, emphasizing how unlikely that was. "This concoction takes three days to brew—the full moon is in two days. We can't wait for the next full moon. The arrows could arrive any day now—we can't risk the potion not working."

Merlow looked at her as if staring down a recalcitrant child. "Could you leave us for a moment please?" he asked the others.

Moira left with a knowing smile, Baruch looked guilty and Auran and Jacob cast concerned glances over their shoulders.

Merlow pulled up a soundproof barrier. "I am truly sorry," he said. "I do not wish to cause you any more harm. I know this is my fault, yet I see no other way. I feel in my bones Baruch's concoction shall work, and I know you do too."

Iris didn't object because he was right.

"That is a miracle in itself. At times like this I believe there is a higher power who oversees us—steering us in the right direction. A few days ago we would not have known this."

Wouldn't that have been great.

"Thanks to Baruch we have access to his wisdom, and to me that means we must use it. Although I know it will cost you dearly." He paused, then asked hesitantly. "Am I correct to assume you have never been kissed?"

Frustration roared in Iris's head. She wanted to kick something. Her anger rose to the surface, but no longer threatened to burn through her self-restraint. She started pacing out of habit nonetheless.

This is so unfair. She'd always avoided intimacy—not knowing what the emotions might do to her self-control—because she feared she wouldn't have the strength to abstain once she'd tasted the forbidden fruit.

Iris clenched her fists. The idea alone of her having to kiss Auran—of course it had to be him—and under Merlow's supervision…

It was humiliating.

But more—she knew she had to cut Auran loose soon. She was terrified kissing him would break her heart—and his—and that it would impact her powers or her accuracy. *I can afford neither.*

Risking injury to others because she refused to make this sacrifice—or bear the pain—was unthinkable. Merlow knew it was an impossible question.

Her heart sank as Auran approached. She nodded to Merlow and he dropped the barrier, allowing Auran in.

Auran walked up to her and embraced her kindly. "Baruch explained it to me," he whispered gently in her ear. "Please don't feel like you need to save us. We'll find another way."

Iris drank in his fathomless eyes. He must know they were out of options. Even Baruch's concoction was grasping at straws—getting the timing right, trusting the accuracy of the story.

She shivered, thinking of the implications. It had to be done. "How much time do we have?" Without waiting for an answer, she kept firing questions at Merlow. "What do you have in mind to speed up the process? You know we can't wait another month. We need to be sure this will work in time, or it isn't worth the risk."

"I know," he said thoughtfully. "We might use the Faerie realm. Time progresses more swiftly there. We could have the potion steep in Faerieland and bring it back."

"What about water from a sacred stream? Who will collect that?" she asked.

Oh, I guess I will.

"Which stream did you have in mind?" Iris continued, while in her mind scanning the area for possible locations.

"I think we must use a sacred stream from the Faerie realm, which will add to the power. We cannot risk sending you else-where," Merlow said.

"I will come, too," Auran said decisively. "Where do we start?"

"It's going to be another full day," Iris said, feeling exhausted already. "The sacred water, the kiss, deciding on becoming a priestess," she ticked off on her fingers. "Sealing off the watchtower. Anything I missed?"

"I would feel better if we secured the tower area first," Auran said. "I will relocate the guards permanently."

"All right. We'll need Baruch for the spell," Iris said.

"I'll send him over," Auran said as he walked out.

"Wear your armor!" Iris called after him.

He held up his hand, indicating he'd heard her.

"Should we layer our spells to fortify them?" Iris asked Merlow.

He nodded.

Iris sat down and started a diagram, combining several spells to create an indestructible enchantment to seal in the arrows. It had to be airtight; it couldn't allow the poison to escape.

Baruch came in and stood over her shoulder. He pointed at the upper left corner of the chart. "We can strengthen this part with an air-shield."

Good thinking. Iris added the spell.

The three of them worked together until they were convinced the spell was fail-safe. One weak spot could collapse the entire enchantment under pressure.

They walked to the watchtower, past groups of guards in the corridor and common room. Their auras still showed signs of grief. Basil had been loved by all.

Auran stood at the edge of the hallway leading to the tower. There was only one road in. "We've evacuated all the guards."

Iris nodded, not wanting to break her concentration.

Merlow, Baruch and Iris positioned themselves in a triangle, to spread the power evenly.

On Merlow's cue they started their incantations. The power inside Iris built slowly. Energy radiated off Baruch as he laid down his spells. She sensed how he pulled energy from his surroundings. *His reach is impressive.*

Merlow was his usual, stable self. She focused on her own chants. The spells came with ease. The danger was in the correct order and balance of the layers.

Timing was crucial.

Iris waited for the men to catch up with her before she started the second layer.

She inhaled—forcing her mind to calm. The familiar buzzing of the energy got louder. She almost saw the shape of the spells in front of her, almost tasted the intensity of the magic on her tongue.

As she pulled off the last spell she noticed Baruch was behind.

Hurry! She stretched her vowels to coincide with the last words from Baruch and Merlow.

They looked at each other and when she nodded they completed their spell together.

A flash nearly blinded her. The pressure shifted as the spells fell into place.

They were blasted from the room.

Iris scrambled to pull her feet out of the way before the room sealed itself off entirely. *Oops.*

As they hurried out through the hallway, Iris cast a glance over her shoulder and saw the spell shimmer in the air. The different energies rubbed off one another: her blue, Merlow's yellow and Baruch's orange created a mini-rainbow. *Hmm.*

The three of them found Auran pacing at the entrance, relieved to see them. "Did it work?"

They nodded in unison, all still turned inward after the intensity of the spells and their co-creation.

Auran pulled some debris in front of the entrance so no one would walk into the spell. "The Earth Faerie left," he said, annoyed. "She claimed her work was done here and asked me to remind you of the deadline of accepting the honor of becoming a Faerie priestess." His face expressed how ludicrous he thought that was.

"You're quite the messenger," Iris said.

"There wasn't much else I could do, standing guard here."

As though that weren't enough.

CHAPTER SEVENTY-EIGHT

Kaale Mountains

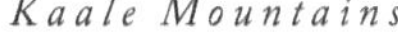

Iris sat with a sigh, relishing the smell of food. Working magic left her ravenous. Simply breathing the scent of broth and grains calmed her nervous system. She spooned down quinoa—the food soothed everyone.

She placed her empty bowl beside her on the floor. The men had already finished. "Sacred water first?"

"Yes," Merlow said. "We shall need permission from the Faerie Queen to enter their realm."

"Will you ask her?" Iris said.

"Certainly."

While Merlow set up a connection with the Faerie Queen, Iris settled against the wall, using her sleeping mat as a cushion.

I need to decide about becoming a Faerie priestess. She couldn't shake the thought there was something very valuable in it for the Faeries, too.

Iris realized the formal decision on whether she would lend herself for the laymen's kiss seemed already made. Her annoyance flared.

She knew she could put her foot down, but she would never risk so many lives. Somehow she felt coerced. Not intentionally, or at least not by anyone here, but she felt backed up against the wall. *I don't like it.*

"We are authorized," Merlow announced. "Both Iris and Auran will enter, and they will be escorted by the Earth Faerie and myself.

I will oversee the procedure and Moira will help us approach the stream without complications."

"All right, let's get to it," Iris said. She pulled on Auran's sleeve. "Whatever happens, don't leave my side." Saying so made her feel safer.

"I've got you," he said.

As an extra precaution Iris added an enchantment to keep herself and Auran connected, with a direct doorway back into this world. It was unusual, but she'd learned to trust her intuition.

They prepared themselves by drinking water as a means of transit and relaxing their minds in meditation. For Merlow and Iris this took a matter of minutes, but Auran needed longer.

Iris grasped Auran's hand to help him ground and slow down his breathing to align with her energy. After a while he sank into a meditative state. When they were all vibrating on theta waves, the physical portal opened.

Baruch monitored the connection on their end.

The Earth Faerie guided the gateway closer to the sacred stream. The only way to create such a specific portal was by having someone in Fae territory direct their energy. Humans could never transport themselves to such a precise location, not unless she were a Faerie priestess. *That's one of the main advantages—connecting to any place within the Faerie realm at will.*

"Step through on my mark," Merlow instructed. "Now."

The soft grass tickled Iris's feet immediately after leaving the hard stone floor. Surrounded by fresh air, they landed in the exact opposite of the gorge. It was light and warm where the cave had been cold and dusky, and full of green plants and flowing water where the gorge was filled with stagnant greys and browns. The entire atmosphere hummed with possibility—as if magic would fall out of the trees if she shook them. Dragonflies and butterflies danced in the sunlight and the flowers were bountiful. The freshness and vibrancy were contagious.

Auran whispered, "I can't blame anyone for wanting to be here."

Iris faced him in surprise.

He narrowed his eyes, and she knew he feared seeing this place might sway her into accepting the priesthood. He was well aware how much flowers made her heart sing.

Her gaze drifted to the beguiling hydrangeas underneath the canopy of fresh green leaves next to her. Iris stretched her arm and gently cupped the pale blue flower head—her heart panged.

"Welcome to Faerieland," Moira said warmly, a knowing smile on her face. "Iris, please walk with me to the stream. The men will have to stay ashore."

Auran observed her, and Iris squeezed his arm. *I'll be fine.* Protocol needed to be followed, and if the situation had been any different, they might not have had access to this stream.

Iris walked—almost bounced—across the lush green grass and took in the faint smell of roses. As she reached the waterfront, the Earth Faerie held out a hand to stop her. "Let us pray and ask the holy water permission to be taken away."

Moira folded her hands over her heart and Iris followed suit—they prayed silently.

When Iris looked up she noticed several priestesses scattered in the bushes alongside the stream, practically absorbed by their environment.

The Earth Faerie caught her eye. "They are here to partake in the ceremony and add strength."

Iris hadn't realized it was so official. *Do they ever do anything straightforwardly?*

"Clear your mind so you can enter the water pure," Moira instructed. "When you go into the creek, you must give first to be able to receive in return."

Clouds blocked out the sun. Iris pressed her lips together.

"Submerge yourself before you take out any water," Moira clarified.

Okay. Iris stepped forward into the water. It was colder than she'd expected. She waded to the middle, where the water came up to her chest, and glanced back.

Merlow nodded encouragingly.

Iris bent her knees and fully immersed herself.

The water felt peculiar—it had a different buoyancy. The creek was filled with freshwater, but it behaved like saltwater. *Very strange.* More proof things were truly different here.

When she stretched her legs to come back up she suffered the pull of the water. For a split second it dragged her under. Iris almost thought she'd imagined it, but when she opened her eyes she registered the shock on Auran's face. *He sensed it too—interesting.*

We're more connected than I'd thought. Iris didn't want the Earth Faerie to see, so she straightened her back and stood up fully as the water cascaded off of her.

The sun pierced through the clouds and she felt illuminated.

Moira handed her an engraved golden bowl, and while silently saying the incantation, Iris sank to her knees. She watched the hollow slowly fill with holy water. The liquid shimmered—enveloped in gold—and the sacred powers pulsed through her hands.

Iris got back up and cast a shield around the bowl so its potency remained.

"Thank you." Iris inclined her head. She glided back to shore and climbed up—careful not to spill a drop.

She handed the bowl to Merlow. Auran immediately joined her side. *I'm ready to go back.* The water hadn't been that cold, but it was chilly in the light breeze.

Moira noticed and offered her a dry cerulean robe. "Here you go."

A fist clenched her heart. Iris's head shot up. In the corner of her eyes she saw Merlow shake his head infinitesimally.

"No, thank you, I'm fine," Iris said politely.

The sun was obscured by clouds again. Iris rubbed her arms.

Moira held up the cotton cerulean garment. "I insist. We would not want you to catch a cold."

"I so appreciate your offer," Iris said. "But I must decline."

There must be something more to accepting this robe. No doubt it was a novice robe, and accepting meant concurring with the responsibilities tied to it. If the Earth Faerie was willing to trick her, then her consenting to join the priesthood must be extremely important to them.

Iris forced herself to smile. "Thank you, again, for granting us access." She turned to Auran and Merlow. "Let's go back."

Iris wobbled and Auran caught her elbow. *The holy water took something from me, too.*

Auran's arm steadied her while Merlow opened the portal back to Baruch. Merlow appeared to realize they had to hurry.

Auran's touch helped ground her. Iris looked over her shoulder at the creek and noticed its vibration had shifted. The water was speeding up, as if the calm stream prepared to thunder down a waterfall. *Like it had been put to a standstill for this occasion specifically.*

That was an eerie thought. *Can the Faeries communicate with water like Baruch does with plants? Perhaps not so different then.*

Auran nudged her shoulder, forcing her attention back to her direct surroundings. The portal was wide open in front of her.

Iris slowed her breathing in preparation and was grateful for Auran's support. She couldn't have stayed upright without him.

They stepped through the portal and Iris choked, landing hard on the floor. Her knees buckled and she slid down.

CHAPTER SEVENTY-NINE

Kaale Mountains

The cold of the rough granite sapped the last bit of warmth from Iris's body.

"Baruch, grab her sleeping mat," Merlow instructed.

Auran lifted her up like a baby and gently laid her on the sheepskin.

Merlow started to strip off her wet clothes.

Iris made a feeble attempt at batting his hand away, but he ignored her. She wanted to object but lacked the strength to speak.

The air around her warmed, and the analytical part of her mind concluded Baruch must've used a heat spell to keep her from shivering.

Warming air costs a lot of magic, she thought drowsily.

Merlow rubbed her firmly with a piece of dry cloth, removing the last water drops from her skin, and draped a woolen robe over her.

Auran tucked the cloth under her calves.

She felt light, as if she drifted above her body to have a splendid eagle eye view of the men working together to support her. She observed the care with which Baruch searched for the imbalance—considerate but firm. How meticulously Merlow tended to her organs, and of course, Auran—gentleness in every touch, their auras intertwined.

Iris felt an aching pain in the distance, but the more she moved toward the light the happier she became.

Why did I ever worry so much? There was so much beauty in life, so much light. It radiated off the three men below her. They worked in unison like a magnificently orchestrated work of art—each element essential to perfection.

Life is perfection. She suddenly understood how every action and each person contributed its own piece to complete the puzzle.

She floated on bliss—basking in the white light.

Merlow vigorously rubbed different herbs on her arm, and Auran massaged her temples with oil while Baruch started several incantations.

Iris glanced back at the portal. *It's not fully closed.* She caught a glimpse of the Earth Faerie. Now she didn't look loving—her pupils narrowing like snake eyes, her aura streaked with black—like that priest, Rex.

I've been poisoned!

The pull she'd felt from the water…it was still dragging her down.

She saw it in her physical body now—an anomaly festering inside, eating away her structure. Iris instinctively knew the Earth Faerie had the antidote—in exchange for accepting the offer to become a priestess.

I'll never give in, not on these conditions.

Iris looked down. *Auran is pressing my chest, huh.*

"She's turning blue!" Auran grunted.

Iris noticed something Baruch had done resonated with her body—as if he'd found the counterpart of the poison wrecking havoc in her bloodstream. He didn't realize he'd struck the right chord, however, because he moved on to another chant.

I need to tell him to stay with this one. She moved toward her physical body and came up against an invisible barrier. *Did Merlow shield us?* She summoned magic to pierce the obstruction. Nothing happened.

Where she normally had access to a well of power she came up blank. *Did the Faeries take my magic?*

Panicking, Iris studied the space around her, frantically searching for something to hold on to.

A golden cord glinted in front of her. Her eyes followed the thread and she realized it was attached to her bellybutton. *Huh?* She tried to grasp the rope, but her hands didn't respond. She cast a glance toward the other end of the cord and saw a mirror image of herself down below. Instinctively Iris tugged on the thread and was catapulted back into her body.

The floating feeling of love and unity was replaced by intense pain. The light gone. *Ouch.*

Iris forced herself to open her eyes—a herculean effort. "Baruch." It was less than a whisper, but they heard her and froze.

Auran bent forward to listen.

She was able to mutter, "Devil's tail."

Auran frowned but passed the message on.

Baruch nodded and immediately returned to the chant for devil's tail. Drop by drop he removed the poison from her body.

As the venom left her system, her ability to breathe slowly increased.

Sweat gleamed on Baruch's forehead. "Her lungs are clear. I will extract the rest," he said.

Merlow moved closer and placed a hand on her navel to repair the damage.

All the while Auran held her hand and stroked her forehead—willing her to stay alive.

Iris wanted to laugh and tell him she had no intention of leaving—not like this and not now—but all she could do was lie there and breathe.

After a few minutes she was able to breathe without having to focus, and she sensed the hope of the men around her. It reminded her of the love and unity she'd seen from above—a bond transcending this lifetime.

We've been brought together for a special purpose. There was more that needed to be done and this most certainly was not her time to leave.

Iris tried to sit up but Auran pushed her back gently.

Merlow's face hovered above her. "Do not exert yourself!" he scolded.

Her body was so heavy she was convinced she could fall through the floor. Exhaustion swept over her. *I could sleep for a week.*

Yet part of her was more alive than it had ever been. She'd brought with her a piece of the clarity she'd felt when floating over her body. A shining knowledge beyond anything she'd ever experienced before.

CHAPTER EIGHTY

Kaale Mountains

Every bone in Iris's body hurt.

Auran helped her sit up so she could drink some of Merlow's concoction. Auran's face was grim as he held the cup to her lips while she drank.

Bitter. Iris recognized some of the herbs, but was too tired to analyze. She glanced at the portal—a crescent of cold silver light leaked around the edges. "Merlow." She threw a pointed look at the opening.

His eyes flared and he closed it immediately.

Iris knew Auran would've been pacing the room if he didn't have to keep her upright. Instead Baruch got up. "What occurred?"

The muscles in Auran's arm tensed, the veins in his face pulsing with the effort of containing his anger. "Something happened in the water," he said. "It pulled at her."

Merlow gasped, and Auran answered the unspoken question. "I don't know why I sensed it—I just did. Perhaps because of that spell you used before we left?" Auran peered at Iris.

"Which spell?" Merlow asked.

"Just something to keep us connected and travel back safely to Earth," Iris answered.

"Why did you deem that necessary?" Merlow asked incredulously.

Iris shrugged her shoulders half-heartedly. "Intuition."

"Why did you not inform me? We should have gone in more prepared. Do you truly believe the Faeries poisoned you on purpose?"

"When you were working on me, I spotted Moira through the portal. Poisoning me was a trick to lure me into accepting the priesthood in return for the antidote. That cerulean robe—that was a novice robe, right?"

Auran cursed.

"Indeed," Merlow said. "Accepting is not without consequences. I was shocked she offered it so casually—twice."

"There must be great importance in your agreeing to become a priestess or the Faeries would not jeopardize their relationship with Merlow," Baruch said, walking back and forth. "What can be so crucial they feel compelled to trick you into consenting? And what kind of person does that?"

Merlow cleared his throat. "There is something else I need to share. I have avoided it for as long as I could, for I did not want to burden you with it."

Merlow faced Iris. "Another prophecy has been made about you."

Another?

"It is the companion to the first part we all know. The second half of the Bright Eyes Prophecy is known by three people only. The Faerie Queen, the Earth Faerie, and me. I was informed by my mentor. This story has been handed down for generations."

Auran helped Iris adjust to be more comfortable and wrapped her shoulders in a woolen blanket. "Should she eat first?"

The thought of food made Iris feel nauseated so she shook her head. "Can I get some water?"

Auran handed her a cup—monitoring her as though she was made of glass. She grimaced. The last thing she needed was his increased concern.

She drained her cup and turned to Merlow.

He sat with his legs folded and slowed his breathing. Iris realized he'd memorized the saga he began to recite. "Right after the Cataclysm, the Oracle of Phortàk, who spoke once every four years—made a prophecy. Much of what she prophesied has already come to pass. This prophecy speaks of a female with bright eyes and immense power. Someone who will sacrifice her life for the greater good."

Iris swallowed. It never got easier to hear.

"When challenged she will remain victorious, provided that particular mortals are in place. Uncovering the required puzzle pieces takes her singular gift and experience. Her fate intervenes with that of the kingdom of the Faeries on multiple occasions. She has the opportunity to save them from harm—and indebt them forever.

However, there is a fork in the road and only one avenue will protect the Faeries. Selecting the other two options means the Faeries will be eliminated. Not by an active deed, but because of where her opponents will strike. She must ultimately face her adversaries and drive out the dark."

Auran reached for his dagger.

"The Faeries will prove a valuable ally if and when they collaborate," Merlow declaimed.

Silence filled the chamber.

"This is the full prophecy. I trust the recent actions of the Faeries indicate we have arrived at the crossroads. I do regret the path they have chosen—to force you into an alliance like that." Merlow lifted his hands and dropped them again.

Iris tried to absorb what she'd heard. If this were true, it meant there were three possible futures and it was up to her to choose one. "So I'm responsible for the continued existence of the Faeries?"

I guess feeling the burden of rescuing Fleuris wasn't enough...

She leaned toward Auran, who was still keeping her upright and lending her some of his bodily warmth. Iris pulled the blanket tighter around her. If only she had clarity on the different parts. "Do you think the prophecy referred to people—with the puzzle pieces? Or insights and actions?"

"It sounded like you're the one to figure that out," Auran offered.

Iris sighed.

"The real question is—do you believe this to be truthful?" he said.

"You mean the prophecy?"

"Yeah."

This was one of the things she so appreciated about him—he never took anything at face value. *Do I believe it?* Iris probed the energy of the tale with a hint of her magic and winced. "It rings true," Iris said. "I don't think it can hurt to follow this guidance."

"What guidance?" Auran exclaimed. "There is no clear path—it only burdens you with more responsibility. There's not a valuable piece of information in there—nothing that helps you decide!"

Iris smiled.

Auran pulled his arm back, and she realized she'd offended him. "I'm not laughing at you," she hastened to add. "You reminded me of something."

He crossed his arms.

"I thought the other day about how synchronistic our being here is. With you meeting Baruch, and the three of us living in Yarden...I believe that *we* are the particular mortals, and we're in place," Iris said almost cheerfully.

"You think that's good news?"

"Well, yes. It says we'll be victorious."

"That's a big assumption. There's enough left to be concerned about. Such as deciding whether you want to alienate the Faeries. As if fighting one enemy isn't enough," Auran sputtered.

"It's key to know why it's so important to them."

"You get to decide whether the Faeries go extinct. I wager that is incentive enough to want to keep you close," Baruch said.

"Yeah, and I have, what, eighteen hours left to decide whether I want to be their priestess?"

Auran and Baruch exchanged a glance.

"Perhaps you should wait until tomorrow," Baruch offered.

Iris peeked at Auran—he'd warned Baruch so she wouldn't exert herself.

We need time to make sure we consider every angle. She nodded and smiled to herself as Auran's brows shot up—surprised she would give in this easily.

But the poison had taken its toll and she needed both sleep and food. "Will you stay?" she asked Auran.

His face showed she couldn't have made him leave if she'd wanted to.

"Perhaps one of us should stay as well," Baruch suggested. "You are too weak to defend yourself and we need you fully protected energetically, too."

Iris realized she had no magic left to shield herself, and was touched he'd thought of that.

"You stay here, Baruch," Merlow said. "I want to work on some potions."

CHAPTER EIGHTY-ONE

Kaale Mountains

The next morning Iris's entire body was tender—each cell still raw from the poison's invasion. She suppressed a groan—not wanting to reveal she was awake.

Today is the day. The thought of kissing Auran was scary exciting. She imagined he would know what to do. Once she'd overheard Auran and Jacob talk about a girl in their class. Auran's aura had flared like her father's when he came home from a long trip and embraced Mama.

Knowing Merlow would supervise slightly dampened her enthusiasm. *I wish I could shield us from sight.* She envisaged Merlow's surprise at their disappearance. *What if I lose control?* She frowned.

"Are you awake?" Auran asked.

Great. "Ahuh."

"How are you feeling?" Auran asked.

"Bruised, but I'll live." She studied his face, wondering whether his stubble would tickle.

Jacob stormed in. "The pipes in the hotroom came loose from their brackets, leaking water and hot steam."

"Morning," Auran said.

The pipes fell?

Auran glanced at Baruch, who was rolling up his sleeping mat.

Baruch nodded. "I will refasten the tubes."

Iris lay back down. Right now she couldn't care less about pipes.

"I'll be right there," Auran said.

"Okay." Jacob walked out.

Has that wrinkle in Jacob's forehead always been there? The men hadn't spoken much about Basil. She knew it hurt them not to be able to give him a traditional funeral. Guards had already begun gathering rocks for a cairn in one of the far-off chambers.

"I've been thinking about the Faeries," Auran said.

Iris pushed herself up against the granite wall. "And?"

"I remembered what Merlow taught you."

She wasn't surprised he'd been paying attention during her lessons. "What's that?"

He held up his thumb. "First of all, the Faeries never operate on impulse, so their actions were planned before we arrived." He raised his index finger. "Second, all the chief Faeries have a direct and permanent link to their Queen. That means she was involved, too."

"How does this tie into the prophecy, other than wanting to secure the survival of their species?"

Baruch stepped in. "I think there is more to it—a deeper layer. My grandmother always said, 'The Faeries are instruments of the Divine. Never take them or their actions for granted. There is a deep wisdom you might miss at first. However, if you are willing to stare into the sun long enough, you will see with clear eyes.'"

Well, that was cryptic. Now what?

A smile tugged at Auran's lips. "You have fun deciphering. We'll fix the pipes." He clapped Baruch on the shoulder as they walked out.

Iris scowled at their backs.

After wolfing down her oatmeal, Iris stilled her mind to connect with Sourni. She frowned.

Something was off.

Normally she felt a brush of her own shield as she extended her senses past the cave. She'd designed the protection so only she and Merlow were able to pass through.

The nudge she'd gotten used to was absent.

Iris scanned the perimeter, hunting for her safeguard.

There was none. *Gods no!*

She should have sensed it if someone attacked or dismantled her shield. She'd been alerted to neither. Iris threw her mind out to Merlow. "We need to reestablish the wards around the cave. They're gone!"

"What? How come?"

"Get the others here, too."

She sent a quick prayer to Seth and Layla that any magic they'd worked hadn't shown up on Apex's readings.

Then it hit her. The pipes.

Spells held as long as a magician was alive. *I must've actually died for a moment yesterday—destroying all my spells. Oh Gods, oh Gods, oh Gods…*

The men barged in. Merlow was breathing heavily. Auran and Jacob now carried their bows, their quivers full, daggers in hand.

Trevor followed in behind them—his viridian aura flaring.

"What happened?" Auran demanded.

"All my spells shattered." Iris looked at Merlow meaningfully.

Auran frowned. "How?"

There was no time to explain or reason to make him feel nervous. "It doesn't matter how. Baruch, can you feed me power so I can restore the shield?"

"Of course."

Energy flowed to her instantly—her pain softened slightly. She smiled at Baruch in thanks for his healing. Then she grabbed the energy he sent and threw magic around the cave, concealing their presence.

It wouldn't hold against a physical attack. There was not enough magic for that. When they'd gotten here, she'd spent three days creating the wards. All she could do now was patch things up.

She sensed Baruch was reaching his limits, too.

Iris cursed herself for not realizing something was off when Jacob first mentioned the pipes. A tingling alerted her to a mindlink. *Sourni.* "I'm so glad you called!"

"They're coming! I overheard one of the guards complaining he was stuck on palace duty."

"What did you hear exactly?"

"Thorn is advancing on the Kaale Mountains with a group of soldiers."

Oh Gods.

"That's where you are, right?"

There was no harm in telling Sourni now. "Yes. Do they suspect you?"

"No, be safe!" Sourni urged.

"May the Gods watch over you. And mind your energy. You're too anxious…"

Damn. I guess that means no kissing anytime soon. Just as she'd gotten used to the idea of doing something so personal in front of Merlow… *First things first.*

Iris opened her eyes. "Cancel the ceremony. How long will it take to evacuate everyone?"

"Evacuate?" Jacob asked.

"Thorn is on his way."

"Damn." Auran kicked the wall. "This gorge is too big to defend. It was meant as a hiding place, not a fortress. Too many angles from which they can approach. Even if we could see them coming, we have no place to go."

"I know that," Jacob said indignantly.

"This place has become a deathtrap. Those two vicious arrows can arrive any moment and we don't have enough magic left to vanquish Thorn. Not in this condition." Iris surveyed her body and cursed the Faeries for taking so much of her power.

"But…" Jacob said.

"Every spell carrying my energy signature has collapsed," Iris explained. "We have to leave."

The cave went pitch black.

Gods.

By Seth, the lighting was Merlow's spell. "Merlow?" Iris asked.

"Yes," he croaked.

Oh good, he's still breathing. "Just making sure. Can you sense where they'll enter?"

"Hmm."

"Baruch, can you send me more power?" Iris asked.

"I am afraid I have depleted any available power, both from the cave and its vicinity," he answered.

"They are approaching from the north. Their numbers are shielded. I recognize Thorn's energy," Merlow said.

Auran cursed.

"I'm empty, so is Baruch. Better tell the guards to prepare," Iris said.

"They do not stand a chance against Thorn," Merlow said.

"I know that! What do you want me to do?!" Iris spit. "Lie down and yield?"

"We need to get you out of here," Auran said. "Merlow can buy you time."

"I'm not leaving you behind," Iris said stubbornly, bracing herself for an argument.

"Jacob, get the guards ready," Auran instructed.

Iris heard Jacob's footsteps disappear into the darkness. It was a miracle he didn't bump into the wall. *Perhaps he does see something.* His sight was unrivaled.

"Baruch, the Lady of the jungle predicted you would prove crucial. I know you can get Iris more power. What if we get you out of the cave?" Auran asked.

"There is no time," Merlow said. "Thorn will be here in ten minutes."

"Think!" Auran urged.

In their silence the black deepened—the damp cold creeped up her ankles. "The crack!" Iris said. "Moira said there's a hairline fissure past the common room, close to the entrance toward the tower."

"Go on," Auran urged.

"Merlow, can you widen the fissure enough to reach daylight— allowing Baruch to tap into the power of the forest?"

"It might be the last thing I do," Merlow said.

"Do it," Iris commanded. "Auran, get us to that crack."

She heard the men fumble for the walls. "Hang on." With the last scraps of her power, she let a spark blossom in the palm of her right hand.

The golden flame illuminated Auran's surprise. He grabbed her other arm, shielding her with his body. "Merlow, take the rear."

Merlow's protection fell in place around them.

"Wait!" Iris snatched her leather notebook and stuffed it down her tunic. *I'm not leaving that for Thorn.*

They half-ran, half-stumbled to the hallway toward the tower with Iris's flame leading the way.

They passed guards taking up strategic positions. Jacob asked, "Merlow, are you absolutely certain no one will engage us from the south?"

Merlow's steps faltered while he reached out with his magic. "North only."

"Spread out two by two," Jacob instructed. "Take up your designated positions. Fall back from the common room."

"Four archers with me," Auran commanded.

"Unit one, follow your captain," Jacob said.

"Sir."

The four archers fell in line behind them, occasionally tripping. Iris raised her hand and increased the intensity of her flame with the last of her strength. She gritted her teeth—a burnout loomed.

Finally they reached the crack.

Merlow searched the fissure with his eyes and his magic.

Iris sensed he enforced their shield—extending the bubble to the archers.

"Stay close together or my shield will not hold," Merlow warned them as he sat on the rock floor right underneath the fissure. Trevor scurried closer to Merlow.

He must be exhausted to risk casting that magnitude of a spell while sitting. Healing must've taken a lot from him.

"You two, guard this side. The both of you, shoot anything coming out of that hallway," Auran ordered.

"I'm afraid I have to extinguish the light," Iris apologized.

"They won't need it," Auran said as he unstrapped his bow. He handed her his spare dagger. "Keep this with you."

Iris gripped the blade, the hilt warm from his hand.

As the light faded she stared at him, forcing herself to smile.

"Battle silence," Auran instructed.

Stillness descended on the cave. The only audible sound was their breath. Merlow's breathing turned heavier as he harnessed his power for what might be his last enchantment.

Iris wished she had power left for a muffling spell.

A loud crack reverberated as the fissure widened.

Merlow trembled beside her as he struggled to contain the widening of the rock. He slouched against her.

Iris said a silent prayer to Seth and Layla. Then added a quick plea. *Father, help us.*

A tingling on her cheek indicated his presence—strengthening her resolve. *We will get out alive.*

She sniffed. *Fresh air.* Taking big breaths, she inhaled the hint of the forest. After the boost of oxygen in Faerieland, the stale air in the cave had been harder to stomach.

On her other side Baruch got to work. She sensed how he reached out through the jagged rock and drew power in, funneling the energy back to her.

It was like finally drinking water when your tongue was parched dry. Her body—so used to ample magic—breathed a sigh of relief when the empty well in her belly refilled. A calm settled over her.

Iris threw her power out to the hallway, inspecting for intruders, while setting up a mindlink with Auran.

She showed him what she discerned at the edges of her magic— at least two hundred men. They were vastly outnumbered.

Someone must've told them about their secret entrance because Thorn was headed straight for the most direct opening.

Iris included Jacob in the mindlink—he didn't blink at the sight of their opponent.

"Get ready," Auran whispered at the archers.

Iris added her own shield around all of them, reaching out to Jacob to shield him, too. She couldn't protect everyone but at least these nine men were safe. Or safer.

She checked in with Baruch to get a feel for how much more magic he was able to access.

The cave shook with a blast of power, and a wave of flames roared down the hallway.

Iris enforced her shield to withstand the flare without blinking. *A lesser magician wouldn't have been able to hold—or one less used to fire…* A flicker of pride rose up.

A second gust battered down her magic. Iris fed power into her shield, hauling the energy down from Baruch almost before he released it.

He sensed her urgency because he picked up his pace.

A volley of arrows hurled around the corner.

One of the guards swore.

Iris's shield tremored. She adjusted her shield so it would allow arrows out from their side, and told Auran via mindlink.

Auran notched an arrow. In the light of the flames Iris noticed how he tilted his head to listen for the intruders.

Iris didn't hear anything past the roaring of the flames, but Auran released his arrow.

She *did* hear the sound of someone crashing to the floor. *One down.*

Auran reached into his quiver for another arrow when his eyes bulged, his arm suspended in midair.

Jacob was shouting over the mindlink. Two guards had been shot in the back.

Merlow was wrong.

Iris threw her awareness out past Jacob. Fifty men came clamoring down the hallway from Merlow's chamber. *How did they get in?*

She let her magic snake past the men, and discovered they'd forced an entry past the hotroom. *How did we miss that?*

Her attention was snagged back to the shield in front of her when more arrows rained down.

"I am coming to the end of my reach," Baruch told her.

Dammit! There was no way out, both sides blocked. *I wish I had enough power to distance-travel everyone out.*

Wait. She considered. *This might work.* "Merlow!" She nudged him.

He looked at her warily.

"Baruch, feed Merlow some magic!" she instructed. "Trevor, you hold Merlow up."

"Certainly, miss." Trevor helped Merlow sit up straight. "Baruch, take the last of my life-power."

"No!" Iris panicked.

"I made a vow to your father," Trevor stated. "If this is how I can be of service then I shall."

Iris closed her eyes. She couldn't be responsible for another person's death.

"I am not even sure how to draw out his power," Baruch said.

And I am, dammit. "It reminds me of what I saw when Thorn seized the little girl's purple magic. Except he took too much." She shook her head. "Do what you did with the rock," Iris suggested. "Pretend he's a plant or something." *Please Seth and Layla, don't let Baruch take too much...*

Baruch placed his hand on Trevor's chest. "I hope this will not hurt."

"Just do it," Trevor said.

Baruch closed his eyes.

Iris saw Trevor's viridian morph with Baruch's orange. *Wow.*

Color returned to Merlow's cheeks as his body was brought back to balance. Trevor breathed heavily. *Good.*

She mindlinked with Merlow, not wanting the others to overhear. "Contact the Faeries. Tell them I will become a Faerie priestess if they will shelter us all for as long as we need. Including our wounded. Effective immediately."

Merlow opened his eyes wide. "Are you sure?"

She bristled. "Yes! Hurry!"

Auran peered at her, sensing something was wrong. "What did you do?"

She mindlinked with him to prevent Thorn from eavesdropping. "I'm negotiating a safe retreat."

"With Thorn?"

She gaped at him in disbelief. "With the Faeries! Tell Jacob to bring everyone here. We'll have to be swift."

Auran cursed under his breath. The stubborn set of his jaw told her exactly what he thought.

She brought Jacob back in on the mindlink and let Auran handle logistics.

A triumphant shout boomed from her left. *Jacob's men must've taken down an opponent. Two hundred forty-eight to go.*

Iris rested her head against the rock wall and focused on maintaining her shield. *Please let it hold.*

From the sounds she knew Jacob's men were taking hits. She'd never thought fighting would make so much noise.

Twenty-four hours ago she'd have been able to shield everyone. Thanks to the stunt the Faeries had pulled, good men were dying. Bile rose in Iris's throat. Agreeing to become a Faerie priestess tasted very much like selling out to her enemy. *Was this what father had felt? He handed himself over to Apex's men so I could live.*

Her nails dug into her hand, but she forced herself to unclench her fist.

There is no comparison, she scolded herself. Her father had embraced death—she sacrificed only love and future bloodlines. *Our family tree ends with me.*

Maybe that was a blessing. The curse would finally die out.

Merlow tapped her mind and she allowed him in. "And?" she asked.

"The Faeries agree to shelter ten men," Merlow said.

"What? They want to leave the rest to die?" Iris was fuming. She'd never expected the Faeries to be this harsh. Images of Wendolyn and Maesie twirling in their iridescent dresses flashed by. *So much for cute Faeries.*

She forced herself to think, to strategize. Her father was a great negotiator, if only she had his skills. Iris tilted her head. "Father?" she reached out tentatively with her mind. She didn't have the incantation Merlow used to invoke his mentor, but she hoped her father was still around.

Iris made herself remember the tingling on her cheek, and traced her father's energy from there. Her father hovered above. "Father?"

His loving energy filled her mind. *"Yes, darling."*

Tears slid down her face and she had to bite back a sob. "Father!" She hid her face behind her hands, not wanting to distract Auran. "What should I do? I can't leave these men behind."

"The Faerie Queen is testing you."

"Now?!"

"The Faeries have long memories," her father explained. *"If you give in now, they'll try to negotiate every next decision. Remember, their future is at stake, too."*

Iris nodded. "Thank you, Father."

"Go now—there's not much time left."

The air caressed her cheek, wiping away a tear.

Iris turned to Merlow. "Tell the Faerie Queen it's all or nothing. And it's now."

Pride showed on Merlow's face. He inclined his head.

Increased pressure on the shield demanded her attention. She searched for the strain—Jacob. The guards had thrown their bows aside and were engaged in hand-to-hand combat. A tall sorcerer was fighting Jacob.

Her shield buckled under the attack from the sorcerer's curved blade chopping toward Jacob. Each impact ate away more of her magic. *Dammit!*

She mindlinked with Jacob—praying it wouldn't distract him. His opening of the link was the only sign he was aware of her.

"That blade is poisoned. Get everyone back here now!"

"Auran has instructed us to hold this line until you are safe."

Iris cursed loudly.

Auran glanced at her in surprise, concern etched on his face.

"I'm fine!" She glared at him.

"Okay, Jacob. Only a few more minutes."

She poked Merlow. "And?"

He held up his hand, imploring her to wait.

She sighed and looked around. *What else?*

Her magic level was dwindling fast. She fed more power to the part protecting Jacob and to where the flames battered relentlessly.

She was impressed Thorn kept up a continuous assault. Being able to maintain such an intense use of power indicated the sorcerer had an enormous reservoir. *He's probably fully rested, pockets full of acorns, and he has never slept on rocks in his entire life.*

In the corner of her left eye, she saw something move. She watched as a portal emerged in front of Merlow.

"Now, Jacob—quickly. All of you," she urged.

"Have you gone through?" Jacob asked.

"No! I can't shield you guys from Faerieland. I won't leave until I can see you."

Auran grabbed her arm to force her through the opening.

Iris glowered at him. "If you shove me through none of you will last long enough to be able to follow! Thorn will take you all out in one swipe!"

Auran let go of her wrist.

"Trevor, go through the portal!"

He hesitated.

"Now! We can't worry about you, too!" Iris called.

Trevor put up his hand and stepped through and out of her sight.

Pain shot through her, her shield wavering. She hissed through her teeth.

Jacob's opponent had forced his way into her shield using his dagger and a cutting spell. The sorcerer slashed at Jacob's thigh—blood rushed out.

Iris patched up the gash in her shield. *Please Gods—let it be slow-working poison.* "Tell Jacob to retreat now."

Auran's eyes widened.

"Baruch—I need more magic." Iris knew she was pushing him beyond his reach.

A little bit of power trickled into her aura.

She drew Jacob and Auran into a mindlink. "I'll hold them off with a blocking spell. Order everyone to run. This won't last."

She murmured the incantation and an energetic barrier formed in front of Jacob and his men.

"Now!" Iris flung the remainder of her magic into the barrier. Footsteps echoed down the hallway. *Good.*

She bit her lip, all her muscles going taut with exertion. Her head throbbed.

Auran lifted her—moving her to the edge of the portal until they heard Jacob shout, "Go!"

Auran shoved her.

Iris fell face down onto the mossy ground in a small glen. She pushed herself up and crawled out of the way. Trevor helped her up.

It's twilight.

She peered back through the portal, afraid of what she might see.

Baruch was lying on the floor. *Did he faint?*

Iris stretched her left hand toward him.

Someone grabbed her from behind and pulled her back.

A shield snapped in place before her. She was captured behind what looked like a glass window—the stretch of moss to the portal was now a no-mans-land. Iris pushed the shield with both hands— it didn't budge.

"You cannot go back," the Earth Faerie told her.

Iris didn't bother to respond. She trained her eyes on the opening into the cave. The rock walls brightly lit by a blaze. *Please Gods keep them safe!* The picture window allowing her to peek in was far too small for her liking.

A few guards tentatively walked through the portal, staring at the enormous pine trees at the edge of the glen, and bumped into the invisible shield.

"Let them through!" Iris yelled.

The shield gave way as if the guards had stretched the glass where their hands thrusted, snapping in place behind them.

The men turned on their heels and stood next to Iris to peer through as well.

An arrow emerged from the cave and hit the invisible barrier—the projectile clattered purposeless to the ground.

Iris prayed to the Gods to let Auran and Jacob through quickly. Nothing happened.

········•●•·········

Auran breathed a sigh of relief when he saw Iris land on the moss, illuminated by the golden light streaming through the towering trees. He turned to Jacob. *Damn.* Bright red blood gushed from the entry wound on his thigh. "Get over here!"

Jacob ignored him and engaged one of Thorn's men.

The second Iris had stepped over the threshold, Thorn's flames had flared—incinerating several of Jacob's men closest to it. Auran prayed the smell of seared flesh didn't make its way to Faerieland.

He shoved three guards toward the portal. "Retreat—that's an order!"

Auran heard the sound of a blade being drawn. He pivoted and jumped forward to fend off an attack on Jacob's unprotected chest. He drove his dagger through the assailant's heart. Blood coated his hilt and dripped on his hands. Auran pulled his dagger back with a sucking sound—and swallowed. He'd never killed a man this close.

An arrow sailed past his head and through the opening. *Thank you Gods.*

More enemies replaced his fallen opponent. Two attackers stood shoulder to shoulder, banked by the walls of the cave. *Thank Seth for the narrowness of this hallway.* Part of him smiled at the irony, after so often cursing the confinement of the cave.

Basil could've held this entire hallway of the cave by himself, buying the rest time to flee.

In the corner of his eye Auran noticed Merlow grab Jacob's shoulders and drag him closer to the portal. *Perfect.*

He threw his head back to avoid having his eye carved out. *I'll ask Merlow to shield this side.* Auran tried to initiate a mindlink.

Ouch. His adversary pummeled his abdomen. *Damn.*

"Merlow!"

"Yes?"

"Shield this side!"

Nothing happened. *Damn.* This was about the worst time for Merlow to run dry.

Clunk.

Auran smiled at the familiar sound. *Thank you, Gods.* "Down!" he yelled.

Around him his men instantly dropped to the stone floor. Thorn's men looked bewildered.

Auran lashed out wildly, forcing the two attackers in front of him to retreat a few steps. Then he threw himself backward, covering his face.

Whoosh!

The blast of the exploding arrow pressed Auran to the floor—his jaw forcing down another guard's boot.

Screaming erupted from the side of the watchtower. *Take that, bastards.* "Out!" he urged the remaining guards.

⋅⋅⋅⋅⋅⋅⋅⋅⋅●⋅⋅⋅⋅⋅⋅⋅⋅⋅⋅

Iris kept staring at the gateway, willing her men to step through. No one had escaped in the past few minutes.

When she thought she could no longer take it, more guards rushed from the cave onto the moss, mystified and overheated.

"Pick up Baruch!" Iris pointed. "Take him with you!" The sound echoed back in her ears.

The guards frowned and looked at each other confused. They were beckoned by their compatriots.

Hurry!

"The barrier blocks your sound, too," the Faerie Queen said.

Iris ignored the Queen. She couldn't see Auran or Merlow, and Baruch was still immobile on the wrong side of the portal.

"How many?" she asked the guard flanking her.

"Five down," he answered.

Iris shuddered. *Five men.*

"When we left," his colleague added.

Gods.

At long last Auran stepped into view. He hauled Baruch up from the granite floor. Jacob limped to his side and both slung an arm under Baruch's armpit. They dragged the Amazonian between them.

"Shield them!" Iris implored the Faeries.

Magic tingled by her ear. *Just in time.*

A blast shook the men from behind. Jacob collapsed.

Iris pushed forward against the barrier. She hammered the shield with both hands. "Let me through!"

"We will not risk your safety," Moira said.

The guard next to her jerked his head to the Earth Faerie. "Let me pass!" he thundered.

To Iris's surprise the shield opened for him. The guard rushed through and hoisted Jacob over his shoulder like a sack of potatoes, then staggered through the glass-like barrier. Iris and Trevor helped him lower Jacob to the ground.

Auran dropped Baruch on the moss next to Jacob, bracing his hands on his knees, breathing heavily. He turned back around.

Iris grabbed his sleeve. "Where are you going?"

"Merlow." Exhaustion was etched on Auran's face.

Auran sounded so weary.

Iris realized she was surrounded by magic—the Faerie air humming with power—and she hurled a shield around Auran. "Hurry!"

She prayed her shield would hold past the invisible barrier.

Auran paused at the edge of the portal. "Merlow!" he bellowed.

Merlow's signature robe appeared, strips of cobalt fabric flapping.

No!

Merlow stumbled into view. Blood gushed from multiple wounds on his torso and arms.

Auran stepped to the side of the portal, near the trees, making room for Merlow to enter Faerieland.

Merlow lurched sideways as magic slashed into his chest, laying open his skin.

He's drained. Why doesn't Auran pull him in?

"It is a one-way portal from Earth into Faerieland," the Queen answered.

Iris was too distressed to be bothered by the mindreading. She didn't want to look at Merlow, but she couldn't avert her eyes.

Merlow's consciousness faded—his aura turning from hay to cream. He fell backward through the portal.

Time stood still as Iris watched Merlow's slashed robes billow around him. Her heart sank in her chest.

His head thumped as he fell onto a tree stump. Merlow's aura flickered—exactly the way her mother's bubble had faltered.

Iris fell forward on her hands. *No!*

Auran grabbed Merlow by his shoulders and yanked him away from the portal. Merlow's feet dragged a trail through the pine needles.

The Queen flung a shield in place, preventing anyone from following Merlow into Fae territory.

Why didn't she do that earlier?

Thorn's livid face emerged at the portal. His grey eyes shooting daggers, violent lips mumbling a curse.

CHAPTER EIGHTY-TWO

Faerieland

Iris cringed as Thorn's curse ricocheted off the Faerie Queen's shield. Crimson light erupted from the friction.

She didn't dare breathe as the barrier wobbled from impact. It held—narrowly.

Iris pivoted to the Queen, but her Majesty was already feeding more magic into her protective layer.

Iris nodded and jumped forward to Merlow, placing a hand on his chest to assess the damage. His aura was barely visible. She drew upon the Faerie magic swirling around her, noticing how much more compact it was, brimming with power. Thorn had cut Merlow open with magic, making the wounds much harder to close.

It meant Merlow had been utterly empty—not even enough power left for a basic shield. *Why hadn't he stepped through the portal sooner?*

Iris sent the Faerie power into Merlow's depleted body, encouraging his system to restore the energy-starved cells, while she used rudimentary battle healing to patch up his biggest wounds.

Gradually his body absorbed the energy and his aura stopped wavering. *Thank you Gods.*

There was still a long way to go but at least he wouldn't die in the next few minutes.

Iris rocked back on her heels and looked around. "Trevor, can you stay with Merlow? Come get me when he gets worse."

"Of course."

Baruch was still out cold and Jacob's trousers were saturated with blood—Auran pressed both hands on his best friend's thigh.

Iris faced the Faerie Queen. "Could you send for your healers, please?" She was not familiar enough with Faerie magic to dare try anything as intricate as closing the artery in Jacob's thigh. Her own magic wouldn't be refilled for another couple of hours.

The Queen arched her brows. "We each take care of our own."

The callousness of the statement rung in Iris's ears. *So only sheltering, huh.*

Iris cursed herself for not including healing in the bargain.

Think! She nodded. "Of course." She walked over to Baruch and probed him with magic. His energy level was dangerously low, his blood pressure nearly nonexistent. *I pushed him too far.* She gently transferred power into his system, praying his magic would replenish the depleted reserve around his vital functions first, hoping the lack of oxygen hadn't damaged his brain.

As if an afterthought, Iris asked one of the younger Faeries hovering closest to her, "Do you know Wendolyn or Maesie?" She forced herself to smile. "I would love to see my childhood friends."

The Faerie's fawn eyes lighted and she eagerly bobbed her head.

"Could you ask them to come over?"

The short Faerie turned to the Faerie Queen. The Queen inclined her head and the Faerie bounded away, her ash-blonde locks swinging.

This had better work. Iris sensed the Queen's attention and kneeled next to Jacob. *We need to close his artery.*

She ignored Auran's stare. It was hard enough to control her thoughts as it was. She indicated Auran should keep pressure on the wound, and searched Jacob's body for other damage. She glanced at the increasing puddle of blood soaking into the dirt.

Closing her eyes, she sent her awareness into Jacob's body, reliving healing him in the cave. *If only I had the magic reserve I had then.* She pushed the thought aside and examined his body.

Her eyes fluttered open.

"And?" Auran urged.

"Luckily the flow of blood washed away most of the poison, though we need to extract the remnants before closing the wound. But he lost... a lot of blood." She couldn't bear saying 'too much.'

She wasn't up to this kind of healing. The damage was too severe. Merlow didn't look like he would be supporting Jacob soon, or Baruch for that matter. Tears fought their way up, but she shoved them down. She didn't dare show any weakness surrounded by Faeries and with the eyes of every guard trained on her.

In the corner of her eyes she noticed a blonde Faerie approaching. "Maesie!" Iris got up and smiled as her childhood friend ran to her. She held up a hand, "Don't hug me, I'm filthy."

"Come here silly." Maesie enveloped her in a bear hug. "My dress has seen worse."

Oh.

Iris savored the hug, allowing herself to relax and breathe in Maesie's familiar scent, now enriched with a layer of herbs. "Look at you!" Gone were the blonde ringlets, the iridescent dress replaced by a more elegant linen gown. "How are you?"

"I am well." Maesie beamed. "How are you faring?" she brushed at the still-wet blood on Iris's tunic with her pointer finger "Did you forget to use magic repellent?"

"We came seeking refuge." Iris took in the amethyst of Maesie's dress—somehow free of stains. *If I'm not mistaken...* "Are you studying to be a healer?"

The Faerie Queen cleared her throat.

Maesie glanced between Iris and the Queen.

Iris's hands tingled and she studied Maesie's face. *Are they mindlinking?*

"I..." Maesie started, avoiding Iris's stare.

Oh no, this won't do.

"I invoke the Universal Words," Iris declared.

The Queen started. "What do you mean?"

Maesie hunched. "I...we...several years ago I affirmed the Universal Words, ratifying the binding magic."

The Queen narrowed her eyes. Even without seeing her aura, Iris sensed her discontent.

"The what?" Auran demanded.

Iris turned to him. "An ancient custom and powerful incantation to ensure truth is spoken." She faced Maesie. "Are you a healer?"

Maesie nodded, fumbling with the lavender embroidered on her sleeve.

"Can you please help my friend?" Iris trusted even Faerie healers were sworn to do no harm and aid those in need.

"I will."

Auran's shoulders relaxed.

Maesie sank to her knees at Jacob's chest and leaned forward. *Is she smelling him?*

"Bring me my bag and a tincture of turpentine." A fawn-eyed Faerie ran off.

Turpentine?

Iris's hands tingled as Maesie worked her magic. The density of the magic around her decreased. *Is she tapping into a particular element of the magic rather than using it as a whole?* Jacob's artery sealed itself until only a tiny opening remained, all the while oozing purple blood, expelling the last dregs of poison.

No wonder the Faeries are considered superior healers. Being able to purge and mend simultaneously would save many lives. *Wow. Being able to learn this will be priceless.* Iris glanced at Auran.

The flow of blood lessened.

"Don't take the pressure off yet," Maesie instructed Auran.

The fawn-eyed Faerie returned with a woven basket filled with cloth, bottles and knives. She handed Maesie a glass vial with a light yellow liquid.

Maesie uncorked the bottle, and Iris coughed at the pungent resin-rich scent. Iris was grateful the lack of auras in Faerieland didn't extend to herbs and plants. The tincture's aura told her its properties would accelerate healing of the wound. *Good.*

She nodded encouragingly when Auran gave her a questioning look—he cringed when Maesie laid gauze drenched in turpentine on Jacob's thigh. Apparently the scent was abrasive even to his nose.

Maesie bandaged the wound in silence—securing the gauze in place. Slowly some color returned to Jacob's aura. *Thank you, Seth and Layla!*

Iris crossed the glen to where most of the guards stood—some propped against broad tree trunks. She separated those who needed medical attention from those who only needed a bath and a bandage. She recognized Evan, the archer Auran had brought into her chamber. *Auran must have faith in him.*

She walked up to Evan—noting his empty quiver and the bloody scratches on his muscular arms.

He caught her look. "It's nothing."

"Could you gather a few men to set up camp?"

"Sure." His chest expanded.

"Let's find out where we can stay." Iris jerked her head toward the Queen, instantly regretting the motion. She massaged her temples, hoping to lessen her headache.

Iris faced the Queen. "May I introduce you to Evan, third in command."

His eyebrows shot up in surprise.

Well, someone needs to replace Basil. She pushed away thoughts of his lifeless hand in hers.

Evan attempted an awkward bow.

Iris noticed the paleness of his aura around his arms.

The Queen nodded curtly.

"Where will we stay?" Iris asked.

The Queen waved at a courtier. "Take them to the clearing beyond the forest. They can set up shelter there."

The courtier bowed to the Queen and turned to Iris. "May I escort you?"

Iris jerked her head at Evan and hissed. *By Seth. This better not swell to a full-blown migraine. I need my...the guards need me.*

Evan flanked her, and they set out to follow the courtier.

"Not her," the Queen said. "She stays with me."

Iris inhaled a great breath and looked Evan in the eye.

He winced.

"Make sure you can set up camp and let me know what else you need. Get that arm disinfected first."

"Yes…ma'am."

Iris suppressed a smile. "Thank you."

She wondered what game the Queen was playing. There was no need to forbid her to examine the campsite. Slowly, she turned toward the Queen—mindful her every thought was on display. "What's so important it can't wait?" Iris was too exhausted to be polite.

"Walk with me."

She fell into step beside the Queen. Endless questions popped up. *Don't think!*

The Queen strode for the tree line opposite of where the guards hovered. When the silver birch trees were within touching distance Iris glanced over her shoulder.

Auran and Maesie still knelt beside Jacob. Merlow and Baruch remained immobile on the ground, watched over by a pale Trevor. Merlow's aura was still precariously faint—ivory rather than his usual buttery-yellow. *I must create a reviving potion to ensure his condition remains stable.* She knew his age was starting to count.

Iris tore her eyes away and ducked under an overhanging branch. She started to feel nauseated—a sense of foreboding growing in her stomach. Intently she scanned her surroundings to see what was off.

The Queen remained silent until they reached a serene stream—the water so peaceful it reflected the surrounding trees perfectly. A young girl in the same linen amethyst dress as Maesie sat waiting on a boulder. She sprang up and dropped into a deep curtsy as the Queen neared.

"Rise," the Queen commanded.

The girl straightened, keeping her eyes lowered.

The Queen turned to Iris. "Go with her."

What? Is she nuts? … Dammit. "What for?" Iris asked as politely as she could muster, hoping to mask her slipup.

The Queen threw her a cold look. "To uphold your end of the bargain. We have provided sanctuary. Now you take up your priestess training."

"*Now?*"

The Queen didn't deign to answer.

"Can't we wait until, I don't know, tomorrow?" Iris remembered Merlow saying, *"The Faeries don't understand sarcasm. But they can be cruel."* By Seth, not again. This was a conundrum. *Think!*

She grounded herself, tucking her anchoring cord deep into the earth.

The Queen watched her with a wry smile.

She doesn't care—cajole, Iris quickly covered her impolite thought by rubbing some muck off her sleeve. "What about Thorn's attack? Apex won't go away by himself. Or by me studying."

"First things first. You struck a bargain. I have not yet seen you inclined to uphold your end," the Queen answered haughtily.

"What?" Iris was baffled. "We just got here, straight from battle. People are still bleeding! I don't know too much about the Faerie ways, but we don't let our injured fend for themselves!"

"You don't want to make an enemy of me."

Iris threw her hands in the air. "An enemy? What in Seth's name are you thinking? We sought you out for sanctuary. I've given up any chance…" Iris fought back her tears. "I've accepted the rules of becoming a Faerie priestess. I am *here*. What more do you want?"

"There is a great deal more, but that is neither here nor there."

Great. Iris sat down, suddenly too tired to stand.

She wiped furiously at her tears. Merlow had taught her to never show the Faeries her weakness. She really wanted to ask him how she was supposed to do that while they read her mind like village gossip.

Her tongue stuck to the roof of her mouth. She eyed the water. It was clear enough. She shuddered—her body recalling the pull of the water and the chill seeping into her veins.

Iris didn't dare drink it. She exhaled. "Can you tell me more about becoming a priestess. How does it work?"

The Queen raised her brow. "The details are known solely to sworn healers."

"Okay."

"Larissa will bring you to the healer's village. Once you arrive you will be prepped for your apprentice initiation. Once your body is purified you will immerse yourself in silent retreat lasting a moon cycle."

A moon cycle? "You mean twenty-eight days?"

The Queen inclined her head.

"But…I…how…" Iris pushed herself up. "I can't be away this long! We need to strategize on how to defeat Apex!"

"They shall have to do without you."

"They are injured!" Iris protested.

"If you do not uphold your end, I shall have to send you all back."

And we wouldn't survive. Not with two healers gravely wounded. *By Seth.*

Iris followed the amethyst dress, oblivious to the beauty of her surroundings. Some deep buried instinct made her steer away from the jasmine-like shrubs and hold her breath—her subconscious recognizing the venomous plant from Merlow's story even when her mind was preoccupied.

After a long walk the foliage became less dense, light permeated the leaves. A circle of terracotta colored houses loomed before them. *It looks almost normal.*

Iris gasped as she moved through the wards. It felt like invisible hands groping her.

She shook off the feeling.

Larissa led her to a cabin somewhat apart from the rest. Inside, they were awaited by a woman whose silk dress was a shade darker than the girl's.

"Mother," the young girl curtsied.

"Leave us."

Iris glanced at Larissa and suppressed the thought that came to mind, instead focusing on the rush mats on the floor.

The stern look on the chief priestess's face told Iris the woman was none too pleased. Iris trained her eyes on the woman's neck—forcing her mind to think of literally anything else. *She has lavender embroidered on her collar!*

"Indeed. As Principal Priestess I earned the markings of the Goddess."

The Goddess?

"I see you have much to learn."

"Yes, ma'am."

"First, we will get you out of these filthy, earthly clothes. You shall not be allowed to enter our sacred baths before your initiation starts. Larissa will show you where you can wash in the river."

Iris swallowed.

LARISSA POINTED AT a tributary of the stream, glinting with sunlight. Iris scanned the water with both her eyes and her magic. *It feels safe enough.* She walked to the overhanging willow and started to unbelt her tunic, glancing at Larissa. The girl was bent over a pink blooming shrub, rubbing the leathery camelia leaves between her fingers.

Iris quickly hid her cherished diary under a nearby bush. She gingerly stepped on the pebbles, then sank to her knees in the water—bracing herself for its pull. Warily, she held her breath, gathering magic.

The water lapped calmly at her legs.

Iris blew out her breath.

"Use this." Larissa handed her a wavy-leafed plant.

"What for?"

"To cleanse yourself."

A soaproot. Merlow had mentioned the existence of soap plants, but she'd never seen one.

Iris bent down and squeezed the bulb under water. She used the lather to rub off the blood and grime. *Chilly.*

She shivered after the cold creek and gratefully accepted the cerulean novice robe Larissa held out to her. After tying the sash, she bent to retrieve her dirty clothes.

"Don't touch them!"

Iris pulled her hand back.

"You would have to cleanse yourself again!"

"So we just leave them here?"

"Someone will come and burn them tonight."

What? Oh no! "All right. Can you give me a minute to say a prayer of thanks for the protection they gave me?"

Larissa's eyes widened. "S…sure." She politely turned around.

Iris dove down, yanked the diary from underneath the shrubs, and stuffed her notebook down her robe, praying it would stay put. Heart hammering, she said, "Thank you Layla." She walked up the incline and joined the Faerie girl.

Larissa gestured for her to follow. She led Iris to a cabin on the other side of the village and motioned she should enter.

Is she no longer allowed to speak? "Thank you." Iris said.

Larissa nodded and left.

CHAPTER EIGHTY-THREE

Arbres

"What do you mean they escaped?" Apex raged. He swept the breakfast platter off the table, sending the apple compote crashing on the floor.

"They must have struck a bargain with the Faerie Queen. They left through a portal." Thorn bristled. "Merlow has always been thick with those conniving witches."

"Why has no one told me we could access Faerieland?" Apex thundered. His green ring glimmered.

"You rule the country, but you don't know about gateways into other dimensions?" Thorn scoffed.

Apex dabbed a finger at Thorn. "You tell me all about them. And how we can get that girl back."

"And Merlow. He's mine."

"You can have the magician if you take care of the girl first," Apex promised.

"Excellent."

"How did the Strong Ones do?" Apex demanded.

"They did well for their first battle. We only lost a handful of footmen," Thorn answered. "I'll be in the dungeon. Let's see what else their precious guard can tell me."

Apex rose. "You captured one?" He pulled the cord behind his desk.

"We trapped one of their pickets." Thorn shook his head. "I can't believe Merlow didn't shield them from sorcery. I was able to… encourage the man to show us the best way in." The sorcerer smiled.

••••••••●•••••••

Sourni forced herself to eat something. She hadn't heard back from Iris. Her tea had gotten cold, but she drank it anyway. *Dear Seth, please keep them safe!* She usually didn't call upon the God of War, but this was an exception. *Send them your strength.*

"Sourni!" Anne ran up to her. "I's so glad ye is here!" She panted. "Apex needs a new breakfast tray, but the maid is afraid to go back in. Can ye take it to him, eh?"

She grabbed the opportunity to hear more and followed Anne into the kitchen. The silver tray was heavy. When she stepped into the deserted hallway, the cut-glass tumbler tinkled against the water carafe. *Breathe.* Sourni tightened her grip to stop the shaking.

The sentinel at Apex's study opened the door for her.

"Your breakfast, monsignor."

"Put it on my desk," Apex commanded.

Sourni navigated past the shards of crystal and porcelain on the soaked carpet, and carefully placed the tray between two stacks of paper. She bent down to pick up the broken pieces, struggling to school her features. *So many apples wasted.*

"Leave it."

Souni curtsied and backed away. As she closed the door she overheard Apex: "Search the library for anything about the Faeries."

"The Faeries?" his curate asked.

"Apparently that's where the cowards are hiding."

They made it!

CHAPTER EIGHTY-FOUR

Faerieland

I ris entered the hut assigned to her—its layout identical to the other cabin. She glanced at the window over her bed. *At least it has more light than the cave.*

She pulled up the mattress and hid her notebook underneath—*not exactly inconspicuous*—then plonked down on her bed and grumbled. *Should have brought my sheepskin.* Iris stretched out her legs, leaned back against the wall, and tried to initiate a mind-link with Auran.

Nothing. Not even the tingling of an ignored call.

I guess that was too much to hope for.

She went up to the chief priestess's home—she couldn't bear to think of her as mother—and knocked.

"Come in."

Iris stepped inside and curtsied. She glanced at the candles in the room, an idea sparked in her mind. "I would like to write a letter to my…friends. Could I borrow a pen and some paper, please? Also a candle, perhaps?"

The woman silently handed her writing materials and a beeswax candle.

"Thank you." The parchment was thick and rough.

Auran,

The Faeries want me to start my priestess training immediately. I don't know what else to do. The Queen is unyielding. I'm not even allowed to visit and tell you in person.

Iris absentmindedly wiped away a tear.

I don't want to do this, but I must. We need this alliance to have a chance at succeeding, and we can't go back to the cave. After thirty days I am allowed a family visit. I put your name on the list.

Iris broke down crying, clutching the letter to her chest. Even though she'd never believed in a romantic future between her and Auran, she'd assumed he would always be there. Even when she and Merlow were hiding in the forest, each day brought the anticipation and exhilaration of a potential visit. In the cave, she'd gotten so used to seeing him often, soothed by his presence. The prospect of not seeing him for thirty days—not even knowing whether he would be allowed in for the family visit…

Her magic stirred—the little she had left. Her reservoir was replenishing slowly.

Use Maesie and Wendolyn as contacts as much as you can. Hopefully the Universal Words will rub off on you. Merlow might know how you can make use of that, even though the promise was made to me. Ask him also about the bargain he struck, and to negotiate a way for me to be a part of this uprising.

I wish I were there with you.

Iris

It took a few minutes for the pounding in her head to recede. Once she was certain she wouldn't vomit Iris pushed herself up, not bothering to suppress her wince. She lit the candle and looked for something to use as a seal. The smell of honeycomb filled her nose.

Yes!

Iris grabbed her diary and carefully opened the hollow spine—shaking out one of the hidden acorns. She poured candlewax on the folds of the letter and pressed the acorn in the hot wax. *There.*

In the village she found Wendolyn, dressed in healer's amethyst.

"Iris, welcome!" Wendolyn took one step closer and froze. "I cannot touch you now—not until your initiation is complete."

Iris fought to control her expression. "Sure. Can you take a message to one of my people?"

"I can."

"This is for Auran. He's tall and blond and…Maesie can point him out. Or in fact any of the guards. Will you give this to him?" Iris handed Wendolyn the sealed note—careful not to touch her.

Wendolyn nodded.

"Do you promise to take this message straight to him, right now? Only to him."

"I do."

Iris watched as Wendolyn disappeared into the forest.

Feeling like her heart had been wrenched from her chest, she turned and entered the small cabin that would be her home for the coming month.

Keeping in mind the ritual her mother taught her, Iris lit the candle again.

Dear Ayna, I ask you watch over my loved ones. Give them strength and fill their hearts with love. Let Auran and Merlow feel my presence. Let Baruch and Jacob feel my gratitude. I pray you keep them safe in this life and the afterlife. And so it is.

Iris stared into the flame—willing her prayer into being—and drawing strength from where the light burned blue-hot. It was time to uphold her end of the bargain to secure the safety of the others.

Iris straightened her back and blew out the candle. She stepped outside to report to the chief priestess and start her training.

THE STORY CONTINUES!

KEEP AN EYE OUT FOR PART TWO OF THE

BRIGHT EYES TRILOGY.

FOLLOW STORY UPDATES AND NEWS ON

WWW.POISONEDARROW.NL

JOIN THE COMMUNITY ON

WWW.FACEBOOK.COM/POISONEDARROWBOOK

OR CONNECT WITH IRIS ON

TWITTER @IRISVANOOYEN

GRATITUDE

"If at first the idea is not absurd, there is no hope for it."

—Einstein

The very notion of me writing a novel did, indeed, seem absurd at first. There was nothing logical about it nor did I seem in any way prepared to write such a thing when these sentences came to me one late summer evening:

They do it again.

I'm so tired.

Did I turn them on?

I realized this could be a book and put the concept aside. However, the idea kept coming back, badgering me relentlessly until I finally gave in. At last I realized this book would not be something I would write *someday*, but today, and the following weeks, months and almost three years. Once I surrendered and embraced the idea, I thoroughly enjoyed the process. So I would like to thank this story for not giving up on me, and my intuition for picking up on the importance of engaging in this endeavor.

Of course this book would not be here if it weren't for the help and support of many people.

First of all, eternal gratitude goes to my darling mom and dad. You are the best parents I could have hoped for! I am so glad I picked you :) Thank you for supporting me—even when I strayed from the beaten path—and believing in me. It means the world. (And it's so convenient when your mother is a walking Wikipedia, and your father knows the rest!)

Thank you, Paul, for being my dear brother and for being there when I need you. Even though that's what siblings are for, I never take it for granted. I am still waiting for our song to hit the charts ;)

To my belle sœur Géraldine. Thank you for brainstorming location names during your vacation and for being such a wonderful sister-in-law. I am so very happy you joined the family!

This book is dedicated to my grandmothers, but I am well aware I am incredibly blessed with such a warm and loving (extended) family all around. I love you all!

I am extremely grateful for one my best friends, Brigitte, our almost daily conversations have kept me sane—not just while writing this book, but in running my business and living life as well. So glad we're in this adventure together!

Reading many acknowledgements over the years I often wondered why authors became friends with their editors, but having gone through the process I can't imagine how you could *not*. To my amazing editor Allison! Without you this book would not be what it is now. Thank you for encouraging me and teaching me about the craft of writing (and thank you for journeying into book two with me as there is still so much to learn!). Your feedback was so empowering that I actually looked forward to your emails. Your comments often made me laugh out loud. The Unkind Editor is crystal clear and brutally honest, but never unkind. I cherish our Skype calls and meetings at Schiphol airport—and laughing and crying together.

I would like to thank my beta readers: Annemieke, Arjen, Brigitte, Jane, Manon, Marcy, and Monique. I so appreciate your feedback and thoughts. Your comments have been invaluable in strengthening the story. With a special mention for my cousin Marc-Peter. Thank you for your extremely detailed response—I guess perfectionism runs in the family ;)

Lots of thanks to my proofreaders Jacqueline, Karen and Tim for crossing t's and dotting i's!

I feel blessed that I have been able to rearrange my life in the past years so I could fit in writing a novel while running my business. I love my clients, and I love them even more for understanding I sometimes wasn't as available as I had wanted to be.

Of course I must mention my favorite bookstore, Latte's & Literature, and its enthusiastic owner Ronald. I've spent many hours enjoying rooibos tea while discovering new must-read books and celebrating each milestone in the writing of *Poisoned Arrow* with your famous chocolate cake! Thank you for thinking along on my book journey.

Huge thanks to everyone who supported me along the way. Your encouragement and interest in my book has kept me going. You know who you are!

Last but certainly not least thank *you*, dear reader, for picking up this book. I hope you enjoyed reading this novel as much as I enjoyed writing my first book!

Iris van Ooyen is a creative entrepreneur who wrote this novel because it was too much fun not to. She lives in the south of The Netherlands, has a closet with too many dresses and doesn't go anywhere without organic dark chocolate and a bottle of filtered water. Nothing makes her smile as much as the huge fragrant roses from her garden. Except perhaps books.

www.ingramcontent.com/pod-product-compliance
Lightning Source LLC
Chambersburg PA
CBHW030100310726
48970CB00004B/1088